MOLLY GREEN has travelled the world, unpacking her suitcase in a score of countries. On returning to England, Molly decided to pursue her life-long passion for writing. She now writes in a cabin in her garden on the outskirts of Tunbridge Wells, Kent, ably assisted by her white rescued cat, Dougie.

Also by Molly Green

The Dr Barnardo's Orphanage series:
An Orphan in the Snow
An Orphan's War
An Orphan's Wish

The Victory Sisters series:
A Sister's Courage
A Sister's Song

A Sister's War

MOLLY GREEN

avon.

Published by AVON
A division of HarperCollins*Publishers* Ltd
1 London Bridge Street
London SE1 9GF

www.harpercollins.co.uk

HarperCollins*Publishers*
1st Floor, Watermarque Building, Ringsend Road
Dublin 4, Ireland

A Paperback Original 2021

3

A catalogue copy of this book is available from the British Library.

ISBN: 978-0-00-833250-1

Typeset in Minion Pro 11/14pt by
Palimpsest Book Production Limited, Falkirk, Stirlingshire
Printed and bound in UK by CPI Group (UK) Ltd, Croydon CR0 4YY

MIX
Paper from responsible sources
FSC™ C007454

This book is produced from independently certified FSC™ paper to ensure responsible forest management.

For more information visit: www.harpercollins.co.uk/green

To my dear sister, Carole Ann, who for two pins would live on a narrow boat!

To all the women and girls who worked on the Grand Union Canal Carrying Company Ltd during the Second World War, taking their narrowboats filled with cargo such as wool, steel, coal, timber, cement, sand, iron, shells for explosives, and even dates used for sauce (!) on scores of trips from London to Birmingham and back.

In 1948 they were finally acknowledged for their valuable contribution in the war and given badges with the initials IW (Inland Waterways), and thereafter jokingly became known as the Idle Women. Nothing could be further from the truth!

Chapter One

Downe, near Bromley, Kent
October 1943

The lights dimmed in the cinema until the auditorium went dark. The chattering audience stopped with one accord. All Ronnie could see was the swirl of cigarette smoke and the silhouette of the heads and women's hats in the rows in front of her. She felt her friend, Lois, give her a nudge.

'Not long now 'til the film.' Lois was breathless with excitement.

'It's Pathé News first,' Ronnie whispered.

'That's the bit I hate. It's always more bad news. I just came to see the main film.' Lois pulled a small bag of boiled sweets from her handbag and handed one to Ronnie. 'Joan Crawford is my favourite. She always plays good parts – makes mincemeat of the men.' She gave a giggle.

'Shhhh!' A man with a large head, and boxer's shoulders, who was sitting in front of them, half turned, waving his hand towards her. 'Some of us would like to hear the news.'

Ronnie recoiled. 'It hasn't actually started yet,' she said, feeling a rise of annoyance.

'This is Pathé News.' The newsreader's voice cut across any further argument. 'Today, the 13th October, Italy has declared war on Nazi Germany, just one month after Italy surrendered to the Allies.'

The audience sent up a roar of approval and several people clapped, Ronnie and Lois amongst them.

'Best news we've heard for ages,' Lois said, turning to Ronnie. The light from the cinema screen showed her eyes dancing with excitement.

The newsreader continued a few moments longer and then switched subjects.

'Women and girls are taking over more and more of the men's jobs. Here are some of the girls in the Land Army doing a marvellous job keeping food on our tables . . . just look at this young lady actually driving a *tractor*!' The newsreader's voice rose in disbelief. 'These girls are certainly wearing the trousers.'

There were a few male chuckles. One man in the audience called out, 'Not in my house, they're not.' More laughter.

Ronnie watched the film intently. Three Land Girls dressed in jodhpurs, their jumpers tucked into their waists and belted, were working on a farm. Ronnie immediately slumped back in her seat. She'd applied three weeks ago to join the Land Army – actually, three weeks and two days to be precise – convinced they would grab her. Several posters she'd seen pinned up in the library and the village hall hoping to persuade girls to join, especially one colourful poster, had really caught her eye. It showed a smiling Land Girl with dark curly hair, a little longer but not unlike her own, her hand resting on a horse's neck, and an amiable pipe-smoking farmer looking on. The message along the top of the poster read: '*We could do with thousands more like you . . .*' and underneath the picture was a yellow banner with black writing: *Join the Women's Land Army*.

She'd dashed home, breathless with excitement that her chance had come, and filled in the application form without telling her mother. What would have been the point? Ronnie had mentioned it a couple of times to her sisters and although Raine and Suzy had cautioned her about the hard, monotonous work, which didn't worry Ronnie one jot, Maman had shot her idea down in flames. She couldn't bear the idea that one of her daughters had dirty, broken fingernails and wore men's clothes while working on the vegetable plot at home, let alone milking cows and mucking out sheds for some unknown farmer.

Every morning when she'd heard Micky, the postboy, rattle the letterbox, Ronnie had flown downstairs, followed by an exuberant Rusty barking his head off. This morning she'd been certain that today would be the day she'd hear. But there had been nothing . . . until the second post at noon.

'*Chérie*, you have a letter in the front room on the mantelpiece,' Maman had said, leaning over the banister when Ronnie had come in from tending the vegetable plot. 'It came a few minutes ago. I will be down in one minute so do not open it until I am there with you. We will read it together.'

Ronnie's heart gave a flip. It must be about the Land Army. And Maman was trying to take control as usual. Ronnie set her jaw. She was almost seventeen – perfectly old enough to open her own letters. She'd wanted to be indoors before the noon post came for this very reason but Rusty had begged her to take him for a walk, the way he'd looked at her with his warm, brown, beseeching eyes.

Please don't come downstairs before I've read it on my own, Maman.

'Come on, Rusty. I'll allow you to read it with me.'

Rusty followed her into the front room, his claws making a clicking sound on the hall lino.

Ronnie grabbed the long envelope tucked behind one of a pair of silver candlesticks, a remnant of the old life they'd had before Dad had lost a lot of money and gone into debt. Probably one of the reasons why he'd died so suddenly at only sixty, she thought grimly. He'd always tried to keep up with Maman's demands and standards. Ronnie's heart squeezed at the thought of her dearest dad and the stress it must have given him when he realised what he'd brought upon the family.

All this was racing through her head as she ripped open the envelope and pulled out the single sheet. She glanced at the heading. She was right. It was from the Ministry of Agriculture and Fisheries; the Land Army came under their umbrella. Heart beating in her ears she read:

Dear Miss Linfoot,

We thank you for your application form to join the Land Army but regret—

Ronnie broke off reading. Regret? Surely . . . Biting her lip and willing herself to go on, she continued:

. . . but regret we must on this occasion turn down your application. Our minimum age is seventeen and a half, and you are not yet seventeen. This is because the work is often heavy, having been carried out by the men before war was declared. However, we are encouraged by your enthusiasm and hope that in a year's time you will apply again, whereupon we would expect you to be successful.

Thank you for your interest.

Yours sincerely,

Ministry of Agriculture and Fisheries

Ronnie was disgusted to see that the person who'd written the letter hadn't even had the courtesy to sign it.

'You are reading your letter without me,' Maman said,

sweeping into the room in her usual style of a Thirties' actress. 'Did you not hear me?' For once, she didn't ask Ronnie to remove 'that dog'.

Ronnie shoved the letter back into the envelope, her eyes stinging with anger. The war would be over by the time she reapplied.

'Yes, I heard you – but, Maman, it's addressed to *me*. I should be allowed to open my own post.'

'Who is it from?'

'No one important.'

'Let me look.' Simone stretched her hand out.

Ronnie was on the brink of refusing to give it to her. But what difference did it make? She hadn't been offered an interview and she'd already told her mother she wasn't going back to school. She wasn't brainy like Raine, or musical like Suzy, and didn't see the need for two more years of mathematics and history and French and all the other subjects she wasn't good at. But she always got top marks in biology and natural history. She knew she had a way with animals and was happiest when outdoors. The Land Army would have given her all those things. Now her hopes were in pieces.

Sulkily, she handed over the envelope.

Simone pursed her lips as she read the letter. Then she looked up. Ronnie noticed a gleam in her mother's eyes.

'*Chérie,* I do not like that you go behind my back to write to these people. We have already discussed this. Winter will come soon and I will not have my daughter digging up turnips. What would people say? They will think we are in poverty. What would your father say if he was here? He would be angry that I allow such a thing. So I am very happy they will not take you. This will be the end of the conversation, even when you are of the right age. You will find a worthwhile job or I will send you back to school.'

Simone had torn the letter into pieces and thrown them on the unlit fire.

Still bristling with Maman's unfair dismissal of the Land Army earlier that day, Ronnie was brought back to Pathé News with the newsreader's latest clip.

'Yes, women and girls are working in the munitions factories . . . Here they are, cheerfully changing into boiler suits and rubber shoes, wearing gloves and masks as protection against poison and dangerous fumes from the explosive material . . . Here's one of the girls filling the exploder and finishing the shells. If it wasn't for the fair sex performing what was once considered men's work, there wouldn't be enough ammunition to send to our boys in the fields. We couldn't carry on the fight. That's how important this work is.'

I'd hate it. Ronnie pulled a face in the darkness. Having to repeat the same movements hour after hour, day after day, cooped up in a room with constant clanging and clattering above the chatter of the girls. It was a wonder they weren't all deafened with the row. Besides, it was obviously dangerous to be amongst all those poisonous fumes, mask or no mask. But I do admire them, she thought. They're getting on with it – and doing their bit for the war effort. And that's what I need to get cracking with.

'. . . and women and girls are even working on the canals, some of them as young as seventeen, taking critical supplies from London to Birmingham and back again on the Grand Union Canal. They work together in threes, from all walks of life. Here's one group in charge of a seventy-foot canal boat with a second boat being towed behind, both of them carrying the cargo. It's a hard, dirty, backbreaking job but these girls are putting their backs into it and look fit and healthy working outside all day . . .'

Ronnie sat bolt upright, staring hard at the screen. She couldn't hear what they were saying but they were tying two boats together, working as a team. One of them, a pretty girl with a cap perched on her blonde curls, looked up and smiled and waved at the camera. The good thing was that they didn't appear to be wearing any kind of uniform, Ronnie noticed, although they all wore trousers. How sensible.

She was barely aware of the other news. And when the film, *Above Suspicion* – a wartime drama that hadn't really appealed, but Lois had gone on and on about it until she'd finally agreed to go with her – eventually came on, Ronnie scarcely paid any attention. Watching a far-fetched story about a honeymooning couple in Europe being asked to spy on the Nazis for the British intelligence, and Joan Crawford, the bride, looking ever more glamorous in every scene, didn't ring true. It all looked so artificial against the horrors she'd seen so many times on Pathé News of the brave boys, many whose lives were being snuffed out before they'd even properly begun to live, or so horribly injured and disfigured they'd never lead a normal life again. Co-star, heartthrob Fred MacMurray, didn't accelerate Ronnie's heartbeat one scrap. No, what was making her heart thump so hard she felt it might burst through her chest was the thought of doing something worthwhile – something she'd be good at.

She'd never been on a boat, but what did that matter? She knew as sure as Lois was sitting next to her that working on the canals would not only be exciting but would be her contribution. She grew more and more convinced as she continued to let the sound of the film roll over her. If she was being grand, she'd say it was her destiny.

But how would she talk Maman round to giving her permission?

Chapter Two

'I wanted to see the Joan Crawford film,' were Maman's first words to greet Ronnie when she arrived home. 'I would have come with you if it was not for this cold.' She sniffed and blew her nose. 'Will you make your *maman* a cup of cocoa, *chérie,* and then you must tell me all about it. I want to hear the clothes she wore.' She gave a violent sneeze.

Ronnie inwardly groaned. She busied herself in the kitchen, spooning out the cocoa in two cups, waiting for the milk to boil, all the while wondering how to approach her mother about working on the canals. Maman would think it even worse than joining the Land Army. She was so engrossed in her thoughts that she couldn't stop the milk from suddenly bubbling up and frothing over the side of the saucepan.

'Damn,' she said aloud, turning off the gas and grabbing a dishcloth to wipe up the liquid. She'd used up all the milk and half of it had spilled over. Thank goodness they could rely on the milkman doing his early morning rounds. No matter how much her mother grumbled about the English insisting on tea first thing, she would be most upset if Ronnie didn't bring her a cup. Sighing, she boiled the kettle, then poured the remains of the milk over the two cups and topped them up with boiling water. She stirred half a teaspoon of sugar into her mother's cup, then found two mismatching saucers. The cups didn't quite fit into the shallow indents but they would have to do.

'Véronique, where is my cocoa?'

Her mother's plaintive voice floated along the hallway, as Ronnie took the hot drinks into the front room.

'What has taken you so long?' Simone demanded, taking the cup and saucer from her. The cup wobbled and overturned, spilling the contents over her dressing gown. She screamed and shot up, letting both the cup and saucer fall to the rug.

'Oh, Maman, I'm sorry. I'll get a cloth,' Ronnie said and rushed to the kitchen for a towel and a bowl of cold water, all the time swearing under her breath, as she doubled back.

'Here, Maman, let me mop it up. Did it burn your legs?'

'Of course it did, child. It was boiling hot.'

'Let me soak them with cold water. That's what we were told in St John's Ambulance. It will stop it blistering.'

'I will bathe myself upstairs,' her mother said. 'You know, Véronique, I worry about you. This would not have happened if you took the trouble to keep to the standard I have always set.' She stooped to pick up the offending cup and saucer. 'Look' – she tapped the saucer – 'this is not the correct one for this cup so it did not fit securely. That is why there was an accident. As if my cold is not enough to cope with—'

'Maman, I'm truly sorry,' Ronnie cut in. 'Please go and soak the tops of your legs with cold water.'

Simone shook her head at Ronnie and pursed her lips. She walked out without another word, leaving Ronnie feeling guilty that she couldn't match up to her mother's high expectations. But then, Raine, her eldest sister, never had, either. And look what she was doing now – a ferry pilot in the Air Transport Auxiliary, delivering the planes to the boys in combat. And Suzy had been abroad and was now touring the country with ENSA. Ronnie couldn't remember what the letters stood for, but it was some sort of entertainment organisation that Vera Lynn belonged to, and Suzy was singing to the troops. Both her sisters had defied Maman, and that seemed to be the reason her mother was clinging on to her, the youngest daughter. It really was unfair.

She waited for a few minutes but there was no sound from upstairs except a bark or two from Rusty wanting to be let out of her bedroom. She'd better go and see if her mother was all right.

Ronnie ran up the stairs but no one was in the bathroom. She knocked on her mother's bedroom door.

'*Entre.*'

Simone was brushing her hair at the dressing table mirror.

'Did the cocoa leave a burn mark, Maman?'

Simone turned and pulled up her nightdress, showing her shapely legs.

Ronnie stepped closer and saw a red blotch on top of her mother's right thigh. She pushed down the spike of guilt.

'I really am sorry, Maman, but at least it hasn't blistered so I think you caught it in time.'

Her mother rose from the stool.

'I am going to bed,' she said coolly. 'I am not at all well. You will come and see me in the morning with some tea in a cup with a *matching* saucer.'

Oh, dear. If her mother was being this difficult over a minor accident, she wasn't going to be in the right mood to talk about working on a canal boat. But at least it had taken Maman's mind off Joan Crawford's extravagant outfits that Ronnie couldn't for the life of her bring even one to mind.

She set her jaw. Whatever Maman said, she was determined she was going to join the canal company. But how to find out about it. Who to write to. That was the problem.

It was only the next morning when Ronnie took Rusty for a walk that she thought of looking in the library for information. She made her way to the one in the village but all they had were leaflets advertising the military forces for men and women. And that was something she definitely didn't want to do. Like her sisters, she knew she'd hate all that marching and saluting and being shouted at. But Miss Jones, the elderly spinster on the counter, didn't know anything about working on the Grand Union Canal.

'Bromley library might be able to help you, dear,' she said, looking forlorn. 'Oh, I do dislike it if I can't be of any help.'

'I'll try there . . . and thank you. You *have* been a help.'

'We're going to get my bicycle, Rusty,' she told the dog, who gave her a bark of what she fondly decided was wholehearted agreement. He'd turned out to be the sweetest, most intelligent animal. When Ronnie had rescued him he'd been a pitiful creature, his ribs sticking through his mangy coat, shaking with terror in the kind ARP warden's arms. As soon as Ronnie had taken him she'd named him Rusty for his tan-coloured but filthy ears and a few brown spots on his equally dirty coat. When Maman had set eyes on him she'd had a fit and said Ronnie had to put a notice up in the village shop to say he'd been found. No one had claimed him and somehow he'd worked his doggie way into . . . well, Ronnie wouldn't go so far as to say into Maman's heart, but at least her mother now seemed to tolerate him.

Hoping her mother wouldn't be home and demand to know where she was going, Ronnie sneaked into the shed and wheeled out the heavy old bicycle. She picked up the dog and set him in the shopping-sized wicker basket at the front.

'You only just fit in now you've put on some weight,' she said, laughing at him, his body squashed, his tongue hanging out with pure joy that he was off on an adventure with his mistress. 'We're going to Bromley library, Rusty. Their library might have some more government leaflets.'

But the elderly volunteer at the counter didn't seem to know what she was talking about either.

'I'll ask the librarian for you,' she said, her whisper almost a hiss through her buck teeth as she bent her grey head towards Ronnie.

With all the notices around warning, 'Strictly no talking', Ronnie could see the woman took her position as library helper very seriously. She managed to suppress a giggle.

'Miss Lidbetter will know. Wait here, dear. I won't be a moment.'

Several minutes later Ronnie was losing patience. But the helper was back with a short stocky woman, her greying auburn hair pinned into a bun – presumably it was Miss Lidbetter.

'Good morning, dear. Miss Ball tells me you are asking for information on girls working on the canals.'

Ronnie surreptitiously glanced behind her, sure that Maman would spring out of the shadows and confront her.

'Yes, I saw a news clip at the cinema yesterday evening,' she said. 'It was about girls like me taking cargo from London to Birmingham and back again. I'd like to apply but they didn't say how to do it.'

'I wouldn't think you were old enough to take part in something like that,' Miss Lidbetter said, studying Ronnie intently.

'I'm seventeen,' Ronnie said, crossing her fingers behind her back, 'and the man on Pathé News said some of the girls were my age.'

'Hmm.' Miss Lidbetter pursed her plump lips. 'What do your parents say about this?'

What would Dad have said? She had no idea. But she knew exactly what to expect from Maman.

'Oh, they know I'm looking into it, but there's nothing definite yet,' Ronnie said, squeezing her fingers more tightly together.

Miss Lidbetter sighed. 'I suppose there's no harm in your writing to them,' she said eventually. 'Then it will be down to your parents as to whether they give their permission.'

Ronnie sent what she hoped was a sweet smile in Miss Lidbetter's direction. She tapped her foot while the librarian took her time rifling through a box of cards and finally pulled one out. She peered at it, then looked at Ronnie over the top of her glasses.

'I believe you need to write to the Ministry of War Transport, dear. Would you like me to jot down the address?'

'Oh, that would be marvellous . . . thank you.'

The librarian adjusted the comb at the side of her bun that was on the verge of falling out and took the pencil the helper offered. She wrote the address on a piece of scrap paper and handed it to Ronnie.

'Be sure to listen to your parents when making a decision of this nature,' she said. 'You'd be doing a man's job and you're just a young girl. It's not to be taken lightly.'

'I'm really grateful, Miss Lidbetter,' Ronnie said, tucking the precious piece of paper into her coat pocket, desperate to make her escape.

'Are there any books you need today, dear?'

'Oh, no, not at the moment.' Ronnie smiled. 'I'd better go. I've tied my dog up outside and he'll be wondering what's happened to me.'

She didn't bother to inform Miss Lidbetter that the real

truth was that it would be Maman she'd have to face when she got home – who would ask why had she been so long – not Rusty.

Ronnie wasted no time in writing a letter to the Ministry of War Transport, explaining that she'd seen a newsreel on Pathé News which had inspired her to apply for a position on the canal boats to haul cargo. Now she'd have to wait for a reply. It seemed as though she was always waiting. Surely this time she'd get the answer she was looking for.

And this time she wouldn't let Maman come anywhere near it.

It was three weeks later when Micky turned up with the post at seven in the morning. Ronnie was up and dressed and had seen him walk up the path, but she'd given up now on the Ministry of Transport.

'Morning, Micky. What have you got for us?'

'One for your mother from that pilot sister of yours.'

Ronnie hid a smile, imagining how annoyed Maman would have been if *she'd* opened the door to the postboy who loved commenting on everyone's letters. She glanced at the envelope. Yes, it was Raine's large looping writing.

'Anything else?'

'Nah.'

The last flicker of hope died.

Then Micky glanced at the pile of envelopes in his hand, tightly bound together by an elastic band. 'Oh, yes, sorry. One other. For *you*.' He looked up. 'It's typed,' he added as he handed her a long envelope, then hopped onto his bike.

'Thanks, Micky,' she called after him, but he just pulled his cap off and still with his back to her, put his hand up in the air and waved as he pedalled off.

She'd only been indoors long enough to put the kettle on when Maman called downstairs.

'Véronique, please bring my post up to my room with my tea.'

Assuring Rusty she'd be down soon to give him his breakfast, Ronnie took the tray upstairs with the two letters. But first she went to her own room and tucked the typed envelope under her pillow, then picked up the tray again and knocked on her mother's door.

'*Entre, chérie,*' Simone called.

'Ah, the English cup of tea for all evils.' Simone was sitting up in bed expectantly, her hair groomed, her make-up on, and wearing a white fluffy bed-jacket, looking for all the world like an actress who was waiting for the newspapers to be delivered giving the reviews of her successful first night.

'I think you mean "ills", Maman.' Her mother's eyes narrowed. She hated to be corrected on her English. 'I'd bring you coffee if it wasn't so scarce,' Ronnie went on, 'although there's Camp if you'd prefer it to tea.'

'Do not even use that word to me.' Simone grimaced unattractively. 'Camp! How can the manufacturers even *pretend* it is like coffee. It is more unlike coffee than any drink I can imagine.'

Ronnie laughed. 'You'd better drink your tea then. And I have a letter from Lorraine for you.' She used Raine's full name on purpose. She mustn't allow anything to put Maman in a difficult mood.

'It will be for both of us, so hand me my letter-opener and come and sit by me. I will read it to you.'

Simone took the letter and carefully slit it open.

'*Dear Maman and Ronnie*' – Simone stopped and gave a deep sigh. 'I so wish—'

'Maman, you won't stop her using "Ronnie". Besides, I

prefer it. Come on, I want to hear what Lorraine's been doing.'

Simone shook her head but carried on reading:

'I hope this finds you both well. I'm busy as usual but at least the pilot I've been filling in for is now back at work which has taken off some of the pressure. I have managed to get a decent sleep for the last two nights. But you know I'm not complaining – I love every minute of my job and still consider myself incredibly lucky.

'Our American pilot, Dolores, brought us some luxury items from one of the American bases (as they call them) and she always shares everything with us. I now have two pairs of silk stockings – yes, two whole pairs! – a box of chocolates and a bar of soap smelling of roses just for me and a huge tin of biscuits she calls cookies for all of us. What a generous girl.

'You will remember Stephanie who I invited for Christmas last year— Simone broke off and looked up. 'Yes, I liked her, but I thought she was sad.'

'She's all right, isn't she?' Ronnie said anxiously.

Simone bent her head again, then smiled. 'She is very much all right. It seems she has a nice boyfriend – although unfortunately he is another pilot.'

'It must be difficult meeting men who aren't pilots in that sort of place,' Ronnie said.

'Hmm. Now, where was I?'

'Stephanie's boyfriend.'

'Oh, yes. Lorraine does not give any other details. Now she is talking of Miss Gower.'

'That's Raine's boss,' Ronnie said. 'What does she say?'

Simone cleared her throat.

'We women pilots have had some incredible news from

Pauline Gower. She's been telling the powers that be in the ATA that we take exactly the same risks as the men, work just as hard, and fly just as many different planes, yet we are paid a third lower in wages. After much arguing and persuasion they have actually agreed we are to have equal pay to the men! It's not even the money so much as the acknowledgement that we're every bit as good!'

Simone pursed her lips. 'What is she saying – "it is not even the money"?'

'I know exactly what she means,' Ronnie interrupted. 'It's the principle of the thing. And the women have finally won!' She jumped up from the bedside chair and clapped her hands. 'Good for Miss Gower. Is there anything more?'

'*Non*, just she sends her love to us and not to worry . . . she is fine. As if I can stop from worrying.'

'She's happy, Maman, and really that's all that matters.' She smiled at her mother but Simone didn't smile back. 'I'll leave you to get dressed while I put the porridge on.'

'Give me twenty minutes, please,' Simone said, draining her cup.

Ronnie decided not to risk Maman bursting into her bedroom, demanding to see this particular letter and tearing it to shreds, so she retrieved it from under her pillow and ran down the stairs, Rusty flying after her, for once not barking. Outside, she unbolted the shed and perching on an upturned crate, ripped open the envelope. The heading in capitals and underlined was: MINISTRY OF WAR TRANSPORT. Her heart began to pound. She skimmed through the two-page letter trying to see if they'd accepted her, but she couldn't tell so she took in a deep breath and read more slowly from the beginning:

Dear Miss Linfoot,

Re: Training Scheme for Women

Thank you for your letter. The training scheme for women is as follows:-

Training takes at least 8 weeks where you will learn to manage a pair of boats – the motorboat and the butty and how to load and unload cargo etc., as well as rudimentary training on care of the engine. You will live on the boats which will carry the cargo along the Grand Union Canal from London to Birmingham and back.

During training you will be paid £2 per week but you must pay for your own food, national insurance and all personal expenses. You should bring your ration books so we can arrange to issue Emergency Coupons. You may then make purchases in any part of the country. When you are able to operate the boats you will be allotted your own pair of boats working together with two other women.

After training, earnings of around £10 per week must be shared by the three crew members. This figure may vary according to the cargo and distance travelled etc. and will depend upon each member's effort.

When you have completed two trips – usually around three weeks each – you may take three days off unpaid. The more trips you make, the more days you may take (unpaid). After a year you will be paid one week's leave, and the same thereafter.

We must stress that you should be fit and healthy as you will be working long hours over a seven-day week.

If you are still interested in this vital war work, and

are at least 17 years of age, then we will arrange for you to come for an interview at our offices.

Yours sincerely,
D. Hunter (Mrs)
Supervisor
Grand Union Canal Carrying Co.

They hadn't turned her down! She hadn't stated her age so she'd have to take a chance they wouldn't ask for her birth certificate. After all, she'd be seventeen in December – only two months away. With a shiver of excitement she tucked the letter back into its envelope. She'd write back immediately. Then when they gave her a date to attend the interview, only then would she tell Maman her plans.

There was one problem even more insurmountable than Maman – and that was Rusty. Maman would never agree in a million years to look after him. She wondered if she could somehow smuggle him onto the boat. She read the letter again. There was no mention of not being able to take a dog aboard and she'd seen dogs on boats when she'd cycled to Keston Common with Rusty in the front basket. They'd always looked perfectly happy. She was sure Rusty would be thrilled to accompany her – and Maman would be delighted to be rid of him.

But would whoever was in charge of the training allow it?

Chapter Three

At the vet's the following Saturday where Ronnie helped out and earned some useful pocket money, she stood on the opposite side of the table to Mr Lincoln. He was having to put down a perfectly healthy dog because the owner, an elderly lady, said she was no longer able to feed it. She hardly had enough income to keep herself together, she'd said, her chin trembling as she left the mongrel to his destiny.

If she didn't already have Rusty, Ronnie would have immediately taken the little dog home, but the thought of Maman's anger stopped her. Ronnie swallowed hard. This would have been Rusty's fate if she hadn't rescued him, and he'd been in a dreadful condition compared to this boy. She vowed never to witness something like that again. She'd have to confess to Mr Lincoln that she wasn't cut out for this kind of work after all. Not that she was squeamish at assisting the vet with the most gory operations. She rose to the challenge just as she knew Mr Lincoln did. And the glow of happiness she felt every time an animal recovered and was back with its owner was all the reward she would ever want. She loved how Mr Lincoln would celebrate a job well done by making *her* a cup of tea instead of the other way round, and adding a finger of Kit-Kat in the saucer. But poor Oscar being lethally injected after looking up at her with such trusting eyes just moments ago sickened her.

She gulped back her tears and turned to blow her nose.

'I hated doing that,' Mr Lincoln said with a sigh. 'Bad enough having four injured pets brought in yesterday evening, caused by a couple of ignorant youths throwing fireworks at them.' He shook his head in disbelief.

'Maman thought it was a bombing raid,' Ronnie said. 'I must say, Rusty shook with terror every time a banger exploded.'

'If only the owners would keep their animals in on Guy Fawkes night,' Mr Lincoln said. He listened to Oscar's heart, then looked up. 'He's gone.'

Ronnie bit down hard on her lip. She mustn't cry. It wouldn't bring Oscar back.

'This war is having such bad consequences on the animal kingdom. I would have taken the little fellow home with me if I hadn't already taken in two poor little blighters in the last three months. And I tried for a week to find a home for this one.'

'I know you did your best,' Ronnie said, tears streaming down her cheeks as she gazed down at the young dog, now perfectly still.

The vet gently picked him up. 'Let me just take Oscar next door.'

He was back in moments and went to the sink to wash his hands. He turned to her, drying his hands on the nearby roller towel.

'You have a real way with animals, Ronnie, the way you comfort the animals when they're in distress. So I have a proposition for you. How about you coming to work for me as my full-time assistant? I'd train you with the idea of putting you forward to take an exam to obtain a proper veterinary nursing qualification.'

Ronnie startled. This was totally unexpected. A proper job with a certificate at the end. One that even Maman might approve of. And she liked and trusted Mr Lincoln. He was a pleasure to work with and she loved his wry humour. She wanted to say yes immediately. She would have jumped at the chance if they weren't in the middle of this blasted war. But was she being weak? She always prided herself on being a strong person who didn't turn away from something unpalatable. Then she thought of Oscar. She knew she wouldn't be able to face the needless destruction of animals day after day as a result of the strict food rationing. But it would be even worse for the animals if there weren't kind vets like Mr Lincoln who carried out the senseless deed with tender-hearted feeling. Thank goodness he hadn't ever turned his back.

'What do you think, Ronnie? Does it appeal?'

'Yes, it does – in many ways,' she said truthfully. 'You know I really wanted to join the Land Army. When the war started I loved digging our vegetable plots at home and seeing everything grow. They taste wonderful. It's something I'm good at and I don't even mind weeding. But the Land Army won't have me. It's so ridiculous. You have to be seventeen and a half, and I'm not seventeen until December. So for the sake of a few months they've turned me down. They said to apply again in a year and I was bound to be successful, but the war will probably be over with by then and I won't have done my bit.'

'I doubt very much that the war will be over within the year,' Mr Lincoln said, 'but you're obviously looking for more of an outdoor life.' She nodded. 'Well, I can see why the Land Army would have appealed but you're going to have difficulty getting in anywhere at your young age. So why don't you think about working here.' He smiled. 'There's no need to come back to me with an answer straightaway. Take your time. It's a big decision.'

Ronnie took in a breath. She could confide in Mr Lincoln. He would never repeat anything she said in confidence.

'There is another possibility,' she said. 'I've got an interview next week with the Grand Union Canal Carrying Company.'

Mr Lincoln raised his brows. 'Working on the canals? My goodness, Ronnie, that's backbreaking work. Mind you, I think you're physically strong and you're a most determined young lady, so you'll probably survive – maybe even enjoy it.' He took his glasses off and studied her. 'Well, I'm disappointed if that's your decision, but if you need a reference, I'll be more than happy to provide one.'

'Thank you, Mr Lincoln. That's kind of you.' She paused. 'There is one thing. My dog, Rusty. Do you think I'll be able to take him with me on the canal?'

'As far as Rusty's concerned, he'd love it,' Mr Lincoln smiled, 'but you'll have to ask permission at the interview. On second thoughts it's probably better to wait and see how you settle in first in case it doesn't turn out how you think it will.' He paused. 'I'll be sorry to lose you, Ronnie. When the war's over I hope you'll consider my offer – that is, if I haven't got someone permanent by then.' He chuckled. 'But I don't suppose they'll be queuing up. It's not an easy option here for a young person.'

'But I've thoroughly enjoyed it – except today with poor Oscar,' Ronnie said, hoping she wasn't making a terrible mistake by pursuing the canal work. 'And if the canal people don't take me on, I would love to come and work for you.'

The doorbell sounded.

'That'll be Mrs King with her poorly hamster. At least with *his* diet he's safe enough.' Mr Lincoln gave a rueful smile as he laid an old but spotlessly clean white pillowcase on the table. 'Can you bring her and Hammy in, please, Ronnie?'

Ronnie mentally counted the days to her interview. Only six more. How on earth was she going to tell her mother she was going to London? Maman would forbid her to go. *London is too dangerous,* she'd say. *You don't know London. You've never been there. And most definitely I will not allow you to go on your own. And why would you want to, anyway?* Her mother would insist upon accompanying her. Worse than that, it wouldn't end there. Maman wouldn't rest until she'd ferreted out the reason for her daughter's sudden desire to go to London and would be watching her from now on. Ronnie shook her head. No, it was impossible.

And then it came to her. She would say she was meeting Raine. Better still, if Raine could really get a few hours off and go to Southall with her, then Maman couldn't accuse her of telling a lie.

'Beatrice Mortimer has invited me for a real cup of coffee,' Maman said when Ronnie walked through the door after attending to the vegetables, 'but I will be back for lunch. I have made a soup. Please have the table laid ready and slice some bread.'

Ronnie wrinkled her nose. Her mother wasn't best known for her soups – or any of her cooking, for that matter. But at least she'd have the house to herself and could telephone her sister in private.

'All right, Maman. Tell her I said "hello".'

The front door shut. All was wonderfully silent. Ronnie went straight to the telephone.

'Oh, operator, could you please put me through to the aerodrome at White Waltham?'

After half a minute a woman's voice said, 'What department, miss?'

'The Air Transport Auxiliary. I'm trying to reach Lorraine Linfoot – one of the pilots,' she added proudly.

'Your name?'

'Ronnie Linfoot – her sister.'

'One moment, please.'

The minutes ticked by. Then there was the sound of a click.

'Ronnie, is something wrong?' Raine's voice was breathless, as though she'd been running hard.

'No, nothing really,' Ronnie said, delighted her sister was there. 'I just wondered if you could meet me in London on Friday?'

'London?'

'Yes. I've never been and I thought it would be a good opportunity for us to have a proper day together. We never have,' she finished.

There was a pause. Then Raine said, 'I'm not due a day off until Monday. Would that do?'

'No. You see I'm meeting someone on Friday.'

The line crackled. All she could hear was Raine saying 'important'.

'It *is* important,' Ronnie said.

'Are you meeting a boy?'

'Don't be daft. I'll tell you about it when I see you. Is there a chance –?'

More crackling. Ronnie shook the receiver in frustration.

'– I could swap?' Raine finished, and Ronnie could imagine her older sister's eyes gleaming with the idea of a secret. 'No one's going to jump at giving up a Friday for a Monday, but I could probably persuade someone. I'll see what I can do and phone you back. It might not be until this evening as you only just caught me. I've got a couple of deliveries to do.'

'That would be marvellous. I'd clap my hands if I wasn't holding the receiver.'

Raine chuckled, then said, 'Where's Maman at the moment?'

'Having coffee with Mrs Mortimer.'

'Oh, James's mother. I've still not met her, but Suzy says she's lovely.'

'*I* have, and she is,' Ronnie said.

'Right then, I must go. Give Maman my love. I'll have a word with her as well this evening.'

'Thanks, Raine.'

Ronnie put the receiver down. If her sister could organise the swap it would take a load off her mind.

The telephone rang just after six. Ronnie sprang up to grab it but her mother, who was in the front room, got to the hall first.

'Is it Raine?' she mouthed.

Simone put her finger to her lips. There was a long pause. Ronnie was just about to go back to the kitchen when she heard her mother say:

'This is Mrs Linfoot, Véronique's mother.'

Another frustrating pause. Ronnie was beside herself with curiosity.

'*Oui*, I know. I can give her a message.'

'Maman, please let me take it.'

Ronnie put out her hand for the receiver but Simone held on to it.

'Shhhh!' She turned her back to Ronnie. '*Excusez-moi*,' she said into the mouthpiece.

'Yes, I will pass on the message. I am sure she will do this.'

'Maman, please . . .'

'I did not quite hear.' Her mother gripped the receiver more firmly and the caller spoke for some moments. 'Oh, yes, she did mention it.' She nodded. 'Yes, I hope so, too. Thank you, *monsieur.*' She replaced the receiver.

'Maman—'

'That was your Mr Lincoln,' Simone said, walking back to the front room. Ronnie followed. 'He asked if you could go in tomorrow afternoon at two o'clock. He needs you to stay with some animals while he is gone no more than two hours. You heard me. I said I was sure you will do this. You may telephone him to confirm.'

'Why didn't you let me tell him there and then?'

'Because he said something very interesting. He asked me if I could persuade you to accept his offer to work for him permanently.' Simone regarded Ronnie and sighed. 'But you have not told me this.'

Ronnie's chest tightened. 'He only mentioned it yesterday as I was leaving.'

'Surely that is important enough to discuss with your *maman*.'

'I was going to, but I wanted to make a decision first. He asked me to think about it before giving an answer.'

'You must know if you would like to work for this man . . . and do you not love animals?'

'You know I do. If there wasn't a war on I'd jump at the chance but . . .' Oh, what the heck. She plunged in before she could change her mind. 'Maman, I spoke to Raine this morning. We're planning to go to London next week – spend the day together. Just her and me,' she added quickly.

To her amazement her mother smiled. How beautiful she was. If only she would smile more often. Then Ronnie froze at her next words:

'We can all three spend the day together. A mother and her two daughters. It will be wonderful.'

No, Maman. That's not what I want at all. Blast it!

Ronnie tried to control the alarm she felt at Maman's suggestion.

'Véronique, why are you quiet? What is the day you will choose?'

'Um, I'm not sure. Raine's going to telephone this evening. She has to work something out with the other pilots.'

'It must not be Friday,' Maman warned. 'I have promised to help Beatrice Mortimer at the Red Cross.'

They'd just finished supper when Raine rang. This time Ronnie managed to get to the phone.

'Friday's all arranged,' Raine said. 'I'll meet you at Victoria Station at ten o'clock. It's a direct line. But give yourself plenty of time in case of delays. All right?'

'Yes, that'll be perfect.'

'What have you told Maman?'

'Only that you and I want to have a day together. She immediately said how wonderful it will be for the three of us. Oh, Raine—'

She heard Raine heave a sigh. 'Don't worry. Leave it with me and put her on the phone.'

Five minutes later her mother appeared at the kitchen as Ronnie was washing the dishes.

'It is so disappointing. Lorraine can only have the Friday for her day off. I said I am not able to come. But you may go with her. I expect you want to discuss the job with the vet.' She looked Ronnie up and down and frowned. 'I wish I had the money for you to buy a dress to wear to meet your sister in London. I cannot remember the last time I saw you looking pretty.'

'A dress isn't practical for my kind of life,' Ronnie said, breathing out. She was actually going to spend some time with Raine whom she adored. They'd never done anything like this before. Maybe her sister would stop treating her like a kid when she told her about the interview with Mrs Hunter.

Ronnie gave an inward smile. Raine was in for a shock.

Chapter Four

Ronnie could hardly believe she was on the train from Bromley to Victoria Station with Maman's blessing. Her heart was beating wildly. She'd made a special effort to look dressed-up, but not used to wearing a skirt her legs felt cold and she wished she'd worn thicker stockings. As usual, the train wasn't heated and on top of that it was draughty, but nothing marred her anticipation at seeing Raine, and having the luxury of talking to her and asking her advice.

And there was Raine in her ATA uniform, her forage cap perched on the top of her dark head, running along the platform as the train juddered and steamed to a final halt. Ronnie, who was standing in the corridor, her coat still unbuttoned, pushed down the glazed door panel and felt outside for the handle. She swung back the heavy door and jumped down to the platform. She barely noticed the fumes and curling smoke as she threw her arms round her sister.

'Raine! Oh, it's so good to see you.'

Raine laughed and hugged her back. 'I do believe you've grown, kid,' she said.

'Don't call me "kid",' Ronnie said seriously. 'I've got something important to tell you.'

'Then let's go and have a cup of tea in the station café,' Raine said, linking her arm through Ronnie's.

They were soon sharing a table with another couple who couldn't keep their hands off one another. Ronnie badly wanted to laugh every time Raine rolled her eyes. Smothering her giggles she swiftly told Raine about the canal company, and while Raine's eyes widened in surprise she didn't interrupt until Ronnie had finished.

'Mmm.' Raine drained the last of her tea. 'I can see why it would appeal to you. Personally, I'd hate it. It sounds too much like hard work. And I know something – Maman's going to hate the sound of it even more than you going into the Land Army.' She looked at Ronnie. 'Where are we going?'

'Southall. The interview's at noon.'

Raine glanced at her watch and rose to her feet. 'I'm not sure exactly where that is so we'd better get going.' She paused. 'By the way, Ronnie, darling, I'm coming to the interview with you.' Ronnie opened her mouth but Raine cut her off. 'No argument. Maman would never forgive me if I wasn't there, and we don't want to risk her wrath any more than we need.' She chuckled. 'And *I* need to see what you might be getting into. Don't worry – I'll keep out of it unless absolutely necessary.'

Ronnie shrugged and followed Raine out of the warm café. Deep down she was relieved her sister would be by her side.

It had been a long walk from the railway station at Southall to the Grand Union Canal Carrying Company's offices, but eventually the two sisters came to an enormous yard filled with a flurry of workmen.

'Can't see any sign of a canal,' Raine said.

What had she got into? Ronnie braced herself.

A woman in her forties, dressed in a frumpy tweed skirt

and pale blue twinset, came towards Ronnie and Raine. She looked from one to the other. 'Veronica Linfoot?'

'Véronique, actually, though I go by Ronnie.' She extended her hand. 'And this is my sister Lorraine.'

'You haven't come to volunteer as well?' The woman eyed Raine up and down with a hopeful expression.

'Oh, no.' Raine took a step backwards.

'No, of course not. Silly me. You have your pilot's wings. Congratulations.' She gestured for them to follow her, then waved towards two seats in front of an old battered desk in a windowless room and took the seat behind.

'I'm Mrs Hunter, the supervisor, who wrote to you initially,' she said, looking at Ronnie intently. She glanced at Raine again. 'Actually, I'm glad you've come with your sister. She looks very young.'

'I'm seventeen,' Ronnie cut in abruptly.

Raine gave Ronnie a sharp look which she pretended not to notice.

'Right. I'll go through a few questions.' Mrs Hunter regarded Ronnie with keen grey eyes. 'First of all, why are you interested in working for us?'

The interview went on with Mrs Hunter reminding them it was a very responsible job which didn't suit everyone. Raine occasionally interrupted with a question of her own, but mainly the two girls listened.

'Can you swim?' Mrs Hunter asked, her pen poised.

'Oh, yes,' Ronnie said enthusiastically. 'I love swimming.'

'We don't take girls on if they can't,' the supervisor said firmly. 'It's too dangerous.' She paused. 'And your parents are happy about you working on the canals?'

Ronnie swallowed. 'Our father died two years ago. He would have approved if that's what I wanted.'

'And your mother?'

'Our mother just wants Véronique to be happy whatever she decides to do,' Raine said with a smile.

If only that were true, Ronnie thought.

'But as you're not yet twenty-one we would require her permission in writing.' Mrs Hunter removed her glasses.

Raine shot Ronnie a warning look.

'I'll be speaking to her,' Raine said. 'It won't be a problem if I tell her I'm happy with all that you've told us.'

'Good.' Mrs Hunter scribbled a note, then looked up and fixed her gaze on Ronnie. 'And if I offered you the job right this minute, what would you say?'

'I'd say, "Yes, please,"' Ronnie said, grateful to see Raine give her a wink.

'You'll need a medical. I'll wait until I hear your mother has given permission and book one for you as soon as possible.'

'I think they'll find she's as fit as a flea,' Raine said.

'We hope so.' Mrs Hunter made another note. 'Bear in mind that the boat is only seven feet wide and there'll be no room for items such as suitcases' – she tapped her pen on the desk – 'so pack sparingly in a rucksack, if you have one. If not, a pillowcase, which can be stowed more easily than a case. And you'll need bedding – or possibly a sleeping bag. It's not kitted out like a hotel, you understand?' Ronnie nodded. Mrs Hunter took a sheet of paper from a file on her desk and gave it to Ronnie. 'This is a list of things you must bring.'

Ronnie glanced at the list, hardly seeing it, she was so excited. She noticed rucksack and sleeping bag along with items of clothing.

She looked up. 'I have my dad's rucksack from when we went camping once, but we gave our sleeping bags to the Girl Guides when we moved to Downe.'

'That's a shame. It would have been useful. Well, be sure to bring a sheet and a warm blanket.'

Ronnie wondered how on earth she was meant to get all that into a rucksack with her clothes and a few personal belongings, but she didn't dare say anything.

'I have something which might be useful for you.' Mrs Hunter rummaged in her desk drawer and brought out a small paperback book. She passed it across to Ronnie. 'It's a novel but it will give you a good flavour of what it's like to work on the canals.'

Ronnie glanced at the title: *The Water Gipsies.* She wasn't a big reader but this might be interesting.

'Thank you very much,' she said. 'I'll definitely take it with me.' She tucked it into her bag.

'Right, then. Just to recap. All being well with your mother you will start the six weeks' training next week, Friday, the 12th of November, where you'll meet your trainer, Dora Dummitt, and the other trainees at nine o'clock in the morning at Regent's Canal Dock. Any problems of any kind, you must speak to your trainer.' Mrs Hunter smiled and rose to her feet. 'Would you like to come with me and have a look at the boats?'

'Oh, yes, please,' Ronnie said eagerly.

She and Raine followed Mrs Hunter down to the canal. There were a couple of dozen narrowboats – not barges, Ronnie quickly reminded herself. They were painted in vibrant red and blue, with the company's initials GUCC and telephone number, and were riding high in the water. There seemed nothing about them Ronnie could relate to. Her pulse quickened.

One of the workmen appeared from a nearby boat and sprang onto the hard surface of the yard.

'Sorry, Mrs Hunter, if you and the young ladies are intending to have a dekko inside – there's all wet paint.'

'Oh, what a nuisance.' Mrs Hunter turned to Ronnie and Raine. 'Quite a few of the boats are here for repair and repainting and redecorating so we'd best not disturb them, but at least you've caught a glimpse. Just remember they look much bigger than they are inside.'

She put out her hand, first to Raine and then to Ronnie. 'I wish you the very best of luck, Ronnie Linfoot. Always remember why you are there – to release a place so a man can fight for our country. Do your utmost to make sure no one can ever point out the difference between women taking the cargo and men. Don't let the company down.'

Ronnie stood and shook hands. 'I promise to do my very best.'

'See that you do, my dear. I'll show you out.'

'I won't be allowed to go,' Ronnie said sulkily as she and Raine walked back to the station. 'Maman will never give her permission. Oh, why can't I be twenty-one?' she burst out.

Raine laughed. 'Don't wish your time away. And don't worry about Maman. I think she'll give it.' She grinned at her youngest sister. 'It's a pity I couldn't come back with you. It would have been easier to talk to her. But I'll ring her tonight, so don't worry.'

If anything, the journey home took even longer than when Ronnie had started out that morning. Immediately she'd kissed her sister goodbye – at Paddington Station this time – she'd felt lonely.

It was gone five by the time Ronnie arrived in Bromley, but her luck was in when she saw a bus for Downe draw up outside. A woman with bleached blonde hair under a felt hat, and thickly painted cherry lips, plonked next to her.

'Been somewhere nice, have you, dearie?' she said, turning

to Ronnie, who was staring out of the window into the darkness, trying to work out how to tell her mother she'd been accepted to work for the Grand Union Canal Carrying Company. She still hadn't got things worked out in her mind when the conductor dropped her at the nearest stop to home.

Keeping to the regulations, she fixed a small piece of tissue paper over her torch with an elastic band to prevent any rogue aeroplane from spotting her. Her common sense always questioned this – how could a pilot possibly see such a tiny beam from such an altitude? – but she supposed it was to remind people that the enemy wasn't far away and to take every precaution.

Wishing her mother would trust her with her own key, Ronnie walked up the path and rang the bell. She heard Rusty barking.

Simone opened the door so quickly Ronnie thought she must have heard her footsteps.

'I have been very worried,' Simone began immediately. 'You said you will be back before dark. It is now past six.'

'Just let me go and see Rusty,' Ronnie said quickly. 'He'll be wanting his dinner.'

'I have fed him,' her mother said. 'He was driving me crazy. He is in the front room.'

Ronnie stared at her mother. Maman had never fed him before. And allowing him to go in the front room when she wasn't around to control him? Unheard of. Did that mean Maman was finally softening towards him? She felt a sudden warmth towards her and made a step forward to give her a hug, but Simone had already turned to go back along the hall to the kitchen.

'Your supper is ready, Véronique. You will eat and tell me about Raine.'

Even though Ronnie was hungry, the meal her mother

had prepared of tinned sardines, cold mashed potato and overcooked cabbage didn't exactly whet her appetite, but she didn't dare pass any remark, though she noticed Maman hadn't even attempted hers yet.

'Raine looks really well, Maman. You can see how happy she is doing the job she loves.'

'Hmm.' Her mouth turned down at the corners. 'I suppose I must be happy, too, but although she does not think it, I worry about her every day.'

'You shouldn't. She's a very careful pilot.'

'And what did she say about you working for the vet?'

Ronnie felt her cheeks warm. 'I told her about Mr Lincoln's offer. But I also told her about another idea I've had.'

'Digging up turnips? No, I do not allow it.'

'No, Maman, not the Land Army. It's to work for the Grand Union Canal Carrying Company.'

Simone's eyes narrowed. 'What is this?'

Ronnie quickly described her interview with Mrs Hunter, all the while watching her mother's expression turn to horror.

'I am your *maman,*' Simone said, her nostrils flaring. 'Why did you not discuss this with me? I know why. Because you are aware I will not approve of this work.'

'It's what I want to do, Maman.' Ronnie took another mouthful of the limp yellow cabbage and would have spat it out if she'd been on her own. She put her knife and fork down and caught her mother's eye. 'Raine liked Mrs Hunter, the supervisor, and thought it would really suit me.'

How could she make it sound a little easier for Maman to say yes?

'I only have to make up my mind definitely to carry on after I've finished training,' she said after a few moments. 'If I change my mind, they would accept it.'

Her mother's mouth tightened.

'You will have ruined your hands and nails by then. Winter is coming.'

'But you know how I prefer to be outside. And it's something Mrs Hunter says is important for the war effort.'

Simone's eyes narrowed. 'You are underage, Véronique. You will need my permission.'

Here it comes.

'Maman, talk to Raine first. She's going to telephone you this evening.'

Simone gave a jagged sigh. 'My three girls. None of you are doing what I would wish. If only Pi—' She broke off. 'No, he would not interfere.' She briefly closed her eyes. 'But you have made up your mind, I think.'

'I have, Maman. I want to do this more than anything.'

Simone put her knife and fork together on the plate, her supper barely touched.

'Then you must tell the vet tomorrow so he can choose someone else. It is a pity. You would be most suited to the work.'

'I'm not sure about that,' Ronnie said. 'Mr Lincoln had to put to sleep a perfectly fit young dog on Saturday.' Tears gathered as the image danced in front of her. 'Rusty would have gone the same way if I hadn't rescued him. I can't bear anything like that.'

Rusty pricked his ears up and gave a short bark.

Simone looked at Ronnie, her eyes suddenly gleaming. 'If you insist on this canal work, what arrangements have you made for Rusty who you say you love so much?'

Ronnie gulped. 'I think it may be possible to take him with me. Dogs do travel on boats and I think he'd like it.' She wouldn't tell Maman she hadn't brought up the subject with Mrs Hunter.

Her mother looked away but not before Ronnie saw how her face fell. 'Oh, I see.'

What was this? It was almost as though her mother didn't want to see him gone.

'Well, you wouldn't want to look after him.'

'Have you asked me?' Simone brought her gaze back to Ronnie.

'N-no. I never dreamed—'

'You want to leave me, so *everyone* has left me,' Simone said, her voice trembling. 'First your father, then Lorraine, then Suzanne, and now, once again, Pierre.' Her lower lip trembled as a lone tear fell down her cheek. 'I do not know where he is . . . maybe he is back in France.'

Ronnie felt her own eyes well up. It was an extraordinary thing to have happened – Maman's first love reappearing after twenty years, knowing she was married but not that she was now a widow. It was so sweet the way they still carried a torch for one another. Best of all, she and her sisters adored the Frenchman who had managed to escape the Gestapo and after a long circuitous journey, find his way to England . . . and Maman.

'He'll keep safe now he has everything to live for.'

Her mother grimaced. 'His work is dangerous. His name is on the Nazis' list for stealing their documents about their wicked plans for our beloved Paris if they lose the war.' Her hand flew to her mouth. 'I should not have disclosed such a secret, Véronique. You must never mention this to anyone. What was I thinking about?' She put her head in her hands and gave a sob. 'And now there will be no one here when you have gone. At least the dog would be some company to me.'

'Oh, Maman—' Ronnie sprang up and rushed to her mother's side. She put her arms round her. 'I won't take him if you want him to stay. He's a lovely boy. He always knows when I'm unhappy and tries to comfort me in his way.' She reached down to pat him. 'Maman, please don't cry. I want to go with your blessing. They say I can come home for three days after the training, which will fly by in a jiffy. And I'd write to you.'

'When do you propose to go?' Simone sniffed and reached for her handkerchief.

'Friday,' Ronnie said in a small voice, going back to her chair, hardly believing her mother seemed to be accepting the new situation.

'You will need warm clothes.' Simone wiped her eyes and blew her nose. 'We must find you some suitable things. I do not want you to catch pneumonia – another thing to worry about.'

'It's quite a long list, Maman. Things like a coat and boots.' Ronnie hesitated. 'They'll use up a lot of coupons . . . and money. That's what worries *me*.'

'Suzanne is not taking music lessons so that money can go to you.'

'I'll pay you back, I promise. I'll be earning £2 a week to start, and then £3 after I finish training, though we have to buy food out of it.'

Her mother nodded. 'Show me the list.'

Ronnie took it from her bag and handed it over. Her mother read it in silence.

'These things are practical if you are on boats or here through the winter,' Simone said, looking up. 'You need a good raincoat. You have outgrown yours.' She glanced at the list again. 'And you must have a suitcase to pack these things.'

'Oh, no, Maman, no cases. Mrs Hunter specifically said not. They take up too much room. She said either a rucksack or a pillowcase.'

'A *pillowcase*?' Simone's voice rose an octave. 'To pack your clothes in?' Ronnie nodded. '*Non*. That I will not have.

What would the village say to see you carrying a pillowcase like . . . like Dick Whittington?'

Ronnie laughed. 'I don't care what the villagers say.'

'Well, *I* do.' Maman pushed her plate to one side, giving the tinned sardines and the soggy cabbage a final look of disgust. 'We will go to Bromley tomorrow.'

Chapter Five

Regent's Canal Dock, London
November 1943

Laughter greeted Ronnie's ears as she surfaced, spitting and thrashing, from the murky brown canal water, terrified and fighting hard not to be pulled under again by the weight of her sodden gaberdine mac and waterlogged Wellingtons.

'That'll teach yer not to be so cocky, miss. The cut's a dirty little devil and a lock's a dangerous place not to be payin' attention.'

Dora Dummitt, one of the trainers, puffed on her pipe as the five other brand-new trainees stood around on the towpath in the rain. One of them was smirking. Another gave a nervous giggle. The trainer let Ronnie struggle for a few more moments, then thrust out an arm that could sink a battleship and hauled her back onto the towpath.

Ronnie, red-faced with exertion and shame, clung on to the woman's arm, and dripped water and mud splashes over Dora Dummitt's sleeve and down the front of her waterproof jacket, already filthy from months of training girls to man the narrowboats.

The sky that had been gloomy all day was now beginning to darken. This first day hadn't been at all as Ronnie had imagined. Instead of the peace of a canal, Regent's Canal Dock was alive with men and boats and horses. Stevedores and dockers were shouting to one another, warning bells rang and whistles pierced the air, cargo came crashing down into the lighters and barges and narrowboats, factories spewed out foul smoke and steam, trains roared over the railway bridge . . . it was a bewildering cacophony and Ronnie hadn't the faintest idea how she'd fit in.

It had sounded like a job tailor-made for Ronnie when she'd been for her interview and had had her medical and was accepted. Nothing about the training scheme had put her off, even when Mrs Hunter had warned her the work could be heavy. She should never forget she'd be taking the place of a man who'd gone off to fight for King and country, and this could mean working as much as twelve or even fourteen hours a day, non-stop.

Do you think you're up to it? she remembered Mrs Hunter asking her, looking her up and down. Ronnie had ignored Raine's amused grin as she tried to stretch as tall as her five foot three inches would allow. 'At only seventeen you'll be the youngest,' Mrs Hunter had added.

'I'm really strong and not afraid of hard work,' Ronnie had answered.

Little had she known that the trainer, Dora Dummitt, would be a slave driver – and a bully who seemed to enjoy humiliating her in front of the others.

'Wait here, all of yer,' Dora ordered as she sprang like a young girl onto the roof of the narrowboat called *Persephone* and disappeared into the cabin. She was back in a trice holding up the floor mat, her eyes sweeping the group of girls. 'When it happens again – and I say "when", not "if" – and that goes for all of yous – one of the other crew must remove this' – she jerked her head towards the mat – 'and anything else that needs ter keep dry. Then yer don't make the cabin floor into an extra cut.' She gave her strange mirthless bark at the weak joke which Ronnie was sure the woman spouted to every new trainee who fell in. 'The one who's had a dunkin' then goes and puts dry clothes on. Bung any wet things round the engine room and they'll dry soon enough.' She paused and her gaze fell on Ronnie. 'Yer'd better buzz off, Shirley, and change into some dry gear but don't be long. We've got more ter do before it's dark.' The smile she presented came out as a terrifying grin, showing several dark holes between her teeth.

It wasn't the first time today Dora Dummitt had called her Shirley, Ronnie thought, thoroughly tired and miserable as she clambered onto the counter of the motor boat and through the hatch into the cabin. The woman must be muddling her up with someone else.

Inside the cramped space, Ronnie tore off her jacket, then removed her jumper and shirt. Too late she realised her clothes were still in her rucksack in the other boat. Dora hadn't given them a chance to unpack and she needed to get to her second pair of trousers and another shirt and jumper. Ronnie pulled a face as she tried to dry the top part of herself with a towel, hardly bigger than a teacloth, that didn't even begin to absorb the water from the dunking. Tears of frustration pricking her eyes, she flung it on the floor. She'd have to put the sodden clothes back on.

She heard footsteps above and then May's voice.

'Ronnie, are you there?'

'Yes,' Ronnie called. 'Very wet, very dirty, and no hope of drying off. My clothes are in the other boat.'

'I've come to tell you our dear Dora says to take what you need of her spares – they're in one of the drawers. She said to help yourself to underclothes as well!' May burst into giggles as she came down the cabin steps. 'Good luck.'

'I can't imagine anything more horrible than Dora's underclothes against my skin,' Ronnie said crossly, but when she saw May double up she couldn't help joining in the laughter.

When May had controlled herself she pulled out one of the drawers.

'Ooh, look what's in here.'

Ronnie tried to see over May's shoulder. 'We haven't got time for jokes.'

'No, look.'

Ronnie peered in. There were several sets of bloomers and vests, all neatly folded, all spotless white. But what gave her a start of surprise was a lacy brassiere.

'You can't believe it, can you?' May said incredulously, gazing at the very feminine undergarment. 'I'd have thought—'

'And *what* would yous have thought, miss?'

No, not Dora. Ronnie spun round, her face hot with embarrassment as though the comment had come from her own lips.

'Mary, yer can go back to the others. I'll find what Shirley needs.' Dora glanced at Ronnie. 'I see yous've found the undergarments. They'll be a bit big but at least they're dry.' She thrust her hand into a sack and pulled out a pair of men's cord trousers and a man's check shirt. 'Here, put these on. And these.' She threw a pair of thick socks at Ronnie. 'Yer might be needin' a coupla safety pins for the britches.' She put two huge safety pins on a shelf by the engine.

'Thank you very much, Miss Dummitt.'

Dora Dummitt grunted. 'I'll see yer outside in five minutes.'

She didn't mind being dirty and dishevelled, Ronnie thought, as she reluctantly but gratefully pulled on a pair of Dora's oversized knickers and a vest of equally large proportions. At home she could at least have had a proper wash, or even a five-inch bath. She'd often come in from the garden in a grimy, sweaty state, having dug up potatoes and tended the vegetables, though her mother constantly reprimanded her for looking a sight when she said she'd brought her daughters up to look and act like ladies.

No time to worry about looking and acting like ladies with a war on, Maman, Ronnie would mutter under her breath.

'Digging is men's work, Véronique,' Maman often remarked when Ronnie handed her a basket of vegetables. 'I wish you did not have to do it.'

But if she didn't, then who else was there? Besides, she enjoyed it and it saved having to queue for hours for a couple of onions and a cabbage. But what on earth would Maman say if she could see her now? Ronnie already knew the answer. Her mother would be horrified, especially if she ever set eyes on Dora Dummitt with her disgusting pipe.

Yes, Dora was a woman to be reckoned with, Ronnie thought, as she removed a hand bowl displaying a painted castle on its underside from a nail next to the range. She tipped the brown water from her soggy boots into it, then bent to fold up the trouser hems several times so she wouldn't trip over them. She hurried to put the shirt and jumper on, and the dry socks which were miles too big. Perhaps there was a better side to the woman after all.

'Okay, Shirley,' Dora broke into her thoughts as Ronnie came up to the cabin roof. 'Let's not waste no more time. We'll go through how ter open the lock again.'

Now bone-tired, and still feeling damp and thoroughly miserable, Ronnie needed the lavatory, but a cursory glance didn't reveal any nearby pub. She didn't dare mention it under Dora's glare but tried to concentrate on the woman's repeated instructions on how to open a lock.

'What's this called?' Dora challenged as she held up an iron handle.

'A windlass,' a blonde girl called Sally unhesitatingly answered.

'And what do yer do with it?'

'Open and close the lock paddles.'

'That's correct. Yous'll all have yer own windlass, but for now just watch me again.'

After a few seconds listening to the woman's drone, Ronnie's glance fell on May, standing a few feet away from the group. Her golden-brown hair was pinned in a victory roll. At this moment May was staring at Dora, but as the girl turned away, she sent Ronnie a wink with one of her big, baby-blue eyes. It was so unexpected and cheeky coming from someone who was as pretty as a china doll that Ronnie couldn't smother a gurgle of laughter. Dora whipped round, casting her suspicious gaze towards May, but by then May was looking perfectly innocent.

'Can we have a break?' Angela, a plain-featured, tubby girl, asked plaintively. 'I'm knackered.'

Angela was the trainee who'd smirked, Ronnie remembered, now desperate for a drink as well as the lavatory – even a few swigs of water would be welcome, but after the canal dunking she didn't dare draw any more attention to herself. She licked her dry lips, praying Dora would allow the trainees to stop for a while.

Dora took the pipe out of her mouth, then with her free hand drew a chain from her pocket and glanced at the watch face.

'All right. It's gettin' dark. We'll have to split in groups. From now on, you three – Angela, Sally, Margaret – will live in *Persephone*' – she jerked her head towards the motorised narrowboat – 'and Shirley, Jess and Mary will take *Penelope*.'

Would May dare tell Dora she was known as May, not Mary? Ronnie wondered curiously. But May said nothing.

'My luggage is in the motorboat,' Jessica said.

Dora grimaced. 'Anyone who has stuff in the wrong boat can change over after we have a cup of char. And anyone who's been stupid enough to bring a *suitcase*' – her gaze fell on Jessica, who Ronnie noticed had gone pink – 'you'll find there's nowhere to store it, 'cept on the roof. Take it home soon as yer can. The boat'll be very dark inside so yous'll need ter light the oil lamp. Then get the kettle on . . . use the flowered water can. I want ter go over a few things to all of yous so we'll cram inter the butty.'

As Ronnie was the nearest one to the butty, as she'd learnt to call the seventy-foot unmotorised boat, which was to be towed behind the equally long boat with the engine, she turned without a word and climbed down the ladder-like steps to the tiny kitchen below. The others piled in behind her. It was bitterly cold and smelt dank, and so dark Ronnie wondered how she'd be able to even find the kettle, let alone make the tea for seven women. But there it was, standing next to the Primus stove. An aluminium one that had escaped the governmental plea for aluminium to build aeroplanes. As she filled it from the can and set out the mugs, chipped and with rings of old tea stains inside, she was relieved to see Dora light an oil lamp. It flickered into life but the cramped space was still gloomy. Well, what they don't see won't hurt them, Ronnie thought, putting the mug with the deepest stains and a crack to one side especially for Dora. She found a large brown teapot in one of the overhead cupboards but there was no sign of any tea.

'Here, Shirley,' Dora said, reaching up to a shelf and handing her a tin. 'Only use three teaspoons of tea. Rationing is stricter here than home. But *I* take two teaspoons of sugar.

Somewhere there's a tin o' biscuits . . . ah, here they are, if there's any left.' She took the lid off and peered inside, the smoke from her pipe wafting over the contents.

Ronnie hid a grin as she thought of Maman's face.

'Now we're all here,' Dora began, 'I'd better go over some pointers. Yous all got yer ration books, I take it.'

The trainees nodded . . . except Ronnie, whose heart did a somersault. She'd had to lie about her age when she'd registered with their local grocer so she'd be given the fawn-coloured one for people seventeen and over.

'Hold on to 'em tight.' Dora stared at Ronnie. 'Yous old enough ter have yer own, Shirley?'

Ronnie drew in a breath as deep as the tight space allowed her. 'Of course, Miss Dummitt. But my name is Véronique.' She rolled her r's, producing a stifled chuckle from May. 'That's what comes with having a mother who's French,' she added, then gazed at Dora. 'But except for my mother, *everyone* calls me Ronnie. When you call me Shirley, I don't know who you mean.'

'Shirley Temple, o' course,' Dora Dummitt shot back with her bark of laughter. 'With all them curls.' She grimaced, which did nothing for her plain, weather-beaten face. 'Cocky one, her.'

'Actually, Shirley Temple is known for her *ringlets*,' Jessica, the tall young woman with wavy golden hair and brightly painted lips, spoke up.

Jessica still looked elegant after a long hard day's training except for an oily mark on her cheek which she couldn't know about, Ronnie thought with amusement, and her light brogues were now filthy from the towpath.

'And she's *blonde* – unlike Ronnie, who is very *definitely* a brunette – so calling her Shirley seems rather pointless to me,' Jessica finished.

'Yer seem ter know plenty about film stars, miss,' Dora said in a sarcastic tone as she took the mug of tea Ronnie handed her without as much as a thank you, keeping her eyes fixed on Jessica.

'Going to the pictures is one of my hobbies.' Jessica smiled sweetly. She glanced round, still smiling at no one in particular. 'And please, everyone, don't shorten my name to Jess. It's *Jessica*!'

Dora rolled her eyes. 'Anyone else care to tell me how she would prefer to be addressed?' she said, mocking Jessica's upper-class accent.

Jessica flushed, but Ronnie was sure it was from annoyance and not embarrassment.

'Well . . .?' Dora stood with her hand on her hip. 'Mary, *you* got another fancy name?'

'Only that I've already told the others me mam and all me friends call me May.'

'Well, we in't family nor friends,' Dora shot back, 'though that could change for the good or bad, dependin' how yer get on with the other wenches.' She puffed on her pipe, then nodded. 'All right, May it is. But I'm not goin' to keep spoutin "Jess-i-ker".' She threw a look at Jessica. 'Afraid you'll have to put up with Jess – from me, anyway,' she told her. 'And while we're on the subject, I'm Miss Dummitt to you lot. Got that, all of you?'

'Yes, Miss Dummitt.'

'Good. Now, if you'll all allow me to carry on—' Dora Dummitt took a mouthful of tea and spluttered.

'What the hell—?' She rushed to the hand bowl and with a horrible retching, spat it out. She spun round to Ronnie, her eyes streaming with tears. '*What* did you put in my tea, miss?'

'Two teaspoons of sugar, like you asked.'

'Show me,' Dora demanded.

Ronnie picked up a small dish.

'That's SALT!' Dora practically screamed. 'You *stupid* girl.'

'I'm awfully sorry,' Ronnie said, looking contrite. 'I don't know how it could have happened, but it was difficult to see what I was doing in this light.'

'Well, see it don't happen again.' Dora flung the contents of the mug in the hand bowl. The girls silently watched as Dora poured some water from the kettle into the mug and swished it round before taking up the teapot. She turned and glared at Ronnie. 'If yer can't see, stick yer finger in the bowl and *taste* it next time, ter be sure.'

Ronnie hid a smile. That was exactly what she *had* done.

Chapter Six

Wearily, Ronnie followed the other trainees as they climbed up the cabin steps and onto the dry dock to listen to Dora issuing more instructions. If anything, it was raining even harder now. Ronnie turned the collar up of her still wet raincoat as far as it would go, but heavy drops remorselessly found their way inside and dripped down her neck. Dora didn't seem to mind that she, too, was getting soaked.

The old bat is probably used to it, Ronnie thought. She probably doesn't even notice.

'The boats have the same blackout rules as cars and buses, so always pull the curtains over yer portholes at night,' Dora was saying. 'And in winter when we're workin' we have ter learn ter see in the dark. The headlight on the front of the boat – always make sure the dynamo's charged the battery. We need all the light we can get through the tunnels . . . and we get quite a few of 'em,' Dora added with a malicious laugh. 'So where were we? Oh, yes. The locks. We'll go through the procedure once more, and then again, until everyone feels they can be trusted ter work one theirselves.'

Ronnie thought the day would never come to an end. She was frozen and her stomach was rolling from only the tea and a cheese sandwich from the canteen at noon, the cheese so thinly sliced she could hardly taste it. How could Miss

Dummitt possibly show them anything more in the pouring rain?

'All right, that's enough 'til mornin',' Dora said, making Ronnie jump. 'Weather should be drier then. We'll call it a day as it's yer first one and if no one objects, we'll get a fish 'n' chip supper as I don't suppose anyone feels like cookin'. I'll pay in one go and yer can all pay me back termorrer when yer can see inside yer purses.'

There was a delighted murmur of assent.

'But first I'm goin' ter show yer how ter light the fires,' Dora said. 'If we don't do it before we leave, you'll find out how cold it'll be when we come back – enough ter freeze a bat's balls off.' She gave a throaty chuckle.

As soon as Ronnie stepped inside the fish and chip shop the fat-filled warm air from the two deep fryers greeted her. What a comforting smell! Even better were the tables set out with knives and forks on the wooden surface where a dozen people were already eating. She almost cried with relief that she would soon be eating a delicious meal. She took her place in the long queue, noticing Dora was at the front.

'Salt and vinegar?' the boy behind the counter asked when Ronnie finally moved to the front. He didn't even look up but carried on filling another order.

'Oh, yes, please,' Ronnie said. 'I'm with Dora Dummitt's group.'

The boy glanced towards the table where Jessica and Angela were tipping their suppers onto large white plates. Dora was eating hers straight out of the newspaper. He nodded and tossed a piece of fish and a good shovelful of chips onto a thick white plate, shook some salt over the meal and dribbled vinegar on the chips.

'There y'are, miss.'

Ronnie thanked him and joined the others.

'We'll eat first,' Dora said, her mouth full of chips, 'and then I want ter run through a few things while we're all here together in the warm.'

For ten minutes there was very little chatter as each of them tucked into the fish and chips. Dora was the first to finish. She wiped a sleeve over her greasy mouth.

'Right, you lot. I need ter go over the bed situation again for the next few weeks of trainin'. As yer know, there's really only room to sleep two in the motor and the same goes for the butty, which yer now know is mainly used for carryin' cargo. But while we're trainin' there's just about room to put three of yous in each boat.' She paused, a triumphant gleam in her eye. 'There's a small double foldin' bed so two of yous'll have ter get cosy in that – just pull it down from the cupboard next to the foldin' table.' She grinned. 'The third one – choose the smallest of yous – sleeps on the long bench. Yer head goes in the open cupboard. Should be some pillows 'n' all in there.'

Jessica grimaced.

'Anything wrong, Jess?' Dora pounced.

'No, not at all,' Jessica said quickly. 'I was just wondering where *you'll* sleep.'

'Me?' Dora pointed to herself with that grin again. 'There's barely room fer three, let alone four of us, in the boats, so I allus put up at the nearest pub. They all know me by now.'

Letting us all know how comfortable *she's* going to be, Ronnie thought scornfully, even though it wouldn't appeal to her at all to sleep over the top of some smoky pub. She'd prefer the boat any day of the week.

'Termorrer we'll have another lesson goin' through locks,' Dora said. 'It's one of the trickiest things yous'll be doin' and often one of the most dangerous. And don't make the mistake that when you've mastered one yer know how ter work all of 'em. They don't handle all the same.'

Ronnie groaned inwardly. Dora might not have thought she was paying attention when she'd fallen into the canal, but she had been. She just couldn't seem to keep all those instructions in her head.

'Yous'll all have yer own windlass,' Dora was saying. She opened a canvas bag and put six windlasses on the table. 'And woe betide anyone who loses hers because it's the most important bit of kit you can have. Without it, you're stumped. No one lends theirs so don't lend yours nor ask ter borrow one. They're as valuable as diamonds to boat folk.' She glared round at everyone.

'Now who's going to be doin' the cookin'?' Dora went on. 'You can take it in turns but it works better when one person is in charge as she knows what she's goin' ter prepare and what food ter buy.' There was a pause. 'Anyone like ter volunteer? If not, I'll do the choosin'.'

Ronnie was silent. At home she did most of the cooking as Maman not only wasn't very good but she wasn't in the least interested, so there'd been no option when Raine and Suzy had left home. But she didn't want to volunteer to cook in the cramped conditions of the boat. Sure that Dora was about to pick on her, Ronnie was surprised and relieved when Jessica spoke.

'I'll do it.'

'Any experience cookin' on a boat?' Dora said, her eyes narrow with scepticism.

'Plenty.'

'Oh. How's that?' Dora's tone had become steely.

'I've done loads of sailing,' Jessica said in just as firm a voice. 'My father had his own boat and I often cooked. I obviously know quite a bit about boats as well.'

Ronnie glanced at Jessica with new respect.

'Humph. Any experience on sailin' boats you'll soon find is no use whatsoever.' Dora lit her pipe, the smoke mingling with the smell of fish and chips. 'But until yer trainin's finished, when each team of three will be in charge of a pair of boats, yous can cook for all of us.' She threw Jessica a challenging look. 'All right?'

'Perfectly all right,' Jessica answered in a cool tone.

'Good. We stop ter buy food every three days unless there's somethin' really urgent – like my baccy,' she smirked. 'Sometimes when we tie up, the shops're a coupla miles away, so be prepared. When we get back yer need to have unpacked and used the toilet. I'm usin' the fancy word, but when I say "toilet" it's not what yer used to at home. And we can't always use a pub bog like we did earlier as there in't allus one when you need it. So we use a bucket in the engine room for that very purpose. You go behind a curtain. Those in the butty have yer own bucket kept under the counter.'

'Ugh.' Jessica screwed her face horribly. 'What do we do with the bucket afterwards?'

'It's the bucket-and-chuck-it method. Yer chuck it overboard – preferably when there's no one gawpin'.' She gave a mirthless chuckle.

There was some supressed laughter from May and Sally.

'Then allus rinse the bucket in the cut,' she continued. '*Never* with fresh water. And *do not* waste water. We carry very little and we've got more of yous on board than if yer trainin' was completed so yer need ter be creative. Never chuck out water. Use it several times over. Yer want a boiled egg? Afterwards a brew? Then you use the same egg water for yer tea. It don't hurt no one.'

Ronnie threw a glance at Jessica, who was pulling a face

at such a thought. She couldn't help grinning until Dora glared at her and carried on.

'The fresh water can – the one with painted flowers – is in the cabin. Another on the roof. Once it's gone, it's gone, 'til we refill 'em. Is that clear?'

'Yes, Miss Dummitt.' There were a few murmurs.

Dora Dummitt set her mouth in a grim line. 'Bein' a boater in't no picnic. If that's what you thought when you decided to join, you should pack yer things immediately and leave. That's all.' She stood. 'Right, if yer all finished, we need ter get crackin'. And no accidents on the way back.'

Ronnie finally crawled in over Jessica with whom she was sharing the three-foot bed, to take her place tight up against the wall of the narrowboat. She was exhausted, but Jessica never stopped tossing and turning, then throwing off the blanket and moments later suddenly pulling it off Ronnie and tucking it round herself. It was impossible to sleep. For one thing Ronnie didn't feel warm. It was as though the freezing cold water from the canal dunking had reached right into her bones. She was just drifting off when Jessica gave a loud snore and woke herself up. A moan escaped the girl's lips as she shot up in bed, scaring the life out of Ronnie.

'Jessica – are you all right?'

'Who . . .?' Jessica twisted round, patting Ronnie's face as though she had no idea who was in the bed with her.

'It's me . . . Ronnie, trying to go to sleep.'

'Ron . . .?' It was the cry of a wounded animal.

What on earth was the matter?

To Ronnie's horror, her bedfellow burst into tears and fell back onto the pillow.

'Jessica, what's the matter?'

There was no answer. Ronnie lay in the dark, her eyes wide open, fully awake now, listening to Jessica's snuffling.

'Can I get you anything?'

'N-no, nothing. Don't worry about me. I must've been dreaming. Go back to sleep.'

If only it was a case of going back, Ronnie thought grimly. She hadn't even begun.

Ten minutes later Ronnie was relieved when she heard Jessica's steady breathing. May, on the other hand, was lying so quietly Ronnie couldn't even hear her breathing.

I won't be able to put up with Jessica's racket every night, was Ronnie's last frustrated thought before she finally managed, through sheer exhaustion, to fall asleep.

Ronnie was awoken early the next morning by some strange noises outside. She sat up, her shoulder stiff from lying awkwardly. Rubbing it, she stepped over to the porthole to see if she could tell where the sounds were coming from, but it was as dark outside as it was in. What time was it? Her watch wasn't on the shelf above their heads where she thought she'd left it. Ah, it had fallen on the floor. She picked it up and scrutinised it, but there wasn't enough light to read the time. Her stomach was rolling. Her mind travelled back to last night. She couldn't remember washing, or even cleaning her teeth before she'd crawled into bed. She ran her tongue over them and pulled a face, then glanced down at herself. At least she'd changed into a pair of pyjamas, though she couldn't even remember doing that.

Perhaps dear Dora Dummitt had helped her. The ridiculous idea made Ronnie giggle.

'What's funny?' May called.

'Oh, you're awake. It was just something silly I thought of,' Ronnie said. 'I'm going to make some tea. Like one?'

'Yes, please,' May said. 'It'll be a real luxury. No one ever makes one for *me*.'

'Why's that?'

'Oh, my old job. I'll tell you sometime.' May put her legs out on the floor. 'Did you sleep?'

'Not much,' Ronnie admitted, nodding towards Jessica, who by now was irritatingly silent. 'Jessica's a snorer.'

Ronnie carefully poured water from the flowered can and put the kettle on to boil. She wouldn't mention how Jessica had called out in the night and seemed upset about something. It wasn't her business. If the older girl wanted to talk out her problems, that was up to her, and she'd listen and give any advice she could, but only if asked.

'What about you, May? Did you manage to sleep?'

'Slept like a log – woke up in the fireplace.' May chuckled, then said, 'Ronnie, can I ask you something. Did you really mistake the salt for sugar in Dora's tea?'

'What do you think?'

'I don't think you made a mistake.'

Ronnie smiled as she put three mugs out. 'Sugar, May?'

'I'll put my own in, thanks very much,' May said, giggling. 'It's safer. And you knew jolly well what you were doing. So did all of us. We didn't know where to put ourselves. Oh, Ronnie, Dora's face . . .' She threw back her head and laughed until the tears ran down her cheeks.

There was a scuffling noise from above.

'What was that?' May said, the laughter choked back as she looked up.

A pale moon-like face, pipe in mouth, peered through the hatch.

'Talk of the devil,' May muttered to no one.

'It's half-past six,' Dora announced, her pipe moving up and down with the words. 'I've let yous all sleep in on yer first mornin' but from now on I want yous up at half-past five, so the boats're thoroughly cleaned and we let go by six-thirty latest. Today we shan't be away until half-past seven, by the looks o' things.'

'Miss Dummitt, what was all that noise outside earlier on?' Ronnie asked boldly.

Dora removed her pipe. 'That'd be the boats chuggin' by. The boaters often start as early as three or four in the mornin'. They gotta make their money. I 'spect yer heard 'em whippin' the towlines over the top o' yer.'

'Oh.' It was all so strange. Would she ever understand?

'Margaret's makin' porridge for us,' Dora went on. 'One of yous can go and collect it in ten minutes. If yer late you'll eat it cold.' She drew her head back and disappeared.

'It was funny I just said "Dora" and she appears like a genie from a lamp.' May pulled a face. 'As if she knew we was talking about her. Well, it's too bad if she did. She certainly don't mince *her* words.' She leapt off the bed. 'Can I have what's left in the kettle, Ronnie, so's I can have a quick wash?'

'There's only a cupful.'

'That'll do. I'll wash down as far as possible, and up as far as possible, and just have to leave possible out!' May chuckled as she took the kettle off the ring.

'I'd better wake Jess,' Ronnie said, cringing at May's crude expression. 'Deadly Dora's like a sergeant major and Jess doesn't take too kindly to being ordered around.'

'Oh, I love that name for her.' May gave a scream of laughter. 'Deadly Dora.'

'What's the joke?' Jessica's voice startled them, as she swung her long shapely legs out of the bed.

'Ronnie calls our dear trainer "Deadly Dora",' May snorted.

Jessica grinned. 'Sums her up perfectly, I'd say.' She looked at the kettle. 'Anyone making tea?'

'We've had ours,' Ronnie said. 'May's just going to use the last drop of water in the kettle for her wash.'

Jessica threw May a fierce look. 'You can put the kettle back on the ring right now, May. That cupful will just be enough for my tea!'

Ronnie's stomach was rumbling as she knocked on the side of *Persephone*. She swiftly stepped through the hatch to find Margaret ladling out the porridge.

'Is that tall one up?' Dora Dummitt looked at her watch and peered at Ronnie.

'If you mean Jessica, she's choosing what to wear, I expect,' Angela said scornfully.

'This in't a fashion house.' Dora rolled her eyes, then shrugged. 'Well, I won't have her keep us waitin'. If she in't ready at seven-thirty, she can stay behind.'

What an ogre the woman was. Ronnie took the saucepan from Margaret. The porridge looked lumpy, reminding Ronnie of the three bears. She broke into a grin.

'Somethin' funny, Shirley?' Dora demanded as she took up her pipe. The trainer had already wolfed her porridge down.

Ronnie didn't answer.

'You, miss. I'm talkin' to yer.'

'Oh, did you mean *me*?' Ronnie said innocently. 'Sorry, I didn't realise. I thought I'd explained that yesterday – that I don't know who you're talking to when you say Shirley.'

'We've a lot ter get through today, and all the other days,' Dora Dummitt said, completely ignoring Ronnie's remark and making little popping noises with her lips on the pipe stem as she endeavoured to light it. 'So I don't want any backchat. Just concentrate, all of yous at all times. Eat sharpish, then clean and tidy the boat before leavin'. Put yer blankets away so they don't get wet when it rains, fold away yer mattress and put up the cross bed into the bed 'ole so it in't in the way . . .'

Dora gave a few more instructions that Ronnie either didn't understand or couldn't keep up with. She rolled her eyes in frustration.

'Boats are never to be left untidy or dirty,' Dora continued. 'And I mean *never.* There's a routine ter keep 'em clean, and it'll come natural once yous've done it a few times, but for now we need ter get on with the day's run on the cut.' She paused. 'I'm goin' outside. There's no room to breathe in here. Until then I want everyone outside by five to eight.' She disappeared.

'I'm off then,' Ronnie said. But before she could put the lid on the saucepan there was a muffled noise above them and Jessica's feet clad in brogues, newly polished after their beating yesterday, appeared through the hatch. She was down in a flash, her long figure causing the small eating space to become even more squashed.

'I came to see where you were,' Jessica said, glancing at Ronnie accusingly. 'You've been gone ages and May and I are starving.'

'Just coming,' Ronnie said.

'I really dislike that woman,' Jessica said when she and Ronnie were back with May in the butty and they were eating the by now lukewarm porridge. 'If she can get a dig in, she will. And she seems to have it in for Ronnie even more than me.'

'She'd bleedin' jump on *any* of us if we put a foot wrong,' May said. 'It's just her way. I wouldn't take no notice.'

'Well, she did come up trumps when she lent me some of her clothes,' Ronnie said. 'My spares were all in here.

Anyway, we haven't got time to moan about her. We'll get our heads chopped off if we're not outside by five to eight.'

Everyone except Jessica had gathered on the dock wall before eight. The minutes ticked by. Dora sniffed and looked at her watch.

'Where the bloody hell is she?' She looked at Ronnie and May. 'Well? You two live with her.'

'She was doing her face when Ronnie and I left,' May said with a giggle. 'Though who's going to take notice of her in this weather, I don't know.'

At least it wasn't raining, Ronnie thought, but the wind whistled through the thin leafless branches which overhung the canal. She shivered in her new raincoat even though it had a warm lining and she had a thick jumper on underneath. She wished she was still wearing one of Dora's vests. It was much thicker than the one she'd packed.

The other girls were beginning to fidget and mutter.

'Someone, go and fetch her,' Dora said, her face screwed in irritation. 'She's to come *now*!'

'Here I am, everybody.' A smiling Jessica appeared on the roof and agilely jumped up onto the dock wall to join them.

'Yer late,' Dora said. 'I won't be kept waitin'. Yer to be punctual, same as everyone here who managed ter be on time. What was yer doin'?'

'I'm actually only five minutes late,' Jessica said, her smile fading. 'I was emptying the bucket, if you must know. Not a pleasant job as the person who used it before me hadn't left it very clean.'

'Sorry,' May spoke up immediately. 'That must've been me. It's so dark in there you can't see a thing.'

'But yer had time for a full make-up, miss,' Dora snapped at Jessica.

Jessica blinked. 'I do that every day. It's normal routine for me. I have to be ill if I haven't got my lipstick and mascara on.'

'Yer not here to be no fashion model,' Dora said scathingly. 'I'm beginnin' ter have grave doubts you'll make a good boater, miss, even if yer daddy *do* have his own boat. This in't no game and I won't put up with no nonsense from yous or anyone.'

Angela whispered something to Sally and Dora pounced on her.

'If yous've anything ter say, miss, spit it out.' Dora glared at her.

'Just that we were all talking last night,' Angela said. 'We had a bet – that Jessica wouldn't last.'

'Why on earth did you bet that?' Jessica demanded, her eyes sparking.

'I think I know why,' Ronnie blurted out. 'Yesterday when we were all covered in mud you had one small streak on your face. No mud anywhere except your lovely new shoes which you've polished like a mirror. We'd love to know how you could have kept so clean.'

Jessica dropped her gaze on each girl in turn, and Ronnie suddenly felt uncomfortable. She'd gone too far. Her sisters put up with her often tactless remarks – they were used to them – but she didn't know these girls. She gave a sideways look at Jessica whose mouth twitched at the corners. To her relief Jessica gave a sudden hoot of laughter.

'Well, who knows,' she said. 'You may be right about the bet. But then again, you might not be.'

'If yous have finished decidin' who will last the course and who won't,' Dora interrupted, a scathing edge to her voice, 'let me remind yous *I'll* be doin' the decidin'. P'raps yer ready to begin yer second day's trainin' – if it in't too much ter ask.'

Chapter Seven

'Right then, we're ready ter let go, and this time get further than Bull's Bridge.' Dora bent to untie the straps. 'We don't have ter come back ter the depot again. We'll be trainin' as we go. But we need ter be doubly careful terday. Look at them trees.' She pointed beyond the boat depot to light woodland where the trees were swaying alarmingly. 'It's a strong wind and yer need ter watch out for any overhangin' branches. They can be boogers.'

Dora seemed to be in all places at all times, shouting orders to Ronnie and the others. Ronnie could see they had as little idea as *she* did about what was supposed to happen next.

'I need one of yous ter help me get the engine started,' Dora said. She raised her voice. 'Sally?'

'I'm not sure how—'

'Oh, for heaven's sake,' Dora growled. 'I haven't time ter go through it all again.'

Ronnie hesitated. At least if she could do what had looked like a straightforward manoeuvre yesterday when Dora was showing them, the woman might give her a bit of credit. Besides, she was fed-up hanging around outside trying to understand the workings of the locks. It made no difference if the rain stopped; the air was so damp and the cold so raw, it found its way deep into her bones. She was already down to her last socks and even they felt damp still. She must remember to dry them on the stove tonight.

All this whirled through her brain as Dora looked round for a volunteer.

It would be warm inside the engine room.

Before Ronnie could change her mind, she said, '*I'll* come with you.'

Dora threw her a sharp, sceptical look. 'All right. But mind yer pay attention. And watch where yer step. Yer don't want another bath before time.' There was a muffled giggle from Sally which Dora ignored. 'Jess, you come, too. Angela, Sally, May—' She broke off. 'Where's May?'

'I hope she's lighting the stove,' Jessica said. 'It's freezing in the butty and we all need a wash.'

'There's no time for no wash,' Dora said. 'Maybe later this afternoon. We need ter get ter the first lock.' She paused and looked at the group. 'We've got quite a few ter get through,' she added with a smirk.

'When yer on yer own with two others you'll need ter work in pairs ter start the engine,' Dora was saying without looking round as Ronnie stepped into the engine room. 'It's easy when yer know how.'

Ronnie was struck by how unfamiliar all the levers and brass rods looked today. She couldn't remember any of them, only that the flywheel was the most important piece of machinery that kept the engine running smoothly.

'I'll do the starting handle if yer pull over the compression lever,' Dora said to Ronnie.

'What can *I* do?'

Dora twisted her neck round as Jessica stepped forward.

'I'll do the startin' handle. Here. Slowly does it. Careful.

Hold it like this. Then turn it and you'll see the flywheel rotate. When I count to three, Ver-ron-eek—' She paused to let the mocking pronunciation of Ronnie's full name sink in, 'push this lever over. Right. One, two, *three*!'

Ronnie pushed the lever and like magic the engine began to thrum. Dora pulled a cable.

'This' – she tapped it, her voice rising above the thundering of the engine – 'is the governor rod. Makes it go faster, but we're not allowed ter go more 'an four miles an hour – tops. So bear that in mind. It's a safety rule. Yer can be sacked if yer caught speedin'. Another thing ter watch out for is the other boaters. They don't allus take too kindly to the trainees.'

'We can't go all day like this without a proper wash,' Jessica grumbled as Dora disappeared. 'I shall stink.'

'I'll be sure not to stand too close to you.' Ronnie kept her face straight and Jessica raised her eyebrows as though wondering whether or not to take her seriously, which made Ronnie burst into giggles.

Jessica sniffed. 'I'm not sure personal hygiene is exactly foremost on Dora's mind, so I suppose we'll just have to get on with it.'

'Margaret, yer our hobbler this time,' Dora shouted at the short, thin girl when the six trainees had squeezed into the engine room. Ronnie couldn't see at all what was going on. 'You remember what to do?'

'Um, isn't it to do with the locks?' Margaret's fair skin reddened.

'Yes, but what exactly?' Dora barked.

'I have to get off the boat and go ahead of you,' Margaret said, obviously embarrassed that all eyes were on her.

'And then what?' Dora demanded. She glared at Margaret, who lowered her eyes. 'And then what, Margaret?'

Margaret pressed her lips together and shook her head.

'Ter get the lock ready for the boat ter go in,' Dora said, in an irritable tone. 'And how do yer do that?'

Margaret screwed up her face. 'I can't remember exactly . . . something to do with the paddles.'

Dora clicked her tongue. 'Lucky Percy'll be around and he'll show yer. But what must yer allus remember to take with yous?'

Margaret stood there shaking her head.

Dora looked at the small group, her mouth turned down at the edges. 'Sally?'

'The windlass, Miss Dummitt.'

'Correct.'

Margaret turned bright red and immediately scuttled off, returning with a two-foot iron rod in the shape of an 'L'.

'Now yer equipped to do the job, Margaret, we'll see yer at the lock which yous'll have prepared. It's quite aways so you'll have ter get a move on – unless yer ride that fancy bike of yours.'

'It's difficult to ride in the mud, Miss Dummitt,' Margaret said, 'so I think I'd better walk.'

'I s'pose yer don't want to get no mud splashes on it.' Dora turned to the others, a smirk on her face. 'While Margaret's doin' that, I'll show yer how ter tie the boats tergether – side by side. It's called "breastin' up". Then when we're travellin' with empty boats it'll only take one wench to steer.'

Dora mentioned such items as the snubber, a very long rope if the next distance between locks – that they were to call the pound – was flat for a decent period of time, the checking strap, which Ronnie immediately forgot the purpose of when Dora went on to explain about shaft poles, which apparently had all kinds of uses such as pushing the boats away from the bank and clearing rubbish in the locks

. . . Dora reeled off the names of other pieces of vital equipment until Ronnie began to feel she could cram nothing more into her brain.

She didn't remember a thing from yesterday, and today was no better. She felt sorry for Margaret, yet slightly comforted. Dora hadn't been getting just at her and Jessica. She wondered how on earth she could get on the right side of Dora without having the rest of the girls accusing her of 'sucking up'.

'Ver-ron-eek, you take the tiller on the motor!'

Ronnie startled out of her reverie. This was awkward. None of the trainees had done any steering on their own.

Dora called out, 'Take May with yer.'

That wouldn't be a lot of help, Ronnie thought. May wouldn't know any more than *she* did.

'Can you remember what to do, Ronnie?' May said, as the two girls made their way to the stern of the boat.

'The one most important thing,' Ronnie said furrowing her brow. 'Always turn the tiller towards the thing you don't want to hit. In other words, the opposite direction you would expect.'

'Oh, yes, I remember that,' May said, chuckling. 'So nothing can go wrong, then?'

'Don't tempt fate,' Ronnie said soberly, 'or we'll be in deep water – literally.'

To her surprise, Ronnie thoroughly enjoyed steering the narrowboat along the cut. That was until she realised there was quite a bit of traffic on the canal to negotiate, often accompanied by shouts and cheers and waving arms from the children who stared from the roofs of the passing boats.

May pointed. 'Oh, look, Ron, at that man leading his horse to pull the boat – it's not making half such a racket as our engine noise.'

Immediately Ronnie worried it was too heavy a load for

the horse. But when she dared take her eye off the steering by sending quick glances over to the boater and his horse, she couldn't see any sign that the animal was suffering.

'We're coming to the first lock, Ronnie,' May said. 'Dora said as it's right next to the basin we need to breast up before going through it.'

To Ronnie's relief Dora appeared, and with the help of Jessica tied the two boats side by side, all the time calling out instructions.

Ronnie's heart beat hard. There were two pairs of colourfully painted boats behind her, and men shouting, though she couldn't make out what they were saying. They sounded annoyed. Probably only too aware they'd be held up by a bunch of amateurs – especially women, Ronnie thought, her frown of concentration deepening. Oh, if only she knew all the unwritten rules of the cut.

A man of about sixty was talking to Margaret and pointing to the paddles on the lock. Margaret was nodding, so Ronnie hoped she was taking it all in. Frankly, she was worried about her. Margaret was so thin she didn't look strong enough to work the heavy locks, or indeed a lot of the other jobs that constantly needed attention. As she watched, Dora joined the two of them and Ronnie was amused to see that Percy, if that was the lock-keeper, was holding the conversation, not Dora.

'Me and Percy'll work the lock,' Dora called out, as Ronnie drew the boats closer. 'Yous all need ter watch close as yous'll be doin' it termorrer.' She looked up at Ronnie. 'You and May listen to what I tell yer when the two boats are in the lock.'

Ronnie held her breath, her pulse racing, as she steered both boats into the lock that Dora had cautioned them against. This was the tricky bit.

Gently does it. Don't rush.

Ready to sigh with relief when both boats were finally in

position as far as she could make out, May's shout startled her.

'Ron, pull away!'

The warning was too late. Ronnie flinched as a loud scraping noise set her nerves on edge. Then a thump. She'd hit the side of the lock. Furiously, she jerked the tiller.

'Wrong way!' May bellowed.

The motor rammed again into the side. Ronnie thought she could hear Dora cursing above the noise of the water pouring into the lock. Biting back tears of frustration, she turned the tiller to the left this time, and miraculously the motorboat pulled away from the edge, *Penelope* bobbing a few feet away at the side of them.

Taking what seemed like hours but was only minutes, the pair of boats finally passed through the lock and into the calmer waters of the canal. Ronnie swallowed hard, bracing herself for Dora's showdown. But surprisingly, when the trainees had formed a group on the towpath Dora merely grunted.

'Yer'll know better next time, Ver-ron-eek. You in't the first nor the last wench ter do that on yer first time. So all of yous take note.' She glared at the others, then struck a match to light her pipe. 'Both boats'll need paintin' but it in't the end of the world. They never give us lot the best boats anyways.'

'Do you need any help, Jessica?' Ronnie asked as she stepped into the tiny kitchen space that evening. The table was strewn with vegetable peelings, an opened tin of baked beans, a jar of Marmite and a packet of oatmeal. A saucepan of something savoury was simmering on the stove.

'I'm more or less finished,' Jessica said, her face in full concentration as she turned the page of a cookery book. 'But it's been a nightmare trying to find everything I need. I wanted some stewing steak but of course that's impossible to get hold of these days.'

'What are you making?'

'Goulash.' Jessica looked up with a tight smile. 'But I fear for it.'

'So do I,' Ronnie giggled. 'I've never even heard of it.'

'Really?' Jessica slightly curled her lip. 'I thought everyone knew goulash – it's Hungarian.'

'Well, that's why. I've never eaten anything Hungarian.' Ronnie gave a self-conscious laugh. 'Have you done a lot of cooking?'

'Only got my certificate for completing a cordon bleu course in Paris,' Jessica said. 'And before you ask, a cordon bleu cook has attained the highest possible standards. Thankfully, I attended before the war when you could get good quality ingredients. It's almost impossible nowadays to put a delicious meal on the table with everything rationed – or so it feels like. But at least I know how to make a decent meal from nothing.'

'Gosh.' Ronnie blinked. 'I bet you could show my French mother a thing or two. She's an awful cook. I have to do most of it and I'm not really interested.'

'Strange your mother is French and can't cook,' Jessica commented.

Ronnie didn't bother to tell her that they used to have a cook in their old life. What would be the point?

'Maybe you'd become interested if you knew how.' Jessica raised an eyebrow.

Ronnie shook her head. 'No, but I do love growing vegetables. Nothing from the greengrocer's tastes as good as the ones you grow yourself.'

'You see, you're already halfway there if you have beautiful fresh vegetables.' Jessica studied Ronnie. 'I'm surprised you didn't join the Land Army if you like being outdoors so much.' She didn't wait for an answer but frowned. 'What on earth can I use instead of the steak?'

'What about corned beef?'

'Ugh. Dreadful stuff.' This time there was a definite curl of Jessica's lip. 'Can you imagine the chefs in Paris cooking with it? They'd rather die.'

'We won't expect you to go that far,' Ronnie said, laughing. 'But it's a whole lot better than nothing, so why don't you try it? There's bound to be a tin in one of the cupboards.'

'It goes against all my principles,' Jessica said.

'Not mine,' Ronnie grinned. 'And I bet it doesn't go against any of the other girls' principles either – or Dora's . . . especially Dora's.'

'If she's ever had any,' Jessica shot back.

Ronnie lowered the table cupboard and peered at the shelves. Triumphantly, she grabbed hold of a tin of corned beef. 'Just what Chef Jessica has been looking for. I think you'll do very nicely,' she said, addressing the tin.

Jessica looked doubtful. 'I suppose I'll have to give it a go, though I'll know who to blame if it tastes like a dog's dinner.'

'My Rusty would be delighted with it, then,' Ronnie said, grinning. 'It's his favourite – a really good dog's dinner! But there's no need to say anything to the others. After all, there is a war on.'

'That's one thing we *did* learn,' Jessica said. 'When something goes wrong with a dish, never apologise and never explain. But I'd be grateful if you don't mention that I'm a qualified cook. This is *not* going to be one of my successes.'

Dora wiped her mouth from the remnants of Jessica's goulash on the sleeve of her jumper and Ronnie grimaced inwardly, thankful her own jumper had now dried and she was wearing it. The trainer gave Jessica a sharp look. 'What did you say it was?'

'Goulash.'

Ronnie stifled a giggle. It sounded awfully grand for what she'd have termed 'corned beef stew' but everyone had cleaned their plates and said it was delicious.

'Hmm. Sounds a bit foreign ter me,' Dora said, looking at her empty plate as though she couldn't believe she'd eaten every scrap. 'But I'm sure yer did yer best.'

Jessica rolled her eyes, making Ronnie turn what threatened to be a burst of laughter into a cough.

'Anyone fancy the White Swan?' Dora said as Sally and May rinsed the plates and set the saucepan to soak. 'I don't know about you lot, but I'm dyin' for a pint. It's close to Denham where we'll tie up and The Green Man where I'm puttin' my head for the night.'

'I'm up for it,' Jessica said immediately. 'And wouldn't a glass of decent wine go down a treat?'

'Do you think she's gone to change?' May said when they'd moored and Dora had gone to fetch her overnight bag.

'Oh, yes, definitely. She'll be in evening dress and full make-up, no question,' Jessica chuckled. 'Which is what I now propose to do.'

Everyone looked at her in astonishment.

'Are you really?' Sally said.

'Don't be daft.' Jessica's eyes were full of mischief. 'But it wouldn't hurt us to freshen up a bit if we're going out. I just wish I hadn't been so worn out last night that I didn't put my hair in curlers. It looks awful.'

'It doesn't at all,' Ronnie protested. 'It's such an unusual colour – like a fairy story princess.'

'Thank you, kind lady,' Jessica chuckled.

'When you've both finished yapping about Jessica's hair,' Angela cut in, 'maybe we can find out who's going.' She paused. 'I'll say yes.'

'And me,' Sally said. 'What about you, Margaret?'

'All right.'

'May?' Sally turned to her.

'I thought it was a foregone conclusion,' May laughed, 'seeing as how I used to work in a pub.'

'Ronnie, are you coming?' Jessica said.

'No, I won't, thanks. I'm going to have a proper wash. I feel really grimy. Then I'm going to bed with a book.'

'I'd prefer to go to bed with a man meself,' May chimed in with a scream of laughter.

Ronnie felt the heat rise up her neck and into her face. She looked away.

'Sorry, Ronnie,' May said, her laughter dying. 'I didn't mean to offend.'

'You didn't,' Ronnie mumbled. 'Not in the least.'

She couldn't help liking May, but she did sometimes say things a bit close to the mark. Maman would definitely *not* have approved of some of the company she was keeping.

Please let them all just go and leave me in a bit of peace.

She wasn't used to being around so many girls all the time and in such proximity. At home she could just jump on her bicycle, Rusty in the basket, and go off wherever she pleased. Or simply stay in her bedroom with him. Have time and space to think.

At the thought of Rusty her eyes welled.

'What's the matter, Ronnie?' May put her arm round her. 'Come on – I was only teasing.'

'I know.' Ronnie bit her lip. Why wasn't she like the others, all happy to go off to the pub?

'Dora didn't say a time so we'll give ourselves twenty minutes,' Jessica declared. 'That should give her plenty of time to complete her transformation.'

'Don't be bitchy, Jess,' Sally said with a grin.

They'd gone. Ronnie took in a few deep breaths. No voices in her ear. No shrill laughter. No Dora ordering her what to do – making her look and feel small.

To have the whole cabin to herself was sheer luxury. Longing for a bath but making do with a full wash, she dried herself on the same mean-sized towel from yesterday, then slipped into her pyjamas. Her hair felt gritty but it would have to wait a few days more. She cleaned her teeth and delved into her rucksack for one of her books.

It was strangely quiet except for the faint crackle of the coal burning on the fire. It was a homely sound as its warmth spread through the boat, and for the first time in the last two days she thought she might have made the right decision to become a boatwoman. She allowed herself a small smile. Who would have thought it? For a fleeting moment she wondered how Maman was. Dora had mentioned they'd all get three days off when they'd completed their training. Maybe after those weeks away she and Maman would get along better. She just hoped Rusty wasn't missing her too much.

The cabin was quite dark. She looked round for the oil lamp – anything to give her enough light to read, but there didn't appear to be one. She opened all the cupboards and fumbled inside but found nothing except a box of candles. Well, that was all they had in the old days, she told herself. Now where would a candlestick be hiding? Ah, there was one on the shelf above the bed. The candle was on the thin side and wobbled in the holder but it would do. Pleased with herself for finding a box of matches in one of the drawers she lit it. Immediately, part of the cabin glowed with the flickering light. Carefully setting it back on the small shelf she hopped into bed, immediately feeling soothed by the unexpected peace in the cabin and the bed she didn't at the moment have to share. Hopefully, she'd be asleep before Jessica and May returned.

She opened the book Mrs Hunter had recommended, *The Water Gipsies*, but after a couple of pages of squinting at the tiny print she gave up. Maybe she wasn't in the right mood. She reached for her other book: *Little Women*. Suzy had lent it to her, telling her she *must* read it because she was just like fifteen-year-old Jo. Ronnie eagerly turned to the first page and was quickly absorbed in the goings-on of the March sisters, four American girls whose father was away fighting a civil war. It made her think of Raine and Suzy. She swallowed hard.

After half an hour she felt her eyelids begin to droop. She'd just finish the chapter and snuff out the candle. It was Ronnie's last thought before falling asleep.

Chapter Eight

Ronnie shot up in bed, blinking in the darkness, her heart beating in her ears. A fire in the shed! Rusty! She had to save him! She tried to get out of bed but she couldn't move. Her limbs were solid as concrete. She swallowed the long seconds. And then she calmed, her breath settling to its natural rhythm. She told herself not to be so silly. It was just a bad dream. She was on the boat – perfectly safe, and so was Rusty at home, even if Maman didn't give him the cuddles he was used to. But the air around her . . . She sniffed. Then her eyes went wide, her chest tight. She could still smell burning! Her hand flew to her mouth to bite back the scream. The coal stove? The Primus? But there wasn't even a glow. The fire must have already gone out. The candle! What had happened to the candle? She jerked her head upwards to the shelf. Oh, no! That was where the smell was coming from.

How long ago had it overturned? Oh, if only there was a light. Of course! She suddenly remembered she had a torch. Stumbling out of bed she bent low, her arms flailing, trying to feel for her rucksack. There! She dug into the outside pocket and her fingers enclosed it. Thank goodness she'd thought to pack it. Oh, but why hadn't she remembered and used it instead of the candle? She switched it on and pointed it at the shelf, then picked up the fallen candle. To her horror she saw a burn hole and scorched shreds of wood, the damage the size of a saucer. Dear God, she might have set the whole boat on fire and at the same time asphyxiated herself!

Dora would go berserk when she found out. Ronnie clenched her jaw. She mustn't find out. Whatever happened, she mustn't see it. It could be enough for Dora to send her home.

As she stood wondering how to get rid of the smell, she heard laughter and noisy footsteps. They were already returning from the pub. One of them was singing, and another joined in. Well, the girls in the motor boat wouldn't be able to smell anything, but Jessica and May certainly would. She'd have to come clean with them and make them swear not to say anything to Dora.

May was still singing as she dropped through the hatch, Jessica behind her, swearing as her foot slipped on the last step.

'What's that smell?' May hissed.

'Shhh,' Jessica warned loudly. 'Don't wake Ronnie.'

'I'm not asleep.' Ronnie shone her torch onto the two girls' startled faces.

'Something's burning,' May said. 'What happened?'

It was suddenly all too much. Ronnie dropped on the bed and put her head in her hands. Tears trickled between her fingers.

'I couldn't see to read,' she said in a muffled voice. 'I forgot I had a torch so I lit a stupid candle. I was reading and fell asleep. Then I must've turned over and somehow knocked it. Or it could have been the boat rocking . . . I don't know.' She began to sob.

'Dear Lord.' Jessica rushed to the bed and put an arm around her. 'It's a wonder the whole boat didn't go up in flames with all this wood. But thank goodness you're safe. No harm done.'

'Only the shelf,' Ronnie muttered.

'Let me look.' Jessica took the torch and shone it onto the burnt patch. 'It's nothing so terrible. Keep your book over it and no one will be any the wiser.'

'I just don't want Dora to find out,' Ronnie sniffed. 'I know it was inexcusable to be so careless but I don't want to be sent home.'

'You won't be,' May said. 'We won't let you. What are friends for if they can't stick together?'

'Especially against that old bat,' Jessica grinned. 'We won't even let the other girls know about it.'

'Least said, soonest mended, is what I always say,' May added.

Ronnie looked up at the two girls, so very different to one another, but making a vow to keep her secret. It reminded her of Raine and Suzy. Ever since they were children the three of them had made a special pact never to keep secrets from one another, but also never to spill them to Maman or anyone else. She realised how much she missed the camaraderie of her sisters, but to her relief it looked as though May and Jessica wanted to be friends.

'Thank you for standing by me,' she said.

'You didn't think nothing different, did you?' May said.

Ronnie shook her head and wiped her eyes with the back of her hand.

'Here, blow your nose.' Jessica handed her an immaculate white handkerchief embroidered with a 'J'.

'It's too nice to use.'

'Don't be daft. Things can always be washed.'

'Shall I make some cocoa?' May said.

'What's the time?' Ronnie asked.

'Coming up to midnight.'

'Perfect time,' Jessica laughed. 'Be like boarding school when we used to have midnight feasts. I might just have a ciggie.' She glanced at May. 'Would you like one?'

'I've given up.'

'Since when?'

'Since just now,' May said, picking up the water can. 'The stink of smoke in the pub made me feel queasy. And sitting next to Dora with that disgusting pipe didn't help. But all this talk of midnight feasts' – she paused to fill the kettle – 'course I wouldn't know about them. I never went to no posh school. Left at fourteen, I did, to look after three screaming little horrors – but talking of feasts is making me hungry.' She took a half loaf from the bread bin. 'Anyone want a cheese sandwich?'

'Yes, please,' Ronnie and Jessica chorused.

May nodded and cut three thick slices. She looked up, a sly smile hovering over the pretty mouth. 'You know, I've just thought of something. This smell won't be gone in just a few hours and guess who'll be the first to show their ugly mug?' She jerked her head towards the hatch. 'Dora, that's who. So tomorrow morning, who's up first must get the stove lit, then put a couple of slices of bread on the top and leave it on too long so it burns. That will really make it smoke. Then when she comes in and smells burning we can show it to her. It'll put her right off the scent,' she chortled.

'Excellent idea, May,' Jessica laughed, springing up. 'Come on, Ronnie. Up the table for May's midnight buffet.'

Ronnie sat down. 'I don't mind admitting I burnt the toast.'

'Be a lot easier than explaining how *Penelope* came to be a burnt-out shell,' Jessica teased as she carefully fixed her cigarette into a long ebony holder. She flicked her lighter, lit the end, drew a deep breath, rounded her mouth and proceeded to huff out a string of smoke rings. Ronnie watched, awestruck. Jessica was so sophisticated. She'd never met anyone like her before. She wondered if Raine would get on with her. Mmm, she might. But she'd be too much for Suzy, that was certain.

'Just be careful with that fag, Miss Hamilton-Bard,' May said, putting the mugs of cocoa on the table, 'or *you* could be the one doing the explaining.'

But it wasn't Dora who woke them, it was Angela. And all of them were fast asleep when she shouted through the hatch, 'Anybody up? It's six o'clock. Dora says we have to leave at seven latest.'

Ronnie awoke with a jerk. She'd lain awake next to Jessica for at least an hour after they'd all gone to bed, worrying about the candle damage. Thankfully, Jessica hadn't been so restless and finally Ronnie had drifted off, but she'd been in a deep sleep and Angela's loud tone had scared her half to death.

She scrambled out of bed.

'I can smell something,' Angela called down, and to Ronnie's horror the girl dropped heavily into the cabin. 'What is it?' She looked accusingly at Ronnie, who was furious with herself that she'd overslept and had nothing to offer as an explanation.

'Oh, I . . .'

'I had a ciggie in the early hours.' Jessica sat up in bed. 'It must be that. But it was too cold to open the hatch.'

Angela's eyes narrowed. 'I know cigarette smell,' she said. 'It isn't that. Something's burning – or has already burnt.' She looked round and her eyes fell on the candle, now back in the candlestick. 'Did you light a candle when you came in last night, Jessica?'

'No,' Ronnie cut in. 'It was me. I was hungry when the others came in last night and fancied some toast. I burnt it, that's all.'

'I don't believe it.' Angela scanned the small space, then her gaze went back to the candle.

Before Ronnie realised what Angela was about to do, the girl snatched up her book and gave a gasp as she saw the damage. 'What's been going on here?'

'I don't know what you mean,' Ronnie said.

'This is new,' Angela said triumphantly as she fingered the burn. 'And the wick has been used. It looks like the candle toppled over and set fire to the shelf.' She swung round. 'Do you realise you could have set the whole boat on fire – and ours as well?'

'What's going on?' May sat on the edge of her folding bed and rubbed her eyes. 'Oh, it's you, Angela. What d'ya want?'

'To tell you to be ready by seven,' Angela snapped. 'But I'm more worried about Ronnie and her lighted candle last night. Do you know anything about it?'

May shook her head. 'Why should I? We were out, if you remember.' She sniffed the air. 'Oh, you're on about the burning smell. We had some toast when we came in last night and burnt the first round.'

'Don't give me that.' Angela looked from one to the other. 'Ronnie's already told that lie. Just have a look at that shelf. I'm going to have to report this.' She turned to go up the steps.

'I wouldn't do that if I were you, Angela,' Jessica said, her voice steely. 'It was an accident and no harm done.'

Ronnie shivered. Even in the dim light Jessica's eyes were flashing dangerously.

'That's hardly the point.' Angela's voice was cool. 'Ronnie was careless to the point of stupidity, and you know it, Jessica.

Heaven knows what she might do next. She certainly doesn't act like a responsible adult. And quite frankly, I don't believe for one minute she's eighteen next month. I think that's another lie. But that will be easy enough to confirm. And get her sent home to her mummy.'

She was gone before Ronnie could open her mouth to reply.

Chapter Nine

'I want a word in private with yer about last night.' Dora Dummitt surveyed Ronnie from the roof of the *Persephone* as she puffed on what looked like an unlit pipe. She'd beckoned Ronnie over just before they were ready to let go.

'Miss Dummitt, I can explain—'

'I hope yer can. And while the others are gettin' the next lock sorted yous'll have the opportunity.'

Ronnie's heart sank. Angela was acting like the school bully and must have already reported her.

The hour dragged by for Ronnie until they came to the first of several locks. Angela and Margaret were trudging along the muddy towpath to get it ready. This time Sally was at the tiller with Dora warning her not to bash the sides of the boat in what would be another narrow space and Jessica and May were preparing lunch in *Penelope*.

'She's all yours,' Dora told Sally as the boat was safely inside the lock and the water was streaming out. 'Hold it steady until the level's the same as outside.' She paused. 'Ver-ron-eek, me and yous'll sit at the table. I want ter know what's bin goin' on.'

Sally sent Ronnie a swift glance, then looked away, chewing her lip, making Ronnie feel even more nervous.

'So, miss . . .'

Dora Dummitt sat without interrupting, only tapping her pipe on the table while Ronnie recounted the accident. Ronnie had already made up her mind there was no point in lying to the woman. The burnt shelf was proof enough. But she didn't mention Angela.

'Yer know yer coulda set the butty on fire,' Dora said icily. 'And it coulda spread to the motorboat.'

Ronnie bent her head. 'I know,' she mumbled. 'I can't believe I didn't snuff it out. But I've never been so tired in all my life. That's why I fell asleep without even realising.'

'No excuse,' Dora snapped. 'By the end of the week yer goin' ter be worse tired than that. Yer need to keep yer wits about yer, girl, and remember everythin' I tell you. It's like I said yesterday – there are all sorts of dangers on the cut besides drownin'. Folks've lost fingers when workin' the paddles, slippin' on the roof and breakin' a leg – that's happened before – yer never know what's round the corner. Often another impatient boater tryin' to squeeze in front. Yer have to be ready for it.' She gave Ronnie a hard stare. 'Are y'up to it?'

Mrs Hunter had asked her the same question. But did this mean Dora was going to give her another chance?

'Yes, I am. I promise.'

'How old are yer, miss? And don't give me no lies.'

'Seventeen . . . next month,' she added.

Dora frowned, then seemed to come to a decision. 'All right. I won't say nothin' 'bout you bein' underage. A month is neither here nor there, s'far as I'm concerned.' She gave her hideous smile. 'Maybe I'll make a boater out of yer one day!'

Ronnie forced herself to look at Dora Dummitt. She couldn't believe she'd been let off so lightly. Angela must have even told the trainer she didn't believe Ronnie was seventeen, but Dora obviously had her own way of dealing with such matters and was not going to be swayed by anyone. Ronnie wondered what Angela would say. Angela had strongly hinted Ronnie would be sent home.

'Right, that's it,' Dora said, leaping up. 'We've work ter do but let me tell you, miss, I'll be watching yer closely.'

'Thank you, Miss Dummitt. I won't let you down.'

'See yer don't,' Dora grunted. 'Now get the kettle on and make the tea. Two sugars for me – an' don't go puttin' no salt in it, mind.'

'We've just used the last of the condensed milk, Miss Dummitt,' Jessica said when she and May joined them and Ronnie had set a mug in front of everyone. 'We need to top up on food. Can we stop somewhere today?'

Dora nodded. 'Tring. It's a village. We'll be there about four if we put a move on.'

'Is it far from where we tie up?'

'No.'

'I'll go, Miss Dummitt,' Ronnie said, feeling the need for a normal walk to stretch her legs instead of the trudge along the towpath in the mud to the next lock.

'I'll go, too,' Jessica said. 'In the meantime, I'm going to make some soup for lunch, and wash these mugs – if that's okay with you, Miss Dummitt.'

Dora nodded and stood. 'Right, everyone else ready?' She turned to Ronnie. 'And yer can bring me some baccy.'

Ronnie was conscious of several boats queueing behind them, some of the boaters shouting what sounded like swear words about wenches, as she frantically tried to fathom out how this particular lock worked.

She'd managed in the end but as the two narrowboats

approached the next lock and Ronnie was about to jump down onto the towpath a boater, bundled from head to toe in old clothes and a cap and standing on his roof, had put two fingers up at them and without a word gone on his way.

'What a rude man,' Sally said. 'I gave him plenty of room.'

Dora, keeping an eye on Sally at the tiller, threw her head back and roared.

'He weren't makin' no rude sign,' she said between guffaws. 'He were tellin' us he's left two locks ready for us.' She lifted two fingers. 'See – one, two. He were doin' us a favour!' She screamed with laughter again. 'Yer need to learn the rules of the cut. That goes for you, too, Ver-ron-eek.'

It was the longest run of locks they'd experienced but luckily there'd been a nice lock-keeper who'd prepared the last three, to everyone's relief. Ronnie would gladly have put her feet up with a cup of tea, but she still felt the most enormous relief that she wouldn't have to be in Angela's company for the next hour or two. The woman was causing an atmosphere by her withering glances at Ronnie, arguing with everything she said to the point where Ronnie kept her mouth closed. She wondered how Margaret and Sally, who saw a lot more of her, managed to put up with her overbearing attitude.

'What's up with our dear Angela?' Jessica said as she and Ronnie left the towpath to join a hikers' trail which led to the village.

'She's annoyed because Dora didn't send me home.'

'What!' Jessica's pretty mouth fell open. 'Do you mean she ratted on you to Dora about the candle?'

'Yes.'

'Dear Lord, what on earth did Dora say? Did she hit the roof?'

'She warned me about fires and told me being exhausted was no excuse. But you know, Jessica, I don't think she likes being told what to do by anyone – least of all one of the trainees. Angela also told her I wasn't seventeen.'

Jessica swung round. 'Good God, how old are you, then?'

'Well, I'm seventeen next month but I was two months away when I applied. It seemed so silly to be only a few weeks away from the minimum age, so I let them believe I was seventeen already. I was so sure I'd be an asset but I'm not at all sure about that any more.'

Jessica chuckled. 'I'm sure none of us is an asset yet,' she said, 'but we're bound to be at the end of our training.' She looked curiously at Ronnie. 'Did you tell Dora the truth about your age?'

'Yes.'

'And . . .'

'She said it didn't matter. And that she'd make a boater out of me one day.'

Jessica laughed. 'Let's hope she does it for all of us,' she said, 'although I worry about Margaret. She's such a thin little waif. I think she's finding this particularly tough.'

'But she's game,' Ronnie said. 'We'll all have to help her as well as fatten her up.'

After the best part of half an hour the two girls reached the village with its pretty parish church and the usual smattering of local shops.

'This one looks like it sells everything,' Ronnie said, opening the door. Glancing round she took in the variety of items. Second-hand clothes swung on a rail over the newspapers and magazines, cakes and bread jostled with a large shallow box of cheeses and a bowl of eggs, tinned goods sat side by side with fresh vegetables and fruit, there was a bacon and ham slicing machine taking up a third of the counter, with a couple of shelves behind that held tobacco and cigarettes.

The middle-aged lady behind the counter put her pencil down and looked up, her expression sour and her brow furrowing.

'Yes?'

'Good afternoon,' Jessica said firmly. 'We would like to buy some condensed milk – six tins, if possible.'

Ronnie felt uncomfortable as the woman looked them up and down. What was this about country people being so friendly?

'You'll be the new trainees with Dora, I suppose.'

'Yes, that's right.' Jessica gave the woman a bright smile. 'We've moored close by, and now we're all dying for a cup of tea.'

The woman pointed to a high shelf. 'I have to use my steps, but you're tall – you can reach it. But no more'n two, mind.'

'Oh,' Ronnie couldn't help exclaiming. 'Dora – I mean Miss Dummitt – said we were allowed several at a time.'

'Your coupons,' the woman demanded.

Jessica stuck her hands in her mac pockets and brought out an envelope. She glanced at it and tutted. 'Drat! I thought I'd got them. This is my shopping list.' She turned to Ronnie. 'Did you bring them, by any chance?'

'No, I thought *you* had them.'

'I suppose you both know there's a war on?' The woman pursed her thin lips.

'Yes, that's why we're learning to do this job,' Ronnie said, ignoring the woman's sarcasm.

'Hmm. Was there anything else?'

'Some potatoes and a cabbage . . .' Jessica began. 'Two tins of Spam, two tins of corned beef and a packet of rice, please. Oh, and some cheese and a dozen eggs.'

'And you expect me to provide all that with no coupons, no ration book?'

'If you could please let us have these things we'll be back in the morning with the coupons, we promise.' Jessica leaned over the counter. 'Please.'

'I'm sorry, I'm not allowed to do any such thing.' The woman shook her grey head. 'You can have the two tins of milk even though I shouldn't be letting you – it's just been rationed this week, but as it's old stock I'll turn a blind eye. And you can take a few potatoes and a cabbage. That should keep you from starving. Anything more, you'll have to come back.'

'What about dried egg?' Ronnie said, knowing it was rationed and crossing her fingers.

'You've not learnt much from your mother, have you?' the woman snapped. 'It's rationed as well. One tin *only* every two months.'

Jessica stepped forward.

'Allow me to deal with this, Ronnie.' She stared the woman in the eyes. 'We're working hard to get coal to you and everyone else so you don't freeze to death this winter. I think you can trust us to come back tomorrow with the blasted coupons.'

'There's no need to blaspheme,' the woman said, her eyes beady with anger.

'I'm not,' Jessica shot back. 'I'd just be grateful if you could use a bit of wartime spirit, that's all. We're all in this together, in case you haven't heard.'

'I've heard, all right.' The woman's mouth became a grim line. 'Take some potatoes and a cabbage. You've got the milk. That comes to one and eleven pence ha'penny.'

Jessica slammed two coins on the counter. 'Keep the change,' she growled as she flung the items into her basket. 'Thank you for your most kind help.'

'What a sarcastic young woman,' the woman said, looking at Ronnie. 'I sometimes don't know what people are coming to.'

'What time are you open tomorrow?' Ronnie asked, ignoring the shopkeeper's remarks.

'Eight o'clock.'

'I'll be there on the dot to collect the other items,' Ronnie said over her shoulder as she followed Jessica out of the door. When they were out of earshot, Ronnie said, 'Dora's not leaving 'til half-past eight because we had all those locks, one after the other. Even *she* can see there's a limit to how many hours we can keep going.' She grinned at Jessica. 'While you're having a lie-in, I'll be getting the rest of the stuff.'

'It's not absolutely necessary, Ronnie. There's bound to be somewhere else on the way that's open tomorrow.'

'But Dora said specifically we only stop every three days for food shopping. She won't want to waste time again. And we'd have to tell her we forgot the coupons . . . and her blasted "baccy". No, let me do it my way. But for goodness' sake find me the coupons now, so I don't have to search for them in the dark in the morning.'

Jessica chuckled. 'All right. I don't suppose you can come to much harm at that time of day.'

Chapter Ten

Ronnie walked briskly towards the village, pulling the fresh air into her lungs, her thoughts whirling. She still couldn't quite get over Dora not sending her home. Maybe Dora's bark was worse than her bite. She couldn't help smiling, although this train of thought led her to Rusty – and how he was getting on with Maman. Even though her mother had conceded to look after him, Rusty would still miss all the cuddles and conversations he was used to. Well, she'd be home for three days after the training period, although that was still more than five weeks away. Strange. She'd only left home three days ago, yet it seemed much longer.

She looked at her watch. Coming up to five to. It was going to be tight getting the rest of the order and back in time. She just hoped the miserable old bat would be punctual. It occurred to her it would probably have been sensible if she'd arranged to borrow Margaret's bicycle with its roomy saddlebag, but the girl seemed loath to ride it herself let alone lend it to anyone. Maybe it was just as well. Ronnie half ran the last few hundred yards and it was exactly eight when she arrived, a little breathless, outside the village shop. The sign on the door said OPEN. Thank heavens. At least the old bag was punctual.

The bell tinkled as Ronnie pushed the shop door to. No

one was in sight. She waited a few minutes, impatiently tapping her foot, then called: 'Anyone there?' She was just about to call again when the same dour woman came through a door at the back of the shop. Even though she must have recognised her she made no sign.

'Yes?'

'Do you remember I came in with my friend yesterday and we forgot the coupons so we couldn't buy much?'

The woman nodded.

'Well, I have them here, and the list.' Ronnie slid the ration book and Jessica's shopping list across the counter.

The woman was efficient, you could say that about her, Ronnie thought, watching as she swiftly put the items into the string bag. She used a short stubby pencil to tot up the bill.

'That'll be five and three,' the woman said.

Ronnie handed her a ten-shilling note and waited for the change, checking her watch. Just gone quarter past and Dora liked to meet five minutes before letting go. She'd barely make it, even if she ran all the way. And the bag was heavy. It was then that she heard the sound of a motorbike roaring to a halt outside. Seconds later the shop bell sounded and the rider breezed in. Instinctively, she turned and looked up. A pair of sparkling brown eyes met hers. One of them gave her a saucy wink as he whipped off his tweed cap that he'd been wearing back to front. It made his black curly hair stand comically at all angles. He was maybe just a few years older than herself and wearing what looked like Raine's flying jacket. He grinned at her.

Reluctantly she dragged her eyes away from his gaze and turned back to the woman who was silently watching.

'What will it be, Will?' The woman behind the counter looked even grimmer, if that were possible.

Will. So that was his name.

'Come on, Flossie, give us a smile. It'll take years off yer.' He strode up to the counter.

Flossie's mouth tightened into a thin line.

'I'll take no cheek from you, lad,' she said. 'What is it yer after?'

He turned to Ronnie, his grin widening.

'It can wait,' he said, not looking at the woman but keeping his eyes fixed on Ronnie. 'But yer might have a bit of a problem if yer one of them trainee wenches, 'specially if Dora's yer boss. She likes ter leave on time.'

'I know.'

But how did he *know?*

Ronnie picked up her string bag and without another word brushed past him and out of the door.

'Hey, not so fast.' He was right behind her. 'Yer goin' ter be late. I'd better give yer a lift on the bike.' He nodded to the shining black motorbike propped on its stand.

'No, I—'

'Don't be daft,' he said. 'She leaves on the dot and yer not goin' ter make it. Yer don't want to get Dora's goat, now do yer? Come on, I'll help you on.'

She hesitated.

'I'd better introduce meself. William Drake, at yer service.' He made a mocking bow. 'But Will ter me mates.' He paused, his brown eyes gleaming with mischief. 'And yous?' He waited.

'Um, Ronnie Linfoot,' she mumbled, her head bent. He was too much for her. Her chest tightened. She felt the telltale heat rush to her face as she tried to think of something to say.

'Boy's name.' He nodded as though he approved. 'What's that watch of yours say?'

'Nineteen minutes past,' she said, her heart thumping uncomfortably in her ears, hoping against hope that Will Drake couldn't read what was going on in her head. To sit on the back of his motorbike, her arms . . .

'Wasser matter? Don't yer trust me?'

'Yes, but—'

'I'm not takin' "no" for no answer.'

Before she could protest he picked her up as though she weighed no more than the bulky string bag she carried and set her on the pillion, then swung himself up, took the handles and revved the machine.

He twisted round. 'Hold on. We'll be there in two shakes.'

Feeling acutely embarrassed, the bag gripped between her knees, she put her arms round the leather jacket. It felt strange. *He* felt strange. She imagined she could feel the muscles beneath her hands. He twisted his head round.

'That a butterfly sittin' behind me or a real live bird?'

She blushed though she had no idea what he was talking about.

'Put your arms round me really tight. That's better. Yer gotta hold on. And lean with me when we go round corners or we'll both be for it. Just foller my movements and yous'll be okay.'

She was glad he couldn't see her face. For an instant she wondered what it would be like to be kissed by Will Drake. But he wouldn't want to know her – a tongue-tied girl who looked a mess from head to toe – more like a boy than a girl. Her cheeks felt they were on fire and for a few seconds she laid one side of her face softly against the cool smooth leather. He would never know.

Even though she was grateful and relieved when he set her down two minutes before half-past eight on the towpath opposite *Persephone* and *Penelope*, she wished those precious six minutes hadn't sped by as fast as Will Drake's two wheels of his motorbike. She wouldn't be late. And it was all due to Will Drake who'd come to the rescue.

He faced her, then deliberately pulled off one of his gauntlets and stuck his bare hand out.

'Nice ter meet one of Dora's wenches.'

Furious with herself for wearing gloves, and not daring to be so obvious as to remove one, she took his hand. But even through the woollen gloves she felt the warmth of him. The air was cold but her insides were melting.

He grinned, showing white even teeth.

'We're actually called boatwomen,' she said boldly.

He gave a short laugh, reminding her of Dora's usual mocking tone. 'Nah. That takes years of experience afore yer one of them.' He looked at her intently. 'Yer don't look strong enough ter prepare a lock let alone steer a boat – but maybe I'm wrong.'

'Maybe you are,' Ronnie said firmly.

'How d'yer get along with our Dora?'

'She has a lot to put up with, showing the ropes to six of us greenhorns,' Ronnie said, choosing her words carefully.

'That don't say nothing about her as a person,' Will Drake said, chuckling. 'Yer can be honest with *me*.' He pointed to himself. 'If yer want my opinion, she's a right ol' biddy. But she knows the boats and the cuts better'n anyone else around here, I'll say that for 'er.'

Ronnie couldn't think of any suitable reply.

'See yous around sometime,' he said as he stepped on the accelerator. 'Say hello ter Dora from me.'

Before she had time to reply he'd vanished.

It was only when she turned to step onto the roof of the butty that she saw Dora Dummitt silently watching from *Persephone*'s roof.

Ronnie's head swam. Dora hadn't been anywhere in sight when Will had pulled up or surely she would have noticed. But Dora would have seen him ride off, no doubt about that.

Ronnie licked her lips. *Keep calm.*

'Where've yer bin, girl?' Dora said, scowling, not bothering to help her onto the slippery surface.

'I went to the village shop to pick up the rest of the food we needed.' Ronnie held up the bulging string bag, her voice wavering, knowing her face would give her away no matter how hard she tried to explain.

'Why didn't yer get everything yesterday?' Dora growled.

'We forgot the coupons.'

Dora opened her mouth and huffed out a huge sigh.

'And I was worried I was going to be late,' Ronnie gabbled on. 'But luckily Will Drake came into the shop – he said he knows you – and gave me a lift so I'd be back in time.' She hauled herself up. 'It was very kind of him,' she added.

'Hmm.' Dora pulled her mouth tight. 'Yer want ter watch Will Drake. He's a one for the girls. Always got someone new on his arm. Then he loses interest and dumps them for the next poor bitch. I wouldn't like to see you or any of the other trainees get entangled.'

Dora might as well have punched her in the stomach.

'Oh, I-I . . .' Ronnie swallowed hard. 'I'm not interested in him like that.'

But she knew she was lying. For the first time in her life she knew what it felt like to be dumbstruck over some boy. She remembered his warm body through the leather jacket when she'd put her arms round him, holding him more tightly than she needed. The moment when she put her cheek against the back of his jacket, so lightly he would never have known. She took a jagged breath.

'What would you like me to do, Miss Dummitt?'

'You'd better go down and make yerself a cup of tea, girl,' Dora said, 'while the rest of us let go. And put him out of yer 'ead before it's too late.'

Chapter Eleven

But Ronnie couldn't get Will Drake out of her head. What was the matter with her? She'd never been remotely interested in boys before. But Will was more than just any boy. In truth he was a man. But he obviously liked playing around with girls and breaking their hearts, so it was just as well she'd never see him again.

She glanced through the porthole to where Jessica was feeding out the snubber from the stern of the motorboat.

'Loop it over the T stud on the bow, May,' Jessica called.

'Right-o.'

'Now tie it onto the motor.'

Sighing, Ronnie drained her cup, then feeling a little guilty she climbed up to join them.

'Can I do anything?' she asked.

'Nothing at the moment,' Jessica said, glancing up, 'but Dora told me to tell you when you finally emerged – they were her words – that she wants you to come off the boat at Cowroast lock. Then you have to walk to Tring Summit which is a long muddy stretch . . . and if Dora says it's long, you know it is, so be warned. She wants you to open the first downhill lock – on your own.'

Ronnie startled. 'But I've never opened a lock completely on my own.'

'Well, now's the time to learn,' Jessica chuckled. 'It won't be just yet because the pound is quite a long stretch before we get to Marsworth, Dora said.' She turned to May. 'Okay, May, let me feel it's secure enough.'

Ronnie left them to finish the job.

Dora hadn't asked any of the girls to open a lock on their own, Ronnie thought, as she mooched sullenly along the towpath, one hand stuck in her raincoat pocket, the other holding the two-foot iron windlass. Why had Dora picked her out? It was becoming a pattern and she didn't know what to do about it. What would Raine have done? Maybe have it out with her, but Ronnie knew that wouldn't go down with Dora, who would rightly say that she was the trainer and knew best how to do her job. Ronnie pulled a face. She had a strong feeling Dora's suspicious eyes were on her even now.

A roll of thunder broke into Ronnie's train of thought. She stopped and looked up at the overhead sky. The clouds were black and foreboding. She couldn't hear any birds twittering as they normally did. Probably they were already bedded down from any oncoming storm. Unusually, there was no sign of wildlife on the canal, or even any boats coming towards her. She walked on, the wind lashing her face, making it burn.

Forcing herself to concentrate on all that Dora had taught them about opening locks, her heart sinking, she trudged along. How far was the damned thing? She must have been going at least a mile but there was no lock in sight. Maybe there would be a kind lock-keeper who would help her. She glanced behind her. *Persephone* and *Penelope* weren't even in view. More worrying was a thick mist which blocked out the fields she knew were there. It was as though she were the only soul in the world. How much further to the bloody lock? Dora shouldn't have told her to come off the boat so soon. She must have done that on purpose.

Ronnie was beginning to feel her temper rising. She squinted ahead. Oh, thank goodness – that dark shape must be it. It couldn't be that far now.

Without warning the heavens opened, then a crack of lightning zigzagged in front of her, making her jump. It was followed by a roar of thunder. Rivulets of icy water ran down her neck, squelched in her boots, soaked her socks. Her hair hung in sodden corkscrews and the drops of rain ran into her eyes. The towpath became a mire and she felt herself sinking several inches in places. So much for the Wellington boots the woman in the shoe shop had insisted would take her through the worst weather.

She needs to come out here and see how her wonderful boots were holding up.

Finally, Ronnie reached the lock that had been built next to the open reservoir. Without warning a great gust of wind tore her hat off. Cursing, she attempted to catch it but it sailed on in front of her. She peered at her watch. It had taken her almost an hour to walk the pound. Surely Dora could have set her down at one of the bridges she'd passed so it wouldn't have taken her this long. The woman was obviously still testing her. Ronnie twisted her head and stared hard through the rain. To her relief she could see *Persephone* slowly leading the way. She peered into the lock space which was empty. She'd have to fill it. She ran over the procedure in her mind. First open the paddles at the top.

The wind flapping her raincoat, Ronnie fixed her windlass onto the socket and turned the ratchet to slowly raise the paddle, wanting to shout with joy at the sound of running water. It wouldn't be long before it filled and the boats could enter. Then to her dismay she watched as the water ran through the bottom gate, completely running to waste. What a stupid idiot! She should have closed the bottom gate first before trying to fill it. Dora would be furious.

Almost in tears she took hold of one of the bottom paddles and immediately wished she hadn't. It was covered in filth and slime. She opened her hand and spread her fingers, now thick with dirt and grease, in front of her and groaned aloud. She didn't even have a handkerchief. Her raincoat wouldn't stand a chance of keeping clean.

'Put your back against the white bit of the gate,' she heard the echo of Dora's voice in her ears. 'Walk slowly back. The brick path under yer feet will help yer grip.'

Ronnie turned and leaned against the end of the gate, pushing one foot, then the other behind her, but the gate refused to budge. She tried again, more firmly this time, but nothing happened. She bit her lip, remembering Will Drake's words that she didn't look strong enough to him to prepare a lock. She stuck her chin out. She'd show him. She'd show them all – especially Dora. Using every possible ounce of strength she pushed again. Her boot slid and her head banged against the paddle as she landed in a heap.

'Need some help?'

She knew that voice. Holding her throbbing head with her free hand she looked round and into the laughing eyes of Will Drake.

Oh, why did he have to catch her at her worst moment? She needed to get the gates open immediately but Dora would be furious if she saw Will helping her.

'I . . . um . . . yes, that would be very kind,' she said, trying to struggle to her feet. But the country scene in her vision shifted and blurred in front of her and she fell back.

Will bent low and put both arms around her waist.

'Hang on ter me . . . that's it . . . easy does it.' He sat her on one of the beams. 'That's the second time terday I've come to yer rescue.' He grinned, showing white teeth. 'Yous all right?'

Her cheeks flaming and not daring to look him in the eye she said, 'I'm all right but my head isn't.'

He put his hand to her face and lifted the wet curls on her forehead.

'Hmm. That's gonna be a good'un.'

'A bruise?'

''Fraid so. Yous best stay there and I'll finish the job.'

Dazed, her head throbbing madly, she watched as Will Drake opened the gates. His style was slow but focused, and seemingly effortless. He raised his thumb to alert the two boats that they could enter and as soon as they'd eased their way into the narrow space, one behind the other, he closed the bottom gates behind them. Ronnie staggered over to watch how he let the water in, fascinated to see *Persephone* and *Penelope* gently float to the surface. But her fascination only lasted seconds when she spotted Dora at the tiller of the motorboat. If looks could kill, Ronnie thought, she and Will would have keeled over on the spot.

For a moment Will looked as though he would ignore Dora's face, twisted with fury, until she shouted something Ronnie couldn't quite catch.

Will shrugged and opened the front gates to allow the two boats to smoothly go through. Dora steered *Persephone* over to the side of the canal and tied it up; *Penelope,* with May steering, followed in its wake. Dora leapt out.

'What d'ya think yous're playing at, Will?' Dora's eyes were like black slits.

'Your trainee wench had an accident.'

Dora grimaced as she rounded on Ronnie. 'What happened, miss?'

Ronnie pushed her wet curls back off her face, unconsciously mirroring what Will had done.

'Hmm. That wants seein' to,' Dora said, her tone sharp. She put a hand on Ronnie's arm. 'Come on, I'll help yer back on the butty. There's a nurse lives not far along the cut just before Fenny Stratford.'

'I can take her on the bike,' Will said. 'Get her there in no time.'

'She's in no state to be ridin' bikes,' Dora said.

'Then I'll see her on the boat.'

Dora opened her mouth to argue but Will had already got his arm round Ronnie and was leading her towards the two boats.

'Which one's yours?' Will said, turning to her.

She could feel the grip of his arm through her raincoat. She was feeling light-headed. Was it the bang on the head? Or was it to do with Will, so close to her she could feel his breath on her cheek when he spoke?

She pointed to the butty and he helped her onto the deck.

'That's enough,' came Dora's strident voice from behind. 'I'll see to her now.'

'As yer like,' Will said. He glanced at Ronnie. 'Get that seen to.' In a flash, he took her face in his hand and kissed her swiftly on the lips.

'Go!' Dora practically screamed. 'This minute.'

Will whipped off his cap, and with a wide grin gave Ronnie an exaggerated bow.

It was as though they were the only two people in the world. As though Will Drake had created some kind of aura around them that no one else would be able to penetrate. She couldn't understand what was happening to her, only that her pulse quickened and her breath caught.

'Hope I'm there next time yer need a knight in shinin'

armour,' he said, laughing, and sprang from the boat and onto the towpath. With a wave of his hand he disappeared.

Ronnie didn't know how her legs managed to hold her up as she slid through the hatch. She pulled down the folding bed and lay on it, not caring about the lump already forming on her head nor Dora's wrath. She needed to think. Quietly. Nothing like this had ever happened to her before. Will's presence thrilled every bone in her body. Shakily, she put her finger to her lips. They felt bruised. No boy had ever kissed her. And she'd never bothered about 'that sort of thing' as she called it when friends at school went on and on about their boyfriends, or how to meet one, or sobbing over the one who'd finished with her.

Will's kiss had been totally unexpected. And to think he'd done it in front of Dora – well, it made her admire him all the more. Dora certainly didn't intimidate him.

As she lay there trying to calm her beating heart, she heard Dora's voice outside, talking to one of the others. She couldn't hear what Dora was saying but anxiety began to form like a knot in her stomach.

She knew she hadn't heard the last from Dora.

Chapter Twelve

'There. You should be fine now.'

Nurse Martin washed her hands at a sink in the front room of a cottage which faced the canal. Ronnie was lying on the patient's bed where the nurse had cleaned her forehead and dabbed on some TCP, making Ronnie wince and her eyes water with the sudden sting. The room filled with the familiar smell.

'Best antiseptic for minor injuries,' she said, examining Ronnie's forehead again. 'I don't think it needs a plaster. Better to have the air on it. Let it breathe. There's only a bad graze but you've got a superb bruise coming out.'

Ronnie closed her eyes. *Will said that's what would happen.*

'If you have any dizziness, blurred eyesight or memory loss, then you must go to the nearest hospital right away as it's likely to be concussion.' She paused. 'Get up nice and slowly.'

Ronnie took in a shaky breath as she put her feet on the floor, then stood.

'You don't still feel dizzy, do you?' Nurse Martin asked.

'No . . . thank you. I feel all right. Sorry to make a fuss.'

'You did the right thing,' the nurse said. 'And I doubt you'll have any repercussions, but don't do too much today, have an early night and you'll be right as rain in the morning – if today's weather is anything to go by we'll be having more "right rain" tomorrow,' she added with a smile, looking towards the window where it was splashing down the panes in deep rivulets.

'It was the rain which made opening the lock so slippery,' Ronnie said.

'You have to be very careful on the cuts, especially at this time of the year.' The nurse removed the bottom sheet of the bed and deftly folded it. 'We're probably in for a long spell of winter. I take my hat off to you girls working on the boats in bad weather. But many of the trainees don't stick it, and frankly, I don't blame them.' She suddenly cocked her head. 'What's going on? Did you hear that?'

There was the sound of muffled shouting outside. Nurse Martin hurried to the window and peered through the rain-streaked glass.

'It sounds as if someone's in the thick of an argument,' she said.

Ronnie was desperate to get a look over the nurse's shoulder, but it was impossible as she was several inches too short. Frustrated, she jumped up and saw Dora waving her arms and looking agitated. Maybe Will hadn't 'got lost' as Dora had ordered him to.

Ronnie smiled to herself. Will wasn't the type to be ordered around by Dora or anyone.

'It's the police!' Nurse Martin turned to her. 'Two of them. It looks like they want to go on board and Dora's not having any of it. They're all standing there in the pouring rain.'

Ronnie took a step back. The police? What on earth did they want? It flashed across her mind that she was glad Will wasn't still hanging around, though why she would think this she had no idea.

'I'd better go,' she said to Nurse Martin. 'Thank you very much for looking after me. I was feeling quite rough.'

'I could see you were,' the nurse said. 'Now, remember – any trouble at all from that head and you'll have it examined by a doctor. Is that clear?'

'Yes, I promise,' Ronnie said.

'Can you see yourself out?'

'Of course.'

Still feeling a little light-headed, Ronnie held on to the banister rail as she went down the stairs. She opened the front door to hear Dora demanding:

'Show me yer search warrant.'

'Rather than getting soaked, if you'd allow us to come on board, I'll be pleased to show you, madam,' the older and shorter of the two men said.

Dora pursed her lips. 'Yous'd better come with me, then.'

What were they looking for? Ronnie put the collar of her raincoat up and followed them onto *Persephone*'s deck. Dora swung round.

'Oh, there you are.' Dora turned to the sergeant, who briefly put his hand up to his cap in a half salute, and the younger man, who touched his helmet.

Once they were through the hatch they removed their hats. Ronnie noticed the younger one had a thatch of shiny brown hair, almost too long for a policeman.

The older one cleared his throat. 'I'm sorry, we haven't introduced ourselves. I'm Sergeant Sandford and this is Constable Scott, investigators for the Grand Union Canal Carrying Company.' He briefly touched a badge with the letters GUCC on his shoulder, then handed Dora a piece of paper. Her eyes flicked over it.

'Don't mean nothin' to me,' she said, giving it back.

Did that mean Dora couldn't understand it? Or that she couldn't actually read it?

'Would you like me to read it out?' Constable Scott asked.

'No, it don't matter. If yer say it's a search warrant, I'll have ter believe you.'

The constable turned to Ronnie.

'May I have your full name, Miss . . .?'

'Miss Véronique Linfoot,' Ronnie said, rolling her 'r's in the French style. Constable Scott raised his eyebrows. 'But known as Ronnie by everyone except my French mother.'

The constable's mouth twitched at the corners but he didn't say anything, merely nodded and jotted it down in his notebook.

'Well, yous'd better carry on,' Dora said. 'But yer won't find nothin' here suspicious.'

'Thank you, Miss Dummitt.'

The sergeant nodded at the younger man and they began looking through the cabin, opening cupboard doors and peering into them, lifting lids of pots including the water can, and to Ronnie's consternation even checking the lavatory bucket. She hoped to goodness it had been cleaned and disinfected. Constable Scott pulled down the folding table to disclose the pantry cupboard and moved the items of food around, then closed it back up again. He then pulled open a drawer which Ronnie remembered contained Dora's undergarments and pulled out a large pair of bloomers. She stifled a giggle, quickly turning it into a cough.

He swung round and caught her eye, raised an eyebrow and looked down at the offending article. A gurgle of laughter stuck in Ronnie's throat and this time her cough was real.

She shook her head. 'Not mine,' she mouthed.

He gestured his head towards Dora who had her back to them, keeping watch on what the sergeant was checking.

Ronnie nodded. The constable grinned and put the bloomers back in the drawer without looking any further. He lifted the lid of the coal box that formed the step down into the cabin but after a quick glance inside let it down again.

'Where else do you keep your coal?' he asked Dora.

'The back end.' Dora jerked her head. 'Yer surely not goin' ter check in there.' Sergeant Sandford said nothing, merely squeezed past Dora with a mumbled 'excuse me', Dora following him.

'We've got to check everything, madam,' he said, reaching for the shovel and turning over several shovelfuls. 'Last week we looked into a coal bunker we found a kid hiding in it.'

'Well, we ain't got no kid hidin' in there, as yer can see,' Dora said.

The sergeant flashed his torch as he poked around a bit in the dark cavity. Finally, he stood up.

'You have a dekko, Scott,' he said, pulling back his shoulders with a wince. 'Oh, hang on a minute – what's this crate?' He pushed with his foot a cobwebbed crate with a sack inside.

'Don't touch that.'

'Why?' The sergeant narrowed his eyes. 'What's in it?'

'My personal belongin's,' Dora snapped.

'Sorry, Miss Dummitt, we shall have to check. Would you care to take the items out?'

'No, I wouldn't.'

'Then I shall have to look.'

Ronnie was desperate to see what Dora had stored in there but after a cursory glance he only brought out a stoneware bottle. Sniffing the contents he nodded, then put it back in the crate.

'Did you check the coal, Scott?'

'I didn't see anything amiss.'

Ronnie wanted to giggle again. A black blob had appeared on the end of the constable's nose, reminding her of Rusty. Now, anything he said, she wouldn't be able to take seriously.

'What exactly are you gentlemen looking for?' she asked, not daring to catch Constable Scott's eye. She was curious, but mainly she needed to say something – anything – to stop a cry of laughter.

'There's been some smuggling going on along the canals, miss,' the sergeant said. 'Expensive goods that are hard to get hold of these days finding their way onto the black market. It's a serious crime. Even food items that are rationed.' He looked at Dora. 'I think that's it for this boat, so I'll take a look at the other boat.' He turned to the constable. 'You stay here, Scott.'

'As yer like,' Dora said. She sucked at her pipe stem. 'I'd better tell the wenches to come inside the motor as there in't room for all of us.'

'After you,' said Sergeant Sandford.

When the two of them had disappeared, Ronnie exploded into pent-up laughter as she caught sight of the black blob the constable had no idea was smeared all over his nose.

'What is it?' Constable Scott said, joining in the laughter which made Ronnie laugh even more as he wouldn't have known the joke was on him.

'Your nose,' she spluttered. 'Soot.' It was the only word she could manage before she doubled up again. What with that and Dora's knickers . . .

He put his hand up to his face. 'Is there a mirror anywhere?'

She shook her head. Constable Scott pulled out a clean handkerchief from his coat pocket and handed it to her. 'Could you dampen this and wipe it off?'

She took it and poured a few drops of water over one corner. He lowered his head and she wiped the offending mark off the tip of his nose. It was rather a nice nose. She felt her cheeks warm at such a thought.

'Has it gone?' he said, not seeming in the least embarrassed.

'Yes.' She drew away and handed him his handkerchief.

'Thank you.' He put the handkerchief back in his pocket. 'I thought you were laughing about Miss Dummitt's bloomers.'

'That as well,' Ronnie said, smiling. 'I just didn't want you to think they were mine.'

'Hardly,' Constable Scott grinned as he looked at her. 'You could get three of you in that pair. I should have taken everything out but I just couldn't bring myself to look at Miss Dummitt's intimate garments a moment longer and then come face to face with her.'

'I know,' Ronnie chuckled. 'The awful thing is, I had to borrow a pair when I fell in the canal on my first day. My things were in the butty. It was really k-k-kind of h-her to offer—'

And this time Ronnie snorted and then let go of all the emotion of the day. She laughed until the tears streamed down her face. It was only when she stopped that she felt the side of her head pound. She put her hand to her forehead and drew in a sharp intake of breath.

Constable Scott's chuckles immediately died and were replaced by a look of concern. 'Is something the matter with your head?'

'I had an accident when I was opening one of the locks,' Ronnie said. 'It's all right now.'

'May I look?'

She nodded and pushed back the front curls.

'Nasty at the time, I should think.' Constable Scott gazed at her. 'I'm surprised a girl like you wants to do such work. It's tough – more than even some men can handle.'

'Thankfully, I'm not "some man",' Ronnie retorted.

What was it with men? He knew nothing about her at all.

And just as she was beginning to like him. He wasn't handsome like Will Drake, of course, she told herself hurriedly, but she could see that his eyes were an unusual green and he had a cleft in his chin exactly like Cary Grant when she'd seen him for the first time in *His Girl Friday*.

'No, I can see you're not "most men",' he said, grinning now, 'even with a name like Ronnie.'

'What do you mean?' Ronnie flashed.

'Well, it's a boy's name, isn't it?'

'Try explaining my real name to everyone who's never met me: where it comes from, how to spell it, how even to *pronounce* it. It's enough to send me cuckoo.'

He was silent for a few seconds.

'Actually, Véronique is a beautiful name,' he said, pronouncing it in an English way but rather charmingly, still with his eyes on her. 'You should use it – well, at least for special occasions.'

'And this is one of them?' Ronnie's voice was coated with sarcasm.

He grinned again. 'Maybe . . . maybe not.'

There was the sound of voices and one by one Angela, Sally and Margaret appeared.

'All change,' Angela said. 'Oh, who have we here?' She looked at Constable Scott and, giving him an appreciative smile, sidled so close he had to step back.

Ronnie wanted to cringe, but she made her expression one of boredom.

'Right, Miss Linfoot, we'd better get over to the butty then,' Constable Scott said.

He put out a helping hand for her as she negotiated the gunwale, and moments later they joined Dora, Jessica and May.

Dora was no more friendly than she'd been in the motorboat.

'It's all yours,' she said, 'but don't be all day. We got trainin' ter do.'

'I'll put the kettle on while you're carrying out the search,' Jessica said. 'I'm sure everyone would welcome a cup of tea.'

Ronnie was amused to see that Dora didn't argue with Jessica's invitation. The policemen were hardly more than ten minutes with their search and seemed grateful to sit down to a cup of tea instead of facing the rain that was lashing harder than ever on the cabin roof.

'If yous've *quite* finished,' Dora said, the only one who'd refused the tea Jessica had made, 'I must insist we're allowed ter get on with our day. There's no smugglin' goin' on here under my eye, I can assure yer. Yer wastin' yer time. Better spent catchin' some real crooks.'

'Thank you, Miss Dummitt, for your co-operation.' Sergeant Sandford stood and gestured to Constable Scott to follow suit.

Constable Scott flipped his notepad shut and shoved it in the pocket of his raincoat. He nodded to Dora, and glanced at Jessica and May, but his gaze lingered on Ronnie.

'I hope that head heals soon,' he said. 'There's quite a bump already.'

Instinctively, Ronnie put her hand to her forehead. It felt the size of an egg. Oh, she couldn't bear it. What on earth had Will thought when he'd seen it? She must have looked a sight.

She felt the curious stares from Jessica and May as they glanced from her to the constable.

'I'm sure it'll have gone down by tomorrow,' she said.

'We'll see to her, if not,' Dora cut in as she rose to usher the two men through the hatch.

'Well, well, who's made a hit with the good-looking policeman, then?' May chuckled.

'Did you notice the way he looked at Ronnie?' Jessica joined in the laughter. 'He's smitten.'

'Don't be ridiculous,' Ronnie said. 'And even if he is – which he's not – I have no interest in him at all.'

'I don't suppose you have after falling hook, line and sinker for that handsome biker,' May said. 'And we saw him kiss you on the lips right in front of Deadly Dora. He was certainly brave to do that.' She grinned. 'Who is he anyway?'

Ronnie felt her face redden. 'His name is Will Drake. He knows Dora.'

'Whether he knows her or not, she didn't seem too pleased when she saw him kiss you,' Jessica remarked.

'He did it on purpose to annoy her,' Ronnie said. 'It didn't mean anything.'

'Apparently, it meant a lot to you,' May said. 'Have a look in the mirror, why don't you. Shining eyes, flushed cheeks . . .'

'Stop it, both of you,' Ronnie said sharply, her temper rising.

'Only teasing,' Jessica said. 'But seriously, Ronnie, I think you should steer clear of this Will Drake. It's very strange for someone that young to have all that money.'

'I don't know what you mean,' Ronnie said. 'He hasn't flashed any money around *me*.'

'Have you looked at his motorbike?' Jessica said. 'I know a bit about these things. It's a Norton. One of the best brands you can buy. Okay, it's several years old but still . . .' She shook her head. 'And how does he get petrol, is what I want to know. I'm surprised he hasn't been stopped by the police.' She glanced at Ronnie. 'I bet those two canal policemen would be very interested in him.'

Ronnie couldn't think how to answer.

'Even his leather jacket,' Jessica persisted. 'Sheepskin lined – surely you can see how expensive that must have been.'

Ronnie went quiet. She remembered thinking how his jacket had reminded her of Raine's flying jacket, but she hadn't given it any more thought. Now Jessica was making her feel uncomfortable.

'Why hasn't he been called up?' May asked.

'I don't know. I don't know any of those things.' Ronnie looked at both girls, wishing they would just leave her to have a bit of peace. Why were they so determined to put her off Will? He couldn't possibly be interested in her – a girl he'd only met this morning for the first time, and who'd looked like something the cat dragged in when he'd seen her only a few hours later at the lock.

'I think you should find out,' Jessica said. 'I bet he's evading conscription.'

'It's none of my business,' Ronnie said pointedly. 'I have no interest in either Will Drake or the constable you say is so good-looking. You're both making something out of nothing, so please drop the subject.'

She was thankful that Dora banged on the side of the cabin at that moment, then put her head in the hatch.

'We're lettin' go so I want yer in yer places. May can steer the butty, Jessica come with me, and *you*, Ver-ron-eek, I'll give you some lighter chores, seein' as how you've had the accident. Yer can wash out the buckets, fill the water cans, and give a thorough clean to the butty. That means polishin' the brasses and the kettle and anythin' else needs polishin'. Yer'll find Brasso and such behind the folding table.' She stared at Ronnie. 'D'yer think yer can handle it?'

'Yes, of course.'

'And after, it'll be time for you to make us a cup of cocoa. Meantime, we'll fight the storm. Then if yer up to it this afternoon yer can clean the engine room.' Dora withdrew her head.

Ronnie pulled a face when she'd disappeared. Dora had shown the trainees round the engine room on their first day and run through the engine maintenance, but it had been difficult to digest at the time. She vaguely remembered the mudbox – a filter to do with the water-cooling intake from the canal – and the contents hadn't looked at all pleasant. She gave a sigh. She supposed it was important to know what needed doing on both boats, but if Dora's idea of those jobs was that they were light, Ronnie hated the thought of the heavy chores.

Chapter Thirteen

Ronnie's attention was taken up by May, who was at the tiller, steering *Penelope* as the pair of boats made their way along the canal towards Fenny Stratford, where Dora said they could replenish their water cans and buy food. May was singing a folk song Ronnie recognised – 'The Ash Grove'. She used to sing in class at school, or rather attempt to. May had a sweet voice, reminding her of Suzy. She bit her lip. No matter how friendly some of these girls were, they couldn't begin to take the place of her sisters, but they were doing their bit for the war effort and she'd elected to do the same. She mustn't compare them.

'That was lovely,' Ronnie said, joining May on the small rear deck. 'You sound happy.'

'What's "happy"?' May turned to her. 'I don't know anyone who's happy, do you?' When Ronnie didn't answer she went on, 'But I suppose it's a damn sight better than waitress work, on your legs for hours with hardly a break, dealing with customers who haven't a clue how knackered you are—' She broke off, chewing her bottom lip. 'Some of the men thinking they could reach out and touch anywhere on your body – like it was their right because they were paying your wages. One bastard actually grabbed my bosom when I was waiting at his table.'

Ronnie's eyes widened. 'Oh, no. Whatever did you do?'

'He was looking up at me, daring me to challenge him. I swiped him on the face.' She gave a short mirthless laugh. 'I couldn't help it. Filthy bugger. He immediately demanded to speak to the manageress who was a horrible old spinster called Miss Lovedale – can you believe she had such a name? He told her an outright lie – that he'd merely complained that the poached egg was hard and could he have another one, and that's when she – meaning *me* – suddenly slapped his face. Miss Lovedale – I'll never forget her twisted mouth – looked at me and said, "Did you slap the gentleman's face, Miss Parsons?" I said, "Yes, but—" "There are no buts," she practically spat at me, and refused to let me explain what really happened. Then she said, "We will not tolerate such behaviour in the company. Please go and collect your things and leave immediately." I opened my mouth to say something but she shut me up. Then he had the nerve to say to her, "Oh, madam, I didn't want the young lady to lose her job."' May snorted. 'Miss Lovedale said, "I'm afraid it's the rules. The customer must always come first and I can only apologise on her behalf." If looks could kill I should've died right there on the spot. So I was sacked.'

'Someone else must have seen what happened,' Ronnie said. 'One of the other waitresses.'

May shrugged. 'We was busy. They probably didn't even notice. Though there was two customers – gossiping women who stopped immediately they heard what was going on. They could've said something. You'd think women would stick up for one another, wouldn't you?' She paused. 'Women can be bitches. We've had some of that here in the last few days, I reckon.' She looked ahead and turned the tiller in the opposite direction the motor in front was taking, then looked back at Ronnie. 'How about you? What made you join?'

Ronnie briefly told her she'd thought about the Land Army until she'd seen the boatwomen on Pathé News.

'It's okay if we all get along,' May said. 'But I think there's trouble brewing in *Persephone*.'

'With Angela?'

May nodded. 'Sally has hinted as much. Margaret wouldn't say boo to a goose, so she's not made any comment. But that Angela – she's a little madam. I wouldn't trust her further than I could throw her. And as she's quite stocky I shan't even try.' She chuckled. 'No, the sooner I finish training, the better. We'll have much more room to move so we won't get on each other's nerves the way we do at the moment.' She adjusted the steering again, then keeping her eyes fixed ahead, said, 'I'm so glad she's not in our little team.'

'So'm I,' Ronnie said with feeling.

'Is there anything more to eat, Ron? I'm really hungry.'

'I'm going to suggest I make something for lunch,' Ronnie said, 'as I've finished everything Dora asked before I tackle the engine room.'

'I think that was rotten of her when you've banged your head so badly,' May said. 'Don't do it if you're too tired.'

It wasn't anything fancy – just sardines on toast followed by tinned rice pudding – but to Ronnie's chagrin not one girl admired or even noticed her effort on the highly polished brass work or the copper kettle, which she was particularly proud of.

After everyone disappeared Dora surprised Ronnie by saying, 'I'll come and help yer in the engine room. I don't expect yer to do all of it on yer own, being so new, like. But I wanted ter see yer reaction.' She gave one of her terrifying grins. 'Yer pull a good face, no doubt of that.'

Ronnie burst into laughter. 'You weren't supposed to see it.'

'There's not much Dora Dummitt misses,' Dora said, removing her pipe. 'And that goes for Will Drake this mornin' takin' advantage of yer.'

Here it comes. Dora was going to give her a lecture.

'He's bad news, girl. And I should know.'

Ronnie stared at her and Dora stared back.

'What he needs is a firm hand. A boss who sees he's kep' occupied. But s'far as I know, he don't have no job.'

'What does he do?' Ronnie asked curiously. Dora at least seemed in a mood to talk without being so angry for a change.

'What *don't* he do is more like,' Dora said, her unlit pipe bouncing up and down as she spoke. She thought for a minute. 'Well, he's worked in several pubs along the cut. Then he were at a greyhound race-track lookin' after the dogs – he loved them dogs, I'll say that for him. But he had to report some cruel goin's-on with the poor beasts. He couldn't stomach it. They got rid of him but for once it weren't his fault.' She took her pipe out, thrust her thumb into the bowl and struck a match. 'When he were a lad he used to help his dad – 'til his dad—' She looked away, then back again. 'His dad were one of the lock-keepers around these parts when he weren't—' She paused long enough to get her pipe going. 'Well, least said, soonest mended about him. But I always thought young Will liked everything ter do with the boats – he were a natural when he were a kid. But no, it weren't enough for him. He wants ter be like them rich kids he hangs around with.' She shook her head and tutted. 'He don't stick at nothin' for long. Same with girls – just like I warned yer. The best thing for him is when he gets called up.'

So he wasn't even eighteen. At least that will keep May and Jessica quiet when I tell them.

'You must have known him a long time,' Ronnie said, trying to get Dora off the subject of Will's other girls, which made her stomach clench.

'You might say that.' Dora rolled her eyes. 'Anyway, we'd better put a move on.'

They worked together almost in silence, with Dora occasionally breaking it to show her how to do yet another maintenance job. The mudbox was exactly as she'd feared. It was full of slime and grease. Dora ordered her to give it a good clean out when she'd got rid of the contents.

'It's a weekly job,' she said, 'so yer don't want to get landed with it each time. Make sure Jess and May take their turn. Yer know what ter do now.' She disappeared.

Ronnie was not at all sure that Jessica would take her turn, even with the perpetual gloves she always insisted upon wearing so as not to ruin her nails. Heaving a sigh, Ronnie tipped the slime overboard, gagging at the stench. After working at the vet's she ought to be used to this sort of thing, she thought, but this was particularly foul. She swilled water through the box and a splash of disinfectant, but if anything the smell was worse. She'd let it soak a bit.

While she finished cleaning the engine room, Ronnie turned over in her mind all that Dora had said about Will Drake. Dora obviously knew him very well and didn't have much time for him, but at least she'd said how Will loved the dogs at the stadium, although she'd gone on to list more faults. Well, he didn't seem that taken with her either. Ronnie shrugged. It wasn't important so there was no point in dwelling on it.

She rinsed her cloth for the last time and bent low to hang it near the engine, then pulled upright in a swift movement only to feel her head spin.

'Ronnie, you all right?'

Ronnie opened her eyes. She was looking at the ceiling. She blinked. Sally was leaning over her.

'What happened?'

'I heard something fall over. It looks as if you might have fainted. Just stay there quietly for a few moments.'

'No, honestly, I'm all right, thanks,' Ronnie said. She looked up at Sally. 'Weren't you on the tiller?'

'Yes, but I handed over to Jess when I heard the noise.'

'Then go back to it.'

'I should tell Dora—'

'Oh, please don't say anything to Dora. She thinks I'm a liability as it is.'

'I'm sure that's not true. But she needs to know—'

Ronnie struggled up. 'Look, I'm fine.'

'I think you need to lie down for a while in *Penelope*.' Sally glanced round. 'It looks like you've finished here anyway. Trouble is, we're on the snubber so we're going to have to wait for a bridge hole and hop onto the butty as it passes.'

It was twenty minutes or so before they spotted a bridge hole. Still a little unsteady on her feet, Ronnie jumped onto the butty after Sally, at the same time grabbing hold of her extended hand. May was steering and immediately wanted to know what was wrong. Sally quickly told her and then pulled down the folding bed.

'In you get,' she ordered. 'I'm going to make us all a strong cup of tea.'

Sally boiled the kettle and minutes later she handed Ronnie a mug.

'I've given you extra sugar . . . good for shock.' Sally nodded towards the mug. 'And I promise it's sugar and not the alternative you put in Deadly Dora's cup,' she added, grinning.

Ronnie giggled. 'I'm saying nothing.'

'Only because you know you're guilty,' Sally chuckled. 'But I'm curious. Can I ask you something?' She sat on the bench.

'Yes, of course.'

'Do you like working on the boats?'

'Quite well,' Ronnie said cautiously. 'I'll feel a lot better when I know what I'm doing.' She glanced at Sally. 'How about you? Do you like it?'

Sally lifted her shoulders. 'I haven't made up my mind yet.'

'What made you come in the first place?'

'The usual thing – a man. He didn't want the things I wanted, after all. So I thought this would be different enough to take my mind off him. Well, in a way, it does. But it's not quite how I envisaged it.'

Sally was a well-educated girl, Ronnie thought. Rather like Jessica, she didn't look the type to do such mucky, back-breaking work.

'What did you do before?'

'I was a nurse,' Sally said.

Ronnie's brows shot up. 'Goodness, that's quite a difference.'

'Yes. The war started at the same time as my training, and I couldn't wait to help care for the soldiers. But when you saw the things I did, it was shocking. Those poor boys. Day after day, night after night they were brought in, some of them completely broken, and we had to help mend them. I was abroad about a year and then ended up at home. There was hardly any break. We just kept on with little sleep. I was a wreck but I still loved the work. But after Mike . . . well, you don't want to hear about him.' Sally sighed.

'Maybe all you needed was a holiday,' Ronnie said. 'To have a proper rest. You might have seen things differently.'

'That's what Mike said,' Sally replied, the words coated with bitterness.

'Was he a doctor?'

'Yes. The typical nurse falling for the doctor.' She rose to her feet. 'Enough of all that. If you're sure you're all right I'll leave you. At least May can keep an eye on you. But if you feel dizzy again you must tell Dora. It might mean you've got slight concussion, but they can do something about that.'

Ronnie thanked her and closed her eyes. In no time she was asleep.

Ronnie had no idea what the time was or how long she'd slept. She stretched her arms above her head, enjoying the space of the whole three-foot bed to herself. After a few minutes she swung her legs out and stood up, then put her hand to her head. Ouch. That felt sore. Oh, dear. There was rather a lump. But it would go, she told herself. And in the meantime, she had a job to do.

There was no one about in the butty. Her stomach rumbled but there was no sign or smell of any cooking. Dora must be using Jessica for something more important. Ronnie picked up her watch she'd put on the burnt bedside shelf. A quarter to six. She must have slept for several hours! Her stomach rumbled as she swiftly pulled a jumper on, then poked her head through the hatch. It was dark. She made out two shadowy figures coming towards her on *Persephone*'s gunwale.

'Yous'd better wake her as yer the nurse,' Ronnie heard Dora say. 'Make sure she in't concussed.'

'I'm all right,' Ronnie called, waving her arm. 'I was going to start supper.'

'Stay where you are.' It was Sally.

The two women dropped through the hatch, Dora as usual chewing on her pipe.

'How are you feeling, Ronnie?' Sally asked.

'Heaps better – honestly.'

'No more dizziness?'

'No, and no blurry vision or headache,' Ronnie said, remembering Nurse Martin's list of possible symptoms from concussion. 'I'm fine now. I think it was just tiredness.'

'And shock,' Sally added, turning to Dora. 'But she looks a lot better than when I left her.'

'Hmm.' Dora narrowed her eyes. 'Yer seem ter be good at getting yerself in a pickle, miss. Let's see if yer can go the rest of the day without any more mishap.' She bounded up the steps and disappeared.

Sally grimaced. 'She shouldn't have made you clean the engine room. It was a rotten thing to ask when you'd had that accident. I told her the best thing for you was to get some rest and you'd be fine – which you are.'

'Thanks, Sally, but to be fair, Dora did come and help me. I'm just terrified she's going to send me home.'

'I'm sure you'd have to do something much worse for that to happen.' She looked at Ronnie. 'Well, if you're sure you're okay, I'll be getting back to the motor.'

Chapter Fourteen

'Right, you lot,' Dora said. Two days had passed without too much mishap. Ronnie and the two teams were gathered in the cold drizzle on the towpath. 'We're startin' on a tunnel this mornin' – Blisworth Tunnel, ten miles away. It's a long one – nearly two miles. Third longest in the country,' she added with a smirk, her pipe bobbing up and down between her lips. 'Ver-ron-eek will take the tiller on the butty. Keep an eye on her, Jess. See she don't do nothin' daft. Margaret, go with them and watch how to steer as you in't had a turn on yer own yet, and May, clean the cabin and make their drinks. I'll be leadin' the way on the motor with Sally and, Angela, do the same as May – a thorough cleanin' job in the cabin and make us a cocoa at ten o'clock.' She suddenly stared at Angela. 'Well, I see the bugs have taken a likin' to *you*, miss,' she said. 'Funny they've not gone after no one else.'

Five heads turned towards Angela. Her rain hat was pulled low over her face, masking her usual sour expression. Then Ronnie noticed a red rash on Angela's face.

'Thanks for reminding me,' Angela muttered through gritted teeth. 'I couldn't sleep last night for scratching.'

'Makes it worse.' Dora's eyes swept around the group. 'When we tie up I'll give yer a sulphur candle. That usually stops the little boogers in their tracks. And yer have ter seal up all the cracks round the doors and openin's, but for now we need to crack on.' She grinned at her feeble joke, looking at Ronnie. 'Yous've got responsibility this mornin', Ver-ron-eek, and that's exactly why I'm puttin' yer on the tiller because yer only took it for a short time the other day over a long pound and I don't want it forgotten what I learnt yer. It's another experience in the tunnel. All right?'

Ronnie nodded. Then Dora's words hit her. She'd be guiding the butty through a tunnel which the woman had already described as tricky. Never mind that Dora was in the lead. *Persephone* would be a long way ahead on the seventy-foot snubber. Thank goodness Dora had no idea how her stomach was fluttering. Was Dora expecting too much from them? They'd only been training for just over a week. She glanced at Margaret who was standing beside her, her small pinched face looking even paler under her sou'wester.

'Are you okay, Margaret?' Ronnie asked softly.

'I'm claustrophobic,' Margaret said, almost apologetically. 'I can't stand being in the dark. My father used to lock me in a cupboard when I was little. He used to constantly call me a "very bad girl", though I don't remember doing anything to deserve that sort of punishment.' Her eyes filled with tears. 'I was so relieved when he died. I think Mum was, too. She'd had a dreadful life with him. But she met Graham Webb five years later, who's now my stepfather. He's the exact opposite . . . he's lovely. He even adopted me. But I've never forgotten my father and what he did to me.'

Ronnie's jaw dropped. 'Oh, Margaret, how cruel. I can't imagine how frightened you must have been.'

'And now we'll be going through a horrible black tunnel. I could probably manage a short one but this is *two miles*. I won't be able to see the end of it.'

'Didn't you realise you'd be going through tunnels when you signed up?' Ronnie said.

'Not really – oh, I don't know.' Margaret gave her a shaky smile. 'I expect I'll be all right.'

'When you *ladies* have finished yapping,' Dora's strident tones were flung at them from a few yards away, 'p'raps we could all get movin'.'

'Sorry, Miss Dummitt,' Ronnie said. She glanced at Margaret. 'If you want to talk about it later when we're quiet—'

'No,' Margaret said quickly. 'I shouldn't have said what I did. Please forget it. I'm just glad I won't be with Dora in the front.'

'I'm going in to make a cuppa,' Jessica announced when Ronnie was settled at *Penelope*'s tiller, with Margaret sitting on the deck leaning against the low wall nervously chewing her nails. 'I can't wait until ten. Do you both want one?'

'I never turn down a cuppa,' Ronnie chuckled. 'You couldn't do a piece of toast as well, could you?'

'Now you're pushing it,' Jessica laughed. 'Of course I can. Margaret?'

'Yes, please.'

'Back in a jiffy.' Jessica disappeared.

The drizzle had finally stopped. Ronnie shrugged off her raincoat leaving the usual bundle of thick jumpers underneath as she swung one arm above her head. It felt as though it had been released from five days of being trapped inside the sleeve of her coat. She circled her arm, all the time keeping her other hand firmly on the tiller of the seventy-foot narrowboat, then swapped over to swing her other arm. That felt so good. Her faint anxiety about steering through a tunnel was assuaged by knowing the experienced trainer was up ahead. It was actually a relief not to hear Dora constantly ordering everyone about and complaining. She wondered how Angela was getting on with the cleaning and grinned.

She was beginning to enjoy herself. Muscles that had screamed with aches now felt stronger and able to tackle any physical job Dora threw at them. It was still early days and she knew she had masses to learn, yet Dora's instructions didn't terrify her as they once had. She'd begun to familiarise herself with the jobs that had to be done and see the logic in some of Dora's comments that Ronnie had to admit often turned out to be helpful.

It was bliss being deep in the countryside. Just at that moment the sun broke through the cloud, dappling spots of light on the water. There was no warmth in it at this time of year but she lifted her chin towards it for a few moments feeling completely content. She spotted a kingfisher sitting on a dripping, overhanging branch. 'Good morning,' she called out, laughing at the ridiculousness of her greeting. The bird eyed her for a second or two before it streaked in front of her, answering her with its zip-zip call, then soared above *Penelope,* the weak rays of sun catching it in a flash of iridescent blue and orange.

Briefly she closed her eyes to imagine those few moments again. It was as though the bird had been waiting for her to come along, then took flight so he could show off his colours. How privileged she felt. Without warning Maman crossed her mind. Her mother loved cities. She was used to living in the heart of Paris. If only she could try to understand her youngest daughter's love of the outdoors. Guiltily, Ronnie pushed the thought away that she'd left her mother on her own with only Rusty for company and hoped Maman was at this very moment taking him for a walk. If her mother would give him a chance, she'd find him a wonderful companion.

'Snack coming up.' Jessica broke the spell as she tapped

Ronnie on the leg and passed up a tray of three mugs and a plate of toast. 'Sorry I spilt some when I came up the steps. She glanced at the white-faced girl. 'Are you okay, Margaret?'

'Yes.'

'Not worried about the tunnel, are you?'

'She'll be fine,' Ronnie interjected quickly, sure that Margaret wouldn't want Jess to know she was so nervous.

'Do you want to change over with me, Ronnie, while you two have your drink?'

'What about you?' Ronnie said.

'I had my toast down below. I was starving.'

'Okay.' Ronnie reluctantly shifted over for Jessica, and gratefully munched her toast and jam, swigging down her tea in greedy gulps. She noticed Margaret was just sipping her tea, not saying a word.

'This is the life,' Jessica said. 'Well, for us at the moment. May's been given the short straw.'

'Is she all right?'

'Yes, she's stuck in the cabin but at the moment she's got tea and toast and a magazine.'

'I don't think that's quite what Dora had in mind for her,' Ronnie giggled, then became serious. 'I just hope Dora doesn't see you and I have swapped.'

'She won't know. She'll be too busy giving Sally instructions.' She paused, her eyes staring ahead. 'I reckon it won't be long before we come to the tunnel so we'll change over as soon as it's in sight.'

The three girls were quiet for a while as they finished their tea.

'LOOK OUT!' Ronnie jumped up, shouting. 'You're going to hit the side!'

Jessica pulled hard on the tiller. The boat swerved and crashed into the bank.

Ronnie sucked in a breath.

'Bugger and blast!' Jessica said. 'I pulled the tiller the wrong way . . . it's a bloody instinct to pull it the same way you want to go.' She turned to Ronnie, her forehead a band of perspiration.

'Dora's going to be furious,' Ronnie groaned. 'And I shall be the one in trouble as she told *me* to take the tiller.'

'I'll stick up for you,' Jessica said. 'It was my fault for suggesting it. I'll stay where I am so she can see it was me.' She frowned. 'It looks like *Persephone*'s slowing down. For goodness' sake – we're going to bump into them if they don't move along.'

Ronnie's eyes were transfixed as the snubber shortened. She could clearly see Sally coiling it onto the counter as she pulled it in.

'Dammit, here comes Deadly Dora,' Jessica said. 'And she doesn't look happy.'

The three girls watched as Dora jumped onto the fore end of the butty and practically ran along the top planks and the cabin to where they were sitting.

'What happened?' she demanded. 'Why is Jess at the tiller?'

Ronnie opened her mouth but Jessica cut in before she could speak.

'It was only while Ronnie had a cup of tea. I lost concentration for a few moments and pulled the tiller the wrong way. It won't ever happen again.' She paused. 'I hope I haven't caused any damage.'

'If yer have, it'll come out of yer wages,' Dora said tightly. 'I'm goin' ter take a look.'

'Bloody Nora.' Jessica blew out her cheeks as Dora jumped down and then stepped onto the towpath. 'Come on, Ronnie. We'd better go and have a look, too.'

The two girls watched as Dora got down on her haunches to inspect the boat.

'I don't think there'll be any damage,' Jessica said. 'It was only a bit of a prang.'

'Don't speak too soon,' Dora snapped. 'It's well scraped.' She lifted her frizzy yellow head. 'Yous'll have to pay for the paint and the painter,' she finished triumphantly.

By this time the other four girls had clustered round on the towpath.

'So, Ronnie, you can't be trusted even on the flat pound, let alone a tunnel,' Angela said.

'I believe yer was cleaning the motor cabin when it happened.' Dora eyed Angela narrowly.

'Yes, but—'

'So don't jump ter no conclusions, miss. It weren't Ver-ron-eek at the tiller.' She glared at the group.

Angela's lips thinned. 'Then who was?'

'Obviously that only leaves me,' Jessica said. 'But quite frankly, I don't need your comments, Angela. It's nothing to do with you what arrangements Dor – Miss Dummitt and I make between us.'

Ronnie stepped closer to have a look at the side of the butty. There was what looked like a new scrape, but no more than several others which trainees before them had most probably made. She had to be honest and pointed out another deep scratch.

'Miss Dummitt, I think this is the one I did in the lock. It looks exactly the same, so I don't think it's fair to blame Jessica.'

Dora leaned over, her pipe half falling from her mouth. She put her hand up to steady it.

'Yer may be right, miss,' she said, turning to Ronnie, 'so let's say no more about it.' She took a few puffs. 'It's time ter press on so I'm goin' to start the engine.' She glared at the group. 'All get back in yer places where I put yous.'

It was half an hour, and after much grumbling and cursing – words that Ronnie didn't even know existed – before the engine turned over. But there was no movement of the boats.

'We're stuck well and truly,' Dora said, tutting and rolling her eyes. 'Yous'd best jump down, Jess. You, miss' – she jerked her head towards Ronnie – 'you stay with the tiller on the butty.'

'Damn and blast,' Ronnie heard Jessica mutter as she hurriedly climbed down.

'Sally, lean yer weight with Jess on the shafts,' Dora directed. 'When you feel it move, shout up and I'll reverse the engine while yer keep pushin'.' She wiped her face with the sleeve of her filthy jacket.

Ronnie braced herself at the butty's tiller. Dora was going to be furious with her and Jess. Just as everything had been going so well. If it hadn't been for Jessica insisting on a cup of tea, none of this would have happened. She stopped that thought. It was unfair. The tea and toast couldn't have come at a better time, and she was just as likely to have swerved into the bank as Jessica, if her steering in the lock was anything to go by.

'Well, it don't seem we can do this ourselves.' Dora jumped down again. She knocked out her pipe against the heel of her boot as she surveyed the situation, then turned to the others. 'Angela, go over ter the pub there and see if anyone'll help. We need at least two – if not three – tough-lookin' blokes ter get us out of this. Blokes who knows what they're doin'.'

'Why should it be me?' Angela said sulkily. 'I didn't cause any of this.'

'Because I said so.' Dora's voice was icy.

'If Angela will take over, I'll go,' Ronnie said quickly.

She hopped down and sped off before Dora could stop her.

The Golden Eagle was only a couple of hundred yards from the towpath. Without hesitating she opened the door. It was the first time she'd ever entered a pub, let alone entered one on her own.

It was difficult at first to take in the scene with the clouds of smoke. Warmth emanated from an open fire in the ingle-nook on one side of the room and she vaguely noticed a few men sitting around it, talking loudly and adding to the smoke with their cigarettes. She headed towards the bar in front of her. Two men sitting on stools with their backs to her turned at the sound of her step.

'Well, well, if it in't one of them trainee wenches.'

Will Drake unfolded his legs and stood tall and solid, looking down at her with an amused grin.

'What can I do for yer this time?' he said to her.

His companion smirked. 'Yer can introduce me, for one thing,' he interrupted as he rose to his feet. Almost as tall as Will, he was more heavily built.

'This is Ronnie, one of Dora's lot,' Will said, grinning at his friend. He looked back at Ronnie. 'This here is Dave. Yer haven't come here to have a drink on yer own, now have yer?'

'N-no,' Ronnie stammered. She swallowed, feeling nervous with him standing so close to her in the gloomy atmosphere, and his mate watching them with interest. 'We're stuck in the mud. Dora asked me to see whether anyone here could help.'

Will's grin broadened. 'Well, I've rescued yer twice before,' he said, 'so one more time i'nt goin' to hurt, I reckon. Let's see if the two of us can get you *ladies* on yer merry way.' He threw some coins onto the counter and strode towards the door, Dave close behind.

Deadly Dora will go mad when she sees who I've brought with me to help, Ronnie thought, as she stumbled after them, her Wellingtons squelching on the rain-sodden towpath.

'Not *yous* again,' Dora grimaced from the deck of *Persephone* as they approached the boats.

'Nice ter have a warm welcome,' Will said with a grin. 'I've brought Dave. He's come ter help.'

Ronnie watched as the two men threw their whole weight upon the shafts.

'Now reverse the engine,' Will ordered Dora.

'I think I know what ter do,' she said, scowling at him.

Five minutes later *Persephone* was free.

Without looking at either Will or Dave, Dora said, 'Thanks for the help.' Her tone sounded the complete opposite. She glanced down at Ronnie. 'Come on, miss. You can stop yer gawpin'.'

'Not so fast.' Will turned to Ronnie. 'I want ter have a word with yer.'

'I can't, Will,' Ronnie said, conscious of Dora's glare. 'We've got to go.'

He caught her arm. 'When's yer birthday?' he said in an undertone.

Ronnie gave a start. 'What?'

'Well, when is it?'

'December – the twenty-third. Why do you want to know?'

He shrugged. 'Maybe there's somethin' yer want and yer can't git hold of. Maybe nylon stockin's. It's not just the Yanks that can get 'em.'

'Where do I go that I'd need nylons?' Ronnie said, chuckling at the absurdity.

'*Ver-ron-eek,* get up here right now!' Dora shouted.

'Coming, Miss Dummitt.'

'We best make ourselves scarce,' Dave said, pulling Will's arm and jerking his head in the distance.

Will squinted. 'Yer right,' he said. 'Time ter go.' He glanced at Ronnie. 'I'll be seein' yer.' With that he and Dave vanished.

In two minutes flat Ronnie heard the roar of Will's motorbike.

Chapter Fifteen

Because of the delay with the mud, Dora wouldn't allow them to stop for lunch before entering Blisworth Tunnel.

'Biscuits and tea is all yer gettin',' she said. 'If we start ditherin' we won't be where we're s'posed to be before dark.'

'Is it a village?' May asked.

'Gayton Junction?' Dora snorted. 'Yous'll be lucky. There in't no villages near the junction.'

There was much grumbling as everyone took their places on *Penelope,* Dora shouting the final instructions.

'Keep the tiller within the sides of the boat, miss,' Dora called. 'That way it don't jam against the wall. If yer swerve do *not* use the wall ter push away with yer hands. It's too dangerous. Take it slowly. Any major trouble, use yer oil lamp as a signal. The tunnel's narrer but it'll just take another seven-footer ter pass us.'

'My stomach's already rumbling,' Ronnie said to Jessica and Margaret as she felt the familiar movement of the butty.

'I'll cook something special tonight and plenty of it,' Jessica said. 'In fact, I'm going to start it if you're happy on the tiller. And I'll make a snack for us for lunch. We can all eat as we're going along. I'm not missing a meal for anyone – and that includes Deadly Dora.'

'She won't like it if you're not watching me,' Ronnie said as she pulled away.

Jessica chuckled. 'Too bad. We've got to eat.'

'Suits me,' Ronnie said. 'I feel hungry all the time.'

'I'd better get started then,' Jessica smiled as she disappeared.

'Ronnie—' Margaret began.

'Don't talk for a minute. I need to concentrate.' Ronnie chewed her lips. 'Bend coming up and— Oh, damn!' she cried as the boat swerved into the middle of the canal.

Pull back. Keep following close as you can round the bend.

Ronnie managed to pull the boat back into the curve of the canal as she followed the trail of the motor in front. Feeling pleased with herself she righted the butty as the canal straightened, but her moment of pleasure faded as she saw not far in the distance, looming before *Persephone,* the black hole of the tunnel entrance. She had to get this right. Bring *Penelope* safely out to the other side or Dora would lose her patience.

Stiffening her shoulders, she said, 'Margaret, keep an eye and tell me if I'm doing anything wrong.'

'I'm not sure I'd know.'

Margaret's voice was so low Ronnie could barely hear her. Oh, if only she hadn't told Jess how hungry she was, Jess would be here now. Margaret's confession that she was terrified of going into the tunnel didn't exactly do anything for her own nervousness. Ronnie wasn't scared of the dark – that wasn't it at all – but she was apprehensive of trying to steer the butty in a narrow space and not allowing it to smash into the sides as had happened on the bank a little while ago. And she could tell Margaret was not going to be any help.

Trying not to alarm the girl, Ronnie smiled. 'Don't worry,' she said. 'You'll be fine.'

Margaret didn't answer but kept her eyes wide as she fixed

them straight ahead. *Persephone* disappeared through the entrance.

Ronnie, sensing Margaret's fear, patted her hand as the tunnel entrance loomed. 'We're going in. Hold on.'

The atmosphere immediately changed from a watery winter sun to blackness. The dank foul air hit Ronnie's nostrils and it took all her concentration to keep her focus, though she couldn't really make out anything in front of her. It was like steering into a dungeon and the dim light from the oil lamp wasn't helping matters. Margaret said something but Ronnie couldn't hear what she was saying above the noise and vibration of *Persephone*'s engine echoing round the walls on either side.

It couldn't have been more than five minutes before Margaret suddenly gave a groan that made Ronnie's blood run cold.

Ronnie swung round. 'What is it?'

She could barely see the outline of the girl's face, it was so dark.

'I don't feel very—' Margaret broke off. There was a silence.

'Speak up! I can't hear you. What's the matter? Tell me!'

'I'm going to be sick.'

'WHAT!'

'I'm so scared, Ronnie. I told you . . . it's so black. Please get me out of here.'

'How can I?' Ronnie shouted above the noise of the motorboat in front, its engine thrumming and its exhaust reverberating around the dripping tunnel walls. She tried to quell her impatience. 'There's nowhere to turn round. You can see that. We have to just carry on. It's too dangerous for you to go down below when you can't see where you're going but you can't be sick up here. We won't see where you've been and one of us could slip.'

And I don't want it to be me, she thought grimly. Was this the time to use the light to signal if there was a problem? But who would see it?

'I feel faint.'

'Put your head down between your knees!'

'I daren't move,' Margaret said in a choked voice.

Ronnie felt for Margaret's hand. It was as cold and clammy as the tunnel and she could hear Margaret's breath coming in quick jerky bursts. Ronnie gave a start. Maybe Margaret really was ill. But they were trapped. She felt in her jacket pocket where she usually kept a few boiled sweets to stop herself thinking of food. She brought one out and unwrapped it.

'Open your mouth,' she said. 'I'm giving you a sweet. Just keep thinking you'll be all right. *I* know you'll be all right.'

'I'm not brave like you, Ronnie.'

'Yes, you are,' Ronnie said, trying to put some conviction into the words. 'You're as brave as anyone else here, me included. You wouldn't be doing this if you weren't.'

Margaret's answer was lost in the engine noise ahead.

'I can't hear you,' Ronnie said, giving Margaret's trembling arm a light squeeze. Poor Margaret. She didn't sound as though she'd had a particularly happy life. Ronnie remembered all the times she'd grumbled at her mother. Yes, Raine and Suzy and I have all been at the sharp end of Maman trying to stop us doing what we love and treating us like naughty children, Ronnie thought, but she doesn't do it out of spite or cruelty. Suzy always says it's out of fear.

Talking of fear, Margaret was certainly terrified of the tunnel and if Ronnie was honest, she wasn't so keen on the dark damp passage herself. She'd imagined a tunnel – dark, of course, but well lit by the boats' lights. As it was, she could barely make out the brick walls that *Penelope* was almost brushing on one side. She gave a thought to the men who'd built it. There must have been many accidents from the explosives they were bound to have used. She and the others would be coming into daylight soon but those men would have spent all day and every day in the dark. What a horrible existence. The image made her shudder.

She realised Margaret had gone very quiet.

'Margaret, are you feeling any better?'

But there was only silence.

'For God's sake, Margaret, speak to me!'

And then in front of her a pinprick of light appeared. At first she thought they must be about to come out of the tunnel until Margaret screamed, piercing her ears, slicing through her eardrums, making her heart pound.

'LOOK OUT!' Margaret screamed again.

'What is it? I can't see a thing. What's happened to the oil lamp? The light's completely gone!' Ronnie fought to keep the panic from her voice but her lips trembled and she didn't know if her words made sense. It must have gone out with all that water from the tunnel walls dripping onto it.

'BOAT COMING!' Margaret screamed.

Oh, dear God. Surely there wasn't room for another boat to pass. Ronnie's stomach churned. If only she could see – judge the space. See where Dora was. She'd said a seven-footer could squeeze by but Ronnie couldn't tell if she was close enough to the wall to allow it. Grimly hanging on to the tiller, she felt the butty moving faster, knowing she had no control. No brakes. Heart pounding in her ears, she realised her speed was set by the motor in front.

In her panic Ronnie pulled the tiller too hard and felt the butty bump against the wall. Forgetting Dora's warning, she frantically used her fist to push against the dripping wall, allowing the boat to pull away, wincing as her knuckles scraped the slimy brick surface. Any moment the other motorboat would crash into them but she still couldn't even make out the shape of any boat. Dear God, had they spotted Dora's headlights?

'Blow the horn!' Ronnie shouted to Margaret, hoping against hope that *Penelope* was hugging the wall. Seconds that felt like hours passed, and finally she felt the vibration in the water from the other boat. Smoke she couldn't even see made her cough as several voices, sounding like an entire family, shouted obscenities. Ronnie hardly dared breathe until she was sure the other motorboat must have passed by.

'Yer silly boogers,' bawled one of the men. 'Where's yer light? Yer've no business steerin' somethin' yer can't handle with no lights.'

'You got by, didn't you?' Ronnie shouted back to the bodiless voice, her temper rising.

'You wimmen make me sick,' came another voice. 'Yer shouldna be allowed on the cut.'

'We're doing a job, same as you,' Ronnie shouted back, her temper flaring. 'Doing our bit for the war.'

'Yer need ter git back home ter mummy, where yer belong,' came the growled response.

'It's no good arguing,' Margaret said, as the other boat's voices faded. 'They've gone now.' She patted Ronnie's arm. 'They could easily have crashed into us but you kept your nerve.'

With Margaret's confidence seemingly restored as a result of warning her about the other boat, Ronnie breathed a long sigh, her heart slowing to an even tempo as *Penelope* inched its way behind *Persephone* on the tow rope through the long, dank, watery passage.

'Oh, look! Isn't that a tiny pinprick of daylight? We must

be coming to the end of the tunnel.' Margaret's voice rose with relief and excitement.

'What the blazes happened to you two in the tunnel?' Dora demanded when they were tying up.

'Our oil lamp went out,' Ronnie said. 'Luckily, Margaret heard that other boat above the engine noise and warned me.'

'What was Jess doin'?'

Ronnie's heart sank. She might as well tell Dora the truth. 'She was making lunch.'

'I said she was ter watch yer,' Dora said tersely. 'Did yer keep away from the wall?'

'I did feel a bump once when I was trying to get really close so the other boat could pass.'

'I warned yer it were narrer. So more damage, I don't doubt.' Dora's tone was grim.

'I didn't scrape anything,' Ronnie said defensively, 'except my hand when I pushed us away.'

'That's what I told yer *not* to do. Yer don't seem ter listen when I'm speakin'.'

'That's not fair. I do.'

Ronnie watched Dora's lips pursing in disbelief, but she didn't care. For once, she wasn't scared of the trainer. She'd done her best and all was well, as far as she was concerned. Even Margaret appeared to have fully recovered from her bad case of nerves.

'It's true, Miss Dummitt,' Margaret said. 'Ronnie was marvellous and kept calm. It was the men in the other boat who started shouting at us.'

'I'm not surprised when they saw a boat comin' towards them with no space to pass,' Dora said, having the last word as usual.

Chapter Sixteen

'Wouldn't it be fun if one of us could play an instrument?' Jessica said after supper. 'We could have a singsong.'

She'd made a delicious macaroni cheese and taken the other trainees half the dish. To Ronnie's relief Dora had decided to have her supper at the nearest pub.

'I play the ukulele,' May said unexpectedly.

'You never said,' Ronnie piped up.

'You never asked,' May chuckled. 'I'm no professional but I'll play a few songs if you like.' She stood with a teacloth in her hand, ready to dry the dishes Ronnie had washed and left in the bowl.

'It would definitely break the monotony,' Jessica said.

'Shouldn't we invite the others?' Ronnie gave the macaroni saucepan an extra scrub to remove the bits of clinging cheese and sauce.

'Yes, we should, though it'll be a frightful squash.' Jessica wiped the foldaway table.

'Do we have to invite Angela?' Ronnie said.

'No, we don't have to. She'd put a real dampener on it.' The corners of Jessica's mouth turned down as though at the very thought.

'We can't ask Margaret and Sally without her,' May said.

'I don't see why not,' Jessica said.

'Maybe she won't come,' May ventured.

'I bet she will,' Jessica said. 'She's the sort of person who likes to be in on everything.'

'I'll go and see what they're doing,' Ronnie said. 'Tonight would be good as we haven't got Deadly Dora peering at us with her disapproving look. She's another one who'd take all the fun out of it.'

'I'll get the uke tuned up while you're gone.' May hung the wet tea towel over the range.

'Where on earth did you hide it in such a cramped space?' Jessica asked curiously.

'I kept it under the cratch, but after the police finished their search that time I moved it where we keep the extra coal.'

She disappeared to the back of the boat and returned with a sack. Five minutes later Ronnie came through the hatch.

'Margaret's not coming,' she said. 'She wants an early night. I think she's exhausted from the tunnel. You know she had a bit of a panic in there. I was quite scared for a while that she was going to be sick.'

'Poor Margaret. I'm not sure she's suited to this job,' Jessica said. 'She's such a frail little thing.' She paused. 'So is it just Sally coming?' She raised an eyebrow.

'And Angela,' Ronnie added with a grimace. 'She said yes immediately.'

'Oh, no. Oh, well, we'll have to make the best of it.'

May tuned her ukulele, which sounded awful at first but settled into a tune Ronnie recognised.

'Let's try one and see how it goes,' May said. 'You must all know this one.' She strummed a few bars and began to sing:

'*Cruising down the river*

'*On a Sunday afternoon . . .*' Ronnie and Jessica joined in.

The three girls were in full voice when Sally and Angela emerged from the hatch. Sally joined in immediately, but Angela barely acknowledged everyone except for a slight nod.

'Not sure where you're all going to sit,' Jessica said. 'I suppose three of you could get on our bed if we pull it down. I'll squash on the seat with someone.'

Ronnie was pleased she knew the words to some of the songs May played, but she knew herself she had no voice.

'If my sister Suzy was here she'd show you,' Ronnie said. 'She's a professional singer. She's sung abroad in—' She stopped herself just in time. Everyone was looking towards her expectantly. 'Mum's the word,' she said with a self-conscious giggle. 'I'm not allowed to say. She's home now and singing to the troops over here. You'd love her voice. They say it's like Judy Garland's.'

Ronnie stole a glance at Angela who was rolling her eyes. She opened her mouth to say something but decided against it. You could never make Angela happy no matter how hard you tried. Then something mischievous made her say, 'Did you enjoy that, Angela?'

Angela puffed out a sigh. 'All right, if you like that kind of thing. I prefer classical myself.'

'That's what Suzy plays when she's not singing,' Ronnie said proudly. 'She can play the violin and the piano.'

'Good for her,' was all Angela said in a tone which meant the exact opposite. She rose up, yawning. 'I'll be going now.' She glanced at Sally. 'Are you ready?'

'No,' Sally said. 'I'll stay a little longer. You carry on.'

Angela pursed her lips. 'All right.'

'Get her,' Jessica said when Angela had disappeared. 'She really is a madam. Why can't she be gracious for a change?'

'She doesn't know the meaning of the word,' Sally said.

'She's an awkward cow. But she's pretty good on handling the motorboat – certainly better than us.'

'That's the last one,' May said, putting her instrument to one side. 'I'm getting tired.'

'Me, too,' Sally said, standing up. 'I just hope Angela's in a bit better mood.'

They were still discussing Angela when there was a sharp bang on the side of the butty.

'Who is it?' Jessica called.

'Me. Open up!' Angela demanded.

'*Now* what does she want?' Jessica grumbled as Ronnie went to open the hatch.

Angela jumped down and handed her a folded sheet of paper. 'Read this,' she said.

Ronnie took the sheet and unfolded it. Her eyes flicked down the page and her jaw dropped in disbelief.

'Who's it from?' Jessica asked impatiently.

'It's from Margaret,' Ronnie said, glancing at Angela, who simply shrugged.

'Read it out then,' Jessica ordered.

Ronnie cleared her throat.

'Dear Miss Dummitt,

I realise I am not suited to this kind of work and have decided it is best to give in my notice now rather than let it drag on. I have enjoyed the company of the other girls and please thank Ronnie especially for her kindness today.

I would like to go first thing in the morning. I know I am doing the right thing but apologise for any inconvenience I have caused.

Yours sincerely,

Margaret Webb.'

Ronnie looked up. 'She never mentioned anything like this earlier when we went through the tunnel and there was just the two of us. I'd have thought she would've said something then. If she had I would've tried to talk her out of it. None of us feels that confident yet after such a short time.'

'Speak for yourself,' Angela put in, but Ronnie glared at her so hard Angela didn't continue.

'Well, well.' May shook her head. 'So she made up her mind this evening when we were having our singsong.'

'Looks like it,' Angela said. 'But she's not in the cabin.'

'Hang on, Angela,' Jessica said picking up the envelope. 'It's addressed to Miss D. Dummitt.'

'Let me finish,' Angela said in a rude tone. 'Margaret wasn't there. Then I saw the envelope addressed to Miss Dummitt, so I thought I might as well walk over to the pub and give it to her.'

'Didn't you wonder where Margaret was?' Jessica said.

'I thought she'd gone to the pub to see Miss Dummitt to discuss something in private. I knew she wasn't taking to the canal life.'

'How did you know?' Jessica demanded.

'I live with her. It's the odd remark she drops.'

'But why wouldn't she have given Dora the letter herself?' Ronnie said, frowning.

'I didn't know what the contents were at that point,' Angela said. 'I didn't even know it was Margaret's writing. To me it was just a letter that needed to be delivered.' She paused. 'Anyway, when I got there Miss Dummitt asked me to open it and read it out. She can't read, can she?' Angela finished on a contemptuous note.

'Why did Dora let you keep the letter?' Jessica demanded.

'She didn't. I must have put it in my bag by mistake.'

'So what did Dora say?' Ronnie asked, ignoring Angela's last remark that didn't ring quite true.

'She wanted to know why Margaret hadn't got the guts to tell her herself, instead of writing, but said she wasn't surprised. And it was for the best because she'd already decided to get rid of her.'

'She actually said that?' Sally stared at her.

'Well, words to that effect,' Angela said. 'Anyway, at that point I didn't know how long Margaret had been gone. It might only have been a few minutes, as far as I knew. So I didn't make anything of it. But now I've been back three-quarters of an hour and there's still no sign of her. I thought I ought to tell you all.'

'Something's not right,' Ronnie said. 'Why did she go out at this time of the evening in the first place? It's freezing outside.'

'You know, I don't like the sound of it.' Jessica's voice had become serious. 'She disappears when we were all out of the way for a couple of hours and leaves a note to say she's going home tomorrow. So where's she gone? It doesn't make sense. In fact I think something really bad has happened to her.'

'What do you mean?' Ronnie said, her heart thumping uncomfortably.

Jessica looked directly at her. 'I mean she might have had an accident.' She paused. 'Can she swim?'

'I'm sure she can.' Sally looked at Ronnie and May. 'Like Dora said, you're not allowed to join if you can't swim. Unless she lied to Dora.'

Ronnie gasped. 'Oh, no, she wouldn't have.'

'It's perfectly possible. We may have to call the police.' Jessica glanced at the others. 'I think one of us has to go and tell Dora right away that she's been gone at least an hour – maybe more. It'd better be me.'

'I'll come with you,' Ronnie said quickly.

'Anyone got the time?' Jessica said.

May glanced at her watch. 'Twenty-five past nine.'

'You, Sally and Angela stay here until we get back,' Jessica ordered. 'Don't get undressed. We may all be needed to help search for her.'

Ronnie and Jessica were silent as they walked towards the pub Dora was staying at. Once, when they were only two hundred yards away, Jessica tripped and swore, but Ronnie shot her arm out and the older girl managed to keep her balance.

'Thanks, Ronnie.' She paused. 'Look! Isn't that Dora coming out of the pub?'

The moon's light picked out the short sturdy figure, head lowered as she hurried towards them.

'You're right. Thank goodness. I was dreading going in.'

They waited for Dora to get nearer.

'Don't tell me you two are goin' ter have a drink? Yer shoulda come earlier and joined the party—'

'Angela showed us the letter Margaret wrote,' Ronnie cut in before Dora could go on any longer. 'When Angela left you and went back to the motorboat she said Margaret still wasn't back.'

Dora's unkempt brows drew together. 'D'yer have any idea where she is?'

'None,' Ronnie said.

'Has she taken anythin' with her?'

'Angela didn't say,' Jessica answered.

Dora stood stock-still. 'Are yer sayin' what I think yer sayin'?'

'I think she may have had an accident,' Jessica said. 'She's been gone ages. Even if you fancied a walk in this freezing wind, you wouldn't normally want to be out for long, would you?'

Dora was silent for a few seconds. 'We need ter get back straightaway.' She spat on the ground. 'Damn tobacco. Not fit to be sold.' She looked at Ronnie. 'You go into the pub, miss, and call the canal police, and me and Jess'll go back ter the boats and decide what's best ter do.'

When Ronnie explained to the grinning man behind the bar that they'd lost one of the boat trainees his grin faded, and he nodded towards the telephone hanging from a wall.

'Oh, yes, operator, would you get me the Grand Union Canal police?' She cupped her hand round her ear to hear above the cacophony. 'Thank you.'

There was a minute's pause. Ronnie could feel her heart thumping.

Please hurry.

'Could you say your name and your location, please?'

She knew that voice. Efficient, but with an undertone of concern. Oh, thank goodness. He would treat it urgently.

'It's Ronnie Linfoot,' she managed.

'Miss Linfoot – Ronnie. It's Michael Scott here. Where are you?'

She couldn't remember what the pub sign said. Taking her mouth away from the receiver she spoke to the barman, who was watching her curiously.

'What's the name of this pub?'

'The White Hart,' the barman answered. 'Gayton Junction. They'll know it.'

She repeated it to Constable Scott.

'What is the problem?'

'We-we don't know exactly . . . One of our trainees is missing. She left a note to say the work didn't agree with her and she was going home in the morning and sorry to inconvenience us. Nothing more.'

'Her name?'

'Margaret Webb.'

'Do you know where she lives?'

'I don't know, but Dora will.'

'How long is it since she was last seen?'

'Um, probably' – Ronnie glanced at her watch, trying to work it out – 'roughly two hours ago.'

'What does Margaret look like?'

Ronnie frowned. 'About my height, thin, with long light brown hair she mostly wears in plaits—' She broke off, tears pricking the back of her eyes. Something bad had happened to Margaret. 'Oh, please can you come right away?'

'I'll get someone over immediately. Presumably you're moored close by.'

'Yes,' she said, for some reason disappointed it wouldn't be him coming.

'Go back to the boat. We don't want to be looking for two of you. I promise it won't be long.'

'Thank you.' Ronnie set the receiver in its holder. She remembered how Margaret got herself into such a panic in the tunnel. She always seemed nervous and Dora didn't help by the way she pounced on any of the trainees' weaknesses.

Ronnie dreaded walking back to the boats on her own. Not because she was scared someone undesirable would step from the shadows and attack her, but because she was terrified to come across Margaret's body. And when the towpath followed the canal for a hundred yards or so to the pair of boats, she had to turn her head away, so strong was the image of Margaret floating on her back in the cold black oily water.

Maybe she's already returned, Ronnie thought. *Wondering what the fuss is all about.*

But when she dropped through the hatch of the motor where everyone had crammed in, Dora simply grimaced.

'Did yer get hold of the police?' she said, her voice quieter and more sombre than usual.

'Yes,' Ronnie answered. She wouldn't tell Dora she'd spoken to the same constable who came yesterday with the sergeant to look for any black-market items. 'Someone's coming right away.'

Dora nodded. 'Good. There's not much we can do 'til they get here.' She glanced at Sally. 'Yer nearest the stove, miss. Put the kettle on and we'll have a cuppa. And don't start worryin' 'til we know somethin' definite.'

The bang on the side of the motor was so sudden and loud that it startled Ronnie. Her tea splashed from the mug onto the foldaway table.

'Police!'

Ronnie scrambled round the others to open the hatch to look into the warm hazel eyes of Constable Scott.

'I thought you—' she started.

'I thought it best for me to come, seeing as I've met you all,' he said, stepping onto the floor. 'Now you're all together I remember Margaret. Little waif of a thing.' He asked a few routine questions and scribbled down the answers.

'Have you the letter she wrote?' he asked, looking up.

Slightly flushed, Angela handed him the piece of paper. He quickly read it.

'Let's see,' he said. 'Margaret wrote this letter to Miss Dummitt who at the time was in the White Hart. As Margaret wasn't in the cabin Angela went to the pub and gave it to Miss Dummitt.' He paused. 'Is that right?'

'That's right, Constable,' Dora said.

'I didn't know how long Margaret had been gone,' Angela said eagerly. 'So I told the others and then Ronnie phoned the police.'

Michael Scott nodded. 'I've arranged a search party,' he

said, 'so they'll be here in a few minutes. Meanwhile, you must all keep calm.'

'I'd like to help search for her,' Ronnie said immediately.

'No, not tonight,' Constable Scott said. 'If we don't have any luck we may need all of you in the morning.'

'You don't think—' May started, but the constable put up his hand.

'I don't think anything at the moment,' he said. 'Anything's possible, but I can assure you we'll find her.' He cocked his head at the sound of footsteps. 'Ah, that sounds like someone.'

Not letting anyone see, Ronnie crossed her fingers tightly, praying it was Margaret. But a minute later they heard male voices.

'I'd better go.' Constable Scott rose to his feet. He glanced at Dora. 'Obviously, I'll let you know when we have some news. I'll phone the pub if I can't get here myself. Someone from there will come and tell you.'

'Thank you,' Dora said. 'We're not goin' nowhere.'

Constable Scott's eyes lingered on Ronnie. 'Thank you for reporting this,' he said. 'I'll do my best to keep you in the picture.' With that he was gone.

'You three best get ter the butty,' Dora said. 'We can't do nothin' more here 'less we hear otherwise.'

'What do you think, then?' May said, when the three of them were back in *Penelope*. 'She could just be enjoying a bit of peace on her own. Angela can be quite hard to take at the best of times.'

'I don't think it's that,' Ronnie said. 'It's ages now since Angela saw her. And I'm going to help look for her.'

'You'll do nothing of the kind,' Jessica said. 'I'm the eldest and what I say goes if Dora's not around.'

'Sorry, but I've made up my mind.' Ronnie slipped on her raincoat. She wound a scarf around her neck.

'Then I'm coming with you,' May said, taking off her pyjama jacket and pulling on a thick jumper, then a second one, and finally her coat.

'Oh, very well, then,' Jessica said firmly. 'We'll split up. That'll give us more chance to find her. And bring torches.'

The three girls gathered on the towpath and moments later Dora and Sally joined them. For once, Dora didn't even stop to light her pipe.

'She's a silly girl goin' off on her own at this time o' night,' she said, popping her lips as though she were actually pulling on the stem of her pipe. 'I just hope she in't fallen in the cut. The cold water wouldn't take long to kill her.'

Ronnie shuddered. Dora was voicing her worst thoughts.

'Anyway, we'll go in pairs,' Dora said. 'We don't want no more worry with another of yous missing.' She looked at Ronnie. 'You go with Jess along the cut that way' – she pointed – 'and May goes with Sally the opposite way.'

'What about you, Miss Dummitt?' Sally said.

'I know these parts,' Dora said. 'I'll be on my own – away from the cut.'

'Where's Angela?' Jessica demanded.

'Stayin' here. Said it were police work.' Dora's lip curled. 'She's right, in a way, but that attitude don't help Margaret.' She popped her lips again. 'Right, let's be off. Keep quiet so's yer can listen fer any noise.'

Ronnie and Jessica set off, Ronnie's heart thudding in her ears. After some minutes the numbing cold penetrated her raincoat and her two thick jumpers, but she forced herself to ignore it. The air smelt stale along the canal and several times she almost called out in fright when something brushed against her trousers. She shone her torch but as far as she could make out, it was only bits from the overhanging branches, blown by the wind onto the towpath.

'Listen!' Jessica hissed. She cocked her ear. 'Can you hear something?'

Ronnie stood still, hardly daring to breathe. A groaning sound, then a whimper.

'It sounds like some animal in pain,' she said, dreading the sight of an injured creature.

'That's what I thought,' Jessica said. 'Well, we can't do anything about it.'

'We can't leave it to die in agony,' Ronnie muttered.

'We're trying to find Margaret,' Jessica reminded her. 'Let's concentrate on that.'

'I'm going to have a look,' Ronnie said. 'You go on. I'll catch you up.'

'No, Dora said we have to stick together. Come on, Ronnie.' Jessica's tone was an order.

'I'll only be five minutes, I promise.'

Jessica shrugged. 'Up to you. You'll be the one to explain to Dora. But mind it's no more than five minutes.'

Ronnie crept towards the sound, not wanting to frighten the creature. The moaning became louder. It sounded like a large animal. Maybe a dog. She tried to remember how Mr Lincoln dealt with a wounded animal who was terrified. He kept his voice calm and soothing. She called out softly.

'Hello, boy. Don't be frightened. I'm going to find you and help you. Where are you?'

And then she stood paralysed. A voice answered her – thin and despairing.

'Help, someone! Oh, please help!'

Chapter Seventeen

Ronnie stood rooted. And then she gathered her wits and half ran, half stumbled, towards that desperate-sounding voice, praying it was Margaret.

'Margaret, it's me, Ronnie. Where are you?'

An owl hooted in the eerie silence. She tried again.

'Margaret! Where are you?'

'Someone, help! Please help me!'

It sounded further away than before.

'Shout again!' Ronnie belted out, cupping her cold ears.

But there was nothing.

Almost crying with frustration, Ronnie climbed up a gentle slope away from the towpath towards where she judged was the village. If only she could hear the others. Tell them she'd heard someone. But it was as though she were alone in the world with only that frightened bodiless voice.

'Margaret! I'm coming!' she shouted again.

'Ronnie?' It sounded as far away as a whisper – but she heard.

'Yes, it's me,' Ronnie called, relief flooding through her bones as she waved her torch this way and that. 'Can you stand to let me know where you are?'

'No.'

Margaret's voice was stronger now. She must be on the right track.

'Are you hurt?' Furious with the dim light of her torch, she tore off the regulatory tissue covering, and shone it in the direction the voice seemed to come from, trying desperately to pick out Margaret. And then she saw an arm reach up.

'I see you,' Ronnie called. 'Hang on.'

Two minutes later she was at Margaret's side. The girl was sitting on the wet grass, her coat bundled around her, but with no hat or scarf. She was shivering violently. Ronnie put her hand out to help her to her feet, but Margaret screamed, 'Don't touch me!'

'What is it?' Ronnie said, shining her torch onto the girl. To her horror she saw that Margaret's coat was dripping with water and her hair hung in wet strings. 'Oh, Margaret, did you fall into the canal?'

Margaret nodded.

'Here, before you say anything . . .' Ronnie bent to unbutton Margaret's coat, but the girl pulled back.

'I want you to have my raincoat,' Ronnie said.

'N-no.' Margaret clutched her hand to her chest. 'You need it.'

'I don't. I've got three jumpers on.' The small lie wouldn't hurt.

'No, I'm all right, honestly.'

'You're not,' Ronnie said. 'I shall get angry if you don't let me get that coat off you.'

'This is why I fell in,' Margaret said. She opened the top buttons of her coat and a small black head peered out, its fur in wet spikes. It opened its mouth but no sound came out.

Ronnie peeled off her raincoat.

'Give him to me,' she said. 'He'll be fine underneath my jumper.'

Margaret handed over the petrified creature and Ronnie gently tucked him under her top jumper.

'He's not much more than a kitten,' Margaret said through chattering teeth, as Ronnie draped her raincoat over the girl's shoulders with her other hand. 'Thank you,' she managed.

'What were you doing?'

'I was going for a last walk along the canal and this man came along. He didn't see me. He was carrying some sort of bag which he threw into the canal, then took off like a bullet. I was suspicious. Why did he act like that? Then I realised why. That bastard. This little creature would've drowned if I hadn't rescued him.' Even in the dim light Ronnie could see her eyes sparking with anger. 'It was desperately trying to swim. It was quite near the bank but when I reached to save it I slipped in the mud and fell in the water. But I managed to get it in the end.'

'We have to get you back and dried off,' Ronnie said urgently. 'You're going to catch your death of cold if you don't. I bet your clothes are sodden underneath. Mine were when I fell in.'

'I can't move,' Margaret winced. 'I must've twisted my ankle. The pain is awful.'

'You'll have to lean on me,' Ronnie insisted. 'We have to get back. You can't sit on wet grass all night. Here, pull up by my hand.'

But when Margaret tried to take it, half standing, she fell back in a heap.

'I can't stand,' she said. 'Pain's making me feel sick.'

'You've got to try. We'll both come down with a chill if you don't. I'll put my arm round you and you'll have to hop.'

'I'm sorry, I can't.'

'Then I'll have to scream.' Still holding the kitten firmly under her jumper, Ronnie cupped the other hand round her mouth and yelled as loudly as she could. 'HELP! PLEASE HELP!'

But all she could hear was silence.

She began to breathe too fast. Surely the others couldn't be that far away. She called again and again, but panic gripped her throat and stifled her voice. No one would be able to hear her. Her heartbeat pounded in her ears.

Someone please come . . . please come.

Did she hear voices? She cocked her ear. A muffled shout.

'Here. We're here!' Ronnie croaked, waving her arms frantically.

'Police!' A man's voice called some way away behind her.

She let her breath out in a gasp of relief as she whirled round to see a pinprick of light. And then it got brighter. A figure running over rough ground.

'Constable Scott!'

He glanced at her. 'Thank God you've found her!' Then he hunkered down to Margaret. 'What happened to you, young lady?'

'Ronnie will explain.' Margaret's voice was thin with exhaustion.

'She fell in the canal and sprained her ankle, and she can't move. She's soaking wet and needs to get dry quickly. But I couldn't support her. We did try,' Ronnie added defensively.

'You'll be fine now, Margaret,' Constable Scott told her in a gentle tone, patting her arm. 'Don't you worry. I'll soon get help.' He put a whistle to his lips. 'They won't be long.'

'Thank you, Constable,' Margaret managed, her teeth chattering. 'I'm just so cold.'

'We'll have you safely back to the boat in no time.' His gaze flickered to Ronnie. 'Why aren't you wearing—?'

'Shhhh,' Ronnie hissed, jerking her head to Margaret's wet coat, now in a heap.

Michael Scott nodded in understanding. 'Then take mine,' he said, undoing the belt.

'No, I've—' Ronnie began, pressing the kitten more firmly. It let out a howl of protest.

'Ah, I see,' he said. 'But it'll be easier keeping a cat inside a coat than up your jumper. And as you're not in any shape to disregard my instructions, I'm ordering you to take my raincoat.' He paused. 'I'm better dressed than you. I've got a jacket on underneath.'

He handed it to her and reluctantly she took it and draped it round her shoulders as Margaret had done with hers.

'Ah, here they come,' he said as two dark figures pounded towards them.

'Is she all right?' The plumper of the two policemen gasped out the question.

'Yes, but she's got a bad ankle,' Constable Scott said. 'She can't walk.'

'Right-o. We'll carry her back.'

'What will you do with the cat?' Margaret's voice held alarm.

'Take it back to the butty, of course,' Ronnie said. 'It'll be our mascot.'

'Dora won't allow it.'

'Dora won't see it – until it's too late. Don't worry – I won't let it come to any harm. Just go with the policemen, Margaret. You're shivering like mad. If you don't catch cold, I'll be amazed.'

She watched as the two policemen locked each of their arms to the other, then Constable Scott lifted Margaret into the "seat" they'd created.

'Put your arms round their necks,' he told her, 'and they'll get you in the warm before you know it.'

'Ronnie . . .' Margaret's voice was a whisper '. . . thank you.'

'Right.' One of the policemen nodded to the other. 'Let's get cracking.'

Ronnie watched numbly as the awkward little group moved off. She felt Michael Scott's gaze on her and turned. He was staring at her but she couldn't make out his expression in the dark. For a few seconds they didn't speak.

Michael Scott seemed to rally himself. 'Right,' he said in a businesslike tone, 'are you ready? We don't want to hang around here in the cold. Your friend looked to me in quite a state.'

'I'm sure she'll be fine when she's got a cup of cocoa inside her and tucked up in bed,' she said, picking up Margaret's coat, heavy with the dunking.

'I sincerely hope so.' His eyes alighted on the coat. 'Here, give me that.'

It was no use arguing with him. She handed it over.

'I want to thank you,' she stuttered, as she carefully picked her way towards the towpath, one hand holding her torch, the other trying to stop the kitten from clawing through her jumpers with the movement. 'I don't know what I'd have done without your help.'

'All in the line of duty.'

She wished he hadn't put it quite like that – but how else could he have replied? He was a policeman and simply doing his job.

'You said you were sending someone else,' she said quietly. 'I didn't expect it to be you.'

To her surprise he said, 'I thought you might prefer it to be me.'

It was as though the two of them were walking through

the night completely alone. Concentrating more on his words than looking where she was going, Ronnie stumbled over an exposed tree root and would have fallen if he hadn't shot out his hand to stay her. The kitten let out a squeal. For long seconds Ronnie's eyes locked with his. Then he put his free hand under her elbow and they walked on. Somehow the pressure of his hand was reassuring even though he didn't say another word until they reached the boats.

'Margaret lives in the motorboat,' Ronnie told him, breaking the silence, 'but I'll need to put the cat in the butty before I go and see how she is.'

'Why don't I find out and let you know. I need to talk to my two colleagues anyway and it'll be more than crowded in there.'

'Are you sure it's not too much trouble?'

He smiled. 'I'm sure.'

Ronnie nodded and handed him back his coat. Pressing the little cat firmly to her chest she banged on the side of the butty. To her surprise Angela put her head through the hatch.

'They're all in *Persephone,*' she said.

'I'm coming in anyway,' Ronnie said, her heart plummeting, hoping her hand over her chest would look casual, as though she was cold – which was true. It *would* be Angela. She was sure to tell Dora there was a cat on board.

'Well, did you find her?' Angela asked in her clipped tone.

'Yes, we found her,' Ronnie answered. 'She'd fallen in the canal but managed to pull herself out.'

'What a stupid girl! What on earth was she doing so near the edge at this time of night?' Angela's tone was tinged with disbelief.

'Actually, Margaret's not stupid,' Ronnie said with a rise of irritation. 'And I don't know what she was doing.'

Trying to have a bit of peace away from you, she badly wanted to say.

'I expect she saw something and went too close to have a look,' Ronnie went on, then shrugged. 'Something like that, anyway.'

There was a muffled mew. Ronnie coughed, trying to disguise it.

'What was that noise?' Angela screwed up her face.

'What noise?' Ronnie's eyebrows shot up. 'I didn't hear anything.'

'Like a cat mewing.'

'Oh, you're imagining it.'

'Where's your coat?' Angela said, narrowing her eyes.

Before she could think of an answer, Ronnie heard footsteps on the roof.

'Ronnie, it's Michael. Can you open up?'

'Oh, it's "Ronnie" and "Michael" now, is it?' Angela said, rolling her eyes as she went to open the hatch.

Ronnie's cheeks warmed but she was determined not to rise to Angela's sarcastic comment. Michael Scott bounded down the steps with Ronnie's raincoat.

'Oh, it's Constable Scott,' Angela said, edging towards him. 'How nice to see you again – and so soon.'

'I believe you're wanted on the motorboat, Miss . . .?' He fixed his eyes on her. 'Sorry, I don't remember your name.'

'Why should you?' She sent him a smile. 'It's Angela . . . Angela Pearson.' She took her empty cup and placed it in the hand bowl without rinsing it. 'I suppose it's Miss Dummitt asking for me. She seems to have made me her right-hand woman,' she added perfectly seriously, 'so I'll go and see what I can do.'

Constable Scott nodded, then glanced at Ronnie who rolled her eyes.

'Dora's never said or indicated anything of the kind,' Ronnie said when Angela left. She took the little cat from underneath her jumper and set it on one of the seats. 'I'd better get you something to eat, Puss,' she said, stroking him. 'You look a bit thin. Don't you have a home to go to?' The cat began to purr.

Michael Scott grinned as he moved to stroke the cat who'd jumped onto her raincoat and was washing its face. 'No, Dora never mentioned anything like that, but it was the only thing I could think of to get rid of her,' he said, his fingers lightly brushing Ronnie's as he fondled the cat's ears. She moved her hand away.

'Good thing you're a lucky black cat,' Michael addressed it. 'That's what you might have to be called – Lucky. You could easily have drowned if the other nice lady hadn't rescued you . . .' His smile faded as he looked at Ronnie. 'I'm not sure Margaret is as lucky. My colleagues decided they would have to take her into hospital.'

'Oh, no. Why?'

'Sally – I believe she used to be a nurse – said she was hot and clammy but still shivering, so she's obviously got a temperature. She told Miss Dummitt hospital was the best place for her.'

'I'll go and see Margaret before they leave,' Ronnie said, quickly moving to the steps. 'She'll be worried about the cat.'

'You'll be too late,' he said. 'They were just leaving. The police car's parked close by and I don't think they wanted to waste any more time.'

Ronnie's eyes widened with alarm. 'Constable Scott, she's going to be all right, isn't she?'

'She's young,' he said. 'I'm sure she will be.'

Chapter Eighteen

There'd been no point after all in going over to *Persephone* now that the policemen had taken Margaret to hospital. Ronnie's head was still whirling after Constable Scott left. What a piece of luck that he'd heard her call out. She sighed heavily. It had been one thing after another and she felt drained. The cat began to meow and weave in and out of her legs. Thankfully, he didn't seem a bit scared once he was on the boat. She pulled the folding table down to expose the small pantry cupboard to see if there was anything to give him. Yes, a bowl of leftovers from Jessica's stew. She scooped a spoonful out onto a saucer and put it on the floor. The cat jumped to the floor and began to wolf down this unexpected treat. While he was occupied, Ronnie got undressed and pulled on her pyjamas. Snuggling up in bed, even though the hard mattress couldn't compare with her one at home, couldn't come soon enough.

Poor Margaret. What bad luck to have fallen in. And all for one little animal. Ronnie had felt immediate sympathy with her, knowing she, too, loved animals, but Margaret had risked her life to save one little cat. And if she wasn't much of a swimmer it was an incredibly brave thing to do. A chill snaked down Ronnie's spine to think of the frail girl in that cold murky water where she'd been herself only a week ago.

Childishly, she crossed her fingers, telling herself Margaret would be back tomorrow, good as new.

But then her stomach turned over. Constable Scott hadn't sounded absolutely convinced. But it was no use worrying. The doctor at the hospital would know what to do. But she needed to find out where Margaret had been taken, and if they kept her in another day she'd ask Dora if she might be allowed to visit her.

She was just pulling back the blanket when a thought struck her. She needed to make a dirt box for the cat. But the last thing she wanted was to go out again and start digging earth up. She was so bone-tired and she'd never get away with not being caught by Dora's sharp eyes. She looked round the small space of the cabin. There must be something. Her eyes alighted on the stove. Maybe she could collect some ashes if she could find a box to put them in. She hunted around and discovered a small cardboard box that held tinned food. She removed the tins and set them inside the tiny pantry cupboard, then shovelled some ashes into the box, most of them floating in the air before settling. But it would have to do. After Lucky had polished off the scrap of stew and licked clean a small saucer of milk she picked him up and put him in the cardboard box she'd set by the range. He immediately jumped out and leapt onto the bed, just as though he knew that's where she slept, and his place was going to be with her.

'So you've bagged your sleeping spot, Lucky,' she said, smiling at Michael Scott's name for him, 'but that could all change when Jessica comes to bed.' She started to chuckle when Lucky began digging his claws into the eiderdown, a blissful expression on his face. He yawned and curled up into a ball, tucking his chin under his hind leg, perfectly content with his new situation.

* * *

'Oh, God, what's that!'

A terrifying screech, then a hiss, woke Ronnie with a jerk. 'Wasser matter?' she said.

'A cat's got in . . . I nearly squashed it.' Jessica's voice rose.

Ronnie chuckled. 'It's only Lucky.'

'What're you talking about?'

Ronnie sat up. 'Margaret. It's the reason she fell into the canal. The cat was drowning and she rescued him.'

Jessica shook her head. 'You won't be able to keep him – Dora will soon see to that.'

'She's not going to know.'

'Hmm.' She paused. 'How silly of Margaret to put herself into such danger over a cat.'

'I don't suppose she realised it at the time.'

'You know the police took her to hospital?'

'Yes. Mich—' She caught herself. 'Constable Scott told me.'

Jessica shot her a look but didn't comment.

'What did Dora say about it all?' Ronnie asked.

'She didn't say much until they took Margaret off.' Jessica picked up her toothbrush. 'But she gave us another lecture about not wandering around in the dark alone, and you could see she was very cross that her warnings hadn't been obeyed. I must say, I wish Margaret hadn't taken off like that.'

'I suppose she wanted a quiet walk by herself – maybe she was having second thoughts about going home.'

'Maybe.' Jessica's voice was a gurgle as she swilled her mouth and her toothbrush in a mugful of water.

'Is May coming?'

'She'll be over shortly.'

'I'm too tired to wait up for her,' Ronnie said, putting her hand out to stroke Lucky's stomach. He'd rolled over on his back against the boat wall, as far away from Jessica as possible. 'Just a minute, Lucky. Let me have a proper look at you.' Ronnie leaned closer. 'Jess, can you pass my torch on the shelf?' Jessica put the torch in Ronnie's hand and she shone it on his underside. 'So you're not a boy after all,' she said, rubbing the furry stomach. 'You're a sweet little girl pussycat.' Lucky purred in acknowledgement. Ronnie looked up at Jessica. 'Lucky's a girl.'

'Yes, I heard you tell her,' Jessica chuckled. 'Well, boy or girl, I don't mind you having it/him/her so long as you keep it out of the space we laughingly call the kitchen. They're not the most hygienic creatures ever to be wandering about where food's being prepared.'

'Lucky's as clean as a whistle,' Ronnie said, cuddling her.

Her last waking thought was wondering what Rusty would think of the little cat.

When Ronnie woke the following morning May and Jessica were both up and dressed.

'I can't believe I didn't hear either of you,' she said, as May handed her a cup of tea.

'We were practically tiptoeing,' May said. 'You looked done in, if I may say so, Ron.'

'I was,' Ronnie said, taking a deep swallow. 'Oh, this tastes wonderful. Thank you.'

'And I see we have a new visitor.' May jerked her head towards Lucky who was still fast asleep.

Ronnie grinned. 'I've told her she has to be on her best behaviour.'

'And does she have a name?' May asked.

'Her name's Lucky,' Ronnie said. 'Well, it couldn't be anything else, her being a black cat and being pulled out of the canal when she was drowning.' She looked at May. 'Are you sure you don't mind?'

'No, I like cats,' May said. 'We always had one at home.'

'My parents would never let me have an animal,' Jessica said, spooning out the porridge, 'so I can't say I'm used to them, but as long as she's clean, I'll keep her secret.'

'What – away from Dora, d'ya mean?' May said with a smirk.

'Yes,' Ronnie answered for Jessica. 'Dora will make me give her up and I'm not going to. Margaret fell in the water to rescue her. She's special.'

'Poor Margaret.' May sat at the table while Jessica set down the porridge bowls. 'Sally said the best place for her was hospital but I'm worried. She looked terrible.'

'Give her a couple of days rest and I'm sure she'll be fine,' Jessica said firmly.

After the three of them had finished a rather sombre breakfast there was a rap on the side of the butty. Lucky startled and jumped off her cushion and Ronnie saw her squeeze into a tiny space near the stove.

Dora slid back the hatch.

'We need ter plan our day,' she said. 'We can't press on 'til we know about Margaret. I've spoken ter the barman, who said the police rang early this morning. They're keepin' her in as she's got a cough. I'm not surprised.' Dora tutted. 'This job in't right for her at all and she knows it by her letter yesterday.'

'I'd like to go and see her,' Ronnie said.

'Certainly not, miss. Yer not goin' anywhere but stayin' here where I can keep an eye on yer.'

'Miss Dummitt, I was the one who found her,' Ronnie said, quelling her temper as she felt her face flush. 'I'm asking you please to let me visit her. She'll be feeling so strange without knowing anyone.'

'How will yer get there then? The hospital's more'n five miles away.'

'I could borrow Margaret's bike.'

'Not in this weather, you fallin' off and another disaster.'

'Then I'll walk to the pub. I'm sure someone there would have transport.'

'Hmm.' Dora wrinkled her brow. 'Maybe Jack Soames might. He's got a van and the old devil can usually find a can of petrol. But I in't happy about it.'

'Oh, that would be marvellous,' Ronnie said, jumping up before Dora could change her mind. 'I'll go over straightaway.' She stopped. 'Which hospital is she in?'

'King's Park. Jack'll know it,' Dora said. 'Don't stay long, now . . . an' tell her we wish her the best,' she added unexpectedly, as she withdrew her head.

Ronnie dressed hurriedly in her only pair of clean trousers and her usual two thick jumpers, relieved Dora hadn't spotted Lucky.

'Anyone seen what the weather's like?' she said to May and Jessica.

'You won't believe it,' May said. 'I went outside before you emerged. The sun's out. It's a beautiful crisp morning.'

'How wonderful. I was getting sick of all the rain and the mud. But I'll still have to go in my raincoat. I didn't bring a proper coat. There was no room.' She didn't add that there was also no spare money. It would be too disloyal to Dad's memory.

'Good luck on your adventure,' Jessica said as Ronnie left. 'Tell her to get better soon.'

'I will.'

Ronnie half ran to the pub, thankful it was so near the mooring. The ground was still soft and squelchy but she hardly noticed. Her main thought was to find out how Margaret was. She was at the pub in less than five minutes.

She heard a motorcar draw up just as she was about to enter the building. She looked round and saw it was a police car. The door opened and Michael Scott sprang out.

'Ronnie! What are you doing?'

'I'm looking for Jack Soames. He works in the pub and Dora said he might be able to give me a lift in his van to the hospital.'

'You'll do nothing of the kind. I don't want to see you go off in some rusty old van with a man you've never set eyes on. *I'll* take you there.'

Ronnie hesitated. Then she nodded. She'd rather be in a car with Michael Scott than Jack Soames, whoever he was, any day.

'Hop in, then.' He smiled and opened the passenger door for her.

'How did you know I'd be here?' she asked.

'I didn't,' he said, switching on the ignition key. 'I just guessed you might use the pub to phone the hospital.'

'So Dora let you off then?' he said when he'd started the engine. He glanced at her.

'Reluctantly,' Ronnie said.

'Has she spotted the cat yet?' He turned his focus to the road.

'No, and she's not going to, if I can help it. And it's not "the cat",' she added. 'It's a "she" called Lucky – just as you told her she was.'

Michael Scott smiled. Even in profile he had a nice face, she thought. Actually, when he had his helmet off so you could see his face, he was rather good-looking.

'What did the hospital say when you rang them this morning?' Ronnie asked, thankful he couldn't read her last thought.

'Not much. I'm not a relative but when I mentioned

"police" Sister said Margaret definitely wouldn't be coming out today.'

'I've just thought – do you think they'll allow *me* to visit her when I'm not a relative?'

'We'll have to play it by ear,' he said. 'It probably depends on her condition.'

The seat was well padded and clean but she couldn't get comfortable worrying about Margaret.

As though he understood, he patted her arm briefly. 'Try not to worry until we find out exactly what the situation is. And by the way,' he added, 'there's no need to call me Constable Scott when I'm not in uniform. I'm just about to go off-duty for the day, so you can call me Michael.'

She nodded.

At the hospital Michael strode up to one of the receptionists.

'Constable Scott.' He handed her his identification and she glanced at it, then waited. 'I telephoned this morning about Margaret Webb. We brought her in last night – the young lady who'd fallen into the canal. Is it possible to see her?'

'Visiting hours are strictly two 'til four every afternoon.'

'We can't come then,' Ronnie said, standing near Michael. 'Margaret and I are trainees for the Grand Union Canal Carrying Company. I know she'd like to see us, if possible.'

The receptionist put her glasses on and ran her finger down a page from an open book.

'Ah, yes,' she said. 'Margaret Webb.' She stopped a passing young student nurse. 'Nurse Brown, could you go upstairs and speak to Sister Harris in Ward 6. Tell her it's a police officer who wants to see her patient, Margaret Webb.'

'And her fellow crew member, Ronnie,' Ronnie added quickly.

The young nurse nodded and hurried away. She was back in no time.

'You may both go up but Sister Harris is very strict. She's given you no more than five minutes.'

'Thank you.' Michael turned to Ronnie. 'Shall we go?'

His expression was calm. He was certainly the kind of person to be around in an emergency, Ronnie thought, as she allowed him to guide her down a long dreary corridor, the lower half of the walls olive green and the upper half what may have once been cream. Michael's steady but swift footsteps squeaked on the linoleum and she had to take little skips to keep pace.

They walked through the door of Ward 6 to see a line of patients on both sides – maybe fifteen apiece. Ronnie's heart-beat quickened with anticipation that her fears would soon be alleviated. A brisk plump woman with grey hair tucked under her cap came towards them and Ronnie saw her badge: Sister Harris.

'We've come to see Margaret Webb,' she said. 'I think you've allowed us a few minutes.'

'That's right,' Sister Harris said in clipped tones. 'The patients in here must be kept very quiet. They are seriously ill.'

Ronnie's stomach lurched.

'Do you mean—?' Her words choked.

'Yes. Miss Webb is very poorly. I'm afraid she has pneu-monia.'

Michael took Ronnie's hand but she scarcely noticed. Biting her lip to stop herself from crying out, she looked directly at the Sister. It couldn't be true. Margaret was only twenty.

'Isn't pneumonia something that only happens to older people?' she asked, her voice tremulous.

'No, I'm afraid not. Babies can get it.'

'She won't die, will she?' Ronnie licked her lips, her mouth suddenly dry.

'She's young,' the Sister said, unknowingly repeating Michael Scott's words. 'That's in her favour.'

Margaret's eyes were closed as Ronnie, her insides quivering, tiptoed over to her bed, Michael a few paces behind. Her friend's face was as pale as the stark white of the pillow. Ronnie sucked in a breath. She looked so small and frail. Pneumonia. Was it really possible? Margaret's hand was outside the bedcover and Ronnie gently took it. Instantly, Margaret's eyes opened and when she saw who it was she smiled.

'Ronnie. How did you know where I was?'

Dear God, her voice was so weak.

'Constable Scott told me. Do you remember he found us last night?'

'Oh, yes. Is he—?'

'He's right here,' Ronnie said, letting go Margaret's hand and moving aside. Michael shook his head.

'Let me thank him,' Margaret said, trying to raise herself.

Michael stepped into view. 'Don't try to move, Margaret,' he said. 'We're only allowed a few minutes as we're not relatives.' He paused. 'Before I left the station this morning they said they'd received contact details for your parents, so by now they will have let them know where you are.'

'Thank you.' Margaret scrunched the corner of her sheet with her restless fingers. 'Mum and Graham are going to be so upset. They thought I was going home today. That's what I told them. But now . . .' She closed her eyes, exhausted with the effort of speaking.

'Is there anything you want, Margaret?' Ronnie said, desperate to do something for the sick girl.

'Nothing.' Then Margaret's eyes opened. 'Just one thing. Please look after the little cat or it would have been in vain.'

Ronnie's eyes pricked with tears.

'I've thought of a name for him,' Margaret said, turning her head to look directly at Ronnie with her cornflower-blue eyes.

'He's actually a "she",' Ronnie said, managing to stop herself from blurting out that the cat had already been given a name. 'What do you want to call her?'

'Lucky,' Margaret said. 'Because black cats are lucky – and *she* certainly is.'

Ronnie swallowed hard. 'Do you know,' she said, 'Constable Scott came up with the same one.' She glanced at him and gave a half smile, and he smiled back warmly. 'So Lucky it is. I think she'll soon get used to her new name.'

Margaret smiled. 'Will you come and see me again, Ronnie?'

How could she answer? She had no idea of Dora's plans: whether she still expected her trainees to continue along the canal today or wait until they knew Margaret was safely at home.

'I'll come if I'm allowed to,' was all she could say, taking Margaret's hand again and giving it a gentle squeeze.

'I'm glad.' Margaret gave a deep sigh. 'You can tell me how Lucky's getting on.' She closed her eyes again and Ronnie watched for a few seconds as the girl's chest rose and fell under the blanket.

'We should leave,' Michael said softly, just as Sister Harris bustled over and pointedly looked at her watch.

Back in the police car Ronnie was silent. She stole a glance at Michael, his hands firm on the steering wheel, concentrating on the road. She wished he'd say something – some words of comfort. As though he knew what she was thinking he turned his head towards her.

'Try not to worry,' he said. 'She's in the best place and Sister Harris seems very capable. You have to have faith that they'll look after her and she'll recover.'

'I'm not sure I do,' Ronnie said. 'I have a horrible feeling . . .' She trailed off.

'It's because we're not medical people,' Michael said. 'They know a lot more about pneumonia now and it's not always a death sentence like it used to be in the old days.'

'Don't even talk about death,' Ronnie said sharply.

Michael turned back to the road. He glanced out of his window, and suddenly she felt him tense beside her as his hands clenched the steering wheel.

'What's that twerp up to?' he said, glancing in his mirror.

Ronnie turned her head to follow his gaze. She couldn't see anyone, so twisted right round in her seat. Then felt her body go rigid. Will Drake stormed by on his motorbike, giving them both a cheery wave as he made his front wheel tip up and leave the ground before it thumped back onto the road again.

'Young idiot,' Michael fumed. 'He could easily cause an accident doing something so foolhardy. And I'd certainly be interested to know where he gets his petrol and what reason he gives to be allowed it.'

Ronnie couldn't answer. Her heart was hammering so loudly in her eardrums she was sure Michael Scott could hear it. She swallowed. What *was* Will Drake doing? By his behaviour he obviously had little fear of the police.

Chapter Nineteen

Michael Scott drew up as near as he could get to *Persephone* and *Penelope,* then hopped out to open the passenger door of the car for Ronnie. Dora strode towards them.

'How is she?' Dora said, after acknowledging Michael with a brief nod.

Ronnie hesitated and turned to Michael.

'I don't think she'll be coming out very soon,' he said to Dora.

'Have you any idea how long?'

'No,' Ronnie said. 'But she does look very poorly. They said she had pneumonia.'

Dora paused for a moment then shook her head. 'I need ter think about this,' she said. 'We have a schedule ter keep. I'll have ter have a word with the office.' She looked at Ronnie. 'You'd better come with me and allow Constable Scott ter carry on with his duties.'

'Oh, I was just about to go off-duty,' Michael said, smiling. He glanced at Ronnie. 'But I was glad to be of service, Ronnie.'

'Thank you . . . Michael,' she added under her breath so Dora couldn't hear her use his Christian name.

He grinned in acknowledgement. 'Let's hope we hear some better news soon.' He jerked his head to Dora's departing figure. 'I'll call the hospital tomorrow and let you all know how Margaret gets along.'

'How can you?' Ronnie said. 'I'm sure Deadly Dora will want to move off today and you won't know where we are.'

'We're not the canal police for nothing,' Michael grinned. 'And the canal isn't going anywhere so I'm sure I can catch you up.'

Ronnie nodded and hurried after Dora. Michael would do his best – of that she was certain.

'We'll wait until termorrer mornin',' Dora addressed the group when she returned from making her phone call at the pub. 'Then I'll phone the hospital and if she's makin' progress we'll be on our way.'

'What about her things?' Ronnie asked. 'Her clothes . . . oh, and her bicycle?'

'Her ma and pa will take over from now,' Dora said.

Ronnie swallowed. Should she say something?

'Miss Dummitt, I promised Margaret—' she started.

'No arguments, miss,' Dora snapped. 'They're orders from head office. We have ter keep on the move.' She lit her pipe. 'There's a war on, case yer hadn't noticed, and we in't anywhere near ready to take cargo.' She gave the others a sly look. 'Yous'll all want ter let go when I tell yer at the next moorin' you lot should be pickin' up some post at The Swan.'

There was a cheer from Sally. Ronnie didn't say anything. Yes, it would be lovely if she had letters waiting from her sisters and Maman, but she was far more worried about Margaret. She bit her lip. There was nothing more she could do.

'It's most inconvenient,' Angela said when she and Ronnie and the other trainees got together to discuss Margaret's plight. 'I wanted to continue the training today. We've still got loads to learn. Margaret was going home today anyway, so I don't see why we have to hang around. We can't do anything, can we?' She looked round at the others as if she was hoping for the group's approval. But no one spoke. Ronnie found she was the only one to look Angela directly in the eye.

'That sounds a bit harsh,' she said.

'Well, as Miss Dummitt says, she's got her parents to see to her. It's not as though she's being abandoned.'

'Really?' Jessica said with raised eyebrows. 'It certainly sounds like it to me.'

Dora returned from the pub the following morning, smiling for once.

'I spoke ter one of the nurses,' she said, pulling on her pipe, 'and Margaret's doin' okay. They say she's goin' to be all right though she'll be there a bit longer. Her folks know where we're headin' so we can now carry on without worryin'. When she's out I'll let them know where we are and they can catch us up.'

Ronnie drew in a huge breath of relief, even though she was still reluctant to leave until she knew Margaret was fully recovered. But she supposed Dora was right to want to carry on today. As Angela had pointed out, Margaret had intended to leave the canal this morning anyway.

They had several locks to negotiate but once through Ronnie became more confident with four more under her belt, until Angela began to criticise her for not getting to the next lock gate fast enough. There'd been a long pound between the last two locks and Ronnie had made as fast a progress as she could, hampered by her Wellington boots and the thick muddy towpath. She forced down her temper but Angela's constant nagging – never in Dora's hearing, of course – made Ronnie so nervous she dropped the windlass in the canal, much to Dora's irritation. But when Angela dared to start on Jessica, Ronnie was relieved and cheered to see this time the trainee had overstepped the mark.

'We only have one boss, Angela,' Jessica snapped, her nostrils flaring. 'And it's not *you*.'

'We're makin' a few changes here,' Dora said, her dark eyes narrowing as her gaze swept the little group that afternoon straight after they'd picked up the post from the toll office. 'May, you'll be livin' in the motor from now on, and Angela will go ter the butty.'

Ronnie sucked in her breath. 'But why?' she blurted. 'We make a good team in the butty.'

'Because I said so.' Dora's tone was challenging. 'Yer need to get used to workin' with different folks.'

'I don't agree,' Jessica said, an angry frown spoiling her lovely features. 'We get along perfectly well as we are.'

'It's not fer you to question,' Dora said, not bothering to remove her pipe. 'Yer need to be flexible in this game – so no more from any of yous.'

'May, you're the only one who didn't object,' Jessica said as the three of them walked back to the butty.

'Well, I like Sally, and I liked Margaret,' May said. 'I'm not keen on Angela so I'd rather be moved than have to live with her, though it's damned annoying to have to pack everything up, even though I haven't brought much.'

'I know something,' Jessica said. 'I'm not going to put up with any of her nonsense. She can bloody well toe the line so far as I'm concerned.'

'It's no good getting cross,' Ronnie said. 'We all need a cup of tea and to read our letters.'

She was longing to read her two letters, one in Raine's looping writing and one from Downe, the writing of which she thought she recognised but couldn't quite place. She was relieved to see that Jessica had a letter, and May had a couple like herself. It would have been embarrassing if one of them hadn't received anything.

But how she wished she had some privacy, she thought yet again as she filled the kettle from the decorated can of water. Too impatient to wait for it to boil, she opened the letter from Downe.

Dear Ronnie,

I hope this finds you well and the work is going along how you hoped and expected.

Curiously, she turned over the sheet, her eyes flicking to the signature. Her old boss, Mr Lincoln. Oh, dear. Had something bad happened to Rusty? Her eyes flicked down the page. This side said nothing about him. She flipped it over to read from the beginning.

The surgery has been very busy lately, but nothing too major except a Dalmatian this morning who practically filled the room! He was the size of a pony and did not want to be held down while I endeavoured to examine him. His owner, an old boy from the next village, wasn't much help, so in the end I told him to go and sit in the waiting room – him, not the dog, haha! I managed to quieten the animal with a man-sized shot of phenobarbitone and it did the trick! I should have given the old boy a dose as well!

A giggle escaped Ronnie's lips as she imagined it.

'What's so funny?' Jessica demanded.

Ronnie swung round. 'I've had a letter from the vet I used

to work for on Saturdays,' she said. 'He made me laugh about one of the animals – and its owner.'

'You can share the joke,' May said.

'Let me finish the letter first,' Ronnie answered as the kettle began to boil. 'Can you make the tea, May?'

Your mother brought Rusty in yesterday.

Ronnie's heart jumped. She *knew* something must have happened to Rusty for Mr Lincoln to be writing to her.

> *Don't worry – he's perfectly all right. She said he kept her awake every night howling and whining. I told her he was pining for you and to give him a bit of attention. I suggested she put his basket in* her *bedroom, as he's used to company at night. She was horrified and said it was out of the question. Rusty pricked his ears up at that exact moment and gave her such a pleading look that she said, 'I'll think about it.' I looked him over and he seemed fine, but animals do miss people and you can't explain they'll come back. I asked if she was taking him for regular walks and she said she was. I think she's secretly beginning to like his company, but she would never admit it, although the bedroom bit was probably a suggestion too far!*

My goodness, what a change. Ronnie smiled at the image of Maman's horrified expression.

> *Anyway, I thought you'd like to know as from what you've told me she might not mention it when she next writes.*
>
> *Take care of yourself, Ronnie. You can always drop me a note if you feel like talking to anyone outside the family. It can be helpful sometimes.*
>
> *Terence Lincoln*

Ronnie glanced at May who raised her head from her letter and winked. 'Well, tell us the joke.'

She read it out to May who giggled, but when she glanced over to Jessica, Ronnie saw the older girl was sitting with one hand to her forehead, staring into space. A small piece of card fell to the floor and Ronnie bent to retrieve it. She couldn't help a quick glance as she put it back on Jessica's lap where the girl had placed her opened letter and another similar card. They looked like tickets to something.

'Are you all right, Jessica?' Ronnie asked. She paused. 'Jess?'

'Oh, yes . . . um, sorry, what did you say?'

'You've gone quiet. Not bad news, I hope?' She suddenly remembered how Jess had sobbed on their first night in the cabin, then fobbed her off that she must have been dreaming.

'You could call it that,' Jessica replied dully, folding the letter. 'But don't question me – I don't want to talk about it.'

Why would a pair of tickets – if that's what they were – upset her so much? Ronnie frowned. There was something going on in Jess's home life – or love life – that was obviously making her friend unhappy.

She was just about to risk saying something more when there was a sudden loud banging on the side of the boat, making them all jump. Then Angela's strident voice shouted, 'Open up, please.'

The three of them looked at one another. No one stirred. Then the hatch in the roof slid open and Angela's head appeared. She threw down a soft bulging bag.

'Thanks for your help,' she said sarcastically, as she climbed down the steps and retrieved her bag. She looked around. 'I'll take the double bed with Ronnie.'

'You won't,' Jessica said quickly. 'That's where Ronnie and I sleep. You'll take May's bed.'

'What, that little space?'

Ronnie suppressed a giggle. It really was difficult to imagine Angela's plump body squeezed onto what barely consisted of a narrow bench. May had never grumbled, but May was slim. Well, at least Jess had spoken up.

'What's that cat doing here?' Angela suddenly shrieked. 'I'm allergic to cats. And it's unhygienic in such a small space so you can get it out of here at once or I'll report you to Miss Dummitt.'

Ronnie was about to argue when Jessica sent her a warning glance.

'You will do no such thing,' Jessica hissed, standing close to Angela and glowering from her lofty height.

'You can't stop me.' Angela's lips pursed.

'Oh, yes, I can. *I'm* in charge of cooking so there'll be no complaints about hygiene. The cat is the reason why Margaret is lying in hospital and we're going to look after it for her. And *you* will keep your mouth shut. Meantime, do us all a favour and put your damned stuff away.'

Angela gave one of her disapproving sniffs and opened the two drawers, banging them back when she saw they were full.

'I'll be off then,' May said, rolling her eyes towards Angela. She pressed her jumpers down in the pillowcase she was using for a suitcase, then blew Ronnie and Jessica a kiss and disappeared through the hatch.

Ronnie pulled down the bed and sat on the edge. With happy anticipation she opened the envelope covered by her sister's large looping writing. She pulled out a sheet of notepaper, written on both sides.

Dear Ronnie,

I keep thinking about you and wondering how you're getting on in the canal boat. I bet there's a lot to take in. And I bet it's jolly hard dirty work as well. But that probably suits you. I'd hate it!

As usual we're very busy here at the ferry pool but I hope to be taking a couple of days' leave in the not too distant future. Be good if it ties in with you. I believe you said you get three days after your training, so let me know and I'll do my best.

I heard from Maman a few days ago. She wrote it on the day you left. It was full of woe about all her girls leaving her to cope on her own and all she had for company was a mangy dog! Maybe she and Rusty will become friends. But I reckon the sooner Pierre manages to see her again, the better. She was a changed woman, wasn't she, in his company? I didn't recognise her as my mother! Neither did Suzanne, haha.

Well, there's no real news from me. We just keep doing our job, hoping it makes a difference. I long for the war to end all this misery, and yet if it wasn't for the war I'd never be doing the job I love more than anything in the world. Or met Alec. Isn't that awful? But it's the truth.

I'd better go. They're ringing the supper bell and I'm starving.

Lots of love and take care of yourself, little sis,

Raine XX

Ronnie read her sister's letter again, stopping at Raine's observation of Maman. She grinned to herself. Her sister was right. Maman wasn't just a changed woman that evening, she was transformed. But as soon as Pierre had had to leave the following day it hadn't taken long before she'd slipped back into some of her old habits. Yet her love for him had never wavered.

Did first love always last?

The image of a dark curly-haired youth with a man's physique popped into her head. What was Will up to when he'd zoomed past the police car yesterday, and cheekily waved? Surely he couldn't have seen who it was in the passenger seat. He certainly didn't seem to be perturbed by the police even though Michael Scott had made that comment about the petrol. It was against the law to have any petrol unless you were one of the emergency services, but she hadn't dared say anything at the time. She wasn't about to let Constable Scott know she held any special interest for Will Drake.

Chapter Twenty

Constable Michael Scott propped his bicycle against the wall of The White Hart pub, sure he would never warm up again. The air was so icy he hardly dared breathe in. When he did it was like sucking sharp nails into his nostrils. Brrrr! Underneath his cape he banged his hands on his upper arms. He'd never known it so cold. It was turning into a real blizzard. The waterproof cape kept the damp out but it was no match for this freezing weather. He should have worn his greatcoat. The realisation made him think of Ronnie Linfoot – how she'd given Margaret her raincoat on such a cold night. What a kind and generous girl – and with a wonderful sense of humour. He grinned and wished he hadn't as his face felt so numb, but he couldn't help remembering Ronnie's choked laughter when he'd pulled out Dora's undergarments. He'd enjoyed that shared moment. Even when she'd caught sight of the soot on his nose and had nearly collapsed with laughter. The way she'd gently wiped it away. Mmm. He could still smell the scent of her. She was pretty, too. And those eyes. They were the colour of purple pansies. He wondered what she'd look like underneath the layers of jumpers, then shook himself. He was on duty, and that meant not daydreaming about a pretty girl.

Before entering the pub he took off his cape and shook

out the worst of the wet snowflakes, then pushed open the heavy oak door to a world in complete contrast with the outside. The heat, for one thing. And the familiar smoke. He wished he could light up but it was frowned upon when they were on duty. A couple of lads were playing darts, and the smell of beer from men grouped at tables as close to the fire as they could get made him long to join them in a pint. He sighed inwardly. That little luxury would have to be shelved until the evening, though he doubted he'd venture out again in this snowstorm.

He hung his cape on the coat stand and walked purposefully over to the bar. The barmaid was serving two middle-aged men, both wearing battered trilbies. He looked round. Most of the men here were more than likely boaters, probably not able to go far when this part of the canal was more fit for ice skates than boats. His casual glance fell on the profile of a youth with long dark curly hair at the end of the bar. He was tipping back a pint with two other men. Michael's instinct told him that although the youth looked old enough to drink, from his build and his being half a head taller than his companions, he was probably underage. He looked up at that precise moment with a shifty expression, then quickly lowered his eyes.

When it was Michael's turn, he showed the barmaid his identity card and said in a low voice, 'Excuse me, miss, but I wonder if you might happen to know the whereabouts of Miss Dora Dummitt. I understand she was here a few days ago—'

Before he could stop her, the barmaid took up her hammer for calling 'Last orders', then belted out, 'Anyone here know where Dora Dummitt's boats're moored?'

Out of the corner of his eye, Michael saw the same curly-haired youth tip his head back to finish his beer and saunter towards him.

'Wot's it worth, officer?' He spoke in a loud voice, laying a cheeky emphasis on the word 'officer'.

Michael looked him up and down, taking in the expensive jacket and boots, the dark eyes, almost black, challenging him.

'I'm not quite sure what you mean by that,' he said.

'Oo-er, we got a posh plod here.' The youth looked round and laughed. Two or three men let out a chuckle. The youth looked back at Michael. 'Wot I mean, officer, is wot's it worth to yer if I tells yer where she is?'

There was a palpable silence. The customers set their mugs down, waiting to see what would happen next.

'And you know for sure, do you?' Michael said crisply.

'Course I do.' A secretive smile hovered around the youth's lips. 'I make it my business ter know where our Dora is.'

'Is that because you have your eye on the trainees?' Michael said, guessing, but sure he was close to the truth.

'Maybe . . . maybe not.' The youth fixed his stare. 'I'll tell yer for a pint. That's a bargain, that is.'

'What's your name, son?'

'First off, you ain't my dad. I got one of them already and I don't need no other.'

'Okay. We'll start again. What's your name?'

'William Drake.'

'How old are you, William?'

'Goin' on twenty-two.'

'That's a laugh,' the barmaid said. She slammed a tankard down in front of one of the customers so hard that the froth spilled over the side. 'Our Will's barely out of nappies. I'm not allowed to sell him alcohol but his mates bought it for him. What could I say?' She shrugged.

'Hmm. Interesting,' Michael said. 'So how old are you?' he repeated. 'The truth.'

Will lowered his eyelids. 'I don't have ter answer that,' he muttered.

'Right, let's go off to the station and you can say that to the sarge,' Michael said, taking his arm in a grip.

'Leave off.' Will rounded on Michael. 'She's a lyin' bitch.'

'Don't you dare call me a bitch.' The barmaid's blue eyes sparked with anger. Her expression relaxed as she looked at Michael. 'He's always rude to me these days, officer, ever since I found out his real age and stopped goin' out with him. I didn't want ter be no cradle-snatcher.'

Will leaned menacingly over the counter. 'Yer lyin' again, Mavis—'

Mavis rewarded him with a stinging slap on the face. 'That's for callin' me a bitch.' She gave Michael a smile. 'I can tell yer his age,' she said. 'I found out he's only just turned seventeen.'

His hand raised, Will swivelled round to face Michael. 'You goin' ter stand there? She bleedin' attacked me. You should arrest her.'

'Afraid you deserved that, for speaking to a lady in such a manner,' Michael said, gripping Will's arm again.

'She ain't no lady.' Will's mouth was sullen.

'That's enough,' Michael said, thinking quickly. 'You tell me where Dora Dummitt is, and I won't book you for juvenile drinking.'

Will snorted. 'I ain't no juvenile.'

'Where is Dora?' Michael spoke softly.

Will gave a heavy sigh. 'They're yonder . . .' He waved his left arm in the direction. 'I reckon they'll be stuck in the ice.'

'Name of the village?'

'Bugbrooke.' Will grinned. 'Or Buggerbrooke, as it's known round here.'

Five miles on a bike in this atrocious weather. Michael groaned inwardly.

‘Thank you.’ He turned to the barmaid. ‘Thanks, Mavis. Just clip him another one if he acts up again.’

She grinned, showing a gap in her front teeth. ‘I will, officer, now I have yer permission.’

Michael nodded and made for the door. He took his cape from the coat stand and people started talking again. He turned his head to give a last look and they immediately stopped. He paused, and then he said loudly and clearly to the youth called Will, now sitting on a bar stool watching and smirking:

‘Just one more thing, Will. We take a very dim view of people who deliberately break the law, especially in wartime, so any more trouble from you and you won’t know what’s hit you. And that’s a promise.’

He shut the door behind him but not before he heard a roar of laughter from the customers. He wasn’t sure if it was directed at him or young Will Drake.

Chapter Twenty-One

Ronnie hated the idea that Dora planned to move on after they'd all had a morning cup of cocoa. She knew she was probably being over-cautious, but she wished Dora would stay put until they knew Margaret was definitely out of hospital. Should she say anything? If she was going to, she needed to say it now, because Dora was already preparing to let go.

She gathered her courage. Dora was emerging from the motorboat after having inspected it for being shipshape and ready to leave.

'Miss Dummitt—'

'What is it now, miss?' Dora said impatiently, jumping down and onto the towpath.

'I'm worried about Margaret.'

'Well, don't be,' Dora said without looking up. 'Get back ter the butty. We're lettin' go in fifteen minutes. You need to be helpin' Angela at the tiller.'

'She said she could manage on her own.'

Dora nodded. 'Well, maybe she don't need help but you could do with watchin'.'

Ronnie bit her lip to stop herself from saying she had no problem at the tiller and in fact liked that part of the job best of all. Dora was so contrary that she might not allow her to take the tiller on her own if she thought she enjoyed it too much.

'I just wanted to ask – couldn't we stay a couple more days – just to make sure Margaret's all right?'

'No, we couldn't, miss.' Dora flexed her fingers and glared at Ronnie. 'I have a schedule ter keep and Margaret's irresponsible behaviour in't helped. There's no more ter be said. So off yer go.'

She'd tried. For once Ronnie was grateful there were several locks to negotiate. It took her mind off Margaret.

Dora tilted her head upwards. 'I don't like the look of that sky,' she said that afternoon. 'It's full of snow.'

'How do you know that?' Sally asked curiously.

'Yer only have ter look at them clouds,' Dora said. 'Some of them have a yeller look and some pink.' She grimaced. 'That's a sure sign, though I must say it's a bit early fer the time o' year.' She looked at her watch as she puffed away on her pipe. 'Three o'clock, near to. I don't think we oughta go further. We could be in for a big snowstorm so we'll tether the boats and tie up at Bugbrooke. Better safe than sorry.'

Ronnie breathed a sigh of relief. They hadn't come far today after a much later start. If there was any news of Margaret the hospital would soon find out where Dora was and let her know. And anyway, she consoled herself, no news was good news.

The afternoon and evening wore on. Jessica went to bed early with a headache.

'You're not coming down with anything, are you?' Angela asked in a challenging tone.

'If I am, I shan't ask you to look after me,' was Jessica's retort. 'Don't wake me, either of you. I've taken a couple of aspirin.' She pulled the blanket almost over her head and told Ronnie not to wake her until morning.

It was difficult for Ronnie to have any conversation with Angela. How she missed May and her chatter and cheerful smile – so different from Angela's turned-down mouth. She wondered how Sally and May were getting on with Dora, as for once Dora didn't need to find the nearest pub to sleep in with Margaret gone. The thought of Margaret made the niggling worry start again. She knew she was being silly. The hospital wouldn't have said Margaret was improving if it wasn't true.

Ronnie awoke from a night where she'd had little sleep, mostly being kept awake by Jessica's heavy breathing and frequent thrashing of her long legs. It was only this last hour or so she'd finally dropped off. Rubbing her eyes and yawning, she realised every part of her body was freezing cold, yet for a change Jess hadn't grabbed more than her share of the blankets. Ronnie sneezed, waking the sleeping girl.

'Wassup?'

'Nothing. Except I'm absolutely frozen.'

Jessica put her head on one side. 'Listen.'

'I don't hear anything.'

'That's just it. It's completely silent. Where are the quacking ducks, the splashes of the otters . . . even the wind rustling in the branches? There's just nothing.'

Jessica was right. The silence was eerie. As though Mother Nature was holding her breath.

Shivering, Ronnie reached for one of her jumpers and slung it round her shoulders. She got out of bed and undid the hatch. Immediately a fall of snow dropped onto her head and she started to giggle.

'What the hell's going on?' Angela's peeved tones made Ronnie giggle even louder.

'Oh, my God, it's snowing,' Angela said, looking horrified at Ronnie's head.

'You look like an old lady, Ronnie.' Jessica sat up, joining in the laughter. 'Literally with snow-white hair.' Feeling for her bag she pulled out a gold compact, then snapped it open. She handed it to Ronnie. 'Take a look at yourself in fifty years' time,' she said.

Ronnie threw her head back so that a lump of snow fell off, showering Angela.

'You stupid girl,' Angela said, furiously brushing the flakes away. 'What did you want to go and do that for?'

'To annoy you, of course,' Ronnie said, still laughing when she saw herself in the tiny mirror. 'I'm going to put my coat on and have a proper look.'

She quickly pulled on her socks and shoes, then threw on her coat and climbed through the hatch.

She gasped. It was as though she'd stumbled into fairyland. It was dark but there was still a crescent moon, and its soft light glistened on every tree, every branch, every twig that was covered with snow. It was such a beautiful sight that Ronnie's mouth opened, causing her breath to puff out in hazy rings. There was no sound of the usual gentle lapping of the water at the sides of the boat. No sound of any creatures. Any not already hibernating would be hidden away in this weather, she thought, hoping it wasn't cold enough to kill them.

'Come down, Ronnie,' Jessica shouted. 'Put your proper trousers on and some more jumpers or you'll catch your death. We don't want another casualty.'

'All right.' Ronnie came down the steps shaking the snow from her raincoat.

'Couldn't you have done that outside?' Angela demanded.

'No. Jessica's right – it's much colder than I thought.'

'I'm getting up,' Jessica said. 'Someone needs to start the porridge.'

'It's not even six o'clock,' Angela grumbled. 'I'm going to have another hour.'

'Fine.' Jessica hopped out of bed and pulled on her tartan dressing gown, then pulled the pipe cleaners from her head and ran her fingers through her hair, shaking it and letting the golden waves tumble to her shoulders.

She looked lovely, Ronnie thought. For an instant she wished she hadn't cut her hair quite so short. She could easily be mistaken for a boy in her filthy clothes. But every time she changed into clean clothes the new set became just as disgusting by the end of the same day. Maman would go on and on if she saw her like it.

Ronnie pictured Suzy looking glamorous in her evening dress, singing her heart out to the weary soldiers. It must be heaven to have a proper bath, wash her hair with shampoo instead of soap, wear something pretty for a change. Just to see what it felt like. She wouldn't want it all the time – of course not, she told herself fiercely. But just to experience it occasionally. Even Raine in her uniform had looked fabulous when they'd met in London to go and see Mrs Hunter about working on the canals. If anything, the uniform made her look even more feminine. Well, uniforms and evening gowns weren't her at all. She was always happier in trousers.

After breakfast when Ronnie was washing the dishes, Dora banged on the side of the boat to let them know she was coming in.

'It's very slippery out there,' she warned as she stepped into the cabin, 'so watch yerselves. We won't be goin' nowhere today – maybe not even termorrer if the snow don't let up. We'd never see where we was headin'.' She looked at Ronnie. 'Yer might have yer wish after all,' she added, 'unless we see one of the boaters comin' the other way ter give us some news.'

But all was quiet on the canal. They didn't spot another boat that day or the next.

'The boaters know in advance what the weather's goin' ter do,' Dora said. 'It's typical of 'em ter make theirselves scarce. They'll all be in the pub!'

Ronnie thought she would go mad with Angela's moaning and groaning, often complaining about Lucky in an undertone, but managed to bite her tongue, though Jessica was more vocal.

'I could cheerfully wring her bloody neck,' she said to Ronnie when Angela decided to go and inspect the weather situation for herself. 'Who does she think she is?'

'Somewhere above us,' Ronnie said.

'Speak for yourself.' Jessica's eyes flashed. Then she looked contrite as Ronnie flinched. 'Sorry, Ronnie, that didn't come out how I meant it. You're as good as me any day of the week. And by the way, I don't mind *you* calling me "Jess".'

'I didn't think you would,' Ronnie grinned, wiping down the wooden top they used as a draining board, and hung the wet cloth over the handle of the kettle. 'I just want May to come back. She was such fun with her ukulele. Maybe we'll ask her to give us a tune this evening after supper.'

'She won't want to brave the slippery gunwale holding an instrument.'

'Then we'll go to *Persephone,*' Ronnie said decisively.

But to her disappointment, May said she really wasn't in the mood. The only good thing was that Jessica had more time to be experimental with the cooking. Until the third day when she said she was running out of ingredients.

'Yous'll need to stock up,' Dora said when she arrived the same minute Jessica was flinging open the cupboards and swearing that there was nothing to make for supper.

'How? We can't walk to the village in this weather.'

'That's the reason yer was told ter bring boots,' Dora said. 'Those brogues yer wear are for summer when yer doin' this sorta work.' She looked at Ronnie. 'And yous've only got wellies that might keep out the water but not the freezing cold.'

'I'll go,' Angela said surprisingly. 'I've got all the correct gear.'

She would, Ronnie thought. But she wasn't going to let Angela go on her own. She had to get outside too. Breathe some fresh air. Stretch her cramped legs. See someone else besides Dora and the others.

'I'll help you, Angela,' she said. 'Jess needs quite a bit of stuff so I can help carry everything.'

For a moment Angela looked as though she was going to oppose the suggestion, but then she shrugged. 'Okay, you'd better wrap up and bring a couple of bags . . . and your coupons would help this time,' she added with a twist of her lips to presumably remind Ronnie of her previous lapse.

The two girls trod painstakingly through the snow. To Ronnie's amusement Angela slipped more in her winter boots than Ronnie in her Wellingtons. The village was further away than Dora had implied. At any other time Ronnie would have enjoyed the walk, loving the sound of the snow crunching under the rubber soles of her boots, but her anxiety about her feet, which felt as if they were becoming more and more frozen with every step, took away any enjoyment. There was no sign of the snow melting, and by the look of yet another sullen grey sky there was no hope for any breakthrough later on. By the time they arrived at the village Ronnie's feet were numb.

'Oh, no, the shop's closed,' Angela said. She shook her head. 'There must be somewhere else open.'

'What day is it?'

'Wednesday,' Angela said.

'If this place is the same as Downe, where I live, the whole village will be shut on a Wednesday afternoon – half-day closing at one o'clock.' She glanced at her watch. 'And it's ten past.'

'What on earth do we do? We can't go back empty-handed.'

For once Angela seemed to be at a loss.

'There's the pub not far,' Ronnie said, pointing to a Tudor building, 'and that's where I'm heading.'

'Miss Dummitt won't like it.'

Ronnie rounded on her. 'You know something, Angela? I don't care whether Deadly Dora likes it or not. I'm not wandering around and still not find anything. I'm going in to warm up my feet. And see if there's anything they might be able to let me have. And you can please yourself whether you come with me.'

'I'm going back,' Angela said.

Ronnie turned without another word, so intent was she on thawing her poor feet. With extra care she covered the short distance to The Crown, then almost slipped on the step of the pub door. Grabbing a snow-covered bush to steady herself she opened the door and was nearly knocked backwards by the heat of the log fire roaring in the inglenook. The place was heaving – almost all with men. They stopped speaking as every head turned towards her. Ronnie gulped, wishing Angela had stayed with her. She shoved her hands in her pockets to stop anyone from seeing them tremble.

'What can I do for you, love?' the man behind the bar asked. He was a tubby man who wore a spotless white apron, and spectacles perched upon his bald head.

Face flushing with embarrassment she forced herself to

put one lifeless foot in front of the other towards the bar, aware of her every move under the stares of the customers.

She swallowed. 'I'm one of the boat trainees,' she began, keeping her voice down, trying not to draw attention to herself, 'and I'm—'

There were a few incredulous guffaws to those near enough to hear her.

'You boat wenches are more trouble than yer worth,' one man with only socks on his feet and his legs thrust out in the inglenook shouted. 'Stuck in the snow, are yer?' Without waiting for a reply, he said, 'I s'pose yer askin' for help.'

'We don't know what the girl wants, so let her finish,' a man at the bar called out, then caught her eye and gave her a wink.

Ronnie's cheeks burned. 'We've almost run out of food,' she said. 'In fact, we don't even have anything for supper. And the shop's on half-day closing.'

'And cold enough to freeze your ba—' He stopped himself and chuckled. 'Oh, dear – better watch me language. We're not used to pretty girls coming in here.'

Ronnie drew herself up. 'If you can't help me—'

'Why don't you sit down, love, over by the fire, and I'll get you a drink to warm you up. You look frozen to death.'

Before she could reply, he said, 'I'm Bob, and I'm doing the cooking. There's some meat and veg pie left over I could pack for you and your pals, but it'd be dangerous you walking in the snow holding a dish.' His eyes fell on the man who'd stuck up for her. 'Sid, could you help this young lady back to the boat when I've got her dinner ready?'

Sid's face split in two with delight.

'Oh, aye, I'll see she don't come to no harm . . . or the dinner,' he added with a black-toothed grin.

'Will it take long?' Ronnie asked, her mouth watering at

the sound of the pie. At least it would tide them over until tomorrow. And tomorrow the snow might have melted and they could do some proper food shopping. 'I shall be in trouble if I don't soon get back.'

'Well, no one's going anywhere in this lot.'

He emerged from behind his counter. 'You sit here, love . . .' He tapped on one of the chairs at the side of the inglenook and put a glass of ginger ale on the round table. 'Take your boots off and let your feet warm up.' He turned to the man who'd spoken up for her. 'Look after her, Sid. I shan't be long.'

Sid looked at Ronnie and grinned, showing three sparse teeth at the top and none at the bottom. 'Yous'll be all right with me,' he said. 'It's the others yer want ter watch.'

The stuffy atmosphere felt as though it was stifling her. She couldn't breathe. Unnerved by so many eyes staring at her, she jumped up.

'Where yer goin'?' Sid called. 'I gotta keep an eye on yer. Yer heard Bob tell me, didn't yer?'

Ronnie sat down again and gulped down half of her drink. It was cool and sharp. She prayed Bob wouldn't be long so she could just get out of here.

The minutes ticked by. She watched the clock. Ten minutes. Quarter of an hour. Now twenty. Ronnie finished her drink, thankful her feet had finally thawed and were tingling. At least it meant there was some life. She looked up as Bob appeared, carrying a basket that exuded a wonderfully enticing smell. He was grinning.

'Tell the ladies to have this on me,' he said, putting up his other hand to stop any argument. 'And don't worry about being late back.' He paused. 'Who's your trainer, anyway?'

'Dora—'

'Dora Dummitt?' he interrupted.

'You know her?'

'All the folk round here know her. She'll understand better than anyone if you're stopping for a drink.' He gave a hoot of laughter, then suddenly tapped the side of his head. 'I've just thought. Old Jack Soames from the White Hart telephoned here no more than half an hour ago, asking if I'd seen her. Apparently, the police are trying to get hold of her.' He roared with laughter again. 'I wonder what she's been up to this time.'

Ronnie's heart jolted. She glanced at Sid who was just heaving out of his chair. She didn't want him with her, being nosy about Dora.

'I really can manage on my own now you've put the dish in a basket,' she told Bob.

He looked over to Sid, then back to Ronnie. Seeming to understand, he nodded to her. 'If you're sure, love.'

'I am.' Ronnie smiled at him, taking the basket before he changed his mind. 'And thank you so much for not charging. It's really kind of you.'

'Hope you and the ladies enjoy it,' he said, 'though I will have me dish and basket back.'

'Of course. I'll bring them back tomorrow morning.'

Twice Ronnie almost slipped and twice she managed to keep upright but it took all her concentration to stop herself from falling over. Thank goodness. There were the boats. Even before she approached the motorboat she could hear the girls talking. Well, she'd give Dora the message privately. It was none of her or the other girls' business to know the reason why the police wanted to question their trainer.

Chapter Twenty-Two

She'd made it! Ronnie almost laughed aloud thinking how pleased Dora would be when she saw the dinner Bob had kindly packed for everyone. She hadn't managed to buy any food but at least they'd be all right tonight, and she knew there was plenty of porridge and evaporated milk for the morning. The village shop would be open tomorrow when surely the sun would finally come out and melt the snow.

Ronnie was just about to climb on board, balancing the basket, when a figure stepped from the hatch of *Persephone*. Constable Michael Scott! So he'd already found Dora. Why was he so intent on interviewing her again? Surely they'd found out all they needed to know when he and the sergeant came to inspect the boats that time.

Those men at the pub hinted Dora was probably up to no good. Oh, it was too embarrassing for words.

She waited for Michael to recognise her and when he did, his expression was grim. Her heart lurched. Supposing Dora was arrested. She and the others were still training. They wouldn't have a clue what to do or even where to go. All this was muddling through her head when he reached her on the towpath.

'Ronnie! Everyone's wondering where you'd got to. Dora's not at all pleased you've been gone so long.'

'She knew I was going to the village to get some rations,' Ronnie said defensively. She held out the basket. 'Look! I've brought them dinner tonight. That should put Dora in a better mood.'

'I doubt it.' Michael Scott regarded her. 'But of course you wouldn't know what I've come for.'

'No, I don't, unless it's checking for stuff on the black market again.'

'No, it wasn't, though I wish it were.'

Ronnie frowned. 'What is it, then?'

He was silent as though wondering what to say. A terrible foreboding flooded through her.

He cleared his throat. 'I'm sorry, Ronnie, I don't know how to say this . . .' His eyes were fixed on her. 'You must be brave.'

Her heart began to pound. He was about to say something awful – she knew it. Not Raine or Suzy. Don't let anything have happened to them. Panic clawed at her throat.

'Not one of my sisters? Or my mother?' She grabbed his arm.

He shook his head. 'No, love, it's not them.'

'It's Margaret, isn't it?' This time her voice was hardly more than a whisper.

'Yes. She took a turn for the worse this morning.'

Ronnie flinched. 'W-will she be all right?' She pulled at his coat sleeve, willing him to say what she wanted to hear.

'I'm afraid not.' He looked down at her, his eyes warm with compassion. 'I'm so sorry but there's no easy way to tell you – Margaret died early this morning.'

Ronnie's basket fell from her grasp but she was hardly aware. Her eyes went wide as she fixed them on him. It couldn't be true.

'B-but she was getting better . . . the hospital said so. Why would they say such a thing if it wasn't true?'

'I know that's what we were told,' he said, watching her. 'But sometimes pneumonia plays tricks.'

'I can't believe it. She's so young. She's—'

Ronnie broke off sobbing. Strong arms encircled her, supporting her, then drew her closer.

'I just can't believe it.' Ronnie's voice was muffled against his coat. She felt Michael's hand stroke her hair.

'Shhhh.' He tilted up her face until her eyes were almost level with his. 'I feel badly, too. It's because I knew her, even though it was just that brief time, but enough to see that she was a real person – a girl who risked her life rescuing a little cat – not just another unknown victim of the canal.'

'If only I'd—'

'No "if only"s,' he said. 'It doesn't help. You did your absolute best. More than anyone you tried so hard to save her.'

'What did Dora say when you told her?'

'She said it was a pity but it was one of those things.'

Ronnie turned her head and began to cry again, still holding on to Michael.

'Come on, Ronnie. Poor Margaret's at peace now.'

She gulped, then sniffed, wiping her eyes with the sleeve of her raincoat. Michael found her a handkerchief and held it to her nose.

'Blow,' he said, as though she were a child. 'Good.' He studied her. 'Are you feeling better?'

She couldn't speak.

He nodded. 'I understand,' he said. 'You'll remember her for the kind girl she was, but she wouldn't want you to be miserable on her behalf.'

Suddenly Ronnie looked at her arm and then with horror

at the ground. The meat pie had been flung into the snow. He followed her gaze and picked up the basket, then crouched down and rescued the pie.

'Here, it's not broken up too much. You should be able to piece it together but it might need a little more time heating up, that's all.'

She knew he was trying to lighten the moment and smiled weakly. 'Thank you . . . Constable,' she managed.

'I've told you before – Michael will do when we're off-duty.'

'Michael,' she repeated, and took the basket from him. 'Thank you for taking the trouble to come and tell us.' Without another word she climbed aboard *Penelope*, somehow comforted by his warmth and understanding.

To her relief Jessica was the only one in the butty. She was making tea and turned when she heard Ronnie's step.

'Did you just this minute bump into Constable Scott?'

'Yes.' Ronnie flushed with embarrassment remembering how she'd blubbed on his coat. Whatever must he have thought? 'He told me about Margaret.' She sat down. 'I can't believe it. She was improving – the hospital said so.'

'These things happen.' Jessica poured her a mug of tea. 'Drink this, Ronnie. I offered our lovely Constable Scott a cup but he wouldn't stay. He was bent on finding you and telling you in person – I suppose he thought he should as you knew her better than the rest of us.' She looked at Ronnie closely. 'Unless, of course, he had another reason.' She gave a knowing smile.

'Stop it, Jess. I'm not in the mood for your nonsense.'

'Look, Ronnie, you can't keep this up. We've got a job to do.'

Jessica left without another word. Ronnie put her hands round the hot enamel mug, trying to draw some comfort from its warmth. How kind Michael had been when she'd made such a fool of herself. It was almost as if he'd gone out of his way – surely beyond what would have been considered his normal duties. If it were true, then why?

It wouldn't sink in. No matter how Ronnie told herself it was true, she still couldn't quite believe Margaret was dead. Nothing to do with the war but something that could so easily have been avoided. Going for a walk by the canal when it was pitch-dark was madness. Whatever had made her think of doing such a thing? How much easier it would have been to have learnt that a bomb had killed her. She bit her lip. That was a terrible thought as well. It didn't matter now how she'd died. Nothing could alter the fact that Margaret, a young girl with all her life before her, was dead.

Ronnie swallowed her tears.

'The officer told me Margaret's ma and pa are comin' to collect her things,' Dora finished when she appeared in the butty a few minutes later, puffing more furiously on her pipe than usual. 'They should be here termorrer mornin' so we'll be tyin' up until they've done their business.' She looked at Ronnie for the first time. 'What's the matter with you, miss? Yer eyes are all red and swollen.'

'It's such a shock about Margaret,' Ronnie gulped.

'Yes, most unfortunate.'

Is that all the woman can say?

As if Dora read her mind, her expression softened a fraction. 'Like I keep tellin' yer – the cut's a dangerous place. Yer have ter learn to respect 'em. Let this be a warnin'. An' it's not worth rescuin' some poor creature what's fallen in.'

Bob, who'd turned out to be the landlord of The Crown, had kindly offered Dora and Ronnie shelter in the pub while they waited for Margaret's parents to arrive.

'Miss Dummitt, I think that's them. They're both carrying suitcases.'

'Go and see,' Dora said. 'No good both of us freezin' to death.'

Ronnie stood outside, banging her arms together to keep warm. She watched as the couple slowly walked from the bus stop towards the pub.

'Mr and Mrs Webb?' she asked. Mr Webb nodded. 'I'm Ronnie.'

'Pleased to meet you, my dear. This is my wife.'

Mrs Webb's face was set as though she was determined to hold herself together, but Ronnie noticed Mr Webb had tears rolling down his cheeks which he wiped away, coughing loudly into his handkerchief as he did so. Ronnie remembered how fondly Margaret spoke of him.

'It's a sad day all right,' Dora said, coming up to them. 'Yous'd better come on board and one of the wenches will make a cuppa.'

'No, thank you,' Mr Webb said. 'It's very kind of you but we want to be on our way as quickly as possible with this snow.'

'Ver-ron-eek, here, has packed Margaret's things,' Dora said, briefly touching Ronnie's arm to show Margaret's parents who she was. 'She was the one what found yer daughter.'

'Oh, my goodness,' Mr Webb exclaimed. 'The nurse told us a friend visited her in hospital a couple of hours before we got there. The weather held the bus up. Was it you, my dear?' Ronnie nodded. 'Margaret said you'd been a good friend and she was sorry to have put you to so much trouble and worry.'

'It was nothing,' Ronnie said. 'I only wish I'd found her sooner – that I'd known she'd disappeared sooner, and maybe . . .' She broke off, choking with tears.

'You mustn't upset yourself,' Mr Webb said. 'But she did want to make sure you were looking after the cat.'

Dora swung round to Ronnie. 'Why weren't I asked about yous lookin' after it?'

Ronnie felt her cheeks flush. 'We were worried you'd be annoyed and not allow it on the boat.'

'I like cats,' Dora said, surprisingly. 'I like all animals, matter o' fact. What d'ya think keeps me goin' on the cut if it weren't for the love of nature?'

'So it's all right, then, if I take care of Lucky?'

Dora gave a short bark of laughter. 'So that's its name. I suppose I can only agree to let it stay with a name like that.' She glanced at the other girls who had silently gathered. 'One of yer, go in and get Margaret's bag.' She turned to Mr and Mrs Webb. 'Margaret's bike is under the cratch' – she nodded towards the motorboat – 'but it'll only take a moment to get it.'

'The cratch?' Mrs Webb sounded puzzled.

'It's at the foreend of the motor,' Dora said impatiently. 'Margaret kept it underneath as it's nice and dry.' She turned to Ronnie. 'You'd better get it, miss.'

Mr Webb wiped his eyes again and trumpeted into his handkerchief. 'Please don't,' he said. 'My wife and I already discussed it.' He looked at Ronnie. 'I'm sorry, I didn't catch your name, my dear.'

'Ronnie . . . Ronnie Linfoot.'

'Then if you could use Margaret's bicycle we'd like you to have it.'

Ronnie startled. 'Really? Are you sure?'

'We're very sure,' Mrs Webb joined in. 'Margaret loved that bicycle. We gave it to her on her eighteenth birthday. She hasn't used it that much as she takes . . . took such pride in it. We bought her the very best. She deserved it. She's always been a good girl but we never thought she was strong enough to do this sort of work. We were so relieved when she telephoned to say she was leaving – coming home to us. And now she never will.' Mrs Webb broke down in sobs.

'Hush, now, love,' Mr Webb said, seeming to gather himself and putting his arm around her broad shoulder. 'We've used up enough of Miss Dummitt's time already.' He looked at Dora. 'We'll be on our way.' He picked up the bag with Margaret's belongings and nodded to the little group. 'Thank you for everything.' His eyes fell on Ronnie. 'Especially we want to thank you, my dear, for your kindness to Margaret and we hope you make good use of her bicycle.'

'I will,' Ronnie said, her cheeks warming with embarrassment. 'And I promise I'll look after it. But anyone would have done the same for Margaret.'

'But you were the one who *did*,' Mr Webb said emphatically, 'and we'll never forget it.'

'Well,' Dora said crisply when they'd gone. 'I'm sure yer didn't expect that, miss. I think different to Margaret's ma and pa. I think it should be the bike any one of yous can use when we need shoppin' or walkin' on a long pound to the next lock.' She stared at Ronnie. 'So what do you say to that?'

'I say no,' Ronnie said, surprising herself under Dora's piercing eyes. 'It will be up to me if I lend it to anyone. Margaret wouldn't ever lend her bicycle because it was her pride and joy, and her parents gave it to me so I'd keep it in perfect condition the way Margaret did. I bought my bicycle at home for half a crown from a jumble sale and it's a heavy uncomfortable old thing to ride.' She stared challengingly at Dora. 'I can't wait to try Margaret's.'

'No good will come of bein' so selfish,' Dora said. 'Mark my words.'

Chapter Twenty-Three

Although Margaret's untimely death hung like a cloud over Ronnie and the others, apart from Angela who never actually referred to her, except to say how silly she was to take such a risk in the dark, Bob's meat and vegetable pie was a great success that evening. Ronnie had told Jessica on the quiet what had happened.

'I'll disguise it,' Jessica chuckled. 'I guarantee Angela won't notice the difference.'

Although the potatoes had run out, there was plenty of cabbage, making a hearty meal. Ronnie was so hungry she forced herself to put all thoughts of poor Margaret to one side and enjoy it. She'd think about Margaret when she was quiet and on her own. She grimaced. Whenever that would be possible.

'Such a treat having pastry,' Jessica said, licking her lips after she laid down her knife and fork. 'I'd make it in the boat if there was room.'

Ronnie couldn't help a smile. If Angela knew the dinner had fallen into the snow she'd have thrown a fit. Dad used to say, when they were on that one and only camping holiday, what people didn't know wouldn't hurt them. He was referring to Maman though he was too loyal to say so. She looked at Angela, who was eating slowly and, judging by her satisfied expression, savouring every mouthful, even though she'd made no comment at all. Suddenly, Ronnie felt the devil in her.

'Are you enjoying it, Angela?'

'Best meal I've had since we've been on this trip,' Angela said, concentrating on her fork where a small piece of meat and carrot clung to the prongs.

'Good job Constable Scott saved it.'

Angela's head shot up. 'What are you talking about?'

'Oh, I dropped the basket and the pie fell out of the dish into the snow. But he came to the rescue and picked it all up again and shoved the broken pieces back together. It was so thoughtful of him.' She gave a peal of laughter. 'Jess had to make some extra gravy so you couldn't tell when she dished up.' She winked at Jessica who gave a surreptitious nod.

'You mean this pie's been rolling about in the snow?' Angela said, her fork frozen in mid-air, her pale eyes staring at Ronnie.

'There was no damage to the dish,' Ronnie said. 'Thank goodness. It would have been embarrassing having to explain to the landlord who cooked it, after his kindness.'

'I don't care a monkey's about the blasted dish,' Angela's voice rose. She banged her knife and fork down on the plate and sprang up. 'I'm going to the motor to warn the others that their dinner's been in the snow.' She glared at Ronnie. 'You're disgusting.'

'The snow was perfectly clean, if that's what you're worried about,' Ronnie said, biting back her laughter. 'There was no sign of any footprints.'

'And I'm sure that reheating it has probably killed *most* of the germs,' Jessica called to Angela's stocky figure as the woman disappeared through the hatch.

Ronnie couldn't contain herself any longer. All the pent-up emotion of the day gushed out and she clung on to Jess, screaming with laughter.

'You little scamp,' Jessica said, joining in. 'You said that on purpose.'

'So did you,' Ronnie stuttered, another wave of merriment overpowering her again. 'And she deserved it.'

'Well, she won't have much comfort from reporting it to Dora.' Jessica stood to collect the plates. 'She will have polished hers off ages ago, the speed she eats. And wouldn't have cared tuppence about the snow. She'll have seen far worse in her time. And I bet Sally and May have finished as well.' She looked at the remains of the pie on Angela's plate. 'I hate to waste this.'

Ronnie heard a soft pad as Lucky landed from the top of the coal bunker. She scooped her up and put her nose near the plate. Lucky pawed at it and Jessica laughed.

'You'd better cut it up for her,' she said, 'but don't let her have any pastry. It's not good for animals to digest.'

'I'm going to chop it *all* up,' Ronnie said, still chuckling. 'Lucky doesn't need us to decide what she should and shouldn't have. She'll soon sort it out.'

She cut the pie in small pieces and set it on the floor. 'And' – she turned to Jessica – 'she doesn't care a monkey's about it being dropped in the snow.'

That set the two of them laughing again.

When they'd washed up and put the dishes away Jessica was silent for a few moments. Ronnie stole a curious glance. Jessica caught her and smiled, seeming to have come to a decision. 'Ronnie,' she said, 'do you like swing bands?'

'Yes, from what I've heard on the wireless,' Ronnie said, surprised at the question. Nobody had ever asked her taste in music, although Maman had always tried to get her interested in Suzanne's classical concerts when she played the violin in the village hall. 'My sister Suzy is the musician – she's the one I told you about who sings to the troops. I forget which band she's with but it's one of the swing bands.' She glanced at Jessica. 'Why are you asking?'

'A friend of mine' – Jessica paused and Ronnie noticed her mouth tighten a fraction – 'sent me two tickets for Jack Payne's band at the Palais de Danse in Leamington Spa. He was born there so he's doing a special visit. I think they're playing there at least two weekends and tickets will be like gold dust. I've calculated we should be there about the same time as the band.' She looked at Ronnie. 'My friend can't go after all and I wondered if you'd like to come with me. It'd make a nice change for both of us.'

'Is he a boyfriend?' Ronnie's eyes were wide with curiosity.

'Not exactly,' Jessica said abruptly.

'What does that mean?'

'It means I don't want to talk about him.' Jessica averted her eyes and Ronnie was sure that whoever this man was, he wasn't treating her very well. But she mustn't even hint at such a thing as she knew by now that Jess became easily upset.

'Surely you should be going with a man to this Palais – whatever you called it.'

'Why must I be going with a man?' Jessica demanded.

'Well . . . oh, I don't know. That's what seems right – to have a proper partner.'

'There's no law, Ronnie, that says two girls can't go to a dance together. Friends do it all the time.'

'But this sounds quite formal.'

'No, it's not.'

'Is your friend working on the day?' Ronnie persisted.

'No.'

'Then why—'

'You ask too many questions, Ronnie. He wanted to go but I told him we're finished, so he sent me the tickets he'd already booked and told me I was welcome to take someone else.'

'He must have been upset.'

'*He* was upset?' Jessica flared. 'He deserved everything that came to him.'

She was obviously very hurt, Ronnie thought. Maybe that was what upset her that first night when she had the bad dream and woke up crying. And that letter she'd received when one of the tickets had fallen out. Poor Jess. But she didn't want to take the place of some man.

'So how about it?' Jessica stared at her.

'I can't.'

'Why not?'

'I've never been to a dance in my life.'

'Then it's time you did.'

It was Ronnie's turn to be silent. Eventually she said, 'It sounds a bit posh – a famous band playing in the dance hall. Suzy would be really envious. But I haven't anything suitable to wear, even if I wanted to go. I didn't bring anything other than work things except one skirt and blouse I wear for church. It wouldn't be right at all for the evening.' She paused. 'It's just not me, Jess.'

'Nonsense,' Jessica said. 'You have to start somewhere. I'll hold you by the hand – see you don't come to any harm.'

'I'd only embarrass you.'

'I'll take the risk,' Jessica said, looking her up and down. 'I'm a lot taller than you, so my things wouldn't fit, but I'm sure we could find you something when we stop at the next town.'

'No, I can't—' Ronnie started, flushing with embarrassment.

Jessica gave her a pointed look. 'Is money the problem, Ronnie?'

Ronnie nodded miserably.

'Leave it with me,' Jessica said mysteriously. 'I'll come up with something.'

The 'something' was in the shape of May.

'I hear you've been invited to the ball, Cinders, and haven't a thing to wear,' she giggled, holding a carrier bag. 'So I'm your Fairy Godmother.' She removed a bundle of deep cherry-red material and shook it into a dress, then held it up against Ronnie.

'Perfect,' Jessica said. 'It looks fabulous against your dark curls.'

'I knew it would,' May grinned. 'The colour suits your dark hair better, but I love wearing it because it clashes with my red mop. I just hope it fits as it's the only dress I've brought with me in case I sang a few songs in a pub and needed to look the part. It's not really an evening dress – more a tea-dress – but I think it would do the trick.'

'I wouldn't feel right borrowing it,' Ronnie said.

'Why not? If you had something I needed, wouldn't you lend it?' May challenged.

'Yes, of course I would.'

'There you are then. You can't hurt it, if that's what you're thinking. It's not new.'

'Try it on, Ronnie,' Jessica urged, 'but take those boots off first. I don't think they'd be doing the dress any favours.'

There was barely enough space to pull it over her head, but with May's help it fell into place, the pleated top snuggly fitting over Ronnie's curving bust, skimming her waist, then the skirt swinging in soft wide pleats to just below her knees.

May stepped back. 'You look a treat,' she said. 'You fill the top out better than me with my little fried eggs.' She cupped them in her hands and patted them. 'I have to stuff my bra with cotton wool. D'ya know, Ron, you've changed from a tomboy into a flirty woman in one easy movement of sliding a dress over your head,' she giggled.

'I agree,' Jessica said. 'The transformation is amazing. I love the V neck. Tantalising.'

'I don't want to be tantalising . . . or flirty,' Ronnie protested.

'Don't be daft. It's not cut low enough to show off those gorgeous breasts,' Jessica said. 'It just gives the beholder a hint.' She turned to May. 'Oh, dear – I've made her blush.'

'Jess is teasing you, Ron,' May said. 'Don't take any notice.' She pursed her lips as she looked at Ronnie. 'If only we had a proper full-length mirror.'

'You know, I've got something that would make it look more evening.' Jessica searched for a minute or two in her toilet bag. 'Here it is,' she said triumphantly. In the palm of her hand was a glittering brooch in the shape of a swan. 'I'll pin it on one of the lapels.'

'No, don't,' Ronnie protested. 'If I lost that . . .'

'You won't,' Jessica said as she pinned it on. 'And they're not real diamonds. I keep those in the safe at home.' Ronnie raised her eyebrows. 'Just kidding,' Jessica chuckled. 'There – all nice and firm.' She cast a critical eye. 'Yes, that was exactly what was missing for an evening do. What do you think, May?'

May nodded. 'You'll be the belle of the ball.'

'I won't have to dance, will I?' Ronnie said, her heart beating with terror.

'Oh, no,' Jessica said. 'The two of us are going to stand around the edge like ruddy wallflowers.' She snorted. 'Of *course* we're going to dance – if anyone asks us, that is.'

Ronnie's heart squeezed at the thought. She imagined Will walking towards her, looking at her with admiration in those dark eyes, asking her to dance. No, it was too much.

She swallowed. 'I'm sorry, May, it was a lovely idea and so kind of you, but I can't go.'

'Why not?' May and Jessica chorused.

'I haven't got the right shoes. Unless I go in my wellies?' She pointed to them, thick with grime and caked mud.

'You could start a new craze,' Jessica grinned.

'What size are you?' May said.

'Four.'

'No good looking at me,' Jessica sighed. 'I'm a seven.'

May tutted. 'I'm a five. Damn.' She thought for a moment. 'I'll ask Sally. And don't worry, I shan't mention this to Angela.'

'She'd be the last person to lend me anything,' Ronnie said. 'You're all very kind but really it's not me, this dance band stuff. The only dancing I've ever done was at school and it was horrible. Boys treading on your toes, seeing their pimples close up. Ugh!' She shuddered at the memory. 'Why don't you go with Jess, May?'

'I'm more at home in a pub than on a dance floor,' May said, 'but you're different, Ron.'

'How?'

'I don't know.' May shrugged. 'The way me and you've been brought up, I s'pose.'

'I don't know what you mean.'

'You're such an innocent, Ronnie,' Jessica cut in. 'I'm determined to get you there by hook or by crook – even if you have to be dragged there on bare feet!'

Chapter Twenty-Four

Ronnie woke with a start. That noise! A terrific banging and cracking, sounding as though the boat was breaking up beneath her. Alarmed, she shot up in bed. Something terrible must be happening. She fumbled for her watch under her pillow, but it was too dark to make out the time. The creaking and cracking noise was even louder.

Gingerly, she pulled back the blanket, stepping over Jess, and managed to put her feet down in the tiny space. If she was careful she wouldn't wake the others while she pulled on her trousers and jumpers over the top of her pyjamas.

'What are you doing waking everyone up at this time of the morning?'

Damn. She'd woken Angela. Jess was still breathing steadily. She seemed to be able to sleep through anything.

'I was woken up by the noise.'

'What noise?' Angela demanded. 'It's probably the damned cat. I'm itching all over with his fleas.'

'Lucky doesn't have fleas. It's more likely your bedbugs.'

'I know bedbugs – if you remember, I've had them before.' Angela's tone was sour.

Ronnie glanced over to her, then grinned. 'They've obviously taken a shine to you. But they're all over your face like last time. And they're not flea bites. They're bedbugs.'

Angela opened her mouth to argue, then startled as there was another loud bang and more cracking and creaking.

'*That's* the noise.' Ronnie didn't bother to keep the sarcasm from her tone. 'Aghh!' Her feet slipped. She shot out her hand on one of the shelves to steady herself.

'What's going on?' Jessica sat up and threw her dressing gown around her shoulders.

'The boat feels like it's going over.'

'Don't be ridiculous,' Angela said.

'Stand up and you'll see. We're tipping.'

Muttering under her breath Angela stood up, then lost her balance and grabbed on to Ronnie. 'Oh, God, the boat's going over!'

'Don't be daft.' Jessica pulled on her clothes. 'It'll be the ice. I've heard the canals can completely freeze over in winter and you can actually skate on them.' She paused. 'Though it does seem early this year – we're not even halfway through December. But it's probably well below zero outside and the boat's probably stuck in it.'

There was a hushed silence as the three of them took in Jessica's words.

Ronnie was the first to speak. 'I'd better put the kettle on.' She looked at Angela who was standing nearest the stove. 'Can you hand me the water can?'

Angela picked it up. 'It's practically empty,' she said. 'There's barely enough for tea.'

'Whose turn was it to refill it?' Jessica demanded. Then she caught sight of Angela's face. 'Oh, my God, you've got bedbugs again.'

'I haven't,' Angela's tone was furious. 'I've caught fleas off that damned cat.' She jerked her head towards Lucky who was soundly asleep on her favourite cushion.

Jessica pulled out the small mirror from her handbag and

held it in front of Angela. She immediately pushed Jessica's arm away.

'They're definitely bedbugs,' Jessica said, 'so I hope you brought the special candle with you. We need to light it immediately because Ronnie and I don't want to catch them.' She put the mirror away. 'Back to my question about the water can.'

'I don't know,' Angela said. 'I only came last night and found everything completely disorganised.'

'I'd keep those sorts of remarks to yourself, Angela.' Jessica glared at her. 'Well, it's no good even thinking of going outside and bringing in the spare. It'll be frozen solid. Ronnie, get the kettle on with what little we've got. We need a drink to warm us up. Angela, get the stove going again. It looks like it's about to die – and find the sulphur candle.'

'Why have *I*—'

'Because I say so!' Jessica roared. 'If you're going to live with us, then you damned well better move your behind.'

'Don't you dare speak to me—' Angela began, turning red with rage.

'One of us – and one only – is in charge around here,' Jessica interrupted. 'I've had some experience of sailing. I'm the eldest. And I'm in charge. And you'd better get that through your thick head. And if you don't like it then go and complain to Dora.'

Angela turned and went to light the stove.

Jessica rolled her eyes. 'I'll start on the porridge.'

'I wonder if *Persephone* has overbalanced,' Ronnie said, her feet not feeling entirely stable as she laid the table.

'If it has, I'm sure Dora will right it single-handedly,' Jess said grimly.

'OPEN UP!'

The three girls startled.

'Coming, Miss Dummitt,' Ronnie shouted as she rushed to the hatch to slide it back. Talk of the devil. But the hatch was well and truly stuck. 'I can't open it!' she shouted.

'I'm going ter freeze ter bloody death out here,' Dora shouted back. 'Soak a cloth in boilin' water and keep pushin' it inter the frame.'

'We're trapped if no one can open the hatch,' Angela said, her voice rising with panic.

'Just calm down,' Jessica said. 'We can't use our precious one can of water willy-nilly. We don't know how long this is going to last and when we'll get an opportunity to refill them.' She looked at Ronnie. 'Didn't you have a hot water bottle last night.'

'Yes. What's that got to do—?' She broke off. 'Oh, I see. We can tip it into the saucepan and heat it up.'

'No flies on you.' Jessica cast a glance at Angela who was looking white. 'And we'll stand the milk bottle in it to thaw it out afterwards. Angela, you can tell Dora we should have it open in a few minutes.'

But there was no answer.

'Well, she's either frozen to death as she'd warned us or she's gone back to the motor,' Jessica said.

It was several minutes later before Ronnie managed to slide the hatch free, half expecting to see a frozen corpse outside, but all was deathly quiet. Then she spotted the water can. Good old Dora. She'd put it by the hatch knowing they'd need it, frozen or not. She lifted it and came back into the cabin.

'No sign of her,' she said, putting the can down near the stove Angela had fired up. 'I think I ought to go and see if everyone's all right.'

'Put your coat on and for God's sake be careful,' Jessica warned. 'It'll be very slippery.'

'Dora did it.'

'Dora's used to it.'

Ronnie stepped through the hatch and cautiously climbed out. Almost immediately her foot shot from under her on solid ice. Desperately trying to stop herself from plunging headfirst over the low wall round the edge of the deck she clung on to the chimney, the searing heat penetrating her woollen gloves, then screamed as her foot slipped again.

'What is it?' Jessica's head poked through. 'Oh, dear God. Hang on, Ronnie. I'm coming.' She was by her side in an instant, taking Ronnie's arms in a firm grip.

'What's happenin'?' Dora's head shot from *Persephone*'s cabin in front.

'Don't worry – I've got her, Miss Dummitt.'

There was a pause. Then Dora barked, 'Jess, yous and Angela come out and start bashin' the ice round the boats with the poles. After an hour me and Sally will do it. We gotta stop the boats icin' up.'

'All right,' Jessica called, pulling Ronnie back through the safety of the hatch. 'We're just going to have our porridge and Angela and I will be out.'

'It's lethal,' Ronnie grunted. 'You need to be really careful.'

'Why did she pick me and not Ronnie?' Angela demanded.

'It's not for us to question,' Jessica snapped. 'Just shut up if you haven't got anything constructive to say.' She turned to Ronnie. 'You clean the cabin and make drinks for us, love.'

Jessica put a meagre lunch on the table – baked beans on toast – and told them it might have to be their supper as well, their supplies were so low. The three of them were eating in silence when a loud bang, as though someone was battering the side of the boat with a plank of wood, made them leap up.

'Anyone at home?' a voice shouted.

Ronnie's heart thudded. Will? It couldn't be.

With difficulty she managed to prise open the hatch again, and there he was, grinning all over, and carrying a cardboard box.

'I reckon yous'll be wantin' some grub sooner or later.' He dumped the box on the table and took the items out one by one with a triumphant flourish. 'A loaf, condensed milk, two quarters of tea, porridge oats . . . oh, and a packet of powdered eggs – I didn't trust meself to bring the real ones,' he chuckled. 'But there's real butter—'

'Real butter!' Jessica exclaimed. 'We haven't seen that since we started on the boats.' She pounced on a tin. 'Nescafé instant coffee? And Golden Shred marmalade?' Her eyes suddenly narrowed. 'Will, how did you get these things. They're luxury items these days. You can't even get them if you've got the money . . . unless—' She paused and looked directly at him.

Will tapped the side of his nose. 'Unless you know the right folks,' he said, chuckling. He peered in the box and took out something flat, wrapped in greaseproof paper. 'Bacon,' he said. 'Bet yer not had that since yer started on the boats neither.'

'I can't believe it,' Ronnie said, eyeing the food, her mouth watering at the thought of fried bacon.

He looked round at the three girls. 'That should do yer for a few days.'

'It's wonderful, Will,' Ronnie said and was treated to a huge wink, making her giggle.

What a kind person. Why did everyone always say such horrible things about him? Especially Dora.

'I suppose we'll have to share it with Miss Dummit and the others,' Angela said, squeezing nearer to have a look.

'Nah. This here's all yours. Me mate's gone to them and taken a box. 'Cept theirs don't have them extra special things.'

Ronnie glanced at Jess, wondering why she'd gone quiet. Her face, beautifully made up as usual, was set like a mask. She was watching Will intently. Ronnie's stomach gave an unexpected flutter. Was something wrong? Impatiently she dismissed the idea. Jess made no bones about disliking Will either, but surely now she'd seen how he'd brought them food when they were desperate, knowing they were trapped in the ice with no means of getting to a shop, she'd change her mind.

'How did you know we're running really low?' Angela asked him.

'Stands to reason,' Will said. He brought out the last items. 'That's it – three tins o' sardines.' His gaze fell on Ronnie.

'It's really kind of you,' Ronnie said, 'especially in this awful weather.'

'I'm used to it.' Will held her gaze. 'It's not kind – I'll be wantin' payment for me services.'

'Of course. How much do we owe you?' Angela said.

'That depends.'

'On what?'

'On *her*,' he said, his eyes not leaving Ronnie's even though he was answering Angela.

'Who's *her*?' Jessica said. 'Doesn't she have a name?'

'A boy's name,' Will grinned, allowing his gaze to rest on Ronnie's chest. 'But she ain't no boy underneath them jumpers. So give us a kiss, Ron.'

Ronnie felt the heat rise to her face. Will was rather cheeky, but she couldn't help the frisson of excitement he gave her just by one penetrating dark look.

'All right,' she said recklessly. 'One kiss. That's all. Do you promise?'

'Yeah, I promise.'

He bridged the small distance between them in one leap, then grabbed hold of her and half flung her over his arm. She glimpsed the wooden ceiling for the space of a second before his mouth came down on hers, crushing her lips, blocking everything out, as though she and Will were completely alone. For a few mad moments it was thrilling, but then she felt something not hers – hot and wet, whirling into the private space that used to be the inside of her mouth. She felt something hard pressing against her thigh.

Almost choking, she put her hands on his chest and with all her might shoved him backwards. Will laughed.

'That was prob'ly your first proper kiss,' he grunted. 'You'll like it better next time.'

'There isn't going to be a next time!' Jessica roared, grabbing hold of him. 'How dare you!'

'Jess—' Ronnie started, her face and neck feeling as though it were on fire, but Jessica took no notice.

'Clear out!' she bellowed. 'And don't show your face again.'

'That's nice, that is, when I've brought you some grub.' Will eyed the items as though weighing up whether he should snatch them back.

Jessica released her grip on him and reached for her bag. She drew out a pound note.

'This should just about cover it,' she said, slapping it into his hand. 'But you can take those extra goods we can't afford back where they came from . . . then Ronnie owes you nothing.'

'That's fer Ronnie to decide, not you.' Will threw Jessica a furious look. 'And I in't takin' nothin' back. They're special for Ronnie and *you* don't have to eat them.'

Ronnie's breath came in short bursts. She felt shaken. This wasn't how it was meant to be in her dreams. She'd longed for him to kiss her properly but not like this. And in front of the others. He'd ruined a romantic moment. But it hadn't been romantic. She'd been frightened. Now, angry for not standing up to him – telling him how upset she was, and letting Jess take over – Ronnie forced herself to face him.

'You'd better go, Will,' she said, a sheen of moisture beading on her forehead. She drew in a deep breath, glad Jess and Angela were with her as she met his penetrating gaze.

Long seconds passed. Will didn't take his eyes off her.

'If you don't leave this minute I'm fetching Miss Dummitt,' Jessica said, 'and I don't suppose you want *her* to know what Angela and I have just witnessed.'

Will muttered something under his breath. He looked at Ronnie and smiled – a slow smile that made her skin prickle. 'I'll see you when you least expect it. I 'spect you'll soon be needin' rescuin' again. And then I'll be collectin' my reward good and proper . . . with no one gawpin'.'

He was gone.

Ronnie felt the back of her eyes begin to sting. She wouldn't cry. She wouldn't.

Angela sniffed. 'If you want my opinion, he was showing off.'

'I'm afraid I agree with Angela.' Jessica went to take Ronnie's hand, but Ronnie flapped it away.

'I can stand up for myself,' Ronnie said. 'You needn't have interfered.'

'Someone had to. How he behaved was unforgivable. And that last remark about collecting his reward . . . to me it sounded like a threat. Not the sort of tone you'd expect from a boyfriend.'

'For the last time he's *not* my boyfriend,' Ronnie snapped, her temper rising, knowing she was being unfair to Jess who'd only been trying to protect her. If Jess only knew what

Will had done that had made her feel so peculiar. So light-headed. It must have been a proper adult kiss that she hadn't been ready for. And that odd sensation against her thigh. She felt the heat rush to her cheeks again. All she knew was that it should have been a special private moment. She glared at Jessica, her confusion with Will bursting out as anger to her friend. 'You never have a good word to say about him, even though he's brought us food when we were nearly out.'

Why am I defending him?

'Look, Ronnie, I'm older than you—'

'Please don't use that excuse.' Ronnie pressed her lips together. 'Raine used to say exactly the same when she wanted to give me her uncalled-for advice. Age doesn't mean to say you're always right.'

'I want you to listen to me. I know how you feel.'

'How can you possibly know how I feel?'

'Because I have more experience than you. I've—'

'Oh, just drop it.'

In bed that night Ronnie lay wide-eyed, staring at the wooden ceiling, wishing she and Jess hadn't fallen out. It was Will she should have told off, not Jess. Raine would have sat her down and given her a good talking-to. She bit her lip. How she missed her and Suzy. And Maman. Ronnie let her lids fall. The realisation of being so far away from everything and everyone she loved swept over her. All she could do was console herself that when the training ended Dora had promised them three whole days off. She couldn't wait. It was then that she gave way to her tears, muffling them under the blanket so Jess wouldn't hear.

She wiped her eyes with the edge of the sheet and with the tip of her finger touched her bruised lips, still not sure exactly what had happened between her and Will.

Chapter Twenty-Five

When Ronnie opened her eyes the following morning she sleepily put her arm out but there was only a warm space where Jess had lain, and a sharp, salty tang she hadn't smelt for months. Bacon sizzling!

'You're awake?' Jessica touched her arm.

'Oh, Jess.' Ronnie didn't know what else to say. Suddenly she felt ashamed. What had Jess started to say yesterday? Whatever it was, she hadn't given her a chance to explain.

'Jess, I'm sorry—'

'Forget it, Ronnie. I have. Here, I've made you a cuppa. And a bacon sandwich. However your friend got it, it shouldn't go to waste. And it'll perk you up.' She handed Ronnie a plate.

'Mmm. It smells wonderful. Oh, what a treat.' She glanced at up. 'Where's yours?'

Jessica smiled. 'I couldn't wait. I've had mine but I'll bring my tea to bed so we don't disturb madam.'

Angela was giving a vicious snore on every intake of breath.

'Jess, listen, I'm sorry about yesterday. I can just hear my mother. "I 'ave not brought you up to be so rude",' Ronnie quoted, imitating Maman's accent.

Jessica smiled. 'I don't want you hurt, that's all. And I

really didn't like that display of Will Drake's. Angela was right. He was showing off to let us know you were his property. And I despise men who treat women like that.'

Ronnie was silent.

'And I'm not at all happy about some of those goods he brought.' Jessica took a sip of tea. 'I think he's a shady character who only does nice things for his own benefit. Certainly his parting shot sent shivers down my spine. All that about collecting his reward with no one looking on. That rang alarm bells for me and it should you.' She gave Ronnie a direct look. 'Your sister wouldn't thank me if I didn't warn you, so here goes – I don't want you to ever be alone with that boy.'

'I'm used to looking after myself. I'm pretty sensible.'

'More sensible girls than you have been swept off their feet . . . and raped.'

Ronnie drew in a quick breath. 'Will wouldn't—'

'How do you know what he would and wouldn't do?' Jessica said fiercely. 'If you don't take any notice of me, then at least take notice of Dora. She seems to know him better than anyone, and she doesn't have a good word to say about him.'

Ronnie opened her mouth to argue but it wouldn't do any good. To change the subject, she said, 'What were you about to say yesterday?'

Jessica paused, studying her as if wondering if she should divulge something personal. 'All right, I'll tell you,' she said eventually. 'I was very much in love with someone for a long time. He said he loved me. We had so much fun together and I didn't for one moment question anything about him. But as the time went on I couldn't understand, if we loved each other so much, why we weren't making plans to get married. My friends kept saying how lucky I was to have such a handsome, charming man who obviously adored me and asking when was the happy day. I came to the conclusion it was obviously *me* who was being unreasonable – trying to rush things. So I tried hard to just enjoy the time I spent with him and not worry.

'And then the war started. By this time he'd joined the RAF. He told me he was being sent abroad and wasn't allowed to tell me where as he'd had to sign the Official Secrets Act. I believed him. Until one day my friend said she'd seen him in London – in Selfridges – with a woman on his arm and twins.' Jessica briefly closed her eyes as though the pain was still fresh. 'My friend doesn't think he recognised her. He'd only met her briefly once.'

Ronnie swallowed the last bite of her sandwich, her eyes fixed on Jess.

'At first I thought she must be mistaken. But when she overheard the woman call him by name, I knew she was speaking the truth. At first he denied it, but then he broke down, begging me not to leave him. He said he was going to ask his wife for a divorce. Can you believe it? Married with a couple of kids. I wasn't stupid. I knew he'd never leave his family for me. He was like most men – wanted to have his cake and eat it.'

She sighed, but Ronnie saw her eyes fill, then look away. She obviously wasn't over him yet.

'Will's too young to be married with twins,' Ronnie said lightly, then was ashamed. How could she be so thoughtless. She took Jessica's hand. 'I'm sorry, Jess. I don't mean to belittle your horrible experience, but you've got to believe me – Will's not like your ex-boyfriend. And anyway, we've never even been out together so there's not much chance of falling in love with him.' She looked steadily at Jessica. 'Is this man the same one who sent the tickets?'

'Yes.'

Before Ronnie could change her mind, she said, 'Then we'll have a fabulous evening at his expense, the swine.'

Jessica broke into a broad smile. 'Really? You'll come with me to the dance?'

'Even if I have to dance in my wellies,' Ronnie chuckled. 'Come on, Jess. Let's get going before Angela wakes up.'

It was another three days before the sun appeared and began to melt the ice. Three days listening to Angela's moaning and groaning. That morning Dora told them she'd managed to flag down a boatman and his family, and according to Dora he had two strapping sons. Upon opening the hatch Ronnie could hear a commotion outside – loud noises of banging and cracking – and a roar from what sounded like the boatman ordering his boys what to do and getting some stick back from the pair of them.

'Break the h'ice round t'hull first,' he bellowed, 'or them timbers'll break, sure as eggs.'

'Bleedin' wind's a booger t'day,' one of the sons shouted back. 'It keeps blowin' the moty inter the rhubarb.'

What on earth did he mean? Ronnie wondered. It was like another language. She had to watch. Perhaps she could help in some way. Pushing her way through the hatch she crawled onto the roof. It was bitterly cold. Too late she realised she hadn't got her hat and gloves on. It was too precarious to shove her hands in her pockets. The boatman on his narrow boat with an enormous pole in his hand caught sight of her and waved frantically. Was he trying to tell her something? If he was, she had no idea what he meant. She was about to brave it and see how the others were faring in the motorboat when a sudden gust of wind caught her off-guard, threatening to sweep her off her feet.

'Back inside, miss,' Dora screamed above the noise. 'I'm not havin' no more accidents from any of yous.'

Using every ounce of her strength, her heart racing, Ronnie managed to scramble back as Dora instructed. Relief flooded through her as her boots touched the floor of the cabin, and the warmth from the stove enveloped her, making steam rise in puffs from her raincoat.

'Take your coat off at once, young lady,' Jessica ordered.

'In a minute,' Ronnie said through chattering teeth. 'I didn't think it would be that cold when I saw it was sunny out.' She spread her hands towards the fire. 'It's the wind. The men were having a terrible time trying to break the ice with the wind nearly knocking them over.' She wouldn't tell them how close she'd been to being swept over the side. She took in a few slow breaths, willing her heart to stop hammering. 'By the looks of things, I can't see us going anywhere today.'

The boatmen were several hours before they were able to break the ice and free *Persephone* and *Penelope*. By then it was dusk and Dora came to give the trainees instructions for tomorrow morning.

'If the cut's iced up again we'll have ter untie the boats and use the motor ter clear a passage in front, then come back for the butty.' She glared at the little group. 'It'll take twice as long, so mind yer ready half seven sharp.'

'I'll barely have time to put my make-up on,' Jessica grumbled.

Ronnie glanced at her and smiled. Jessica grinned back. Even if they didn't agree on Will Drake, Ronnie was happy they were friends again. And if she were absolutely honest, she wasn't at all sure she felt quite the same towards Will herself.

Chapter Twenty-Six

Bit by bit *Persephone* and *Penelope* were making their cautious way up the Grand Union Canal towards Royal Leamington Spa, Dora ensuring the trainees all took turns on every aspect of handling the pair of boats.

'Pair of boats comin' towards us,' Dora said, squinting. 'They be trainee wenches' boats.'

Ronnie and the others clambered onto the roofs of their narrow boats, hoping to catch a glimpse. Their trainer had obviously told the crew the same thing as two girls stood atop the butty and another pair on the motor, their cargo sheeted up against the weather.

Ronnie cupped her hands round her mouth.

'Hello. Where are you heading?'

But the girls shook their heads and put their hands round their ears.

'They can't hear us,' May said. 'But it's nice to know we're all in the same boat.' She broke off, giggling at the weak joke.

'Somethin' for yous all ter be aimin' for,' Dora smirked.

This time Ronnie steered the motor through Braunston Tunnel. Almost immediately she came upon a very sharp bend. Heart in mouth she carefully negotiated it. Enjoying a rare moment of pride, she was relieved to find the tunnel was shorter than that awful one when Margaret had panicked, and there was no further mishap.

Ronnie began to relax, finally getting to grips with the various manoeuvres, grateful that the wind wasn't quite so raw and as unsettling as it had been. They were passing through open countryside, still snowy but glittering in the sun, and after the bustle of Braunston itself, it was wonderfully peaceful, except for the occasional birdsong which was a beautiful sound, and the crackle of the ice breaking in the trees. She briefly closed her eyes, breathing in the cold crisp air. Being in tune with nature must feel the same as Raine felt being in tune with the sky, and Suzy in tune with her music. Ronnie smiled. She was becoming quite poetical.

That evening, soon after they'd tied up, Dora came to tell them May was going to have a singsong in the motor that evening and had invited them to join in.

'I've put salt on the gunwale,' she said, 'so it should be safe enough.'

'Ronnie and I'll be there,' Jess said. 'I don't know about Angela.'

'I shall stay in and answer my letters.' Angela's mouth was set in her usual lines of disapproval.

Just as well, Ronnie thought. That girl always put such a dampener on everything.

'We aim to get to Stockton termorrer, and if we don't have no more delays we should be in Leamington Spa the next day.'

'Don't forget our night out's in Leamington Spa,' Jessica muttered to Ronnie.

'If yous've got anythin' to say, Jess, then we'd *all* like to know,' Dora said.

'Oh, no, it was nothing.'

'Hmm,' Dora grunted. 'Then don't interrupt when I'm

speakin'. I believe my words might be just a *little* more important than yours.'

Angela sniggered and Jessica rolled her eyes.

'I quite agree, Miss Dummitt,' Jessica said, her eyes now demurely cast down, causing Ronnie to stifle a giggle.

'The twenty-second and twenty-third are the last times the band plays,' Jessica said when Dora disappeared.

Ronnie handed Jess a mug of instant coffee while she was at the tiller. By an unwritten agreement, neither of them mentioned how it might have been obtained. The delicious aroma had wafted into her nostrils as she'd poured the boiling water over the powder. What a marvellous change from tea and cocoa. For a treat she'd put a whole teaspoon of sugar in her own mug.

'One of us will have to ask her,' Jessica said, 'and I suppose it'll have to be me.' She gave a rueful smile.

'It's a shame the others can't go, too, as Dora would be more likely to allow it,' Ronnie said. 'She couldn't very well say no to all of us.' She gave a start as she spotted bunches of brown feathers through the mist. 'Watch out, Jess!'

'Out of the way, you silly ducks.' Jessica moved the tiller gently to the left to give them a wide berth.

'How do we know Dora will let us stay for the evening?' Ronnie said. 'I can see us loading up and turning round to go straight back to London.'

'We've got to let her see she's being unreasonable if she doesn't allow it,' Jessica answered, her brow furrowed in concentration.

'Do you know what I've just realised?' Ronnie said, smiling at the effortless way the pair of mallards swam by, leaving barely a noticeable ripple behind them, the colourful male just a foot or two in the lead. When she was sure they were safely out of danger she said, 'The twenty-third, the Saturday, is my birthday.'

Jessica threw her head back and laughed. 'Ronnie, that's perfect. I'll tell Dora that. She can't possibly say no to a birthday treat.'

Ronnie swallowed the last precious mouthfuls of coffee. Now that she'd decided she *would* go with Jess to the dance, if Dora had different ideas, she'd be quite disappointed.

In the end Ronnie went with Jessica to speak to Dora.

'What makes yer think yer so special that the rest of us will have ter spend the night in Leamington?' Dora demanded. 'We're already behind on our schedule.'

'It's only that I've been given two tickets, Miss Dummitt,' Jessica explained, 'and then I found out that they're on the same day as Ronnie's birthday.'

'So, yer'll finally be seventeen, then, miss,' Dora said with a smirk. 'The minimum age to work the boats.'

Ronnie felt her cheeks warm.

'Yes, you can go red, my girl,' Dora said. 'You didn't tell Mrs Hunter the truth on your interview, did you?'

'Not quite,' Ronnie stuttered.

Dora took her time to light her pipe.

'"Not quite" allus means "no",' she said finally, narrowing her eyes against the smoke. 'Mrs Hunter thought you was lyin' but yer sister assured her you was capable. I told her I'd already guessed, by the look of yer. Barely more than a kid. But I thought yous'd cope. I'll see if I was right when we complete the round trip.'

'Would you give Ronnie and me permission to go and hear the band, Miss Dummitt?' Jessica asked, an impatient edge to her tone, obviously annoyed Dora had deftly changed the subject.

'And what will you be wearin', miss?' Dora said. 'Yer won't be able to turn up in that outfit.' She gave a snort.

Ronnie looked at Jess who rolled her eyes.

'We've sorted her out,' Jessica said. 'May's lent her a dress which fits perfectly. All she needs now are the shoes.'

'And where might they be comin' from?' Dora demanded.

'Maybe when we stop at Leamingon Spa Ronnie can find a pair in the market.'

Dora grunted. 'Yer'll have plenty to do in Leamington, it seems, that's nothin' ter do with workin' the boats.'

'We'll do our work the same as the others,' Ronnie said hotly.

Dora sent Ronnie a hard look.

'Well, I'm not sayin' no, but I'm not sayin' yes, neither, 'til we get there.'

Ronnie was sure Dora kept her and Jess on tenterhooks on purpose.

'We're not going to give her the satisfaction that we're at all worried,' Jessica said, when Ronnie voiced her thoughts.

The two of them were in the cabin and Ronnie was helping Jessica prepare lunch while Angela was at the tiller.

'Keep your voice down,' Jessica said, jerking her head towards Angela's feet, no more than eighteen inches away.

Ronnie grinned. It was just as well Jess reminded her. Not having an engine, the butty was quiet, especially without Angela's perpetual cutting in on the conversation. This usually amounted to a 'better' suggestion or doing something a different way – *her* way – that irritated Ronnie so much.

She turned as the cabin door opened. It was Dora holding a drawstring bag.

'Will these do yer?' she said as she opened the bag and tipped out a pair of shoes onto the draining board.

Ronnie gasped. They were quite beautiful. White with silver sequins and high heels. She picked one up and Jessica picked up the other while Dora stood by.

'They're gorgeous, Dora.' Ronnie turned to look at her. 'Are they really yours?'

'I were young once, believe it or not,' Dora said, 'and not so bad as a looker.' She sent them a glare. ''*Course* they're mine. I thought they'd be the right size as I were always known for havin' small feet.'

There was a note of pride as she imparted that piece of surprising information.

'They look the right size but I've never worn high heels before,' Ronnie said. 'I'm not sure I could walk in them.'

'There's only one way to find out,' Jessica said firmly. 'Try them on.'

Ronnie removed her boots and socks and put one on. Then the other. They were obviously good quality shoes the way her feet seemed to mould into them. She stood, but if it hadn't been for Jessica she would have toppled over.

'Steady,' Jessica laughed, her hand on Ronnie's arm. 'If you've never worn heels before it takes a bit of practice and I'll see you do that a few minutes every day.' She turned to Dora. 'They'll be just the job with May's dress, Miss Dummitt. You've solved the problem.'

'Mind you take care of 'em, miss,' Dora said to Ronnie. 'They're a bit special, they are.'

'I can see,' Ronnie said, almost lost for words that Dora should have come up with something so perfect. Who would have thought it?

'Well, I'll be goin'. We've got a way to go yet before tyin' up.'

She disappeared through the hatch before Ronnie could even thank her.

'Well, well, well,' Jessica said, chuckling. 'Wonders will never cease. In my wildest dreams I'd never have thought Deadly Dora had anything like this stored away.'

'I can't believe it,' Ronnie said. 'They seem to have a special meaning to her, yet she's trusting me with them.'

'Also, don't forget, it's her way of giving us permission to go,' Jessica chuckled, 'without having to actually say so.'

'What I'd love to know more than anything,' Ronnie said, 'is why she bought something so glamorous in the first place. I wonder where she'd been planning to go. Wherever it was, I don't think she got there because they look brand new.'

'Our Dora keeps her personal life very close to her lace-clad bosom,' Jessica said mockingly, 'so I doubt we'll ever know the answer to that.'

Chapter Twenty-Seven

Jessica slipped May's dress over Ronnie's head.

'Jess's little compact mirror doesn't show you how super you look, Ron,' May said admiringly.

Ronnie had washed her hair in the hand bowl, wishing she could have a bath. It seemed ages since The Boat Inn at Stockton had let her have a bath for sixpence. The bath itself had been none too clean, the previous bather having left several grey hairs in a tangle on the bar of Lifebuoy. Now in *Penelope* she'd washed every inch of her body, taut and sleeker since she'd been working on the boats. Jessica had tamed her dark curls into a gleaming frame around her face, and even though Ronnie had said she absolutely didn't want any make-up at all, her friend put a puff of Outdoor Girl powder on her nose, and a slick of lipstick on her full mouth.

'It's a transformation,' May said. 'Dora's shoes and Jess's swan brooch have made my dress look much more expensive than it was.'

Jessica stepped back to admire her handiwork.

'I have to agree with May,' she said. 'Finally, you look like a lovely young woman.'

'Instead of a horrible grimy youth,' Ronnie challenged, making the others laugh.

Wearing high heels was incredible. She didn't totter in them any more, under Jess's reminder to practise wearing them for a few minutes every day. Even on the swaying boat she could now keep her balance. She couldn't repress the thrill of excitement that she was going to her first dance, even though she was shaking with fear. But with Jess she somehow knew she'd be all right. But suppose someone actually asked her to dance? Her heart beat fast. She'd have to say she was sitting this one out. She wouldn't – couldn't admit she didn't know the first thing about dancing.

For several long moments she wished with all her heart she hadn't told Jess she would go with her. It was only that she'd felt so sorry when Jess had confided in her about that horrible boyfriend. She'd felt the least she could do was support her friend and keep her company.

She turned her feet this way and that, feeling like Cinderella. Who would have thought Dora, of all people, would have come up with such a pair of shoes? But then Dora had that lacy brassiere tucked in her drawer. But how surprising they had exactly the same shoe size.

May followed Ronnie's glance.

'I know what you're thinking, Ron,' she said gleefully. 'I'd just love to know the story behind Dora's shoes.'

'We all would,' Jessica said, 'but she'll never spill the beans.'

'They were obviously for a very special occasion,' Ronnie said, feeling a little mean that they were having a joke at Dora's expense.

Jessica tucked a stray curl behind Ronnie's ear. 'At least she's allowed us to tie up here so we can go, so she can't be all bad.'

The only pity was that Ronnie had to put one of her old jumpers over the dress and top it off with her now weather-beaten raincoat. And, of course, the Wellington boots. The shoes were safely in the same drawstring bag Dora had delivered them in.

Don't forget the bag . . . don't forget the bag, Ronnie said to herself over and over, like a mantra. The image of dancing with someone in her pretty dress, complete with Wellington boots, made her want to break out into hysterical laughter. She sobered up when Jess shrugged on a beautiful camel coat with a tightly curled black collar. How she'd managed to pack something so bulky, Ronnie couldn't imagine. But standing next to her, Ronnie suddenly felt like the poor relation.

'Are you ready?' Jessica asked, picking up a large and expensive-looking leather shoulder bag.

'About as ready as I'll ever be,' Ronnie said ruefully.

'Got your bag with Dora's shoes?'

'Yes.'

'Have a wonderful time,' May called after them. 'I'll be thinking of you and I'll want to hear all the details.'

It was a difficult walk along the towpath, although thankfully it was no longer icy. But the rough ground wasn't easy to negotiate in the dark and Ronnie was thankful when they were able to leave it for a proper tarmac road. The cold already seeping through her raincoat to the one jumper she'd allowed herself, she was relieved they only had to wait a few minutes for the bus to take them into Leamington Spa.

This was it, Ronnie thought as she swung up on the platform behind Jess and grabbed the handrail to steady herself. No going back now.

'Hold tight.'

'Let's go upstairs,' Jessica said as she twisted her head round to Ronnie. She started up the narrow winding steps and darted to one of the few vacant seats at the very front.

A mother and her three children were crammed together on the other seat across the aisle, and as the driver pulled away the baby on the mother's lap started to howl.

'I wouldn't have sat here if I'd known the kid was going to make that row,' Jessica muttered under her breath.

'There wasn't much choice,' Ronnie said. 'It's pretty full.' She tried to peer through the smeared window. 'If only we could see out. They say Leamington Spa is a beautiful town but in the blackout it's impossible to see anything.'

'We'll have plenty of light inside the dance hall to pick out the best-looking partners,' Jessica said, chuckling.

Ronnie was relieved Jess didn't try to make any more conversation – almost impossible with the baby still sobbing. A feeling of dread lodged in the pit of her stomach. Why had she said she would go? Raine and Suzy would have been so excited to go to a dance and listen to jazz and get up on the dance floor, but to her the thought was terrifying. Those few classes at school dancing with other girls who never stopped giggling wouldn't be any use at all this evening. She jutted her chin. Well, it was too late to change her mind now.

At that moment there was a screeching of brakes and the bus jerked forward, then stopped. Jessica shot out her right arm in front of Ronnie to stop her falling against the front window, but to Ronnie's horror she saw the mother and baby being flung forward. The baby's head met the glass with a horrifying bang. For some seconds there was a heart-stopping silence. Then the baby screamed.

'Everyone all right up there?' the conductor called from below.

'No!' Ronnie shouted down the stairwell. 'There's been an accident. Can you come up?'

The conductor was there in a few swift steps.

'My Tommy's head's bleedin',' the mother told him. 'And I don't know what to do.'

By this time her two other children were crying.

'That looks a nasty graze so we'll have to get you straight to hospital.' He turned to the passengers. 'I'm afraid the driver's had a bit of a fright. Some woman ran out in front of him. She was bloody lucky – excuse my French – not to get run over. So everyone off the bus. We've got to get this lady and her baby to the hospital.'

Jessica grabbed Ronnie's arm and they scrambled down the steep steps with the other passengers, some of them muttering and grumbling, as they were turned out on the pavement.

'Are we anywhere near the Palais de Danse?' Jessica called to the conductor.

'Two hundred yards in front of you,' he called back as he rang the bell. The bus moved off.

Oh, no! Ronnie suddenly ran alongside the moving bus, waving her arms and shouting. But the bus platform was empty. The conductor must have gone upstairs again to tend to the lady and her baby.

'STOP! Please stop!' But her cry was lost in the crowds and she could no longer see the bus in the dark. Panting, she slowed, tears of frustration falling down her cheeks.

Footsteps ran up behind her. 'What is it, Ronnie?'

Ronnie spun round. 'Oh, Jess, I've left Dora's shoebag on the bus! I can't go in!'

Jessica gripped her arm. 'We have to, don't you see? We can telephone the bus station and ask them to hold them for us in Lost Property.'

'I feel sick. Whatever's Dora going to say?'

Dora's words spun through Ronnie's head. *Mind you take care of them. They're a bit special.*

'Don't worry, Ronnie, we'll get them back and she'll never need to know.'

The uniformed doorman sporting an Errol Flynn moustache was checking tickets. He looked up and smiled flirtatiously at Jess but when his gaze fell on Ronnie the smile faded. Fully aware of how she must look in her now tatty raincoat and Wellington boots by the side of her glamorous friend, she felt herself go red. Then something snapped. What right did he have to judge her? She tilted up her chin as she heard Jessica say:

'My friend left something on the bus. Would it be possible to telephone the bus station to ask about it?'

The doorman glanced at Ronnie with a supercilious expression. 'Ask for Mr Booth at the bar.'

Jessica gave him a curt nod. 'Thank you.' Taking Ronnie's arm firmly she guided her inside.

'Jess, I don't want to go into the bar in my raincoat and boots. They'll all be dancing and I'll feel ridiculous.'

'May's dress is halfway down your legs so you can take your coat off,' Jessica said. 'It'll be almost dark in there. No one will notice the boots. But I agree they'll notice you in outdoor clothes. Let's just ask someone where we go, and then we'll find Mr Booth.'

Reluctantly, Ronnie followed Jess through a door marked Cloakroom. It was a large room with coat rails already getting full. There was plenty of chatter going on as a dozen girls were changing. Jessica peeled off her coat and hung it on a nearby hook under the watchful eye of the attendant.

'Oh, Jess, look at you!' Ronnie's mouth opened in awe at the golden-haired beauty standing before her.

'Am I okay?' Jessica tossed her hair. 'If I'm not, it's the only gown I brought with me.'

She was dressed from head to foot in a soft green and

Ronnie noticed for the first time her eyes were exactly the same colour. At the front of the dress the fabric draped across the neckline but when Jess turned around, Ronnie saw her creamy bare back with only a hint of material at the waist.

'You look so sophisticated,' Ronnie said, in awe. 'Anyone looking at you would never dream you worked on the canals and ended up every evening like the rest of us – absolutely filthy.' She grinned, then looked down at herself and pulled a face. 'I can't go in there like this.'

'Yes, you can. Come on, off with that coat.' Jessica suddenly grinned. 'Do you remember what I said when I was trying to persuade you to come with me? I said, ". . . even if I have to drag you there on bare feet." So that's what I'm about to do now. Take off your boots.'

'I can't go in there without shoes,' Ronnie protested. 'I haven't got stockings on underneath these socks. I don't even own a pair.' Strange . . . she felt a flash of disappointment that she wasn't going to have an evening off the boat after all. She could hear the scuffling of dancing feet, the laughter and the music coming from behind a nearby closed door and she was curious to see what was going on.

'Ronnie, we'll find Mr Booth. Make a plan to collect the shoes which our nice conductor will have seen by now. Then stay a little while to listen to the music. You don't have to dance. But we've come to listen to Jack Payne's band. So let's go in. Either that or we'll have to turn around now without making the phone call and go back to the boat. Then you'll have to confess to Dora, when you might not have to.'

Ronnie blew out her cheeks. She was no match for Jess in this mood.

'All right, then,' she said. 'But I'm not going in barefoot. Let's go straight to the bar and find Mr Booth.' She gave Jess an imploring look. 'But promise to stay with me. I don't want to be left on my own – the laughing stock.'

Jessica hesitated. Then she nodded. 'All right, I promise.'

The band was already well under way when another uniformed man held the door open for the two of them to go through. Ronnie saw his glance travel to her feet and his eyes widened in disbelief.

'Forgotten your dancing pumps, love?' he chortled.

Ronnie gave him a frosty look. What a rude man. Maman would want to know where his manners were.

'It's a long story,' Jessica said coolly. 'We wouldn't want to bore you, so if you'd allow us to pass through.'

Conscious of several people's eyebrows raising when they caught sight of her boots, and a few smothered sniggers, Ronnie gazed up at the high domed ceiling, determined not to allow anyone to think she was bothered, but hating every squeaky step as she followed Jess's tall figure striding towards the bar, elbowing her way to the front, apologising profusely as she did so.

With her golden hair and stunning dress, Ronnie saw that Jessica immediately caught the attention of one of the barmen.

'Good evening. Could you tell me where I might find Mr Booth?'

'Sorry, love. He's unwell today so he won't be in. Can I help?'

'I hope so.' Jessica treated him to a smile. 'I need to speak to someone urgently and wonder if I could use your phone.'

The barman shook his head. 'Not allowed without his say-so, I'm afraid. And with such a crowd we're needed behind the bar non-stop or else there'd be a rumpus.'

Jessica twisted round to Ronnie. 'Did you hear that, Ronnie?'

Ronnie nodded.

'We'll do it tomorrow, first thing in the morning – all right?' she added louder.

Ronnie nodded again. It was no good trying to make herself heard with all the background noise and a sultry brunette crooning on the microphone.

'Well, now we're here, what'll you have?'

'Um, just a lemonade or something,' Ronnie muttered, the band drowning out her words.

'Did you say lemonade?' Jessica said. 'It's your birthday. You must have a proper drink to celebrate. What about some punch?'

'All right,' Ronnie said, feeling herself pulled into something beyond her grasp, but not wanting to draw attention to herself, though that seemed impossible with all the ceiling spotlights changing colour as they turned, picking out one area of the floor and then another. Eventually, the lights will pick me out, she thought miserably, and what a fool I shall look.

The barman poured two glasses and Jessica pointed to a table over the other side of the room. Ronnie's heart sank. She would never be able to bring herself to walk across that enormous expanse of dance floor in her rubber boots. But when she looked through the chattering crowds she couldn't see any other vacant seats except a few single spaces on the three-seater sofas lined up against two of the walls, all of which were occupied by courting couples who only had eyes for each other. She certainly wasn't going to intrude on any of *them*.

'I'm sorry, Jess, I can't do it,' she said miserably.

'Well, we'll have to stand here all night then,' Jessica said, taking a gulp of the punch while watching the dancers.

Ronnie smoothed her dress, knowing full well it wouldn't

hang down any further and hide her boots. She'd really messed up poor Jess's evening. She'd made it clear that Jess was not to leave her side, which meant her friend wouldn't even be allowed to have a dance.

She picked up her glass and took a sip. It tasted of different fruits. 'Thanks for this, Jess. It's really refreshing.' She took another sip. 'Don't take any notice of me. It's not your fault. I want you to have fun.'

Out of the corner of her eye Ronnie saw a tall fair-haired officer in RAF uniform approach them. He was making directly for Jess. Ronnie smiled to herself and stepped back so he had a clear path to her friend. At the same moment she felt someone behind her trip over the heel of her boot.

'Careful, young lady.'

She knew that voice! Her pulse racing, she swung away, desperate for him not to recognise her.

Oh, if she could only become invisible. It was too much. The last person she wanted to see her looking so ridiculous. Before he could say another word she'd pushed through the dancers, clinging on to her glass and working her way to the other side where Jess had spotted the empty table. Just as she was about to take possession of one of the chairs and put her bag on the other to save it for Jess, a party of giggling girls deliberately flung themselves in front of her and plonked down.

'Excuse me, but this is *my* table—' Ronnie started.

'Oh, my dear, aren't *we* hoity-toity?' one of them said, giving a horrible impersonation of Ronnie's accent, eyeing her through heavily made-up lids.

'Do you own the table, then?' another challenged.

'No, but—'

'Sorry, no buts. Just clear off.'

Ronnie swallowed. She couldn't just stand there. But she

didn't want to give up the table that she felt was rightfully hers.

One of the girls glanced at Ronnie's feet and dug her friend in the ribs, pointedly jerking her head down. The friend followed her gaze.

'Setting a new fashion trend, are we?' she jeered, then collapsed into shrieking giggles.

Heat flooded Ronnie's cheeks. She was about to turn away when a voice behind her said, 'Can I help?'

Oh, no. Not Michael again.

He put his hand lightly on her arm. This time she couldn't escape.

'Ronnie, I thought it was you. Why don't you come and sit with us? We're just a few tables away.'

Who's 'us'?

'I'm with Jess,' Ronnie muttered.

'That's all right – I met her on the boat that time.' He gave her a knowing grin. 'There are a couple of empty chairs at our table. Do come and join us – both of you. I'm with my sister and a friend.'

Ronnie felt she'd been put on a spot. She peered over the floor at the couples dancing, hoping to catch Jess's eye and let her know where she was sitting, but when she spotted the tall figure firmly held in the arms of the fair-haired officer, she could tell her friend was miles away.

'I should go with him,' the first girl giggled. 'He must be special if he can put up with his girlfriend wearing rubber boots at a posh dance.'

Ronnie glared at her, which made the girl giggle even louder. She had no choice but to follow Michael to a nearby table where two women sat chatting. They both stopped talking as she and Michael approached.

Both looked wide-eyed as they caught sight of Ronnie's boots but one woman, her shining brown hair pulled back in a victory roll, and with an animated expression, quickly regained her composure. The other, a raven-haired beauty, raised an amused eyebrow, and a mocking smile hovered over her lips as she fixed her gaze on Michael.

Ronnie hesitated. She knew instinctively that she didn't want to spend time with this woman. And from the way she was ogling Michael, this one was patently not the sister.

She's too old for him, was her immediate thought. She must be thirty, if a day. Ronnie gave an inward shrug. Why should she care?

'Can I introduce a friend of mine, Ronnie Linfoot,' Michael said. He glanced at Ronnie. 'This is my sister, Kathleen—' he gestured towards the young woman with the victory roll and she smiled warmly and held out her hand. 'And this is Penelope,' he went on, 'a friend of ours.'

'Oh, how funny. I live on a boat that's your namesake,' Ronnie blurted out, her nerves jangling as she attempted to stifle a sudden chortle. By Penelope's glare the woman obviously didn't find her remark in the least bit amusing, though Kathleen's lips twitched upwards.

'Really,' Penelope said languorously as she picked up a silver cigarette holder and popped a cigarette into the small cavity. 'One of the boat girls. I've heard of them.' She looked down her nose.

'I bet it's jolly hard work,' ventured Kathleen.

'But not really for proper women, I wouldn't think,' Penelope said sweetly, 'carting a load of coal or flour or whatever you have to carry back and forth, ruining your nails.' She casually inspected her own beautifully manicured and varnished red . . . well, 'claws' was the only word Ronnie could think of. 'I wondered why you were wearing those rubber boots.' She smiled, but it didn't reach her ice-blue eyes. 'Well, now I see.'

Ronnie forced herself not to put her hands behind her back, feeling like a stupid schoolgirl who'd been caught in a prank as Michael glanced at her feet. He looked up and winked at her.

'I must say, Ronnie, you look very fetching in that dress . . . and the colour suits you to a T.'

She gave him a sharp look. Was he mocking her? Then she saw his warm smile and twinkling eyes. She felt the tension leave her stomach – until a spark of inquisitiveness flashed across Penelope's face.

'So, Ronnie . . . or should that really be Veronica?' she said.

'No, it's not Veronica, but the French version – Véronique.' Ronnie made sure she gave the 'r' the full French roll.

'How delightful.' Penelope threw her head back with a throaty laugh. 'And how very sophisticated.' She stared pointedly at Ronnie's Wellingtons again, then the heavily made-up eyes stared at Ronnie. 'So how do you know Michael?'

'Oh, the sarge and I were carrying out a routine inspection on the canals,' Michael said casually before Ronnie could think of an answer.

She breathed out, thankful he hadn't mentioned anything about Margaret having had a fatal accident. She couldn't have borne it in front of this woman who didn't look as though she could ever muster a grain of sympathy. Kathleen looked so much friendlier with the same twinkle in her eyes as her brother's. Ronnie wondered what Kathleen could possibly have in common with this Penelope.

Fascinated, Ronnie watched as Penelope waved her cigarette in Michael's direction. He didn't appear to notice and she wanted to hug him for it. Then she remembered how he'd held her in his arms when he'd had to tell her Margaret had died. A warmth crept up her neck.

'Michael . . .?'

'What? Oh, sorry, Penelope.'

Ronnie watched, fascinated, as Michael felt in his pocket and produced a lighter. He flicked it on. Penelope leaned forward, cupping her hand possessively around Michael's as she did so, then inhaling deeply before she finally dropped her hand from his and briefly closed her eyes in seeming bliss. What a show-off. Penelope was doing this whole pantomime on purpose, Ronnie was certain, to let her see how close she and Michael were. Well, the show was all in vain, as far as Ronnie was concerned. The woman could have him.

Nevertheless, she was relieved to see Jess rush over and break whatever spell Penelope seemed to have woven around herself.

'There you are, Ronnie. I wondered where you'd got to. Have you had a dance yet? You must . . . on your birthday. It's a lovely sprung floor – just dreamy.' Jessica drew breath. 'Anyway, then I saw you with Constable Scott.' She beamed at him. 'What are the chances of that?'

'Oh, Michael . . . please,' he said, springing to his feet and extending his hand. 'Hello, Jessica. I should be asking you and Ronnie the same question. I was visiting my family in Oxford and Kath told me she and Penelope had tickets for tonight so Penelope managed to wangle an extra one for me.'

I bet she did. Ronnie forced herself to keep her expression neutral.

Michael quickly introduced his sister and Penelope to Jessica. Ronnie noticed Penelope's eyes narrow a fraction as her gaze lingered on Jess, who took the seat Michael pulled out.

Serves her right to have a bit of competition, Ronnie thought, aware she was being childish.

'Do sit down, Ronnie,' Michael said. He cocked his ear and Ronnie noticed the band had changed tempo. 'Better still, as it's your special day, may I ask you for a dance?'

Chapter Twenty-Eight

Ronnie stared at Michael's smiling face. Why on earth had he asked her to dance? He'd seen her boots. Was he laughing at her expense?

'What a scream your Ronnie was,' she imagined Penelope saying to Michael afterwards. 'She must have known you were only joking. Fancy saying yes and clodding around the floor in those rubber boots.'

Ronnie glanced at Kathleen, who gave her a gentle nod. Penelope stared at her, a challenge in those cold eyes. Something snapped. She'd bloody well take him up on his offer. Whether he meant to humiliate her or not, she'd carry it through with as much dignity as she could muster.

She looked directly at Michael. 'Only trouble is' – she began, deliberately hesitating so Penelope would think she was about to decline – 'the last time I tried a quickstep my partner hadn't got a clue and trod all over me.'

'That must be the reason why she's wearing protection on her feet tonight,' Penelope said, looking round the table and smirking.

Ronnie was gratified that no one seemed to be taking any notice of the woman.

'Well, you won't have to worry about that with me,' Michael

said, smiling broadly. 'I'm no Fred Astaire but my mother proudly framed my Beginners' Dancing Certificate.'

'In that case I'll just take my boots off.' She couldn't resist a sidelong glance at Penelope who sent Michael a look of utter astonishment, then tapped the cigarette stub into the ashtray so vehemently that little puffs of ash floated in the air. Ronnie fought a gurgle of laughter as she sat on the chair and bent to take off her left boot.

'You show 'em, Ronnie,' Jessica grinned.

'Here, let me,' Michael said.

Ronnie hesitated, but only for a split second. Aware of Penelope's malevolent gaze, she obediently extended her leg. Michael firmly took hold and pulled each boot off, placing them together at her side. She felt his fingertips briefly touch her skin above her ankles as he removed her socks. For some reason she couldn't comprehend, the small gesture sent a quiver of excitement through her.

'Right then, are you ready?'

'Yes.' She took his hand and tiptoed towards the dance floor, careful not to put her bare feet in the way of some enthusiastic couple not looking where they were treading.

From the first few steps she could tell that Michael was an accomplished dancer. She'd never managed a proper quickstep in her life so had scant experience to compare, but giving no more thought to Penelope and Wellington boots, she urged herself to concentrate. So much so that she felt her back stiffen.

'Just relax and let me guide you,' he whispered.

His breath was warm on her neck.

As she gave herself up to the music she felt her shoulders soften and her hand release its claw-like grip on Michael's. She felt him pull her closer against him, their movements in perfect harmony as he changed direction, twirling her so she was almost dizzy, then danced her at top speed across the width of the floor. She was half conscious of other couples backing away, allowing them space.

She was on wings.

She never wanted it to end.

The music stopped. Michael looked down at her and smiled.

'Did you enjoy it?' he said.

She nodded. She couldn't think of anything to say. The music started up again but he didn't suggest they have a second dance. Maybe he hadn't enjoyed it as much as she had. Maybe he felt self-conscious dancing with a bare-footed partner. Maybe he'd rather have had the glamorous Penelope in his arms. She shrugged off the idea. If it were true, there was nothing she could do to alter it.

But as they approached Michael's table her heart began to beat rapidly. She'd make her excuses to leave, hoping Jess would follow her. She would *not* put up with any more sarcasm from that ghastly Penelope. But there was no one sitting at their table. And she knew it was the right one because her boots were still there where she'd left them.

'They must all be on the floor,' Michael said, as though reading her thoughts. 'Good. That'll give us a chance to have a chat.'

He pulled out her chair and took the seat next to her.

'What would you like to drink?' he said, glancing towards her glass, barely touched. 'And don't say you haven't finished your punch, if that's what it is, as it'll be warm by now.'

'I shan't be able to tell the difference,' she said ruefully, picking it up and taking a sip. Michael was right. It wasn't so good as when it was chilled, but it was something at least to wet her mouth, which had suddenly gone dry. 'I really don't want anything more. Jess and I'll be going soon.'

'You've only just come,' he said, turning towards her.

'How do you know?'

'I saw you walk in.'

'I suppose you recognised Jess.'

'No. I've only met her that one time. But I was sure it was you, even though I admit I did a double take.'

'Because I looked clean, for once?'

'Because you looked so different,' he said. 'Don't forget – I've never seen you in a dress which sets off those lovely dark curls.' He paused. 'I must say both really suit you.'

'You mean you prefer me in a dress rather than my filthy old men's clothes?' she teased, enjoying their banter.

'I like them, too,' he chuckled, 'when they're on Ronnie. But tonight Ronnie's gone and Véronique has taken her place.' He brushed his finger along her jaw. 'I know you don't like your full name, but it's beautiful. Like you.'

Ronnie blinked. Beautiful? Did he mean it? Or was he mocking her?

'So it's your birthday, Véronique.' He studied her. 'Would it be awfully rude of me if I asked how old you are today?'

She hesitated, then said, 'Seventeen.'

'Didn't you have to be at least seventeen when you started working for the GUCC?'

Ronnie grinned. 'That's right.'

'So you fibbed?'

'I'm not admitting anything to a police officer.'

He laughed. 'All right. I won't hand you in. It's just that I now feel positively old compared to you.'

'How old are you, then?'

'Twenty-one.'

'I'll keep that in mind. But you're very nimble on your feet for someone so elderly,' she teased.

He grinned. 'And *you* dance like an angel.' He put his

hand over hers. 'Don't look like that . . . I never say anything I don't mean. You can ask Kath.'

'Good job I wasn't wearing the boots then,' she answered lightly, conscious of the touch of his skin.

'Yes, it's possible angels don't wear boots,' he grinned. 'But I'm sure there's a story behind them. So what really happened? Did you forget to bring your shoes?'

'No, I had them with me, but I left them on the bus. It was because the driver had to brake sharply so he didn't hit some poor woman who ran in front of him. But a mother and baby across the aisle from us fell into the front window. The baby hit its head and the conductor said we all had to get off so he could get them to hospital. So in the rush I forgot.' She hesitated. She might as well tell him the rest. 'The thing is . . . they're Dora's.'

His eyebrows shot up. 'Dora's? You mean you borrowed some dancing shoes from our Dora?'

'The very one,' Ronnie couldn't help chuckling at his astonished expression. 'The strange thing is that our feet are exactly the same size. She told me they were special.' She bit her lip. 'I don't know how I'm going to tell her I've lost them.'

Michael seemed about to say something when the others returned, Kathleen smiling at both of them as she sat down.

'Gosh, it's a while since I did any ballroom dancing,' she said, sounding a little out of breath, 'but I had a good partner – much older than me but he was a dab hand and I really enjoyed it.' She looked at Ronnie. 'How about you? Did my brother give you a twirl?'

Ronnie felt Jess and Penelope's eyes on her, then to her embarrassment they both glanced at Michael's hand still warm on her own.

'Yes, he did,' she said, quickly pulling her hand away. 'He

played it down about his dancing and never once stepped on my bare toes.'

She bent to put on her boots and when she straightened up she caught Penelope watching her closely. The woman immediately busied herself lighting another cigarette.

'Ronnie left her shoes on the bus because there'd been an accident,' Michael said, turning to Ronnie. 'You know, it's not terribly late. Why don't we get a cab and go to the bus depot where they have a Lost Property desk? You said everyone had to vacate the bus so I'm sure the conductor would have noticed the bag and handed it in.'

'It's very kind of you,' Ronnie said, feeling herself stutter with embarrassment under Penelope's gaze, 'but—'

'No buts,' Michael said. 'If we go now and get them, you won't have to spend time tomorrow chasing them when Dora will need all hands on deck, so to speak.'

Ronnie admitted Michael had a point. If she left it until tomorrow she'd have to confess. Dora would be furious and resent time wasted when they needed to press on to Coventry. She saw Penelope's eyes narrow.

'I think it's a good idea, Michael,' Kathleen said. 'Don't worry about us – we'll be fine.'

'But such a shame to break up the evening we'd all been looking forward to.' Penelope inhaled on a fresh cigarette and blew out a stream of smoke rings over their heads.

Michael glanced towards her and Ronnie detected a tightening around his eyes as though he didn't approve of the woman. For some reason she felt an unexpected stab of triumph.

'What about Jess?' she said.

'She comes too. Then the cab will drop you as near as possible to where you're moored – it'll be quicker and safer. But if we're going, we need to go right away,' he added, 'so I'll go and find her.' He vanished.

'Oh, Jess, I'm sorry to drag you away but—' Ronnie began when Jessica reappeared.

'Don't worry about me,' Jessica cut in. 'Michael's explained. In fact, he rescued me from the most awful partner. He had bad breath and kept trying to kiss me. I turned my cheek and ended up with his drool. Ugh.' She fished in her bag and brought out a handkerchief and wiped both cheeks. 'Oh, that's better.' She grinned at Ronnie and Michael. 'Well, what are we waiting for?'

'It was very nice to meet you, Kathleen,' Ronnie said sincerely. She glanced at Penelope and gave her a curt nod, then followed Jessica to the cloakroom, Penelope's peal of laughter sounding in her ears.

A cab was waiting for them when she and Jessica stepped outside, Michael holding the rear door open. The three of them climbed in and Michael pulled down one of the single seats to sit facing them.

'The bus depot's only a few minutes away,' he said.

As they arrived, the man at the Lost Property desk was just rolling down the shutter.

'Sorry, mate,' he said to Michael. 'Yer too late. You'll have ter come back tomorrow – we're open 9 a.m. to 9 p.m.'

'Wait a moment—' Michael began.

'No arguin', mate. I'm closed.'

Michael produced a leather case and flipped it open, then held it up to the man's face.

'Constable Scott,' he said. 'And I'm asking you to open up.'

The man's eyes widened. 'Why didn't you say you was the police?'

'You're wasting my time.' Michael's voice was firm. 'Just open up and tell me if a bag has been handed in, containing a pair of ladies' shoes.'

'What sorta bag?'

'A cotton drawstring bag,' Ronnie said.

'What time was it?'

'About an hour ago,' Ronnie said. 'The bus driver or the conductor would have brought it in.'

'You'll have to give me a minute. I don't work here – I'm just doin' a favour to close up.'

He rolled back the shutter and peered amongst the shelves, taking out left items and putting them back. Ronnie thought she would scream with frustration.

'A drawstring bag, you say?'

'Yes.' Ronnie's eyes roved over the shelves, then excitedly she pointed to one of the pigeonholes. 'That's it!'

The man removed a cotton bag and Ronnie pounced on it. She opened it and pulled out a silver shoe which glittered in the dim electric light.

'Oh, thank goodness, it's hers.' She looked happily up at Michael.

'Goodness, I can't see Dora in these,' Michael grinned. 'But if you say so.'

'Oh, I do.'

'Please sign here, sir,' the man said, putting a book in front of Michael. 'And the date and your address.'

'I'll note down my police number,' Michael said. 'That should be good enough.'

'Quite, sir.'

'Thank you very much,' Ronnie said, smiling and taking Jess's arm, her other hand firmly gripping Dora's shoe bag.

'You were lucky, Ronnie,' Jessica said. 'So come on, Cinders. Let's get home so that Michael can return to the dance hall.'

Ronnie looked at him curiously.

'I'm seeing you both back to the boats and then I'll catch

the train straight back to Oxford,' he said. 'Even for a policeman, I think I've had plenty of excitement for one evening.'

For some inexplicable reason, Ronnie felt a quiver of satisfaction. He wasn't going to dash back to Penelope.

The cab dropped the two girls as close to the boat as possible. Michael got out and gave a hand to Jessica, then Ronnie.

'Goodnight, Michael,' Jessica said. 'Thanks for coming to the rescue. I can't imagine what Dora would have said to Ronnie coming back without her precious shoes.'

'All in the line of duty,' Michael grinned.

A little embarrassed that Jessica had patently left her alone with Michael, Ronnie said, 'It was awfully kind of you to go out of your way like that. You've saved my life.'

'Knowing the little I've seen of Dora, I can believe it,' Michael chuckled. 'Anyway, you're all safe and sound.' Facing her squarely, he gently tilted up her chin. 'You did look beautiful tonight, Véronique,' he said, 'but you're just as pretty in your boat clothes – don't ever forget it.'

And then he bent his head.

As his lips touched hers, Ronnie trembled. His kiss deepened, was so tender. . . Instinctively, she kissed him back. His arms came around her, holding her close . . . so close she imagined she could feel his heart beating beneath his coat.

'I won't ever forget this evening and especially our quickstep,' he said finally, holding her a little away from him.

'I don't suppose you will, having a partner with bare feet?' she laughed, a little breathless, but more sure of herself now.

'That's not the reason why.' She could just make out his grin in the darkness. 'Did you enjoy your birthday?'

'I'd almost forgotten it was,' she said, truthfully, not admitting her mind was now on other things. But she wasn't going to let him know that.

'And tomorrow is Christmas Eve. Are you going home?'

'No,' Ronnie said. 'We can't go on leave again until we've finished our six-week training.'

'Are you sorry?'

'Not really.' She paused. 'Well, I am for my mother as she'll probably be on her own, although Raine might get a couple of days' leave. But I'm quite looking forward to a more unusual Christmas on the boat.'

'You must let me know how it goes,' he chuckled. 'Well, I'd better wish you a merry Christmas.' He kissed her forehead. 'Goodnight, Ronnie,' he said softly. 'Sleep tight.'

'Merry Christmas, Michael,' she said, but he'd already disappeared.

It was only when she was tucked in bed that night, staring up at the wooden ceiling, and still feeling the imprint of Michael's kiss, that she wondered why he'd singled her out. Jess and Penelope were undeniably far more glamorous than she could ever hope to be. Or wanted to be, she thought. But Michael seemed to like her for herself. She smiled in the darkness, enjoying the gentle rocking of the boat and comforted by the warmth of Lucky on her now aching feet at the end of the bed and Jessica's light snoring only inches away. It was at that moment she realised she'd spent most of the evening with another man and hadn't once given Will Drake a thought.

Chapter Twenty-Nine

Ronnie opened her eyes the next morning and yawned. She stretched her arms above her head, the events of last night still on her mind. Walking with Jess into the dance hall wearing May's lovely dress, the effect completely ruined with the Wellington boots instead of Dora's glittery dance shoes. Then bumping into Michael. He was the last person she'd expected to see. Meeting his sister, Kathleen, whom she'd liked straightaway. But not that awful friend, Penelope. Ronnie wondered not for the first time why the two of them were friends. The hard-faced but glamorous Penelope seemed the very opposite to Kathleen. And did Michael realise how the woman made a beeline for him at every possible opportunity? Maybe he liked the attention. But he hadn't chosen to dance with her.

Yet he was willing to dance with me, even in my boots. She chuckled to herself as she recalled the look of astonishment on Penelope's face when she'd removed her boots. Then she felt that same funny little quiver when she remembered the touch of his fingertips on her bare ankles.

She relived those moments in his arms, following his steps in her bare feet, praying no one would step on them. She hadn't wanted the music to end. She supposed it was the novelty of dancing with a man instead of one of her classmates.

But Michael wasn't just any man. She was certain no man would ever have kissed her the way Michael had.

She shook herself. This wasn't getting anywhere. What was the time? She turned over to look at the clock but it was too dark to read. It must be early. She wondered what the plans were for this evening and tomorrow, Christmas Day. Dora certainly hadn't even mentioned Christmas. It would have been fun to put up some decorations in the boat though she doubted anyone had brought any with them. Like her, they'd probably assumed they would be spending Christmas at home.

'When are you going to give Dora's shoes back to her?' Jessica said at breakfast time.

'What's this about Miss Dummitt's shoes?' Angela said suspiciously, her eyes darting from Jessica to Ronnie.

'Oh, nothing, Angela,' Ronnie said quickly. She didn't feel like explaining to Angela how she'd come to borrow something from Dora.

'It must be something,' Angela persisted.

'Oh, all right. Dora lent me her shoes because I didn't have anything quite right to go with May's dress.'

'You sound like a pauper,' Angela said, frowning. 'I understood you came from a decent family.'

Ronnie managed to ignore her. Angela simply wasn't worth arguing with.

'There's no need to be so rude.' Jessica threw Angela a murderous look. 'It shows *you* up, not Ronnie.'

'Are these the shoes in this bag?' Before Ronnie could stop her, Angela shot up and grabbed the bag, tugged the drawstring and shook one of the shoes out.

'Goodness, these can't be Miss Dummitt's,' she said as she handled it, turning it this way and that. 'They look expensive.' Angela glanced up at Ronnie. 'She's not exactly a glamour-puss, is she, but then, neither are you, I wouldn't have thought.'

'Put it back at once!' Ronnie thundered. 'It's nothing to do with you. It was very kind of her to lend them to me – not that *you'd* know anything about kindness.'

'Correct me if I'm wrong, but isn't it *you* who calls her "Deadly Dora"?' Angela shot back. 'That doesn't sound very kind to me.'

'Is that what I'm called?' Dora's face poked through the hatch.

Ronnie sat stock-still. Jessica's mouth twitched.

'Not by *me*, Miss Dummitt,' Angela said, desperately trying to push the shoe back into the bag. 'All the others call you that behind your back and I think you'll find that Ronnie started it off.'

'Yes, you can go red, miss.' Dora stared at Ronnie, who put her hands to her burning cheeks. Then to her amazement, Dora threw her head back and roared with laughter. 'I rather like it. Shows I mean business.' Her laughter stopped abruptly as she squinted at Angela. 'What're you doin' with my shoes, miss? I don't 'ppreciate my belongin's bein' looked over and discussed.'

'Oh, they'd been thrown on the floor so I was just picking them up. Ronnie was laughing about them, saying you lent them to her, and she couldn't believe they were yours. Too glamorous for you, she said.'

There was a stunned silence.

Ronnie found her voice. 'Miss Dummitt, please believe me but I didn't say anything of the kind. Those words were Angela's.'

'Ronnie's speaking the truth,' Jessica said. 'And thank goodness I was here to witness that little scene.'

Dora threw Angela a glare. 'The brasses need cleanin' on

the motor, Angela. You'll find the brass cleaner in the cupboard. And the engine room's in a bit of a mess, so you'd better get over there now and get crackin' with that.'

'Why aren't the girls who live there doing it?' Angela demanded.

'They're occupied with other things,' Dora said. 'And seein' that *I'm* in charge here – and as I'm known as "Deadly Dora" – I don't need to be explainin'. So off yer go, miss.'

If looks could kill, Ronnie thought, stifling a giggle, Dora would have dropped dead right on the spot from Angela's furious gaze. Then without another word Angela slid open the hatch and vanished.

'I'm beginnin' not to be too pleased with that one,' Dora said, jerking her head towards the hatch.

'Now you know how *we* feel,' Jess put in.

'That's as maybe,' Dora grunted. 'What I'm interested in – did the shoes do the trick?'

And when Ronnie told Dora honestly the whole story about what happened, Dora slapped her leg and doubled up laughing until she said her side was 'hurtin' bad'.

'But if it's done one good thing, miss, it's taken yer mind off Will Drake and fixed it more firmly onter Constable Scott,' she roared again. 'And he's a darn sight better for yer than that young tyke!'

'I expect yous'll be goin' to the pub this evenin', bein' as it's Christmas Eve,' Dora said as everyone squashed into *Penelope* after an early supper.

'We thought we'd sing some carols,' May said. She looked at Dora. 'You don't sound like you're coming with us, Miss Dummitt.'

'No, I'm not,' Dora said, to Ronnie's surprise, knowing how Dora loved calling in at the pubs along the cut most evenings, sleeping there overnight. 'I don't go much for Christmas, not bein' religious-like. No, I've got me own plans.'

She didn't mention what they were and Ronnie couldn't help being curious, but Dora didn't say a further word.

Lapworth, the village where Dora had decided to tie up the boats, was only twelve miles distant, but they had to proceed in a painstakingly slow way because parts of the canal had borne the brunt of the blizzard. Branches had come down in the wind and often made it difficult to negotiate the steering, although Ronnie had to admit Angela came into her own on the tiller. Best place for her, Ronnie thought, knowing Angela was out of everyone's way and they didn't have to put up with her barbed comments.

When the girls finally tied up the pair of boats, May eagerly looked across the cut for a pub, but no one could make out any building looking remotely like one. The mist and gloom didn't help. It was only three o'clock but already becoming dark.

'I'm not bothered about going to the pub either,' Ronnie said, smothering yet another yawn when she and Jessica and Angela were in the butty having a welcome cup of tea and the treat of a couple of biscuits each.

'No, I don't suppose you are,' Angela said. 'Long as you've enjoyed *your*self, doesn't matter a hang about the rest of us.'

'What are you talking about?'

'How late you were last night coming home . . . with your *boyfriend*.'

'With my *friend*,' Ronnie quickly corrected. 'What were you doing, Angela? Spying on us?'

Angela snorted. 'As if I'm interested,' she said. 'I was making a cup of cocoa and I heard voices. I wondered who it was. I might have known it was you.'

'You're not a teensy-weensy bit jealous, are you, Angela?' Jessica said.

'Certainly not.' Angela's lip curled. 'I'd hate a man nuzzling round me.'

Ronnie bit back a retort. But it sounded as though Angela had witnessed Michael's kiss. For some reason that bothered her more than anything.

When Jessica and Angela had left for the pub, Ronnie pulled down the double bed. She sat on top of it and opened her novel, *The Water Gipsies,* reminding her of the interview with Mrs Hunter that she and Raine had attended. She shut her eyes, trying to picture her sister's life. She couldn't help thinking Maman was right and that Raine's job was probably far more risky than she let on. A shiver ran across Ronnie's shoulders. *Keep safe, darling Raine.* She wondered if Raine had been given a couple of days off from flying but thought probably not. The boys would want to surprise Jerry, if possible. But how dreadful to be forced to kill people at Christmas. But then how dreadful at any time of the year.

Ronnie swallowed hard and tried to concentrate on her book. But when she'd read the same paragraph three times over, she snapped it shut, wishing she had a portable wireless and could listen to some music. Maybe a jazz programme to remind her of dearest Suzy, singing her heart out to the troops, perhaps not even that far away. What she would give to see her sisters' smiling faces.

She recalled her mother's last letter.

Véronique, ma chérie,

You cannot know how disappointed I am to receive your letter you are not coming home for Christmas. It will be the first Christmas I am left here on my own. There is not even the possibility to see P. All I have is your dog who I think misses you as much as I do.

Maman had gone on a bit longer before telling her she hoped she would have a nice Christmas with her new friends. Pierre would have been the perfect solution, Ronnie thought. But at least her mother would have Rusty. She closed her eyes, seeing his tail wagging and hearing his barks of excitement the minute he laid eyes on her. She choked back a sob, feeling the thin mattress harder than usual under her back and neck with the weight of her guilt and homesickness. She was alone in the world.

Should she have joined the others who were probably by now having a jolly time? She pictured the whole pub singing to May's ukulele and shrugged. No one would want her around when she was in this mood.

What was that noise?

She jolted up, her heart beating hard.

Someone was on the roof! Who was it? Everyone had gone.

Ronnie reached for the poker, waiting, her blood pumping as the hatch slowly slid open.

She didn't realise she was holding her breath until she breathed out her fear. A familiar face appeared in the hatchway.

'Miss Dummitt! Thank goodness. I thought it was a burglar!'

'No burglars out in this weather that's enough to freeze the balls off a brass monkey,' Dora chuckled as she jumped down the last step. 'But this in't no place for a young girl alone on Christmas Eve neither, so I've come to take yer with me.'

'Where?'

'To have a bit o' Christmas cheer with a family I know.'

'I thought you didn't bother about Christmas.'

'Well, *they* do,' Dora said. 'There're five kiddies . . . or rather six, now, with the new'un. Not forgettin' Cobber the horse. So what d'ya say?'

'Where do they live?'

'On a boat, o' course,' Dora said impatiently. Then she grinned, showing the black gaps. 'And if yer want to know where Cobber lives, he gets stabled at the pub opposite so's he can enjoy a pint with the locals.' She threw her head back and roared at Ronnie's disbelieving expression. 'We in't far from them. Their boat's the *Princess Dolly*.' Her laughter faded as the word 'Dolly' seemed to tremble on her lips. She sniffed. 'So no more yakkin'. Are yer comin' with me, or not?' Her dark eyes were as stern as ever. 'If so, bring yer torch – much good as it does.'

Ronnie couldn't help smiling. She stood and for the second time closed her book.

'If they wouldn't mind a stranger, I'd like to. Very much.'

By the weak torchlight Ronnie could make out the boat's name, *Princess Dolly*, decorated with bunches of painted roses at either end. Inside, a baby howled and Ronnie could hear shouts and laughter from what sounded like several children. A man's loud voice rose above the cacophony.

He sounded fierce. Immediately, Ronnie wished she hadn't come. Whatever had she let herself in for? She'd been perfectly all right on her own, quietly with her book. As though Dora read her thoughts she said, 'Don't take no notice of him. He has ter make himself heard with that lot.'

Ronnie nodded and meekly followed Dora onto the deck.

'Open up!' Dora roared. 'I've brought a visitor.'

The hatch instantly slid open and Dora pushed Ronnie

through the space. A man's arm steadied her onto the floor and she found herself crushed against him.

'Thank you.' She looked up at a broad, strong-featured man, so tall he had to bend his auburn head so as not to hit it on the ceiling, which was draped with coloured festive chains like the ones she and Raine and Suzy used to spend hours gluing together. She extricated herself from his grip and stepped backwards.

'Ow,' a small ginger-haired boy shrieked. 'Yer hurt my foot, you did.'

'Oh, I'm sorry.'

There didn't appear to be an inch of space anywhere. How Dora was going to fit in as well, heaven knew.

Dora burst through the hatch, grinning.

'Leave the child be, Fred. She in't used to real boat people.'

'Sooner she be, the better.' Fred looked at Ronnie. 'Don't say yer one of them wenches what takes the cargo up and down the cut without a man. You don't look more'n a kiddie yerself.'

'She's one of 'em, all right,' Dora said before Ronnie could answer. 'And seein' as she in't fully learned yet, she's not givin' a bad hand.'

'Wot's yer name, missus?' A little fair-haired girl, no more than three or four, put her arms round Ronnie's legs.

'It's Ronnie.'

'Can't be.' A boy of about nine muscled into the little group. 'Ronnie in't a girl's name.'

'I know,' Ronnie smiled at him. This one had dark hair and eyes to match. 'But when I was your age, I loved doing all the things boys did like climbing trees, going off on my bike, looking at birds' nests . . .'

The boy nodded, regarding her with new respect.

'Don't bother the lady, Georgie.' A plump woman came in through the door from the hold carrying a bucket of coal.

'Dolly,' Dora said, 'this is Ver-ron-eek, one of my wenches. The youngest as yer can tell. She were on 'er own while the others went to the pub so I took pity on her.'

'Pleased to meet yer.' Dolly wiped her tanned hand on her snow-white apron, then held it out. 'That's a fancy name yer got.'

Even in that brief moment, Ronnie felt Dolly's callouses. 'Very pleased to meet you, too,' she said. 'And please call me Ronnie.' The baby's howl had softened to a whimper. 'Congratulations, Mrs . . .'

'We don't stand on no cere-mony here,' Dolly said, her dimpled face wreathed in smiles. 'Dolly'll do nicely.'

'Dolly,' Ronnie said, 'congratulations on the new baby. May I see him – or is it a her?'

'No need for congrattylations, dearie. She in't mine. Her ma died borning her. Poor little scrap. So we took 'er in. You go 'n' 'ave a peep while Fred' – she swung her attention to her husband – 'you go 'n' fetch the bottle and we'll give the lady a special Christmas drink.'

'Oh, please, not for me,' Ronnie protested, but Fred wouldn't hear of it.

''Ow d'ya think I'll get one if yer refuse?' he said, twinkling down at her. 'Ma won't let me 'ave one on me own.'

'I'll be more'n happy to join yer, Fred,' Dora said quickly.

Ronnie noticed him glance at Dora with a wink and Dora smiled back, looking almost coy.

If Dora got her teeth fixed she'd actually have quite a pretty face, Ronnie thought. *Maman would soon cart her off to the dentist.* She smiled at the image of Maman taking Dora firmly by the arm and dragging her to see Mr Chapman. Ronnie peered into the makeshift crib, which looked as though it had once been the bottom drawer of a chest. The baby stared up at her with round blue eyes.

'Hello, little one, what's your name?'

'She's Rosy. Like them rosies Pa did on the boat,' Georgie piped up.

Ronnie wished she had a little soft toy for Rosy to play with. She stayed a minute or two with the baby's hand locked around one of her fingers, then reluctantly and gently unhooked it and went back to her seat.

The children gathered round her, curious to see this stranger.

'Why d'yer speak funny,' the oldest boy of about thirteen challenged her, staring at her from his stool, his face only inches away from hers.

Ronnie hesitated, not wanting to say 'at home'. 'It's how I learnt at school,' she smiled.

'Y'see, Ma,' the boy said. 'I keeps tellin' yer I need ter get to school. They learn yer all sorta things.'

'I'll learn yer a clip over the ear, Dave, if yer don't stop tormentin' the nice lady,' his mother warned him.

'I'm happy to tell him anything he wants to know about school,' Ronnie said.

'That's as maybe, but first orf I want yous to sit yonder and I'll pour the tea I were makin' 'fore yer came.' She pointed to the seat plank.

Ronnie had no sooner sat down than the little girl climbed up on her lap.

'That's Liza. Shove 'er orf if she's bein' a nuisance,' Fred said. 'Yer gotta learn 'em at that age.'

'I don't know how you manage with five children and a new baby to look after,' Ronnie said in an awed tone as she held Liza firmly and looked around. The cabin was as neat as a pin, positively sparkling in the light from the two oil lamps falling on the gleaming brassware. Wherever her eye took her she spotted picture frames with faded photographs, brasses by the stove – all gleaming and reflecting – making the cabin look larger than it really was. There were hand-embroidered coverings which she'd bet Dolly had made, pictures and decorative plates hung by string . . . really, how on earth *did* Dolly cope, Ronnie thought again, guessing the woman did the lion's share of the work.

'Oh, they in't all mine,' Dolly said, roaring with laughter as she handed Ronnie the tea. 'Mine are them twins.' She jerked her head towards a pair of ginger-haired, freckle-faced boys, one Ronnie had inadvertently trodden on. 'They're six,' she said, a note of pride in her voice. 'The other three are 'vacuees. But for easy sake I told 'em all to call me ma.'

Ronnie gave a sharp intake of breath. This family who had so little had extended their tiny cabin to three other children they'd never set eyes on and blended them in with their own family, not to mention caring for a brand-new baby. What generous-hearted people.

'It's doin' our bit fer the war effort,' Fred said. 'And Doll likes ter be surrounded with kiddies. That's when she's most 'appy.'

'Off you git from the lady's knee, Liza.' The little girl jumped off. 'And like or not, I want yer ter drink this oop, so's Fred can 'ave one and stop crazin' me.' She put a glass half filled with a golden liquid in Ronnie's hand.

Ronnie took a sip, then wished she hadn't. It burned the back of her throat making her cough. She felt the warmth spread inside her body.

Fred gave a rich chuckle. 'All right for yer?' he asked.

'Yes, it's lovely,' she managed.

'I made it meself,' he said. 'I used—'

'Enough, Fred,' Dolly interrupted, chuckling. 'Ronnie don't want to hear all the ins and outs of how yer made it. Why don't yer play 'er a tune on yer squeeze-box. The kiddies like it, 'n' all.'

'I'll do that, Doll.' He picked up a battered-looking concertina, unclipped it and drew out a few scattered notes. 'Let's see. We'd better 'ave a Christmas carol.'

He played the introduction of 'Away in a Manger' and to Ronnie's astonishment everyone, including little Liza, joined in.

'And you, Ver-ron-eek,' Dora said, looking at Ronnie with her terrifying grin.

'You wouldn't say that if you heard me sing, Miss Dummitt,' Ronnie said, smiling, for once not irritated by Dora's mocking pronunciation of her name.

'Don't matter if yer can hold a tune or not – it's the joinin' in what counts,' Dora said.

Fred played several more carols and most of the children – or kiddies, as Ronnie now thought of them – sang with gusto. Ronnie found herself doing just what Dora had ordered – joining in with this amazing family.

'It's gettin' late,' Dora said after several of the children began to yawn. 'The kiddies need to get ter bed.'

Ronnie raised her glass. 'Thank you for making me so welcome,' she said. 'The tea and the special drink and singing the carols – and most of all meeting you and the kiddies. It's made me feel more like Christmas than any Christmas I've ever had – and I mean it.'

'Well, wot d'ya know,' Fred said, looking Dora's way. 'This one's growed up more'n I first seed.' He turned to Ronnie. 'This'll be yous one day, miss,' he said with a wink and a smile. 'Kiddies needin' yer attention all day long. But make sure yer take note of Ma. She allus puts me first, like. That's the only way ter keep yer man 'appy.'

Ronnie politely smiled back but Fred had already turned

his attention to Dora. This time Ronnie noticed it was more than a quick glance.

'Bring Ronnie back agin,' Dolly said as she kissed Dora's cheek. 'We like 'er, don't we, Moi-chap?' Her plump face grinned up at Fred.

'She's a good'un,' he said to his wife, at the same time pumping Ronnie's hand. 'She'll make some geezer 'appy, no doubts about that.'

Fred's words floated through Ronnie's mind as she was drifting off to sleep. That rule of keeping your man happy might well suit him and possibly Dolly too, but it wouldn't suit *her*. Ronnie's lips curved into a wry smile. But what sort of a marriage *would* suit her? Try as she might, she couldn't envision being anyone's wife. For one thing, no one would want to put up with all the animals she'd decided she would shelter when she finally left home and had a place of her own. Briefly, she wondered what sort of Christmas Michael was having. And the other girls in the pub. Well, she wouldn't have swapped this evening for all the tea in Dolly's enormous teapot.

Chapter Thirty

New Year's Eve 1943

'We best go over a few things,' Dora said, when they arrived in Coventry. 'I warn yous, it in't no picnic carryin' coal. But it's vital for the factories to keep goin' – the ones that have survived the bleedin' Jerry – so far, that is.'

Ronnie felt a rush of excitement. This was what they'd been preparing for – actually seeing something worthwhile for their efforts. This was how Pathé News had enticed her to become a boatwoman. Then she realised the implication of what Dora was saying.

'Coventry was bombed heavily at the beginning of the war, wasn't it?' Ronnie said.

'Yes.' Dora concentrated on lighting her pipe in the wind. 'That were a bad night. I weren't too far away when it happened. The sky were that red and yer could hear them bombs all night. Whole town smashed up. Shops, factories, homes . . . and their cathedral.' She shook her head. 'That were a great shame. Not that I ever went inside, mind. But I went ter have a gawp the followin' day and it weren't a pretty sight.'

Ronnie noticed Dora's face had paled as she took some furious puffs of her pipe.

'Will we have the opportunity of going into the city after they finish loading up the coal, Miss Dummitt?' Sally asked.

Dora stared at her. 'If yer really interested, the bus goes in quite frequent from where we're loadin'. Best thing about Coventry for yous, I reckon, is to go in and have a bath. For me, I don't care if I never see the place again s'long as I live. The main thing is we'll be loadin' up the boats first.' Her sharp eyes landed on Ronnie and the others, one by one. 'Before we get there yer need to carry out my instructions to the letter. If yer don't – and even if yer do' – she grinned at them, showing the gaps in her teeth – 'the coal dust – well, it's grit – will get everywhere. In yer hair, up yer nose, in yer throat, and yer won't help swallowin' some of it. It'll be in yer clothes, yer underwear so you'll be itchin' and scratchin'. It'll be on every surface in the cabin . . . so yer have to prepare. Before they load, yer need ter pick up the floorboards and stack them at the fore end so's to keep them clean and dry. And mind how you do it – they're bleedin' heavy – and be careful of the underneath side – it'll be slick with all the oil and water. Then bolt the cabin and engine doors and pull the hatch cover over so's the dust don't fly while the coal comes through the chute. Got that?'

'Yes, Miss Dummitt,' Ronnie joined in the chorus.

'And you, miss?' Dora's glare went straight to Angela.

'Yes, of course, Miss Dummit,' Angela answered with a sniff.

'Then make sure yer say so next time.'

Somehow the thought of all this preparation didn't worry Ronnie in the least. She'd always loved a challenge. Jessica was not so sanguine.

'We need to wrap our hair up in a scarf,' she said. 'Have you brought one with you, Ronnie?'

'No, but I've got my woolly hat.'

'I brought two scarves,' Jessica said, 'so you're welcome to borrow the other.'

'Thanks, Jess. I'll see how I go.'

'What do you think about a trip into the city?'

'I'm in two minds.'

'I'm definitely going to have a look round. It'll be something to tell my grandchildren one day.'

'Don't you have to have children first for that to happen?' Ronnie teased.

'It would seem so,' Jessica said, and Ronnie wished she hadn't made such a remark when she noticed a sadness in her friend's attempt at a smile.

When Dora and her two teams arrived at the Newdigate collieries loading bay, the wind had got up nearly to gale force.

'I should never have washed my hair,' Jessica grumbled, trying to tighten her scarf for the dozenth time. 'It's too slippery to keep this damned scarf on, but I wanted it to be clean for when we go into into Coventry.'

'The way Dora was talking, you'll have to wash it all over again anyway,' Ronnie said with a grin, pulling her woolly hat further over her forehead.

'Miss Dummitt to you, miss,' Dora said as she jumped into the engine room to do her inspection. Without bothering to wait for a reply she said, 'Right, get them floorboards up.'

Ronnie heard Jess grumble under her breath as the two of them bent down to begin lifting the boards. Dora had lifted several on her own by the time Ronnie and Jessica had struggled with the first one.

'Slide 'em on their sides to the fore end and careful when

you go under them cross beams . . . No, don't straighten up yet, miss!' Dora's voice was shrill. 'Yous'll do yerself an injury with them chains.'

By the time Ronnie had moved ten of the twenty-six floorboards with Jessica's help, she was exhausted. Dora had made carrying the rest of them seem effortless.

She gave them a smile of triumph. 'Yous'll soon build up some muscle doin' this work,' she said. 'Now get everythin' sealed up and I'll check on the others.' She disappeared.

'I'm not sure I want to have muscles,' Jessica muttered. 'It's not very fetching on a woman.'

'Now you know how *I* feel,' Ronnie grinned.

The men loading the boats were a cheerful lot, calling out to one another as they deposited the coal into the chute to fall into the hold.

'All right, love?' one of them called to Ronnie. She held up her thumb in reply. 'Then stand on the pile of coal and grab those girders on the chute to move yer boat along ready for the next load comin' through.'

Thankful she was wearing thick gloves, Ronnie did as she was told, all the while terrified she wouldn't get it right – or worse, slip on the pile of coal. But to her immense satisfaction she felt the boat glide gently along.

'Stop!' The man held his hand up. 'That's it. Here it comes again.'

Another load landed in the hold.

'Now flatten the pile with these,' Dora said, suddenly appearing. She handed Ronnie and Jess a shovel each and stood watching them for some time, then nodded. 'Good. Now we need ter pull the boats back to the moorin' rings as there's a queue behind us gettin' impatient.'

In all, the loading hadn't taken longer than two hours,

but Ronnie was more tired than she cared to admit with all the shovelling, then finally helping to sheet up to stop the coal getting wet.

'Makes it look nice and tidy, too,' Dora said. 'Same with all the cargo.'

Every muscle in Ronnie's body ached handling the heavy sheeting with Jessica and May. They still had to take the boats back to their moorings and thoroughly scrub the cabins which Dora had warned would be in a bad state with all the coal dust. That would probably take at least an hour to get them clean enough to pass Deadly Dora's inspection.

As it was, with everyone, even Angela and Dora, rolling up their sleeves, getting the boats in shipshape was a major task. What dust hadn't settled on every possible surface, even though they'd so carefully covered everything in sight, was still floating in the air. By the time they'd just about finished, two more hours had slipped away, and Ronnie's back ached worse than when she used to spend half a day bending in the garden at home.

'Anyone want tea? she asked, feeling she couldn't do another stroke.

'We all do, miss,' Dora said. 'Just get that kettle on.'

Ronnie picked it up. 'Oh, it's covered in dust.'

'Are yer sayin' yer not?' Dora said with a triumphant grin.

Ronnie looked down at herself. She was filthy. Her hands were black and greasy. She supposed her face was as well, by the looks of the other black faces.

'I don't think it's just me,' she chuckled. 'We look like a bunch of chimney sweeps.'

Dora gave a hearty laugh, and everyone except Angela joined in.

Ronnie made the tea and handed round mugs, Dora slurping hers almost in one go, then giving a loud, open-mouthed sigh of satisfaction before lighting her pipe.

'Is anyone goin' inter Coventry for a bath?'

'I'd love one, but I'm too tired,' Ronnie said.

Dora gave a few puffs of her pipe. 'Let's see. On the way we'll tie up at Sutton Stop. There's plenty o' water taps so yer can have a good wash in the cabin. And we can check for any post. Best of all there's a good boaters' pub, the Greyhound. That's where we're headin' tonight . . . in case yous've all forgot it's New Year's Eve and we're goin' out. No exceptions – even *you*, Ver-ron-eek. So yous best get washed and put yer glad rags on. We're havin' fish 'n' chips, for which I'm treatin' and then we're off to the pub where I'm standin' yous all a drink – just one, mind. We meet outside the boats at eight o'clock sharp.'

'Do you know, I *had* forgotten about New Year's,' Jessica said when Dora, May and Sally had gone back to *Persephone*. She grinned. 'So we'd best get crackin', as Dora would say.'

'I'm not going,' Angela said. 'I've had enough dust down my lungs for one day so the last place I want to be in is a smoky pub.'

Feeling guilty, Ronnie crossed her fingers hoping that Jess wouldn't try to persuade Angela otherwise.

Although Sutton Stop was only a short journey along the canal from the collieries, once they'd tied up and filled the water cans, the girls were becoming irritable.

'I'm washing my hair of all this filth right now,' Angela announced when they were back in the cabin.

'No, you're bloody not,' Jessica flung at her. 'You can do it after Ronnie and I have gone. You'll be nice and quiet on your own. But until then, Ronnie and I will be using the water.' Taking a penny from her trouser pocket she looked at Ronnie. 'We'll toss who goes first. Heads or tails?'

'Tails never fails,' Ronnie said, laughing.

Jessica threw the coin in the air. ''Fraid it does, love,' she said. 'It's heads.'

As soon as Ronnie had taken her turn to wash her hair and every inch of her body in the hand bowl she felt a million times better. It was as though she'd washed away her exhaustion and with the help of Jessica's small hand mirror she hoped she'd managed to make herself look presentable for the evening. Remembering the dress May had lent her for the dance, she wished she had something nice to wear. After all, it was quite special to welcome in another year. She sighed. Maybe this would be the year the war ended.

Jessica looked her up and down.

'It won't do, Ronnie,' she said. 'Not for New Year's Eve.'

'No one's going to take any notice of me,' Ronnie protested, not nearly as bothered as she'd been on the night of the dance.

'That combination of navy skirt and blue blouse looks like a school uniform,' Jessica said, frowning. 'I can at least lend you a top.'

Five minutes later Ronnie was wearing a long-sleeved red top with a scooped neck and a pair of Jessica's pearl studs on her earlobes.

'That's a lot better,' Jessica said, 'though we have the usual shoe problem.'

'You'd better ask Miss Dummitt if you can borrow hers again,' Angela said with a smirk, looking up from her magazine. 'That's if she doesn't want to wear them herself tonight.'

'I shall be wearing my brogues,' Ronnie said, ignoring her and putting on one of her old jumpers.

'At least there's no snow this time,' Jessica grinned, 'so the brogues won't be as noticeable as the wellies.'

Ronnie laughed. 'What an evening that was.'

'And your Michael didn't seem to mind one bit.' Jessica joined in the laughter. 'In fact, I think he was intrigued.'

Ronnie blushed, aware of Angela's eyes on her, and her lip curling in an ugly manner.

'Shows what taste he has,' Angela muttered.

'Are you ready?' Jessica said pointedly to Ronnie.

'Once I get this second jumper on.' Ronnie pulled a baggy piece of knitwear over her head and reached for her raincoat. 'Right. Now I'm ready.'

'Happy New Year,' Angela called after them in a sarcastic tone.

Stomachs full after a delicious fish and chip meal, the group led by Dora walked a hundred yards on to the Greyhound. From the laughter emanating from inside, a large crowd must have already gathered for the long evening ahead. Dora pushed open the door. Angela was correct on one thing, Ronnie thought, as the smoke hit the back of her throat, sending her straight into a bout of coughing.

'What yer havin' ter drink, ladies?' Dora said.

Ronnie hesitated. The last proper drink she'd had was the punch at the dance, and it might have contributed to her somewhat outrageous behaviour of dancing barefoot.

'What about a sweet sherry?' Jessica said, glancing at her.

'Oh, yes, that'll be nice.' At least she'd sampled it one Christmas.

The other three quickly gave their orders and Dora headed straight for the bar, pushing her way through the mostly male drinkers, leaving Ronnie and the others squashed into a corner, with people still coming through the front door.

Dora was back in less than two minutes, a grin spread across her face.

'Good thing I made a bookin',' she said. 'Dick's saved us a table.' She jerked her head. 'Through the arch by the other fire.' Her glance fell on May. 'Yous can come with me, miss, ter help carry the drinks.'

Ronnie followed Jessica and Sally through the archway, Jess bending low so as not to knock her head against the beams. Most of the tables in this smaller room were occupied by couples. Several of the men eyed the girls as they walked over to the vacant oblong table which had a piece of card propped up by an upturned beer mug in the centre with 'RESURVD' scrawled on it.

The three of them removed their coats and hats, chatting about their day, but soon the conversation turned to the missing trainee.

'It's awful to say it, but I'm so pleased Angela decided not to come tonight,' Sally said. 'What a misery she is. Never got anything good to say about anyone.' She sent Ronnie and Jessica a mischievous grin. 'I'm just so pleased Dora swapped her and me over so I don't have to listen to her constant "poor me" act.'

'I doubt she'll stay,' Jessica said. 'All she likes doing is steering and there's a lot more to it, and many more dirty, heavy jobs she's not keen on tackling.' She leaned back and lit a cigarette. 'If she does decide to leave it'll be good riddance, so far as I'm concerned.'

'Dora's certainly unbending, isn't she?' Sally said. 'Did you notice how she called us "ladies"? I'm pretty sure that's a first.'

'Shhhh!' Ronnie warned. 'Here they come.'

Dora and May put the trays on the table, and Dora took a jug of ale and a mug and set it in front of her chair at the head of the table.

'Before we git started I need the lav. Shan't be a mo.'

She picked up her canvas bag and still in her coat and hat disappeared.

The girls chatted on until Jessica looked at her watch.

'Dora's been gone twenty minutes. Do you think she's all right?'

'Shall I—?' Ronnie started, then spotted a woman coming through the archway. 'Dora!' she said in an undertone.

The others followed her gaze. Dora was almost unrecognisable. She was wearing a plain fitted black dress which transformed her stocky figure. She'd smoothed her hair into a tidy knot, leaving a few yellow tendrils at the nape of her neck. But what immediately drew Ronnie's eye were Dora's feet. She was wearing the very shoes she'd lent her for the dance at Leamington Spa! They made Dora appear to glide over to the table, and Ronnie noticed several appreciative pairs of eyes following the woman in black.

Dora smiled as she sat down. 'Well?' she said challengingly.

'You look marvellous,' Ronnie blurted, having sipped half of her sherry. 'Those shoes are so pretty. To think I never got the chance to wear them.'

Dora seemed to bask in the praise of the others. 'I've decided to git my teeth fixed,' she stated to everyone's surprise. 'No good bein' dressed to the nines if there's black gaps in me gnashers.' She roared with laughter as she poured a huge mug of ale and gulped a quarter of it in one go. Then she turned to Ronnie.

'Yous is brave, Ver-ron-eek.'

'Why?' Ronnie braced herself.

'Sittin' next to me,' Dora chuckled.

Ronnie gave a timid smile.

Dora looked round at the others. 'Yous all worked like

real boaters terday,' she said. 'Can't fault any one of yer, so well done.'

'If that's the case, it's down to you, Miss Dummitt,' Jessica said, raising her glass. 'A toast to Miss Dummitt – or Deadly Dora as she's known on the q.t.'

Ronnie gasped at Jess's cheek but Dora grinned.

'To the wenches,' Dora said, raising her mug, then slurping a few more mouthfuls. 'May yous all soon have yer own boats without my nose pokin' in at yer.'

They all laughed and began chatting amongst themselves, though Ronnie was aware Dora was being a little left out. She finished her sherry and, feeling bold, said, 'Miss Dummitt, may I ask you something rather personal?'

'What would that be?' Dora said, narrowing her eyes at the smoke emanating from her newly lit pipe, which Ronnie privately thought spoilt the effect of the black dress.

'You hinted before that your lovely evening shoes were special and I wondered what might have been the occasion.'

There was a deathly silence between the two of them. Only the chattering and laughter in the room reminded Ronnie of just where they were. Dora looked at her and pulled her mouth into a bitter line. She refilled her mug from the jug of ale and took some deep swallows. Ronnie wished she could vanish into the air. She'd gone too far.

'I'm sorry, Miss Dummitt, that was awfully rude of me. Please forget I ever asked.'

'It's not the question I'm bothered with, it's the answer I'm prepared ter give,' Dora said surprisingly. 'I never let on ter anyone how them shoes came about.'

'My mother would be cross with me for asking,' Ronnie said, mortified. 'She'd say she hadn't brought me up to be inquisitive where my elders were concerned.'

'Yer ma is right,' Dora said, drinking some more. 'But I

don't mind yer askin'. But it's too noisy in here. We'll go ter that table in the corner if yer really want ter learn Dora's secret.'

A secret?

Jessica raised her eyebrows when Ronnie and Dora rose from the table, the rest of the contents of Dora's jug now in the mug she held, her pipe in the other hand.

'Where're you going?' Jessica asked.

'Dora wants to have a quiet word with me,' Ronnie said, hoping Jess would think it was the fire warming her cheeks.

'Mmm. Wonder why. Well, she can't be going to tell you off as she's already said how good we've been,' Jessica said, her eyes dancing with curiosity. 'Let me know later what this is all about.'

Ronnie smiled, and followed Dora to the other table.

'D'ya want another drink, miss?' Dora said as Ronnie sat down.

'No, I think I've had enough already,' Ronnie said.

Dora took up her mug and regarded the contents. 'Expect yer right.' Her word were a little slurry. 'Anyway, here goes.' She looked directly at Ronnie. 'Somethin' you don't know, miss, but I were born on a boat.'

'How exciting!'

Dora shook her head vehemently. 'No, it were somethin' to be ashamed of. Still is, outside boater folk.'

'I don't understand.'

'Boat folk are looked down upon as we don't speak la-di-da, and people who don't know any better think the boat families keep their boats filthy and their kiddies as well.'

'But Dolly's was spotless.'

Dora nodded. 'Yes, and most of 'em are. But there're just enough Rodneys – that's what we call the mucky lot – ter give everyone else a bad reputation.'

'I see.' All Ronnie could think of was how ignorant some people were.

'So where was I?' Dolly said, relighting her pipe. 'Oh, yes. The bit about me bein' born on a boat. I were taken in by another family as I were Ma's number thirteen kiddie and she couldn't cope. I were the final straw. I were only a baby so I didn't know no different and I always called them auntie and uncle. When I were older I crazed 'em ter send me ter school but we was always on the move, carryin' cargo and that. I just went to class here and there, most no more'n a few days at any one time. But I always wanted ter make somethin' of meself right from when I were still a kiddie.' She sucked in a breath and studied Ronnie. 'This is probably not very interestin'.'

'Oh, yes it is,' Ronnie said truthfully. 'I love hearing about your life.'

'Hmm,' Dora said, not sounding too sure. 'Well, when I were your age I met a lad—' Her dark eyes settled on Ronnie. 'I fell hook, line and sinker and he felt the same.' She paused a moment. 'He were a boater, too. And six weeks later he asked me to marry him.'

Ronnie gave Dora an encouraging smile, but deep down she knew this wasn't going to end well.

'Gosh, that was quick.'

Dora nodded and gave a small smile. 'O' course I said yes. We was that happy. We had the weddin' date fixed and I bought these shoes to go with a dress me friend lent me. I couldn't afford both things and I wanted them shoes so bad as soon as I saw 'em in the winder. The weddin' was only a week away when he said he had some news I weren't goin' to be too pleased about. He said he'd met a girl before him and me went a-courtin' and she told him she was up the duff.'

'What does that mean?' Ronnie said, puzzled.

'Bun in the oven – havin' a kiddie.' Dora's voice was impatient.

Ronnie gasped. This was worse than she imagined.

'What a shock for you.'

'Yes, it were. I knew how much he wanted kiddies 'cos he was an only one. We'd talked about havin' no more'n four so's they could be brung up decent and go to school, but now there's this girl sayin' she's havin' his kiddie.'

'Do you think he really *was* the father?' Ronnie said.

Dora nodded. 'No doubt about it. He said he wanted ter stay with me – keep ter the weddin', but I knew our happiness wouldn't last. He'd always regret givin' up his kiddie, no matter how many kiddies he and I might have. Maybe I wouldn't be able to have 'em. So I told him he'd have ter marry her and be quick about it. I made him promise not ter ever let her know he'd been about ter marry me, 'cos I didn't want her ter feel bad. It weren't her fault he'd met me.'

'What did he say?'

'He didn't like it but I could see he were relieved. So he said, "All right. I'll do it. But I'll always love yer, Dora, and never forget it." It fair broke my heart, it did.'

Ronnie felt tears pricking. She swallowed. 'Miss Dummitt, that's the saddest story I've ever heard. Do you think he kept to his word about not telling her?'

'Oh, yes.' Dora looked into the smoky distance. 'He never told her. And I know that fer a fact because she allus treats me like a friend. She's never suspected nothin' between the pair of us.'

Something clicked inside Ronnie's brain.

'It was Fred, wasn't it? Who you took me to meet – and Dolly – on Christmas Eve? He's the man you were in love with.'

Dora narrowed her eyes. 'And how might yer know that, miss?'

'I saw by the way he looked at you – several times. I realise now he still loves you.'

Dora smiled. 'And I him. But it in't no good, and it's no good harpin' on about it.' She took a few puffs on her pipe. 'Sad thing is, Dolly lost the kiddie so I coulda had him after all.'

She paused so long Ronnie thought Dora had come to the end.

'And that's the story of them shoes.' Dora stuck one foot out and turned it this way and that. 'Tonight's the first time I've wore 'em. It feels a bit funny but I'm glad I did. Sorta lays the thing to rest.'

'And you never met anyone else?'

Dora grunted. 'Oh, yes, I met someone else. But he weren't no Fred.' She glanced at her watch. 'We'd best be gettin' back to the other wenches. They'll be wonderin' what me and yous is yakking about.'

'I promise never to breathe a word of any of this to the others, or anyone else,' Ronnie said in a low voice.

'See that you don't, miss.' Dora regarded her for a few moments. 'Like I said . . . I don't tell no one my secrets but I feel better this evenin' than I have for quite a time, and that's a fact. But let it be a lesson to yer. Fred were a decent bloke but there's plenty out there that in't. And yer don't want ter get tied up with any of the bad boogers – like Will Drake, f'rinstance.'

'You've warned me about him before,' Ronnie said.

'See that you heed me, miss.'

No matter how Jess pumped her that night about the conversation, Ronnie kept to her word. But something had shifted between herself and Dora – she was sure of it. There was much more to the woman than she'd ever given her credit for. Dora, by losing Fred, had built a protective shell around herself to make sure no one ever came close to her again. What was so astounding was that the woman had poured out her secret to *her* – a trainee whom Ronnie had always thought Dora didn't even like.

Just shows how wrong you can be, Ronnie thought as she snuggled down in the bed she shared with Jess.

Chapter Thirty-One

Regent's Canal Dock, London
January 1944

Dora's relentless orders had lasted six weeks, but to Ronnie it felt more like six months. But a phantom six months where she had never felt so alive. She felt she was truly doing her bit for the war effort and enjoying every minute. They'd had to go all the way back to Camden Town to unload the coal at the A.B.C. bakery, and had made another round trip, this time to Birmingham to take fifty tons of steel bars.

'It's supposed to be six weeks of solid trainin',' Dora told them when Jess grumbled that they were supposed to have a break after the standard six weeks' training, 'but we lost all them days when we were iced in, so yous'll need at least another fortnight.'

Ronnie groaned inwardly.

'I think we're ready to go on our own,' Jessica said.

'*I'll* decide that one.' Dora's voice had a steely edge. 'I hadn't quite finished. Yous'll all get yer time off now. Ver-ron-eek, Sally and May first, and Jess and Angela when they come back. Be back the evenin' of day three.' She paused. 'Is that clear?'

Jessica's face dropped and she muttered something under her breath.

'Yer got something to say?' Dora demanded.

'Yes.' Jessica looked directly at the trainer. 'When we've finished training and are down to three in a team for the pair of boats, I'd like to work with either Ronnie and Sally, or Ronnie and May.'

Dora's eyes were slits. She glanced at Angela. 'Yer got a problem with Angela here?'

Ronnie was silent, her nerves on edge waiting for Dora's answer. Dora seemed to have forgotten that she'd been aggravated herself with Angela over the shoes.

'Let's just say I work well with any of the girls I've mentioned,' Jessica said. 'And I consider teamwork is vital in our work.'

'We'll see,' Dora said.

Ronnie noticed Angela threw Jess a furious look. Jessica simply hardened her jaw.

Thursday couldn't come quickly enough. Ronnie was almost counting the minutes.

'Promise you'll look after Lucky, Jess,' she said. 'She's really settled in well but she needs her food twice a day and some milk and water.'

'I'll see she doesn't starve,' Jessica said, 'but I'm not looking forward to the next three days living with Angela. She's a pain in the bum. But at least when *you're* here it's not quite so bad.'

'Lucky will take the sting out of it,' Ronnie said, chuckling, but grateful not to be left in Jessica's place. 'She's so funny. She always cheers me up.' She looked at her friend. 'You won't let anything happen to her, will you, Jess? She's had a horrible start in life already, poor little thing.'

'I'll try not to.'

'Jess . . .'

'You go and have a good break,' Jessica said. 'I'll take care of Lucky – and more to the point, I'll take care of bloody Angela.'

Ronnie grinned, satisfied. All she now had to face was Maman.

As Ronnie walked up the path to her front door, carrying a bag of washing they'd never had the space or time to do, she wondered if her mother would grumble at her daughter's appearance. She knew she looked dirty and dishevelled, that she was exhausted, but she felt like a different person inside. Stronger. Strangely healthier. And heaps more sure of herself. Would her mother recognise the changes?

'What on earth have you done to yourself?' Maman's tone was a mixture of disbelief and horror.

'It's dirty work, Maman,' Ronnie said, immediately deflated.

'For goodness' sake come in, child,' she said, practically dragging her daughter inside. 'I do not bear to have the neighbours see you in such a state.'

There was a sudden flurry and a tan and white animal flew from the sitting room into the hall and jumped up at Ronnie, licking her hand as she patted him. Still in her raincoat she knelt down and flung her arms round him.

'Oh, Rusty, it's so good to see you again. I've missed you so much.'

'Véronique, you will remove your coat which looks to need a good clean . . .' She glanced at Ronnie's feet. 'And take off those filthy boots. Then you will have a bath.'

Oh, the joy of soaking in hot water. Ronnie leaned back in the bath knowing she couldn't be too long with her mother wanting to grill her. Quickly, she changed into her heavenly clean skirt and jumper, rinsed her face and brushed her short curls. By the time she'd carried out her mother's instructions, hampered by Rusty who was close at her heels with every step, half an hour had passed. But now she was ready for Maman's inspection. Ronnie braced herself for a telling-off for taking too long.

'Maman—'

'Hush, *chérie.* You will have a cup of tea first and some *gâteau*.'

'You made it?' Ronnie said, more astonished at the image of her mother baking than at not being reprimanded.

'*Non.* Beatrice Mortimer made it and gave it to me yesterday. She said it was for when the girls are home. So you are home' her mother smiled, 'and we will try her cake. I will give her my opinion next time we meet.'

Her mother might have made the tea, unusual in itself, but she still sat elegantly, her legs together and slightly angled to the side, as she waited for her daughter to pour. Ronnie suppressed a smile. Yes, Maman had softened a little lately, but she still expected to be waited on. Not irritated in the least, Ronnie poured them both a cup and handed one to her mother.

'*Merci, chérie.* Now you will tell your *maman* that you have stopped this nonsense on the boats and have come home for always.'

'No,' Ronnie protested. 'It's not at all like that. It's not nonsense. I've finished my training and when I go back next week I'll be with two of the others and we'll be on our own, taking cargo to Birmingham and bringing stuff back. I'm a fully trained boatwoman,' she added with a note of pride.

Simone threw her hands in the air. 'I do not know what is 'appening with my daughters,' she said. 'They are not like me, their *maman*, at all. Not one. Not even my Suzanne.'

Ronnie burst out laughing. 'She's probably the closest,' she said. 'You both love music and . . .' She hesitated, trying to think of something else they had in common. 'Well, music is one of the important things you both share,' she finished, giving up.

'Yes, *chérie,* you are right.' Her mother smiled, seeming mollified, and taking a delicate bite of Mrs Mortimer's cake. 'Walnut and raisin. How, I wonder, did she manage to get such ingredients?'

'She probably already had them,' Ronnie said, not having a clue as to where Mrs Mortimer did her shopping. Nor did she particularly care, even though she liked James's mother very much, the little she'd met her. The cake was too good to worry about how it came to be made. To change the subject she said, 'Any idea when Raine and Suzy are coming home?'

'I believe you mean Lorraine and Suzanne,' her mother began, her eyes flashing with annoyance. 'Suzanne writes she will come home next month and Lorraine says she will try to come on her next days off – whenever that might be. And "try" is not good enough. It means I am second-best choice.' She drew her mouth into a disapproving line.

'Well, she probably wants to see Alec when she can,' Ronnie said. 'It can't be easy for them to meet very often when they're working different shifts in different camps.'

Though it would have been good to see her, she thought. She missed her sisters. Rusty gave a short bark as if to say, 'But I'm still here.' She bent down and kissed the top of his head. Something struck her. 'Maman, when I arrived Rusty came flying out of the front room.'

Simone had the grace to blush prettily. 'Sometimes I have him downstairs to give him a change.'

'Are you sure it's not that you want him for a bit of company?'

'Of course not,' her mother retorted.

'So it's all right with you if I take him back with me?'

'What are you talking about?'

'To the boats. Dogs are allowed. We see quite a few on the canals.'

'I do not think he would like life on the water,' Simone flashed. 'He is used to his home here.'

'It was just a thought, Maman,' Ronnie said, hiding a smile. Who would have thought it? Maman was actually calling the cottage Rusty's home!

For Ronnie the novelty of being home wore off quickly. If only Dora had given her more notice about the dates of her leave. As it was, there hadn't been time for her to phone Raine to ask her if she could manage a day off to coincide with her three days until she was already home. The line hadn't been very good, but she thought she heard Raine say she'd see what she could do. But her sister hadn't sounded very hopeful.

Ronnie sighed. Maman's company could be stifling. If it wasn't for Rusty she would have made some excuse to go back early. By the second day she thought she would scream with boredom, listening to Maman's gossip of the neighbours, how frumpy they looked, how difficult it was to shop with more and more items being rationed . . . She hardly showed any interest in what her daughter had been doing these past few weeks, simply repeating that she hoped Ronnie would change her mind and be sensible and find a job in Bromley.

Everywhere she went Maman wanted to accompany her.

'I'm going to see Mr Lincoln tomorrow,' Ronnie announced. To her delight Maman wrinkled her nose. There was no chance her mother would give the vet's a second visit.

'Ugh. He is a very nice man and I am sure very clever, but the smell in that place. I thought I would be sick. I cannot believe you worked there.'

'I didn't know you'd been to the vet's.'

'I took Rusty once as he kept whining. It drove me crazy.'

Yes, Ronnie gathered that from Mr Lincoln's letter but she knew better than to tell Maman he'd written. No, what was so strange was hearing her mother call him Rusty for the very first time instead of 'that dog'. She decided it would be prudent not to draw attention to it.

'Oh, what did Mr Lincoln say about him?'

Simone hesitated.

'Maman, what did he think was the matter?' Ronnie said impatiently.

Simone shrugged. 'Maybe he was missing you.'

'He seems to have settled now,' Ronnie said, twiddling his ears. He gazed up at her with his usual adoring look.

'We get along well enough,' Simone said. 'I make him behave. He is better that way.'

Rusty pricked up his ears and gave a loud bark. Then he rushed to the window, jumping up, his tail wagging madly.

'What is it, boy?' Ronnie said, going over to the window and pulling one side of the blackout curtains to expose an inch of the outside. It was already pitch-dark at only just gone four.

A figure stood on the doorstep but she couldn't make out the face under the umbrella. Someone collecting for charity, she thought, as she went to the front door, Rusty at her heels. She opened it to see her sister with her hand raised to the doorbell.

'Raine! How did you manage it?'

'Let me in – it's freezing out here.' Raine grinned as she folded the umbrella, shook it and came into the hallway. She tossed it into the umbrella stand and shrugged off her wet coat. 'You know, I think it's trying to snow.'

Ronnie flung her arms around her sister who squeezed her tightly in return before letting her go. 'How long have you got?'

Every moment was going to be precious.

'Back tomorrow after lunch,' Raine said, 'but I thought it was better than nothing. I managed to swap a day with someone who owed me a favour.' Rusty thrust his nose in her gloved hand. She peeled off her gloves and stuffed them in her coat pocket, then bent down, laughing, to pet him. 'Yes, I know you're there, Rusty. But just let me get myself sorted.'

'Tell whoever the other pilot is that I love her,' Ronnie beamed. 'You go through. I'll make some more tea. Maman's in the front room.' She dropped her voice. 'I can't believe this, Raine, but she's finally taken to Rusty. She doesn't want me to take him on the boat, though she won't actually come out and say it.'

'So what's she said to make you think that?' Raine laughed, patting the dog's head.

It was at that moment Ronnie gave a gasp of surprise. For on the finger of her sister's left hand was a ring she'd never seen before.

'Raine, is that what I think it is?'

Raine gave her infectious laugh and looked down at her hand. 'Probably. What do *you* think?'

'I think it's an engagement ring.'

'You're absolutely right, kiddo.'

'Why didn't you tell us?'

'It only happened the night before last. Alec and I went out for dinner and he popped the question in the restaurant. It was all very romantic in the candlelight.'

It shouldn't have been that unexpected, but somehow it sent the signal that her sister would one day leave the family to set up her own home with her husband. She was pleased for Raine but things wouldn't ever be the same again. She bit the inside of her lip.

'What did you say?'

'I said yes, you idiot.' Raine ruffled Ronnie's curls. 'And then I said, "Shall we have some champagne to celebrate?" So we did.'

Raine laughed, and even in the dim hallway Ronnie could see her sister's face alight with happiness. She mustn't ever let Raine know her own selfish thoughts. She must be happy for her. Goodness knew, Maman might not be that thrilled with her news. As though to verify the thought she heard her mother call.

'Who is at the door, Véronique?'

'Oh, just someone wanting to know an address,' Ronnie said, giving her sister a wink.

'There is a draught. Please shut the door.'

'I already have.'

Ronnie followed Raine into the front room, the excited dog rushing between their feet. She forgot all about making tea, she was so curious to see Maman's reaction to the engagement ring.

'Hello, Maman.'

'Lorraine, how nice to see you. We didn't expect you. Why did you not telephone me?'

'I didn't know it myself until a few hours ago. But here I am.'

Still seated, Simone turned her cheek for her daughter's kiss. Raine rolled her eyes towards Ronnie who had to bite her lip hard to stop a burst of laughter. Everything was wonderful now her sister was here and she was determined to make the most of it. They had something really lovely to celebrate in this interminable war.

Soon the three of them were drinking tea. Ronnie watched, amused to see Raine making sure her ring flashed under the weak light of the side table lamp.

'Lorraine, do I see you are wearing a new ring?'

'I am, Maman.'

'Allow me to look, please.'

Raine walked over to her mother's chair, holding out her left hand.

'This is an engagement ring.' Simone tilted her head to look up at her eldest daughter, then took Raine's hand to inspect the stone more closely.

'I suppose it must be,' Raine said, staring at it as though for the first time.

'Do not be sarcastic,' Simone admonished. 'It does not suit you.'

'I wasn't really.' Raine gave a short laugh. 'It's only that you stated the obvious, seeing as it's on the wedding ring finger.'

Simone peered down again. 'It is very pretty,' she said at last. 'But you know that emeralds are unlucky.'

'Not another one,' Raine muttered. A slight frown crept between her eyebrows. 'I love it. Don't you think it the most beautiful green?'

'It is – but diamonds are safer.'

'I didn't want safe diamonds,' Raine said, her voice on edge as it often was with Maman. 'Unless it's one like Suzy's gorgeous antique ring,' she added quickly. 'No, Maman, I wanted a risky emerald.'

'And you chose this yourself?' Simone asked.

'Yes, Maman, I actually chose it myself. Alec said I could have whatever ring I wanted.' Raine stared at Simone, challenging her to say more.

Ronnie's stomach clenched. Raine and Maman didn't get along that well at the best of times, but until now they seemed to have called a truce. Was it about to break? To defuse a possible argument, Ronnie was about to ask if anyone wanted more tea when the doorbell rang.

'Who is that now at this time of night?' Simone's voice was sharp with irritation. 'Send them away – whoever they are.'

'I'll get it,' Raine said, springing up.

Ronnie heard the door open, then a man's voice. It went on for a minute or two but she took little notice until Rusty started to growl. Perhaps she should go and see who it was. But before she could move she heard Raine say, 'You'd better come in.'

The front room door opened and Raine stood there, her face strangely pale as she stared at Ronnie.

And then Ronnie saw who was behind her: two policemen followed her sister into the front room. They quickly glanced round. She recognised the shorter man – she'd forgotten his name, but he was the same sergeant who'd come with Michael when they'd searched the boats that time. The other one, a constable, was tall and thin with eager eyes.

What on earth were they doing here?

The sergeant looked straight at Simone.

'Sorry to disturb you, madam, but we need to ask your daughter a few questions.'

Chapter Thirty-Two

'What is the meaning of this?' Simone demanded as her stare bounced off the two policemen, and then alighted on Raine. 'I suppose I must ask you the same question, Lorraine.'

'I think you'd better ask Ronnie, Maman,' Raine said quietly.

'*Véronique?* Is she in some sort of trouble?' Simone's voice rose. She stared at Ronnie.

'That is what we must find out,' the sergeant said, removing his cap. 'I'm Sergeant Sandford and this is Constable Butler of the Grand Union Canal Police. I previously met your daughter when she was working on the canal boats.'

'She still is,' Raine put in. 'So why do you think Ronnie has anything to say to the police?' Before waiting for an answer, she carried on, 'She's only seventeen. What can she possibly have to say that would be of any use to you?'

'Because we think she may be able to help us fill in some gaps in a case we're investigating,' Sergeant Sandford said. 'May we sit down?'

'I'll fetch another chair,' Ronnie said, jumping up, her mind racing. She grabbed a dining-room chair and carried it back to the front room, where the constable took it from her.

Don't say another girl has had an accident.

After the two policemen were seated, the sergeant fixed his gaze on Ronnie.

'I believe you know a William Drake?'

Ronnie's stomach lurched sickeningly. So *that* was it.

'Yes,' she said in a low voice, then forced herself to look directly at him. 'Has something happened to him? Has he had an accident?'

'One thing at a time, miss.'

'To whom is this person you are referring?' Simone interrupted, half rising from her chair and fixing her eyes on Ronnie.

'Just a boy I know.'

'How well do you know him?' asked Sergeant Sandford.

'That is something I would also very much like to know,' Simone interjected.

'Only slightly,' Ronnie said, the heat rising to her cheeks with Raine's and her mother's eyes upon her. 'He came to my rescue a couple of times when I was working on the boats.'

'Were they the only two occasions?'

Ronnie noticed the constable was scribbling in a notebook.

'No. Maybe twice more. But I've only known him since I began working on the canals.'

'And when was that?'

'In November.'

'The exact date?'

'The end of November.' In her nervousness she couldn't remember the exact day.

'And you work for the Grand Union Canal Carrying Company – is that right?'

'Yes.'

'And your trainer is Dora Dummitt?'

'Yes.'

'My sister has a right to know why she's being questioned like this,' Raine interrupted, and to Ronnie's surprise lit a cigarette. She wondered when Raine had started smoking again.

'All in good time,' the sergeant said firmly. 'Now, where were we? Ah, yes. And when he came to your rescue' – he emphasised the word – 'did you happen to notice his motorbike?'

'Of course,' Ronnie said. 'He gave me a lift on it and saved me from getting into trouble with Dora . . . I mean Miss Dummitt. I would've been late if it hadn't been for Will,' she added, hoping it would help him in whatever business the two policemen were here about. 'Please tell me what's the matter.'

'It appears he may be in trouble.'

'What sort of trouble?'

'Black-marketeering . . . theft . . . fraud.'

For a few seconds she couldn't say a word. Then she looked defiantly at the sergeant who was watching her closely. 'I don't think Will could be involved with anything like that at all,' she said. 'He's always been very gentlemanly to me.'

She hadn't forgotten the times he'd come to her rescue, and when he brought that box of food for them. Then the heat rushed to her cheeks as the memory of what had happened only minutes later flooded through her. He hadn't behaved exactly gentlemanly towards her then and Jessica had given her a lecture afterwards about her mistrust of him, calling him 'shady', and making her promise never to be alone with him.

Sergeant Sandford opened his leather bag and pulled out an object.

'Is this yours?' he said, holding out a camera.

'No,' Ronnie said. 'I don't own a camera.'

'And you've never seen this one before now? You're saying it doesn't belong to you?'

'I told you I've never seen it before, so it can't belong to me, can it?' She put her hands to her cheeks, now burning. They were going to think she was guilty. She wished she was anywhere but here in the front room with Maman looking so dismayed and Raine frowning.

'Do not be rude, Véronique,' Simone said. 'You have been brought up with good manners.' Her gaze fell on the camera. 'I can vouch for her. This is not my daughter's. She does not own a camera.'

'What made you think the camera belongs to my sister?' Raine said, blowing out a stream of cigarette smoke.

'Because we found it in her bicycle saddlebag.'

'My daughter's bicycle is here at home – safe and sound,' Simone said triumphantly. 'So you have made a mistake with her bicycle. The one you are talking about is not hers. If you do not believe then you may look in the shed. So the two things you accuse her of, you are wrong. You must interview others. It is obvious Véronique cannot be of any help with your investigations.'

'I am not accusing anybody,' the sergeant said. 'Merely enquiring.' He threw Ronnie a piercing look. 'Does the bicycle on the butty belong to you, Miss Linfoot?'

'Not exactly,' Ronnie said. 'It was Margaret's.'

'Margaret Webb – the young trainee you and Constable Scott found when she'd fallen in the canal?'

Ronnie's heart turned a somersault at the mention of Michael's name. She wished he was here instead of the tall thin one with a face devoid of expression.

'Yes. She died of pneumonia.'

'I heard about that.' The sergeant cleared his throat. 'Very bad business.'

It was more than that, Ronnie thought. Much more. But she couldn't say how upset she still was to these two men. It was best to stick to the facts.

'What happened to Margaret's bicycle?' Constable Butler asked.

Ronnie didn't look at him but kept her eye on Sergeant Sandford.

'Margaret's parents came soon after she died to collect her belongings. They said as I was the one who'd found her I should have her bicycle. But I've never felt it was truly mine and always let anyone else use it if there's a long walk to the next lock. And as far as the saddlebag is concerned, I've only ever kept a spare jumper in it.'

Something didn't feel right in this conversation. She felt the constable's eyes on her – as though he didn't believe a word she said and was determined to catch her out.

'What has all this to do with my daughter?' Simone said.

'Please allow your daughter to explain, Mrs Linfoot,' Sergeant Sandford said curtly.

'Why are you connecting Will Drake with the camera?' Ronnie asked. 'Anyone could have put it there.'

'We found this with the camera.' The constable handed her a creased piece of paper.

Ronnie opened it and read a scrawled message written in pencil.

To the boat wench who hert her head. Hope you like it. I put a film in so its reddy to use. W.D.

Ronnie's chest tightened. Why would he have given her a camera? It didn't make sense.

'We need to check the initials, but Will Drake is an obvious place to start.' Constable Butler's eyes seemed to pierce right through her.

'Let me look at that, Ronnie,' Raine demanded, holding out her hand. She peered at the badly spelt note, frowning. 'It doesn't even mention Ronnie by name,' she said, looking up, a triumphant expression in her eyes. 'He could have written this note to any of the trainees. As Ronnie said, the bike isn't officially hers anyway. All the girls borrow it. If the note is from this Will Drake, why aren't you questioning *him*?'

'We have to conduct our interviews in our own way,' the sergeant said curtly. He looked at Ronnie. 'I believe you had an accident and hit your head and had to go to the nurse. Is that correct?'

Ronnie didn't dare look at Maman. She just nodded.

'You have hurt your head and did not tell me?' Simone made as though to inspect Ronnie's head.

'Maman, calm down,' Raine said. 'You can see Ronnie's fine now.'

Simone shook her head, pursing her lips, but she sank back into her chair.

'It's an expensive camera,' the sergeant went on, 'and alerts us as to how or where he got the money to come by such an item. Are you aware of what he does for a living?'

'I don't know,' Ronnie said. 'Something to do with the boats, I suppose.'

'He rides an expensive motorbike – it might be an older model but it's the top make. How could he afford that on a boater's wages?' He gazed round the room as though looking for someone to provide the answer.

'Isn't there some kind of serial number you can use to trace the camera to see if it's part of stolen goods?' Raine asked in a challenging tone, drawing a last puff of her cigarette, then stubbing it out viciously.

'Yes, and that's what we intend to do' – Sergeant Sandford nodded to his colleague – 'but we needed to know the background as to why it's in your sister's possession.'

'I do not allow my daughters to accept expensive presents from boys,' Simone said firmly. 'And they know this rule. Véronique knows nothing about it. If this boy gave her this camera she will . . . would not accept it. I think I know my own daughter better than anyone.' She glanced over to the two policemen, her eyes flashing.

'My sister has never seen the camera before, as she's told you.' Raine sprang to her feet. 'So if you'll excuse us, I'm only on leave this evening and I'd like to spend it quietly with my mother and sister.'

'Yes – well, that'll be all . . . for the moment,' Sergeant Sandford said, emphasising the last three words as he looked at Ronnie. He stood and jerked his head to the constable.

They weren't going to let this go.

Ronnie was sure the two of them could hear the loud beating of her heart. Forcing herself not to show her alarm, and conscious of Maman's eyes upon her, she said, 'I'm sorry you had a wasted journey,' she said, more confident now they were going.

'Nothing is ever a waste,' Sergeant Sandford returned. 'Well, enjoy the rest of your time at home, though I expect you'll be going back to the boats soon, won't you?'

'I expect so,' she said. She wasn't going to give him any clue as to when she'd be returning.

He nodded briefly. Well, as far as she was concerned they could damned well see themselves out. But Raine sprang up.

'This way,' Ronnie heard her sister say as she escorted the two policemen out of the front door.

Raine came back, a serious expression on her face.

'Well, we could have done without that visit, I must say.'

Ronnie bit her lip. She felt drained now it was over. She turned to her mother who was sitting very still. How on earth was she going to explain it all to Maman and Raine? But what was there to explain? She was innocent. Well, innocent of any wrongdoings where cameras were concerned, but she knew Maman would closely question her on her friendship with someone who seemed to be mixed up in murky dealings.

'I'll go and make a fresh pot of tea,' she said with a false bravado she didn't feel. 'I'll go and make one.'

'I think you need to give your sister and me an explanation first,' Simone said, 'and how it is that you hit your head.'

'Let her make the tea, Maman,' Raine said. 'I'll go and help her.'

'And leave me to think bad things alone?' Simone said. 'No, we will all stay here and Véronique will give us the explanation.'

But Ronnie had already disappeared to the kitchen. She'd just boiled the kettle when Raine appeared at the doorway.

'It's going to take quite a bit of explaining, Ronnie,' she said. 'It sounds like you've got tied up with an unsavoury character.'

'That's all you know,' Ronnie flashed. 'I know he's not well educated but he's helped me when I needed it on the canal and he brought us a box of food when the boat was iced up and we couldn't get out to replenish our larder. But he never mentioned giving me something expensive like that camera. We're not going out together or anything, so I don't understand it.'

'So the note was definitely meant for you, then? And the camera?'

'I suppose so.' Ronnie looked at her sister, her lower lip trembling. 'But I *know* he hasn't done anything wrong.'

'Sorry, Ronnie, but you *don't* know,' Raine said. 'The police don't usually make such serious allegations if they haven't got proof.' She gave Ronnie a stern look. 'You haven't fallen in love with this boy, have you?'

'Don't be ridiculous,' Ronnie said. 'I'm not in love with anyone. He's just a friend.'

'Then why have you gone so red?' Raine demanded.

'Raine, please . . .' Ronnie made a sign towards the front room.

'We'll talk about it later,' Raine said. 'Meanwhile, for goodness' sake let's have that cup of tea.'

Five minutes later the three sat silently drinking their tea. Ronnie chewed a biscuit without really tasting it. Her mind flew in all directions. Was Will really involved in something crooked? If he wasn't and he'd really bought the camera for her with his own money, why had he risked putting it in her saddlebag where anyone could easily lift it out? Maybe he thought it wouldn't come to harm under Dora's beady eye. And what was worse, if he *had* stolen it, she'd be implicated. That's why the police were nosing around. She swallowed. The pair of them obviously suspected she was mixed up in something shady.

'Now, Véronique,' Simone began, as she put her cup down with such force it rattled in the saucer. 'You will start at the beginning and tell me all.'

'There's nothing to tell, Maman,' Ronnie said. 'Will Drake is a boy I've spoken to on about four occasions. He helped me a couple of times, once on one of the locks that was so heavy I couldn't move it. That was when I hit my head, but I didn't come to any harm.'

Simone's mouth tightened with annoyance. 'This is what I told you. It is men's work. I do not know what your father would say to all this.'

He would have calmed you down, Ronnie thought.

'And you have not seen the camera before?'

'No, Maman. I already told the police I've never seen it. Do you think I would lie to them?'

'Maman, for goodness' sake don't keep going over things we already know,' Raine said.

'And as for you, Lorraine, you will not smoke in the house. When did you begin this disgusting habit?'

'When Audrey was killed last year,' Raine said flatly. 'I only have the occasional one.'

'Oh, I remember. That was so awful.' Ronnie bit her lip. No matter how she tried not to think about it, to her mind her sister was still part of a highly risky organisation.

Simone stared at her eldest daughter. 'That poor girl is proof you are doing dangerous work. And she would not want you to smoke because of her.'

'Audrey smoked like a chimney,' Raine said with a short laugh. 'She'd have loved having a fellow smoker.'

'Do not talk lightly of the dead,' Simone snapped. She fixed her gaze on Ronnie. 'It was very nice of Margaret's parents to give you her bicycle. But if it is still on the boat, how did this boy know about this bicycle to put the camera in the bag?'

'I don't know,' Ronnie said, her voice shaking. 'Maybe he came to give it to me and I'd already gone, so Dora or one of the girls must've said to put it in the bag and I'd get it when I was back from my leave. . . Oh, I don't know – it must be something like that.' She burst into tears. 'I don't know anything about black-marketing or stolen goods. Will wouldn't give me anything that was stolen.'

Raine sprang up to put her arms round her sister.

'You can't be sure of that, Ronnie,' she said. 'But it's for the police to find out, and not for you to fret. But I would steer clear of this boy in the future.'

Ronnie pulled away from her sister in fury, tears streaming down her red mottled face. 'Don't you dare tell me who I should and shouldn't have for a friend. You've always been bossy with Suzy and me, especially me, just because I'm the youngest. Well, I'm sick and tired of it.' She leapt up. 'Come on, Rusty, I'm going to my room.'

She ran up the stairs, Rusty only just managing to pull his tail in before she slammed the door shut, then flung herself on her bed and sobbed her heart out.

Chapter Thirty-Three

'Ronnie.'

It was Raine shaking her awake.

'Come on and have supper. Maman's kept it simple. Baked potato topped with scrambled egg – all right, it's powdered, but I seem to remember you don't mind it.'

'I'm not hungry.' Ronnie's voice was muffled.

'You've got to face her sooner or later,' Raine said. 'And *me,* come to that. You know – your bossy sister.' She gave a chuckle as she sat on the bed beside her sister.

Ronnie emerged from the eiderdown.

'She'll go on and on at me.'

'No, she won't. I've told her not to mention anything more about Will Drake, cameras or bicycles, or the police. I told her *I* know you're telling the truth.'

'What did she say?'

'She said, "Véronique has never lied," so I said, "There you are, then. No more to be said." And she agreed.'

'If she sticks to it.' Ronnie gave a half smile. Then she remembered. 'Oh, Raine, I'm sorry I was so nasty to you. I was just—'

'Forget it,' Raine said. 'Having the police turn up unexpectedly in the evening is pretty nerve-wracking for anyone, I should think.'

'But you were so calm and collected.'

'All a front,' Raine laughed. 'With the help of a cigarette.'

'Did you really start smoking because of poor Audrey?'

Raine's laugh stopped abruptly. 'Yes. I have to admit it did shake me. She was a damned good pilot. There was low cloud that day which makes it very difficult to see where to land.' She paused. 'She was the first female pilot to die since I started and was such a character. She became a good friend.' Raine's eyes glistened with tears.

'Poor Raine. And poor Audrey. You know something, I'm sick of this war, even though we're hardly aware of it on the canals. But it's doing such terrible things to people.'

'I know.' Raine patted her arm. 'But your friend Margaret died and it was nothing to do with the war.'

'I thought that at first,' Ronnie said, 'but none of the trainees would even be taking the cargo up and down the canal if it wasn't for so many of the boatmen volunteering to join up. So indirectly it still comes down to the bloody war.'

'Try not to swear,' Raine said mildly. 'You don't want it to slip out in front of Maman. Anyway, splash your face with cold water and come down. I want to hear more about your job.' She rose to her feet. 'By the way, have you heard from Suzy lately?'

'Yes. She sounds as though she still enjoys her singing, doesn't she?'

'I bet she has some rough times in between,' Raine said sombrely. 'She's like me – doesn't let the family know the full story.'

Ronnie looked at her sister. Yes, she thought. Raine would hide anything awful until it was over. It was probably how the pilots all survived. She caught sight of Raine's engagement ring again.

'When are you planning to get married?' she asked in a small voice.

'I've got to help win a war yet,' Raine chuckled. 'And winning is not yet on the horizon – so to speak.'

'When do you think it'll be over?' Ronnie said anxiously.

'It's turning our way,' Raine said with conviction. She ruffled Ronnie's already dishevelled curls. 'It won't be long, I don't think, before we get that madman on the run.'

The house was quiet when Raine left after a quick cup of tea and slice of toast and jam the following morning.

'I didn't think you'd have to go this early,' Ronnie had grumbled.

'It's difficult at this time of the year to be sure of transport,' Raine said. 'I'd rather be too early.'

There'd been nothing more to say.

'Don't look so worried,' Raine said, giving her a hug at the bus stop. 'Rusty will keep you company until you go back this afternoon. And about that police visit – forget it. It's all routine to them. You're innocent, and they both know it.' She smiled and gave Ronnie a kiss. 'They'll be after Will Drake from now on. Meanwhile, don't get into any arguments with Maman. It's not worth it – you know how she likes to win!' She hugged Ronnie again. 'Don't forget to write.'

She was gone in a whirlwind.

Ronnie was thankful to say goodbye to her mother. Simone was looking subdued. At least she had kept to her word and not mentioned the police visit again. Rusty's eyes were doleful as Ronnie told him to be a good boy.

'Telephone me as soon as you arrive,' Simone called as Ronnie had just breathed a sigh of relief that the door would close behind her at any second.

She grimaced. Maman would never understand that she didn't have access to a telephone whenever she wanted.

'Thank God you're back.' Jessica swooped upon Ronnie as soon as she saw her walking along the towpath. 'It's been hell here.'

'What's happened?'

Raine had warned Ronnie not to bring up the black-marketing subject unless anyone else did. 'Someone will, there's no doubt about that,' her sister had said, 'but it will be interesting to hear from them first before you go spouting off – particularly with this Dora woman.'

Ronnie brought herself back to Jess who was regarding her with narrowed eyes.

'Surely you know.' Jessica took one of her bags. 'Didn't the police come and see you about the black-marketing racket? That sergeant who was here before, and a constable – but not our Michael Scott. They talked to all of us and I heard the sergeant ask where you were. Dora was obliged to give them your address. Did they turn up?'

'Oh, them,' Ronnie said, making her voice casual. 'They were just making a few enquiries.'

'From what you've told me about her, I bet your French mother threw a fit.'

'No, she didn't,' Ronnie said untruthfully. 'There was no reason for her to. I wasn't under any suspicion or anything.'

'Really?' Jessica's pencilled brows shot up. 'They showed us an expensive camera and asked us if we'd seen it before. We said no. Then they asked us who the bicycle belonged to and Dora casually told them we all used it, but Angela immediately said it was yours. They asked if we knew anyone with the initials W.D. and Angela chimed in again with "Will Drake, Ronnie's boyfriend".'

'She can't keep her mouth shut, can she?' Ronnie said bitterly. It all fell into place now.

'They implied the camera was stolen property and that as they found it in your bike's saddlebag it was in your possession.'

'I didn't possess it. I never even knew about it until yesterday when the police told me.'

'I believe you – thousands wouldn't,' Jessica chuckled. When Ronnie opened her mouth to protest, she said, 'Sorry, couldn't help that. I know you're not involved with anything crooked. But you already know how I feel about Will Drake.' She gave Ronnie a sharp look as though to ascertain her reaction, then shrugged. 'Well, I'd better warn you that Dora's looking for some answers. But that's the least of it. I can't stand living with bloody Angela. Thank God I can escape for a couple of days.'

'Is Lucky all right?' Ronnie asked, feeling awful she hadn't enquired before now.

'Yes, I've made sure of that – but Angela is making a meal out of sneezing every time Lucky brushes past her. She hasn't forgiven Deadly Dora for allowing Lucky to stay on board. I can't tell whether the sneezing is put on or not, and quite honestly, I don't care. Lucky's a dear little cat. I think I'd have gone even more crazy without her making me laugh.'

Immediately, Ronnie warmed to her friend. She'd been worried about leaving Lucky under Jess's care, but she needn't have. Jess obviously liked cats and had come up trumps.

As for that police visit, she would do as Raine said – forget it.

Chapter Thirty-Four

Ronnie decided that unless Dora brought up the subject of whether she'd had a visit from the police, she wouldn't mention it. Jessica and Angela disappeared for their short leave and Dora was busy giving some last instructions before the five trainees would take over their own boats in a fortnight's time. Ronnie gave an inward sigh of relief. She'd been worrying about nothing.

The two weeks fairly flew by and Ronnie couldn't believe it was now February. The snow had only just begun to melt and it was the last two days that Ronnie and the other girls would be working together with Dora.

Minutes later Dora put her head through the hatch.

'Both boats must be thoroughly cleaned inside and out terday before we split up,' she said. 'And I'll be doin' the inspection.'

Jessica groaned and Dora sent her a stern glance.

'Ver-ron-eek, you and Jess and Angela will keep with the same boats, and May and Sally will be goin' with me to another pair of boats where they'll meet the new member of the team – Laura McKay. She's a Scot, but she can't help it.' Dora roared with laughter.

Oh, no. They weren't going to be stuck with Angela from

now on, surely. Ronnie glanced at Jess. Would she say anything to Dora? To her surprise her friend simply stared ahead. She was probably right. Once Dora had made a decision there was no point in arguing.

Late that afternoon they tied up at Uxbridge.

'Any volunteers to pick up the post at the post office?' Dora asked as the six of them were squashed into *Persephone*'s cabin.

'I'll go,' Ronnie said immediately.

Several of the girls said they would be busy packing with the forthcoming move and as usual Angela didn't volunteer.

'Can yer find yer way, miss?' Dora said.

'Of course, Miss Dummitt. I shall quite enjoy it.'

'Don't make an expedition of it.' She gave a few puffs on her pipe. 'I expect yer back before dark.'

'I will be.'

Ronnie felt a little skip of excitement as she took Margaret's bicycle out of the cratch. An escape. And not having to listen to constant chit-chat. If only she had Rusty it would be perfect. How she missed him. He used to love their walks together.

'I've come to pick up the post for Miss Dora Dummitt,' Ronnie told the short balding man behind the counter. 'There might be some letters with other names on them,' she explained. 'We're working on the boats and are moored on the canal.'

'What names would they all be?' he said, peering myopically at her over the top of his spectacles.

'There's Jessica Hamilton-Bard and Sally—' She hesitated.

'I think you'd better write them all down, miss, so I don't make no mistake.' He handed her a scrap of paper.

Try as she would, she couldn't remember Sally's last name. In the end she just wrote Sally.

'I think it begins with "L",' she said apologetically. 'But I've got all the others. Oh, and me, of course.' She giggled as she wrote her own name and passed the slip over to him.

He looked at it and nodded. 'It might take me a while to get them all together,' he said.

The minutes ticked by. Ronnie tapped her foot impatiently. Where on earth was he? She looked at her watch. Quarter-past four. It'd be getting dark soon and she'd be in trouble. Oh, where was the man?

'Sorry to have kept you, miss, but there was quite a stack to check and tick off in the book that they'd now been collected.' He looked at her. 'Have you identification?'

Blow it. She'd forgotten to bring her letter to say she worked for the Grand Union.

'I'm sorry, I don't seem to have it.'

'Don't worry. You wouldn't know all them names and Miss Dummitt's if you wasn't who you say you are,' he chuckled, handing her a package. 'I've put them all together in here so they keep safe.'

She saw it was addressed to Miss Dummitt with 'To Be Collected' printed in large letters. How she longed to open it and see if there was anything for her, but she didn't dare. Thanking the clerk for his trouble, she stepped out of the building. As she feared, clouds had gathered and what had been a slight mist from the canal had got worse. It wasn't going to be such a pleasant cycle ride back.

Ronnie jumped down the steps into the cabin, surprised to see only Dora sitting at the fold-out table, puffing away on her revolting pipe.

Dora looked up. 'Have yer got the post, miss?'

'Yes, it's all here.' She handed Dora the package.

Dora immediately ripped it open and drew out a small

pile of envelopes held together with an elastic band. She held out the bundle.

'Sort out any for here,' she said, 'and I'll take the rest of 'em back ter the motor.'

Ronnie extracted two envelopes for herself, happy to see one from Suzy and one from her friend Lois, and also two for Jess. None for Angela.

'Where is everyone?' she asked.

'I told 'em I wanted a few minutes with yer on my own,' Dora said.

Now what?

'I never thought you'd make it as a boater,' Dora continued, 'you bein' so fresh-faced. But I don't hear no complaints when yer workin' in the freezin' cold, nor the work which is mucky and heavy, and no complaints neither from the other wenches – well, 'cept one.' She actually gave Ronnie one of her grins.

That'd be Angela. Ronnie felt her skin prickle.

'And I bin watchin' how yer carry out what I tell yer to do, and it's good enough fer me.'

Praise indeed, Ronnie thought, a warm glow stealing through her body.

'Thank you, Miss Dummitt—'

A loud banging on the side of the boat made Ronnie jump.

'Drat them girls. I told 'em I wanted a bit o' peace,' Dora grumbled. Ronnie hid a smile. It was usually the way Dora announced herself. Dora opened the hatch to a funnel of cold air. 'Oh, not again!'

'Sorry to disturb, ma'am. May I come in?'

Ronnie startled as a policeman stepped into the cabin. He removed his cap to reveal a shock of iron-grey hair and gave a short nod of acknowledgement to her. Dora glared at him.

'I'm gettin' a little tired of the police turnin' up night and day with no warnin',' she said, her voice sour. 'What's it this time, officer?'

'Inspector Jackson.' He showed his card. 'Are you Dora Dummitt?'

'*Miss* Dummitt, to you,' she flashed.

'I believe you're the trainer for the boatwomen.'

'What of it?'

'I'm enquiring after a Miss Linfoot.'

Dear God, not again.

Dora kept her attention on him. 'On what grounds are you enquirin' after her?'

'Suspicion of involvement in a black-marketing ring.'

'Nonsense.' Dora took a puff of her pipe. 'I know where my trainees are at all times and I can assure you, officer, they none of 'em have time ter be in black-marketin' rings neither any other rings. I work them too hard and too long – so it's impossible. Stealin' and sellin' stuff has bin goin' on long before these wenches arrived on the cut – and yer know it full well.'

He glanced at Ronnie, then back to Dora.

'Is this young lady Miss Veronica Linfoot by any chance?'

'I'm Véronique Linfoot, yes,' Ronnie cut in, annoyed with the anglicised version of her name. 'And I've already said all I know when the police came to my house.'

'Yes, I've read that report. But I'm not entirely satisfied. So I'd like you to come with me to the station to help with our enquiries. Just routine, you understand.'

'No, I don't understand at all.' Dora stood up indignantly, her pipe falling to the floor with the vehemence of her words. 'You don't need to be takin' her anywheres.'

'I'm afraid we do.' The inspector's tone was firm. 'It shouldn't take long.'

Ronnie swallowed hard, Sergeant Stanford's last words in front of Maman and Raine reverberating in her eardrums: *that'll be all – for the moment.* She forced herself to look him in the eye. 'I told the police all I know when they came to my house,' she repeated. 'You *can't* arrest me. I'm innocent.'

He put his hand up to silence her.

'I'm not arresting you – we just need you for further questioning.'

'No. I won't go. I haven't done anything.' Ronnie's mind flew in all directions, trying to take in what he was saying. 'Ask Constable Scott – he knows me. He knows I don't know anything about black-marketing or stolen goods or anything. He and Sergeant Sandford already came to see Miss Dummitt and all us girls and inspected the boats.' She blinked to stop herself from bursting into tears. 'Oh, please talk to Mi . . . Constable Scott.'

He looked at her. 'How old are you, miss?'

'Seventeen.'

'Then you'll need to be accompanied by an adult.' He turned to Dora. 'If you wouldn't mind going with her, Miss Dummitt, we'll be on our way.'

'*Now*?' Dora raised both bushy eyebrows.

'Yes. I have the car and we can get you there and back in no time.'

Dora puffed at her pipe, her head tilted, as though considering whether she should go or not.

'I could ask Jess,' Ronnie said in a small voice, dreading Dora going with her.

'Jess?' Dora glared down at her. 'She in't your trainer. No, miss, I'm the one ter go with you. It in't no use to be arguin'. We need to get this cleared up once and fer all so's we can let go termorrer mornin' for Bull's Bridge. So we best be on our way.'

At least she kept her ear to the ground, Ronnie consoled herself, and always knew what was going on along the canals. And Deadly Dora wasn't intimidated by anyone – least of all the police.

Ronnie sat with Dora, her chin buried in her scarf, in the back seat of the police car. At least it was warm. At the request of the inspector, Dora had put her pipe out and was fidgeting with her hair, grasping one stray yellow curl, then another, and pushing them back under her cloth cap. Every so often Ronnie gave her a sideways glance but Dora stared straight ahead, her mouth moving as though still puffing on her pipe.

Ronnie felt a cold sweat seeping into her vest as she thought of the two of them in an interview room and tried to cling on to the fact that they had nothing on her. She hadn't done anything. But had Will?

In a daze she gave her name at the counter and followed the inspector and Dora along a short dark corridor. He opened a door at the far end and gestured for Dora to go in.

'Ah, Miss Dummitt. Please take a seat.'

That was Michael's voice! Ronnie's heart soared. Everything would be all right. He would explain everything and get this mess sorted out.

She stepped into a room no bigger than their front room at home. She noticed the blackout curtains had already been pulled, and a solitary bulb hanging from the ceiling wasn't giving out much light. The room was bare of any niceties. A steel filing cabinet stood like a sentry at one side of the door, there were a couple of overhead cupboards and a few hardback chairs scattered around a large central table.

Michael came towards her. 'Miss Linfoot, would you like to sit by Miss Dummitt?'

She gave him a half smile but there was no smile in return. Not even a hint. For a moment she was dumbstruck. Then she realised. Of course he couldn't allow himself to show any kind of favouritism. He was on official duty and wouldn't want it to be known that they had shared something much more than a few routine conversations. She took a deep breath.

Inspector Jackson nodded to Michael to be seated, then took the fourth chair. He began to shuffle some papers, then looked across the table at Dora.

'May I have your full name, Miss Dummitt?'

'Dora Edith Maisie Gladys Dummitt.'

'Have you ever been known by any other name?'

'Them's enough names fer anyone, I reckon,' Dora said, with a wry twist of her lips.

'Dora Edith Maisie—' The inspector spoke the names as he began to write, then looked up. 'What was that last one?'

'Gladys.'

'Oh, yes. Dora Edith Maisie Gladys Dummitt. You're sure that's it?'

Dora threw the inspector a frosty look. 'I oughta be sure of me own names, though what that's got ter do with you, or Ver-ron-eek, I can't imagine.' She fumbled in her bag and extracted her pipe.

'I'm sorry, Miss Dummitt, it's no smoking in the interview room,' Michael said, sounding apologetic.

Dora rolled her eyes and tutted but put the pipe back in her bag.

'We've called Miss Linfoot in for some further questioning, Miss Dummitt, about this black-marketing ring, and in particular, her relationship with William Drake, but I'll get back to you in a few moments.'

Dora's eyes flew wide. 'So that's what this is all about,' she said. 'That young rogue, Will Drake.' She glared at both policemen. 'Well, Ver-ron-eek here don't have nothin' ter do with him.'

Ronnie didn't dare look at Michael. How embarrassing that he was sitting opposite, his eyes intently watching her.

'Go ahead, Miss Linfoot,' the inspector said.

'I-um-I don't know what you mean.'

'How well do you know William Drake?'

'Not very well.'

'How often have you met him?'

'I don't meet him,' Ronnie said indignantly. 'I've just bumped into him a few times, but only since I've been training on the boats. Miss Dummitt will verify it.'

Out of the corner of her eye, Ronnie saw Dora's features harden and her hands grip the sides of the chair.

'Is that correct, Miss Dummitt?'

Dora nodded. 'She wouldn'ta known him before then – I can vouch for that.'

'How can you be so certain?'

'She don't mix with his sort. She's from a good family and they in't from this neck of the woods.'

'What did you talk about on the occasions when you "bumped into him"?' the inspector said, looking at Ronnie and emphasising the bumping in.

'He helped me prepare one of the locks once, and he gave me a lift on his motorbike when I went to the village shop one morning and was running late.'

'Is that all?'

'He brought us food the other day – not just for me but for all of us. It was very thoughtful of him.'

'Were there any luxury foods that you never see now in the grocery shops?'

She swallowed. Mustn't mention the bacon and marmalade.

After all, they'd all enjoyed the unexpected treats even though Jess remained suspicious as to how he came by them.

'I didn't notice anything.'

'Cigarettes?'

'No.'

'Hmm.' The inspector stroked his jaw. 'But he regarded you as his girlfriend, did he not?'

'No, I didn't say that,' Ronnie blurted, her face getting hot. Michael was staring at her as though he could tell the way Will had kissed her that time.

'And he never mentioned he could get you items such as stockings?'

You let me know if you want some nylons. It's not just the Yanks that can get 'em.

Ronnie bit her lip hard.

'Well?' The inspector's eyes bored into hers.

'I think he did mention something once about stockings but I just laughed and said where would I wear them when I'm working on the canals all day.'

'I see.' The inspector rose and went to the cupboard. 'And you say you've never seen this camera found in the saddlebag of your bicycle?' He set it in front of her.

'No, I'd never seen it before until Sergeant Sandford showed it to me when I was at home.'

'That's correct,' Michael said. 'It was all in the report, sir.'

'I know. I have it here,' the inspector said impatiently. 'But the note tucked in with the camera and initialled W.D. sounds to me as though young Will thinks of you as his girlfriend.'

'Well, I'm not,' Ronnie snapped. 'I've never even been on a date with him and he'll tell you the same.'

Don't look at Michael even though he's watching me.

'We've already spoken to him,' Inspector Jackson said.

Ronnie saw Dora's back stiffen.

'He said he bought the camera and wanted to give it to you but you were away, and one of the trainees told him to just leave it in your saddlebag.' He paused. 'I think that makes you his girlfriend, doesn't it? Giving someone an expensive camera looks to me like he knows you quite well – even knows you're interested in photography. Doesn't that prove he considers you his girlfriend?'

Ronnie shook her head.

'He said you'd asked for a camera . . . for your birthday.'

She stiffened. 'I said nothing of the kind.'

Why had he lied?

'The camera was part of a haul of stolen goods,' the inspector said, 'and Will Drake has admitted he stole several of the items along with the camera. He had to confess. We had more than enough evidence.'

Shock waves bounced up and down Ronnie's spine. Will was a common criminal. She shifted in the hard chair and gave Michael a surreptitious glance. He was scribbling in a notebook. Well, the inspector had certainly made it clear Will was not to be trusted. Her glance strayed towards Michael's mouth. She fancied she could still feel the touch of his lips when he'd kissed her after the dance and told her she was beautiful. And now their next meeting was taking place in this horrible room. And he wasn't saying anything to stick up for her.

The inspector looked across at Dora. 'Not only were the goods stolen but we also have evidence he's mixed up in this black-marketing ring and we want to know who else is involved. It's not a pleasant situation for a young girl to be in so I'd be grateful, Miss Dummitt, if you'd answer a few questions.'

Dora looked back without blinking.

The inspector cleared his throat. 'Miss Dummitt. I believe you know Will Drake. Is that correct?'

'I've seen him around, same's I have all the other boat folk.' Dora's tone was curt.

'But he doesn't work on the boats, so how is it that you know him?'

Dora's expression was stony.

The inspector waited. 'Miss Dummitt?' He paused, then said very deliberately, 'Or do I mean Mrs Drake?'

Chapter Thirty-Five

The room fell into shocked silence. Her jaw slack, Ronnie twisted her head to look at Dora.

Mrs Drake? Good gracious – Dora must be Will's auntie!

'Is that correct?' the inspector demanded. 'You're Mrs Drake, are you not?'

Dora stared at him. 'Yes,' she stated loud and clear.

'And you are Will Drake's mother?'

Ronnie almost fell off her chair. *Will's mother*! *It couldn't be. No one looked or acted less like a mother than Dora.* She felt Michael's gaze on her as though to see how she was taking this news. There was another pause. Then Dora answered.

'That's it.'

'You are confirming William Drake is your son? Please answer yes or no.'

'I told yer, didn't I?'

'And his father is Leonard Drake? Is that correct?'

'It looks like it, don't it?'

The inspector gave a deep sigh. 'And are you in contact with Mr Drake?'

Dora's head jerked. '*Him*,' she spat. 'I haven't a clue where he is. We in't no longer wed, s'far as I'm concerned. He never was no cop—' She broke off with a snort. 'Sorry, that sounds funny sayin' that in a police station. Anyway,' she went on, 'he were always in and out of jail. Treated me like dirt once he got what he wanted. Lied ter get his own way. Bullied me if he didn't. And Will's off the same block as the old man – goin' exactly the same way. Never would listen ter me. In and out of reform school from eleven. I couldn't never control him. At fourteen he were as tall as any man, always stealin' from my purse, mixin' with a load o' bad uns, breakin' inter houses and worse. When I threatened ter go ter the police he hit me.'

Ronnie gasped.

'The second time he did it he put me in hospital. That were when I told him he weren't no son of mine and I didn't care if I never set eyes on him again.' Dora blew out her cheeks. 'No wonder the name "Drake" turns my stomach.'

She looked at the two policemen. 'But I can tell yer for a start, Ver-ron-eek here is innocent. She in't involved in no black-marking, nor stolen goods, nor nothin' like it. Yer barkin' up the wrong tree.' She took out her pipe again. 'I'm lightin' up, so don't go saying it's agin the rules. I need this for me nerves.'

Ronnie saw the inspector give a slight nod to Michael who produced a lighter.

Dora shook her head. 'No, I'll use me matches, if yer don't mind. The lighter'll burn the baccy.' She struck a match and lit it, then gave a few puffs to get it going. 'That's better – so where was we? Oh, yes. No, Ver-ron-eek in't done no receivin' of stolen goods, nor nothin' like.' She scowled at the two policemen. 'And don't go pinnin' nothin' on me neither. I've always bin as straight as a bloody pub dart. Len Drake put me in jail for twelve months in my young days when I were blinkered about him, him tellin' the cops I were his accomplice even though I had nothin' to do with his bleedin' crooked deals. Never mind that I already had a kiddie – that were Will. I were lucky my friend Dolly took him in. I tell you somethin',' – she sent the inspector a fierce look – 'I never want ter see the inside of that miserable place again so I won't be riskin' *my* skin ter be locked up at the King's pleasure.'

By now, Dora's face was red with fury and frustration.

Inspector Jackson nodded. 'I believe we have all the information we need,' he said, putting a hand lightly on Dora's shoulder, which to Ronnie's admiration she promptly shook off. 'Constable, take Miss Dummitt and Miss Linfoot back to the boats.'

'So yer sayin' we're free ter go, Inspector?'

'You are.'

'That were quick.' Dora narrowed her eyes at him. 'Seems yer knew all along all the answers to them questions.'

Inspector Jackson actually broke into a half smile. 'Perhaps we did, but we have to make certain,' he said, turning to Michael who'd risen to his feet. 'You've got William Drake's report, Constable?'

'Yes, it's here.' Michael handed him a sheaf of papers.

The inspector grimaced. 'Good. We'll charge him. It'll be his third time in his short life.'

Dora walked out of the room, her chin high, Ronnie following, not allowing her eyes to stray one second to Michael who was holding open the door, her mind too desperate to take in all that had transpired at the station just now.

What a shock, Dora being Will's mother. The father sounded a dreadful man and Will didn't sound much better. No wonder Dora never acknowledged him as her son. Poor Dora. Thank goodness Dolly had been such a good friend to her.

Will. Ronnie briefly shut her eyes, ashamed of how foolish she'd been over him, sticking up for him even when Jess had told her bluntly never to be alone with him, and Dora had specifically warned her to stay away. Dora knew only too well that he would let her down. And so he had – telling such an outright lie which might have been enough to send her to some sort of reform place herself. She shuddered. Why? What did he have against her? He was the first boy ever to kiss her. That first time had been swift and cheeky, but it had stayed with her, and she'd built him up to something more than he was. But that second kiss . . . She felt her cheeks flame, recalling how shocked she'd been, tearing herself out of his embrace. That must be it. He was angry that she'd acted like a baby.

But she hadn't been a baby when Michael kissed her. For the first time in her life she'd felt like a woman. His kiss hadn't ended like that one of Will's at all. Michael's was tender and full of affection – or so she'd thought. And she'd instinctively returned his kiss. But the few times he'd spoken in the interview room, he hadn't directed anything whatsoever to her. She could feel a spark of resentment within her, building to something like rage.

Outside, he'd made sure she and Dora were safely in the rear seat before he got into the driver's seat, though he didn't say a word.

Ronnie watched as Michael removed his helmet and laid it on the spare front seat, then started the engine. Sitting immediately behind him, Ronnie could study the back of his head without Dora realising. His nut-brown hair was shiny clean, and she couldn't help noticing his ears were a good shape and lay close to his head. Angrily, she drew herself up. She had no business thinking such things. He couldn't have made it plainer that their dance was something of the moment and now he'd dismissed it. No doubt he'd had a few drinks that evening which would have put him in a rosy mood. He was probably courting Penelope by now.

That thought made her cringe.

As though he'd tapped into her head, Michael twisted his neck round, startling her.

'Are you all right in the back?' He glanced at Dora but his gaze lingered on Ronnie.

Ronnie's mouth was too dry to answer.

'Yes,' Dora said tersely. 'All I want ter do now is get back ter the boats and finish my pipe.'

'I'll get you there in no time,' he said.

True to his word, he pulled up on the slushy road as close as he could to the towpath, then nipped out and opened the rear door.

'Thank you, officer,' Dora said, climbing out of the back of the police car. She looked at Ronnie and frowned as though battling with herself. 'Yous'd better ask the officer in fer a cup of brew, miss.'

'I'd like that very much,' Michael said quickly, as though to pre-empt any argument from Ronnie.

But the thought of her and Michael cramped into the small cabin under the curious stares of Jess and Angela filled Ronnie with alarm, especially the way she felt about him now. But there was nothing she could do.

Dora gave Michael a stern look. 'Don't keep her long, mind. I've got plenty of work ter get through.'

'I won't,' he said, and followed Ronnie to *Penelope*.

He put his hand out for Ronnie to climb over the towpath onto the deck but she pretended not to see it.

Only Lucky looked up as Ronnie dropped into the cabin, thankful neither Jess nor Angela were there. She stroked the little cat's head and told her she was a good girl, then filled the kettle to make the tea, all the while conscious of Michael close behind her, stroking Lucky's ears, making her purr.

'How much sugar?' she asked as she set a mug of tea in front of him with a clatter. A little spilt over the edge.

He shook his head. 'None, thanks. I gave it up when rationing started.' He took a sip of tea, then put the mug down. 'Ronnie, I'm sorry I had to treat you so formally at the station.'

'You could've given me some sort of sign that you were sorry to see me there, at least,' she flashed. 'Why didn't you?'

'I couldn't risk it. Inspector Jackson has eyes in the back of his head. He already suspects I know you a little more than in routine police work, so I knew I'd have to be extra careful.' He hesitated. 'The thing is . . . I knew you were being used.'

Ronnie's back stiffened. 'What do you mean?'

'When he asked you to go with him to the station to help with further enquiries it was Dora he *really* wanted to interrogate – not you. He knew you were underage and it was natural that she'd go with you. Then she'd confirm what we already suspected about Will, but we needed her to admit the relationship and that she wasn't going to cover up for him. Jackson was convinced that Dora knew about the kind of rackets her son was in, though we had no evidence, but he wanted to scare her into thinking she'd be dragged into Will's criminal activities, which would be the last thing she'd want. He knew she'd already spent time in jail.'

'So why was I there if the inspector knew I was innocent?'

Michael cleared his throat. 'So you'd be right in front of Dora. She'd have to look you in the eye – a frightened girl – and he hoped she'd have enough decency not to drag you into this mess and would come out with the truth.'

Ronnie swallowed hard.

'So the police used me as a pawn?'

'If you put it like that – yes.'

A fury as she'd never known shot through her body. She stared at him without blinking. This was far worse than she'd imagined. How could he sit there and tell her Inspector Jackson's twisted plan in this calm way? Why the hell hadn't he warned her?

'Ronnie, what is it?' He tried to pick up her hand but she snatched it away.

'Leave me alone!' she rounded on him, her eyes blazing. 'Do you realise what you've put me through? Thinking I was going to have to ring my mother and sisters and tell them I'd been *detained* in a *police station* . . .' Tears streamed down her cheeks. 'Then face court and maybe even a prison sentence? I was petrified that's what they'd do to me. And all the time you knew.'

'That would never have happened—' Michael started.

She put her head in her hands, the tears spilling through her fingers. She felt Michael's hand on her shoulder and jerked her head up.

'Just go!' she shouted. 'I never want to see you again!'

She heard him give a heavy sigh.

'If that's what you really want, but you might let me explain—'

She sprang up to face him. 'You've already given me an explanation. It wasn't good enough.'

He nodded. She turned her back and heard the hatch slide open, then close.

The only sound was Lucky, still purring contentedly on her cushion.

Chapter Thirty-Six

'What's the matter, Ronnie?' Jessica immediately asked when she and Angela came through the hatch.

'Nothing.' Ronnie pushed back her curls and gave Jessica a wan smile.

'Something or someone's made your eyes all red and puffy.'

Ronnie sent her a warning look. She didn't want to discuss anything in front of Angela.

'Why've you two been gone such a long time?' Angela demanded. She narrowed her eyes. 'Miss Dummitt was very mysterious just now, but said you had the post.' Her gaze darted to the table and she pounced on the package and shook out the individual envelopes.

'I suppose you've already helped yourself to yours,' she said. 'Never mind the rest of us.'

'Oh, do shut up, Angela,' Jessica said irritably, turning to Ronnie. 'Was there anything for me?'

'Yes, a couple,' Ronnie said, keeping her eye on Angela who was looking through the post again.

'Here are yours, Jessica,' Angela said curtly, pushing the two envelopes into Jessica's hand. 'I'd better take these over to the others. They've been waiting ages.'

She disappeared through the hatch.

'Good riddance,' Jessica said. 'I really can't stand that woman. I think I'll have to speak to Dora again about swapping.'

'Don't you go and leave me with her,' Ronnie said.

'I don't mean that,' Jessica grinned. 'I mean swap *her* for a nicer model.'

Ronnie forced a smile.

'I know it's way past teatime but I'm putting the kettle on.' She gave Ronnie a sharp glance. 'You look all done in. Have you had one this afternoon?'

'No, I'm dying for one.'

'Coming up.'

Ronnie ripped open the letter from her sister. She pulled out a sheet of paper, written in Suzanne's neat hand on both sides.

Dearest Ronnie,

I hope this finds you well and they're not working you too hard. It was such a shame I couldn't see you when you had a few days at home but by the time I'd got there I'd have to turn round and go back again. I'm longing to hear about your adventures on the boats and if you've really taken to it. Also what the other girls are like. Do you all get along nicely with one another?

Maman told me something rather worrying in her last letter. She said the police came when you were home, asking questions about stolen goods and cameras. What was that all about? She sounded very upset.

Ronnie bit her lip. Not half so upset as she'd be if she'd known about this afternoon. She was determined never to let her know such an interview had taken place. She read on.

Anyway, I expect it was simply routine but do be careful, Ronnie. You can be a bit headstrong sometimes!

Ronnie lifted her chin. She turned over the page.

I've had an awful cold – it might have been flu – and was laid up all last week. Throat so sore I could only croak. But I'm feeling a lot better now and can't wait to get back to the troops. I miss it now when I don't sing. Isn't that amazing? I do miss my violin as well but I shall take it up again when this is all over.

Well, I suppose I'd better end this. I shall be singing to the boys tonight for the first time since the cold so wish me luck.

Hope it's not too long before the three of us all meet again – the boys now ask me to sing that Vera Lynn song at every concert. I must say it gives me hope as well as the soldiers. I'm thinking of you and Raine much of the time. Remember when things get you down to keep that determined chin up, Ronnie. You're doing an important job that many girls would never be able to tackle!

Much love,

Suzy XX

Ronnie skimmed it again before folding it up and putting it back in the envelope. Her sister's lovely letter had come at exactly the right moment.

She opened the one from Lois.

Hello Ronnie,

You'll never guess. I've joined the WAAFs!! Me. Lois Park. Can you believe it? I realised I had to do something before I was forced into one of the services I didn't want. And as the boys in the RAF look so dashing in their uniforms, I thought that was the one to be in. I start training on Wednesday, so hope you get this letter. In my next one I'll tell you all about it – if I'm allowed!

How are you taking to life on the canals? I don't know any girl who's doing that. Trust you to do something different! Not a very easy place to meet boys though, I shouldn't think. But you never were one to bother about them anyway, so you probably haven't even noticed, haha.

Sorry this is short but I'm in a whirl with packing and saying goodbye to everyone. Don't know where I'll be based so don't bother to answer this until I let you know.

Love and XX

Lois

Ronnie gave a wry smile. Trust Lois to go for what she considered the most glamorous uniform on the men. She shrugged. Lois had already had at least three boyfriends to her none at all. Had her friend learnt anything about boys in that time? Had *she*? Ronnie chewed her lip as she thought of Will. Why had she been so attracted to him? On appearance, or in his speech, he would *never* have met Maman's approval – or Raine and Suzy's. But on those occasions when she'd needed help he'd been there. Surely then, it was what people *did* that mattered. Judging a person by their appearance and the way they spoke was acting like a snob. But Will had spoilt it all by lying.

She gritted her teeth. She was just about to ask Jess's advice when Angela came back, looking on as though she'd just sucked a lemon. Well, it was too bad. The question was burning her.

'Jess?'

'What, Ronnie?'

'When a boy kisses a girl, is it normal that they put their tongue in her mouth?'

Ronnie heard Angela's breath hiss.

'It's vulgar.' Angela practically spat the word. 'No well-brought-up boy – or man – would do something like that.'

'I'll explain,' Jessica said firmly. 'If a boy does it against your will, then it's not nice at all. He's forcing himself on you and is working himself up and wants to go to the next step. And you know what I mean by that?'

'Course I do,' Ronnie stuttered, feeling her cheeks go hot.

'So he feels annoyed if she rejects his advances, as he realises he's not going to get his own way with her. But if the two people love each other, it's absolutely right – in fact, it's wonderful because they've both consented.'

'I don't want to listen to any more of this disgusting conversation,' Angela said. 'I'm going back to the motor. Maybe it will all be over when I come back for supper.'

Jessica burst out laughing. 'I'm only giving her a bit extra of the facts of life,' she said. 'She's such a little innocent.' She looked at Ronnie. 'Because we're talking about *you*, aren't we, Ronnie?'

'And Will,' Angela threw over her shoulder as she slid back the hatch, 'if his disgraceful behaviour when he brought the box of food that time is anything to go by.'

'Angela's right on this occasion,' Jessica said. 'I could tell by his expression he didn't like being pushed away.'

Ronnie was silent. That's why he'd lied. He was getting back at her for pulling away from that kiss, at first thrilling, then turning into something she now admitted she'd found repulsive. She waited until Angela had disappeared. She had to tell someone what had happened this afternoon in the police station – about Will, and Michael's strange behaviour – at least she could trust Jess not to let it go further.

'I must say I'm not surprised at Will.' Jessica poured more tea into Ronnie's mug. 'I tried to warn you about him, if you remember.'

'But he brought those boxes of food for all of us,' Ronnie protested. 'He paid out of his own money. It was such a generous thing to do.'

'Ronnie, he didn't.'

'What do you mean? You saw him come in with it. And his friend took another one to the others.'

'Yes, physically he brought them. But he didn't pay for them with his own money.'

Ronnie stared. 'Who did, then?'

'Don't you remember I gave him a pound?'

'Oh, yes, I'd forgotten.'

'And then, of course, Dora.'

'What did *she* do?'

'Sally saw her hand over some money to both of them as they were leaving.' Jessica's mouth tightened. 'She didn't know I'd already paid Will and the little beggar took it. So he got paid twice. I wouldn't call that a thoughtful gesture – I'd call it downright stealing.' She threw Ronnie a firm look. 'And I was never happy about the marmalade and the coffee. That would have cost an arm and a leg – if you could get your hands on it, that is. And if you did, it would more than likely come from black-marketing practices.'

Ronnie swallowed. She wouldn't mention the stockings. Jess would pounce on it as evidence Will was mixed up in shady dealings. How could she have been so stupid?

'From what you told me at the station this afternoon, Dora wants to discourage any connection with him, particularly where the police are involved. But blood's thicker than water and there's a bond between a mother and . . .' Jessica's voice shook. A tear ran down her cheek and she quickly brushed it away.

Ronnie glanced at her, concerned. Why was Jess so upset?

Jessica pressed her lips together, then without meeting Ronnie's eye, she repeated, 'There's a bond between a mother and her son that's difficult to break.'

A terrible thought struck Ronnie. 'Jess . . . did you . . . have you—?'

'Yes. I had a baby – a little boy.'

Ronnie sprang up and put her arm round her friend. 'Oh, Jess, what happened to him?'

'I had to put him up for adoption.' Jessica bit her lip hard. 'He was so beautiful. Hair the colour of corn and liquid blue eyes. The spitting image of his father. I was only allowed to keep him for six weeks. But that was enough. I loved him to bits.' Her voice wobbled.

'Was . . . is the father the married man you were in love with?'

'Yes. I don't want to go into it, but I'd hate anything similar to happen to you. There's a part of my heart that will never heal.' Jessica gazed at Ronnie. 'I'd understand if you were furious with Will, but I don't understand it where Michael's concerned.'

'Because he didn't stick up for me. I'll never forgive him.'

'Ronnie, he has a career to think about so he daren't argue. He might be up for promotion and has to keep his nose clean.'

'So his promotion comes before an innocent person who's supposed to be a friend gets convicted?'

'No, I'm not saying that. But what do you think would have happened if Michael had tried to intervene? Do you think his sergeant would say, "Oh, all right, Constable, I'll listen to you even though you're way below me in rank. Yes, we'll forgo our plan to trap Will Drake." Jessica sent her a stern look. 'Of *course* he wouldn't. This is the real world, Ronnie, and you need to grow up.'

Ronnie knew her face had turned bright red. But not with guilt. With anger that Jess should be talking like this to her. She was terribly sorry about Jess and her baby, but . . .

'I don't mean to sound harsh, Ronnie,' Jessica went on. 'You've had a ghastly day. But you turned your anger onto the wrong man. Poor Michael. And he *did* apologise to you afterwards. He's as genuine as they come – and he likes you so much. Anyone with half an eye can see it. And if I'm not mistaken it goes deeper than that. I'd say he's head-over-heels in love with you.'

'Don't be ridiculous.'

Why did her heart just now do a funny little somersault?

'I'm not,' Jessica said. 'I'm older than you, that's all. But even if he wasn't in love with you, you still never gave the poor bloke the chance to explain. To defend himself from your accusations. You acted like a kid instead of a grown-up woman. I'm disappointed in you.' She got up and cleared the table. 'I don't want us to fall out over this so let's forget it and I'll go and finish supper.'

'Can I do anything?'

'No,' Jessica answered shortly. 'I'm better doing it on my own.'

Ronnie gave a heavy sigh as she slumped on the plank seat. If only she could put Rusty on a lead and take him for a walk on her own and think about all that Jess had said. Not allowing Michael to have his proper say. And her own muddled angry thoughts. Being away from people is how she'd always tried to work things out in the past. But she was here in a cramped boat, rarely having a moment to herself . . . through her own choice, she reminded herself crossly.

Was Jess right? Had she been unfair to Michael? She'd been so quick to blame him for the terror she'd felt being in that room, petrified she was going to be clapped in jail. The whole set-up had been concocted by the police and Michael had gone along with it. But that didn't mean to say that he agreed, an inner voice said. Well, if he didn't agree then he was weak not to speak up. But Jess didn't seem to think so.

Ronnie recalled all the times he'd been there to help her, how kind he'd been when he'd had to tell her about Margaret, the way she fitted in his arms at the dance . . . She swallowed hard. He hadn't asked for anything in return. Hadn't tried to frighten her or take advantage of her like . . . well, like Will. And now she'd hurt Michael by not giving him a chance to defend himself. She hadn't been brought up like that. The image of Dad slipped into her mind. He was frowning. She knew he would have given her a sharp telling-off.

Suddenly she wanted to see Michael. But it was too late. She had no means of contacting him. And besides . . . she'd told him as clearly as anyone possibly could that she never wanted to set eyes on him again. And he was a gentleman. He'd have taken her at her word. He must have had an inkling that Will had overstepped the line with her and he wouldn't want to do anything more to upset her.

Tears welled. She'd spoilt the special friendship she was sure they'd once had. Jess had even said he was in love with her. If it was true . . . if he really was . . . well, it made everything even worse.

Chapter Thirty-Seven

June 1944

During the following months Ronnie was so busy she hardly had time to dwell on her inner turmoil about Michael. It had been sad saying goodbye to Dora. Ronnie felt the back of her eyes prick with tears as she recalled their parting. She was being stupid, she knew, but she'd become fond of the trainer. And she'd never forget Dora's unhappy love affair.

'It was nice knowin' yer, Ver-ron-eek,' Dora had said, with a teasing smile as she stuck out her hand. 'I believe I've made a boatwoman out of yer.'

'Oh, you have. I was worried at first. I kept thinking you were going to send me home.'

'Not likely,' Dora chuckled. 'Not with them strong arms of yours. You was the perfect trainee. The company's proud of you . . . and so'm I.'

Ronnie couldn't restrain from giving Dora a hug.

'All right, miss, that's enough.'

But the way Dora had grinned, Ronnie knew she wasn't displeased.

Lately the canal girls' work had stepped up and they were working non-stop with no leave in between. But there was always something to hold Ronnie's interest along the cut. It might be the heady almond scent of meadowsweet, the pretty little white flower growing along the bank. Or the rustle of the leaves in the trees. And the first time she saw little tots sitting on the roof of their parents' boat made her suck in her breath, until she noticed they were chained to one of the chimneys. The youngsters pointed and shrieked at the cattle in the field who were curiously watching the boats pass by, making Ronnie laugh out loud.

Several times they'd had to travel through the night to manage the upsurge of deliveries. On these occasions the monotony would often be broken by boatmen singing as they passed by, their voices floating over the water with 'Two Lovely Black Eyes', or some comic music hall song. If Ronnie and the others attempted to join in there'd be shouts and hoots of derisive laughter.

Ronnie was exhausted but she found more peace when she was working hard. After a gruelling day she would go up on deck to steal some quiet moments, thrilling at the sight of bats emerging just as the sun was setting, flying so closely together it was a wonder they didn't bump into one another. She loved hearing the sudden splash of an otter or a water vole, or seeing a red fox slide through the growth on the side of the cut, intent on its evening prowl.

Lucky had taken to sunning herself and dozing on the deck now it was milder. Only yesterday evening in the dusk the little cat had suddenly pricked up her ears when an insect, a water boatman, struck out from the water. Lucky had instantly sprung up and taken a snap at it. The water boatman had only just managed to escape and had flown off.

'Sorry, Lucky, I'm afraid you were *unlucky* that time,' Ronnie laughed as the cat pretended she wasn't a scrap disappointed by licking herself at rapid speed.

There was one piece of good news and Ronnie and Jessica received it with undisguised delight – Angela decided she'd had enough of working with totally inept people and was leaving in the morning.

'It was the last straw when head office told us our leave's been cancelled *again*,' Angela complained.

'I think there's a reason for that,' Jessica said. 'Do you realise all we seem to have been carrying lately are shell cases and steel? What does that tell you? An invasion on the coast of France, that's what I think. And we're helping prepare for it. I'm going to buy a paper today to see if it gives any clue.'

'If it's true, they'll be keeping it secret,' Angela said scathingly. 'But whatever it is, I don't intend to be part of it.'

'I think it's madly exciting,' Ronnie said. 'We'll feel we're doing something really important. Because when you think of it, we're hardly aware of any war unless we walk round a town that's taken a few hits.' She turned to Angela. 'Are you all packed?'

'I know you can't wait to be rid of me,' Angela answered with a curl of her lip.

May and Sally had gone to another boat to make up a new team in February, but as soon as Sally found out Angela was leaving, she'd got in touch with the company to ask if she could make up the third girl on *Penelope* and *Persephone*. It had all been agreed and Sally was due to arrive in the afternoon. Ronnie felt a flutter of joy. Sally was lovely. She'd never forget how kind Sally had been when she'd hit her head on the paddle that time. She couldn't wait to see her. It would be heaven to be part of a happy team again. They'd arranged that Jessica's home would be in *Persephone*, the motor, and Ronnie and Sally would live in *Penelope*. That suited Ronnie down to the ground.

'Sally!' Ronnie said, as a dark-haired girl appeared in the butty an hour later, just as she was making tea.

'It's me all right. Sorry I'm a bit later than I'd said.'

Ronnie and Jessica gave her a hug, both wanting to know all the news about Dora and May.

'One at a time,' Sally laughed, a little breathless. She looked round the butty. 'Where do I sleep?'

'You can have the double bed to yourself as I'm the smallest,' Ronnie said. 'Jess's got a whole boat to herself.'

'I bagged it,' Jessica laughed. 'It now seems too good to be true. No moaning Angela and no Deadly Dora.'

'I have to stick up for Dora,' Ronnie said. 'In spite of everything I can't help liking and admiring her.'

'She's had a bit of a rough deal from what I gather,' Jessica remarked. 'But it's good being on our own without constantly being criticised.'

'Why did you leave the new team?' Ronnie asked Sally curiously.

'The Scot – Laura McKay – stayed a whole fortnight.' Sally shook her head. 'I always thought the Scots were a tough lot. Then the new girl turned up. Lily. And that accurately describes her – lily-livered. I hate to say it but she was useless. Terrified of creepy-crawlies, always losing her windlass, late every morning – you couldn't depend on her. I can't see her lasting.'

'Well, the cut in't everyone's brew,' Jessica said, mocking Dora. 'Speaking of which . . .' She glanced at her watch. 'Let's have a quick cuppa and then get going. We need to be tied up at Brentford by six o'clock latest. That only gives us a couple of hours. But I'm not cooking supper. I say we have fish and chips tonight to celebrate Sally coming back.'

Sally produced a newspaper from the basket she carried. 'This is probably cause for an even greater celebration,' she said. 'Look at this.'

'Good God,' Jessica said, briefly scanning the leading article. She handed the paper to Ronnie. It was today's *Daily Mail,* Tuesday, 6th June 1944, and the front-page headlines screamed out:

OUR ARMIES IN N. FRANCE
4,000 INVASION SHIPS HAVE CROSSED CHANNEL
BRITISH AND CANADIANS
SECURE 2 BEACHHEADS

Ronnie's eyes travelled down the columns, trying to take in such a momentous development.

'You know what this means,' she said, beaming as she handed the paper to Sally. 'We must have delivered some of the ammunition they needed. We said how we were suddenly much busier. I wish we'd known.'

'Probably best we didn't,' Sally chuckled. 'You'd have got so excited you might not have had your mind on the job.'

'Well, I was right,' Jessica said triumphantly. 'I said right at the beginning when Dora wouldn't let us go on leave that our boys could be planning an invasion – and northern France was the obvious choice.'

'My mother's going to be really happy,' Ronnie said. 'Maybe it won't be too long before her beloved Paris is free.'

'The war's really turning in our favour now,' Jessica said, checking her watch. 'But I tell you one thing – if we don't soon get going, we're not going to make it by this evening.'

With exaggerated groans from Ronnie and Sally, the two of them quickly cleared the cups and threw on their jackets.

'Who's going to help me untie?' Jessica asked.

'I will,' Ronnie volunteered. 'Sally can be unpacking.'

'That'll take all of two minutes,' Sally laughed.

* * *

By the time the three of them had moored at Brentford, Ronnie's stomach was rumbling. Instead of tying up at six, as Jessica had planned, Ronnie's watch showed it was coming up to nine, and getting dark. She'd seen *Persephone* and *Penelope* through a couple of locks by herself, but thankfully a surly lock-keeper for once made an appearance to open the particularly tricky Thames lock.

'I don't know about you, Sally,' she said, flopping down in the butty when the two boats were safely moored. 'But I'm too tired to walk to any fish and chip shop.'

'Why don't I make us all some scrambled eggs on toast?' Sally suggested.

'I'll help, when I can just draw breath.' Ronnie gave her a weak grin.

'No, you did more than your fair share with those locks and Jess really had to concentrate getting through them, so let me.'

'That Thames lock was a killer,' Jessica said, coming through the hatch. 'I'd forgotten it was tidal and had a bit of a prang. Good job Deadly Dora's not around. She would have given me hell for it.'

'I think we did an excellent job between us,' Sally said. 'By the way, Jess, Ronnie's exhausted. We thought we'd stay in and have scrambled eggs. Is that okay with you?'

'Suits me,' Jess said. 'We should have some fresh eggs in the cupboard.' She glanced at Ronnie. 'Oh, I nearly forgot. Look what I found in the motor this afternoon – addressed to you.' She tossed an envelope over to Ronnie.

Ronnie stared at it curiously. She didn't recognise the neat writing. It was marked 'Strictly Confidential'. How strange. She glanced at the postmark and her eyes went wide.

'But this was posted in February . . . and it's now June.'

'I know.'

'Where was it?'

'Wedged in the back of one of the drawers. I wondered why it wouldn't open properly.'

Ronnie frowned. She fetched a knife and carefully slit the envelope. She read the first line and her heart jumped. It was from Michael!

12 Polstead Road,
Oxford
12th February 1944

My dear Ronnie,

When you told me you didn't want to ever see me again and I saw how upset you were, I vowed not to be the cause of any more hurt. But after mulling it over I decided I must explain the difficult situation I found myself in, hoping you'll understand. I'm one of the youngest of my colleagues and don't have all their experience but I was completely against bringing you into the station and scaring you into thinking we were going to question you yet again. I'd already argued the day before with the same inspector you saw that you were too young and inexperienced to be put through something like that, and it wasn't fair. He said, 'Nor is black-marketing.' I desperately wanted to tell him we were good friends and you would take a dim view of my role, and the police in general, but that would have made things worse as he would say I'm biased, and the police are supposed to be objective. He had it in his mind that his plan was going to work, and said, 'I'm sure she'll soon forget it.' It's not surprising that he doesn't get on with his own daughter.

And when I saw your white face when you walked into the station, all I wanted to do was to take you in my arms and tell you everything would be all right.

Maybe it was unwise to mention his plan the other day but I couldn't have been anything less than honest with you. I didn't want you to find out some other way. I don't blame you for being angry.

But how I miss you! I keep thinking of that dance we had. You said you'd never had a decent partner but you followed my steps so perfectly – even in bare feet! For me it was a magical evening and I hoped you felt it was a special birthday. And then you let me kiss you. I drove home with my head in the clouds! I couldn't wait to see you again, little knowing what a dreadful meeting that was to be.

Dearest Ronnie, can you find it in your heart to forgive me? I know I mustn't hope to see you again, but at least if I know you are no longer angry with me, it will be of some consolation.

Yours,

Michael

Ronnie gulped, trying to dislodge the lump that had formed in her throat, as she read his last sentence. She'd missed him too. Terribly. Spikes of guilt stabbed her. She hadn't realised how much she'd hurt him. Completely unnecessarily. So he'd thought that evening at the Palais de Danse had been magical as well. A little quiver ran down her spine. She hadn't known men could feel magical about a girl, but there it was in black and white.

'Is it bad news, Ron?' Jessica said.

Ronnie shook her head. 'Not really . . . well, I suppose it is.' Her eyes filled with tears. 'It's from Michael,' she added flatly.

'Michael! What does he say?'

'He's asked me to forgive him. But it wasn't his fault. I never gave him a chance to explain.' She burst into pent-up sobs.

'I don't know about all this,' Sally said. 'What did he do that you have to forgive him?'

Jessica quickly put Sally in the picture and for once Sally just listened, only making sympathetic noises.

'Pass the envelope,' Jessica said. Ronnie handed it to her and she studied it. 'I thought so.' She gave it back to Ronnie. 'Look at the flap. What does that tell you?'

Ronnie shook her head. 'I don't know. It's just where the envelope is stuck down.'

'Let me look,' Sally said. She peered at the back of the envelope and looked straight at Jessica. 'I see what you mean. It's wrinkled, which tells me it's been bloody steamed open, and I've had enough experience with my mother steaming all my post until I left home to do my nursing.'

Ronnie sat in shocked silence. Finally she stuttered, 'B-but who—?'

Sally frowned. 'You know something, Ron. I think Angela has something to do with this.'

Ronnie's head jerked up. 'Angela? What on earth do you mean?'

'Well, I may be wrong but she said something that wasn't very nice just before she left.'

'Oh, yes?' Ronnie raised her eyebrows.

Sally hesitated. 'At the time I just put it down to her general bitchiness, but she said she couldn't bear to share a boat a minute longer with a hoity-toity know-all and a stupid little schoolgirl who was after every man in sight. And as she was living in the butty at the time I could only assume she meant Jess and you.'

Stupid little schoolgirl after every man in sight. Was that how the others saw her? Ronnie's eyes stung with indignation.

'Maybe I shouldn't have said anything,' Sally said.

'No, I'm glad you did. Because if that's how she felt about

me I won't feel awful thinking she may have deliberately held my letter back.'

'Well, that's what it looks like to me,' Sally said.

'And we're sure it wouldn't be Deadly Dora?' Jessica threw out the question.

Sally shook her head. 'Definitely not. We got to know her better as she spent more time with us in *Persephone*. She tells it like it is but I don't see her being devious. And she's actually quite soft underneath that tough exterior.'

'I'd say the same,' Ronnie said, vivid images of the interview room still fresh in her mind.

'Then it's got to be Angela,' Jessica said. 'I don't understand what's wrong with the woman. She never mentioned her family at all. We know absolutely nothing about her.'

'Maybe she was jealous that we all became pals and she felt left out,' Sally put in.

'She didn't bother to make an effort,' Ronnie said. 'I don't remember her ever saying anything nice.'

'Well, we'll never know for sure if she spirited your letter away but I'd take a bet on it.' Jessica looked at Ronnie. 'The important thing is, what are you going to do about the letter, as poor Michael must have given up hope by now?' She patted Ronnie's hand. 'And while you're thinking about it, Sally and I will get some supper on the table.'

Ronnie couldn't rally her brain to think straight. First Angela – if it *was* Angela – holding back her private letter, and then Michael thinking his letter asking her to forgive him hadn't made any difference. He'd written it less than a fortnight after that horrible day in February but it was now June. He'd think she definitely didn't want to make any contact with him. She blinked back the threatening tears. He would have given up on her.

But even after all this time there must be some way she

could let him know it was *her* who'd behaved like a schoolgirl. Angela was right, for once. Or was it too late and she should leave well alone?

What would Dad tell her to do? She didn't have to imagine. She knew he would say, 'When there is anything difficult to face and you must make a decision, then follow your heart. It will never let you down.' She could visualise her father actually saying the words that she'd always thought were rather soppy. But not now. Oh, not now. Her heart, she was sure, was the only thing to be certain of.

Somehow she had to make Michael see she treasured their friendship and she was so sorry she'd allowed it to be threatened. But how? They wouldn't be back to London for two or three more days, and Maman would have first claim on her.

'You've gone awfully quiet, Ronnie,' Jessica said as she laid the little table for their late supper while Sally was breaking the eggs into a basin. 'Is it so difficult for you to admit to him that you were wrong?'

'I just don't know—'

A noise like a hundred lawn mowers sounded overhead. All three stared upwards.

'DUCK!' screeched Jessica.

There was an ominous silence and the cabin was suddenly plunged into darkness. Someone screamed. Ronnie felt the boat tip so hard she was sure it was about to go over. And then her head exploded as she was tossed to the floor and the whole cabin seemed to tumble down on top of her.

Chapter Thirty-Eight

'Ronnie! Sally! You all right?'

It was Jess.

'I'm okay,' Sally's voice sounded muffled to Ronnie's ears. 'But whatever it was knocked me flying.'

Ronnie tried to speak but it was just a whimper. She heard a scuffle, then another silence.

'If only we could see.' Jessica muttered a few more choice words. 'Bloody torch – where the hell is it?'

'One on the shelf . . . by the bed,' Ronnie croaked, sitting up and spitting out dust and what felt like bits of plaster floating around her. She rubbed her stinging eyes. The shadowy figure of Jess shone a light on her face.

'You sure you're all right, Ronnie?'

'I think so.'

'I'm going to feel for the hatch,' Jessica said. 'Have a look outside.'

Ronnie heard her slide back the door. The cabin was immediately flooded with light and she stumbled onto one of the chairs.

'There must have been some kind of explosion from one of the warehouses on the other side of the canal,' Jessica called back. 'It's started a huge fire. The whole bank is lit up as light as day. I'm going to check *Persephone*. Won't be a moment.'

Ronnie watched numbly as Sally swept aside broken crockery, books, wall plates, pots and pans, both lanterns . . . all had come crashing down and were now covered in a slime of food and filth and shards of glass. Thank God no one appeared to be injured although there was an odd throbbing in her hand.

'Be careful, Jess,' Sally called through the hatch. 'There could be another explosion.' She turned to Ronnie. 'I don't think she heard.' Sally stopped in her tracks, alarm spreading over her features. 'Ronnie, what's happened to your face?' She rushed to Ronnie's side and smoothed her hair back. 'You're bleeding but I can't see any cut. Where's it coming from?'

'I don't know. I just rubbed my eyes.' Dazedly, Ronnie held up her right hand, palm towards her face. It was as though she was wearing a bright red glove. As though in slow motion she turned it to show Sally.

She heard Sally's gasp. Moments later Sally was kneeling down in the cramped space in front of Ronnie, attempting to wrap a tea towel round Ronnie's hand.

'Oh, don't touch it,' Ronnie shrieked as pain shot through her head and up her arm.

'I've got to. I've got to stop the bleeding. Keep still and be thankful I'm a trained nurse.'

Ronnie gripped onto the chair with her good hand, desperate not to faint.

'Is it bad?' she murmured.

'It's not good,' Sally said. 'You've got a piece of glass stuck in your hand. I won't be able to extract it. Even if I could you'd need stitches. We're going to have to get you to the hospital.'

'We don't know the nearest one.'

'Then we'll call 999.' Sally quickly rose. 'Press the tea towel down just here—' she demonstrated to Ronnie, 'really firmly. And keep your arm raised above your head. I'm going to tell Jess to find the nearest phone box.'

'She can take my bike,' Ronnie said weakly. 'But don't be long, will you?'

'Don't worry. I won't be two minutes.' Sally disappeared.

Sally had left the hatch door open and Ronnie could hear the clanging of the fire engines. Was Jess right? Was it an explosion caused by chemicals or whatever they were storing in the warehouses? Or was it from a German bomb? She shuddered, then felt her head swim. *I mustn't faint – I mustn't faint – don't let me faint.* The words tumbled over in Ronnie's head. *Don't leave me on my own, Sally. I'm scared.* She looked up at her hand. The blood had already soaked through the tea towel. She felt dizzy. *Recite a poem.*

She began out loud: 'I know a bank where the wild thyme blows, where oxlips and the nodding violet grows, there sleeps Titania sometime of the night.'

No, that wasn't right. She'd left out some lines.

She could barely breathe with the smoke and dust swirling around her. She needed water. Somehow, keeping her hand in the air, she edged her way through the debris to the water can, but it had overturned and what was left of any water was in a slurry under her feet. What was that piece of paper? She bent down to see, but as she touched it with her good hand, it disintegrated into a pulp. In a sickening moment she realised it was Michael's letter. She struggled back to her chair and began to cry, tears of frustration and pain and guilt. Her senses had been so stirred with having received his letter that she hadn't taken in his address and could only remember Oxford. There was no way now of knowing where he lived. No way to answer his dear letter.

'What's the matter, Ronnie?' Sally jumped the step down

into the cabin and hurried over. 'Don't worry. The ambulance is coming. You'll soon be right as rain.'

She couldn't summon up the energy to tell Sally it was the letter, not her hand, that was breaking her heart. The next thing she heard was the sound of cloth being torn.

'Here, Ron, let me look.' Sally gently brought Ronnie's injured hand down and glanced at the blood-soaked towel before letting it drop to the floor. 'I'm going to wrap this new bandage round your hand quite firmly, so you'll just have to bear the pain.'

Ronnie found her handkerchief in her trouser pocket and blew her nose. 'Did you see Jess?'

Sally nodded. 'She's going to wait for the ambulance.'

'Is it really bad out there?'

'The fire's terrible. Apparently, one of the caretakers was blown to pieces.'

Ronnie felt the blood drain from her face. 'What caused it?'

'They say it was one of the new rockets Hitler's bragged about, but we'll have to wait and see.'

Sally worked quickly, looking up every few seconds.

'All right, Ronnie?'

'I keep feeling faint.'

'You won't faint. I'll make sure of that. You're just in shock on an empty stomach.' Sally paused. 'Is your hand very painful?'

'No. I can't feel anything.'

'Hmm.' Sally tore the end piece of the bedsheet in two vertically and used the strips to finish with a loose knot. 'That's all I can do for the time being. Do you think you could walk if I hold your arm? It'll be quicker than waiting for someone to come for you. Long as you can keep your bad hand up above your heart.'

'Yes, I can do that.' Ronnie suddenly looked around. Lucky wasn't curled up on her usual chair. 'Oh, Sally, where's Lucky?'

There was a horrible silence.

'Sally?'

'I'm afraid it's bad news. I thought she was just asleep but when I touched her she didn't move. She wouldn't have known a thing.'

'Oh, no. Not my little Lucky.' Tears poured down Ronnie's cheeks, leaving dirty streams. 'I promised Margaret I'd look after her.'

'But you did.' Sally's voice was soothing.

'Where was she?'

'On the deck. It's been such a nice day she didn't want to come in when I called her earlier. But it wouldn't have made any difference. She wouldn't have survived.'

'I hate them!' Ronnie bellowed, making Sally flinch. 'Bloody Nazis with their bloody bombs. Everyone says they don't have a chance of winning the war but they don't let up.'

'They won't, as long as Hitler is in charge,' Sally said. She took Ronnie gently by her arm. 'Come on, Ron. It really is important that you get seen to quickly. There's nothing more you can do here.'

'What about all this mess?' Ronnie said, for the first time really taking in the devastation. 'It looks terrible. Like the cabin's taken a direct hit.'

'Don't worry. Jess and I'll see to it.'

Reluctantly, Ronnie rose to her feet and allowed Sally to help her through the hatch and out of the butty onto the towpath.

A warden was blocking their way.

'Sorry, love, stand back, and let the firemen do their job.

'My friend's been injured,' Sally said. 'It's quite serious and we need to get her to a hospital. I've called an ambulance.'

The warden looked at the now blood-soaked bandage.

'Oh, dear.' He frowned as though to make a decision. 'Right-o. Stay where you are. We've got one ambulance here already and another on the way. Let me have a word.'

Ronnie shivered. Her teeth began to chatter and Sally glanced at her anxiously.

'Are you cold?'

'Not really,' Ronnie answered.

'It's still quite warm,' Sally said, putting an arm round her. 'You're in shock. I hope to goodness they don't keep us here long.'

The warden was a few minutes but he came back with an older woman in Red Cross uniform.

'I'm Dr Hamlyn,' she said. 'What happened to you, my dear?'

Sally quickly explained, and the doctor nodded. 'We're taking three injured men to hospital right away, so you can come with us.'

'Would I be allowed to go with her?' Sally said.

'Sorry, my dear. We're going to be crowded as it is.'

'What hospital are you taking her to?'

'Queen's Hill.'

Sally nodded and turned to Ronnie who was feeling dizzy again.

'Jess and I'll find out where you are,' she said. 'Don't worry about anything. Just get that hand sorted out.'

Ronnie nodded, too upset about Lucky to argue.

'Miss Linfoot . . . Veronica . . . wake up!'

Ronnie opened her eyes, a smell of disinfectant in her nostrils. She blinked. Where on earth was she? Then a fuzzy white-clad figure came into her line of vision. It bent over her.

'Ah, you're awake.'

'Where am I?'

'In hospital.'

Alarmed, Ronnie tried to jerk into a sitting position.

'Why . . .? What . . .?' She shook her head, trying to clear it. 'How long have I been here?'

'You came in two days ago.' It was a man's voice. A voice of authority. 'A doodle-bug fell on one of the warehouses opposite your boat. I'm Mr Ferris, who operated on your hand.'

Then it came back to her. The explosion. Her hand. Lucky. And Michael's letter. Overwhelmed, she fell back onto the pillows again and began to sob uncontrollably.

'There, there. No reason for that. The operation went well but it's going to take some time for the movement to recover because a nerve was severed. But it will come back, I promise. You've had a temperature as well, but it's almost back to normal. We'll soon have you out of here and back with your mother.' He smiled down at her, transforming his angular features. 'What a charming lady she is.'

Maman had come? Ronnie wiped her eyes with the back of her good hand.

'Why didn't someone tell me she was here?'

'You were sound asleep. She wouldn't let the nurse wake you up, but she stayed by your side yesterday through visiting hours. She'd had quite a tiring journey what with the delays, so I told her you'd be home in a few days and not to try it again as we would let her know how you were doing.' He picked up her chart at the end of the bed and glanced at it. 'Though it'll be a long time before you'll be able to go back to working on the canals,' he continued. 'By then we all hope the war will be over.'

Ronnie lay there, the surgeon's words floating over her head without her really taking them in. All she could think of was that Maman had been worried enough to make a journey fraught with problems to come and see her. The thought warmed her heart.

'And you certainly won't be fit to go back until your own doctor says so,' the surgeon continued.

'How long do you think it will be before I can use it properly?' Ronnie managed.

'It could be several months.'

Ronnie gave a nervous laugh. '*Months*? I can't be away that long because there's only two of them. We're a team of three. We all work together for both boats. They can't manage on their own all that time.'

'I'm afraid they'll have to – or get someone in your place. I know too well what heavy work is involved from the boaters who come in here having had nasty accidents. Big heavy chaps, too.' He looked down at her, his eyes twinkling. 'And you, Miss Linfoot, are no match, trying to do men's work. So dry your tears and I'll look in tomorrow.' He straightened up and left.

Trying to do men's work. A flare of temper rose inside her. She felt as though she was coming alive again after having no recollection at all of how she'd been brought here. Her head cleared. She hadn't been *trying* all these months – she'd been *doing* it. Even Dora said she was doing a good job. No. There was no doubt in her mind she'd be going back to the boats. Be with Jess and Sally. Continue to do her bit in the war that she was secretly proud of and wanting Maman and her sisters to understand and be proud of her too. And Michael. She hadn't even had a chance to answer his letter.

She swallowed. She didn't even *have* his letter. She had no address – no way of contacting him. She'd never be able to tell him how sorry she was she'd been so hateful. She'd let him slip through her fingers because of her own stupidity. Only now did she realise something momentous.

She loved him.

Chapter Thirty-Nine

Downe, near Bromley

The taxi driver pulled up outside Ronnie's home. He sprang out to take her rucksack and left it on the doorstep while she paid him.

'Thank you, miss.' He glanced at her arm. 'You take care of yourself, now.'

Coming home after a long spell working ten, sometimes twelve or more hours a day with no leave, and then the hospital, felt very strange. Maman would want to know every detail of how she came to have the accident. Ronnie sighed, then rang the bell. Almost immediately the door flew open and Rusty hurled himself on her, barking joyfully.

'Rusty! Down, boy!'

'Véronique! My little girl! I have been waiting for this moment. *Entre, chérie.*' Simone glanced at her arm. 'But you are in the sling.'

'That's good,' Ronnie said. 'It reminds me to be careful with it.' She gave her mother an awkward peck on the cheek.

'You have worried me half to death,' her mother said as she took Ronnie's bag. 'Come into the front room. You must tell me all about it when I have made the tea. Did they tell you I came to the hospital?'

'Yes, I wish they'd woken me. I'd love to have seen you. It was a shame you had a wasted journey.'

Her mother smiled. '*Non*, it was no waste. I could see for myself my daughter and speak to the doctor. And I telephoned every day. Did they tell you?'

'Yes,' Ronnie said. 'I always sent my love to you.'

'That bit they did not say.'

'I expect they're very busy.'

Ronnie allowed herself to be guided to her father's chair, Simone chattering non-stop. She was grateful when her mother disappeared to the kitchen. She needed a few minutes to compose herself before Maman began her round of questions.

'When the hospital rang and told me what happened, my first thought was that I should never have let you go to those canals in the first place,' Simone said as she brought in a tray of tea. 'If your father is looking down on me, he will blame me.'

'That's nonsense, Maman. I love the work. It's hard but it's so satisfying. And the rest of the girls are nice. They're from all walks of life but that's what makes them so interesting.' She wouldn't mention Angela, nor would she say at this point that she fully intended to go back as soon as her hand healed. Maman wasn't in the right sort of mood, and Ronnie was too tired to argue.

Simone poured the tea and handed her a cup. Ronnie couldn't remember the last time her mother had made her a cup or fussed over her. She began to think her mother really *had* been worried.

'The very nice doctor said you need rest and that's what your *maman* is here for.' Simone gave Ronnie a sharp look after she'd finished describing the explosion. 'What is wrong with your eyes, *chérie*? They are as red as tomatoes.'

'It's irritation from all the dust and smoke that filled the cabin from the explosion. It'll go in a few days, but I have to put drops in them.'

'Do they hurt?'

'They sting. But I can see, if that's what you mean.' Ronnie gave a short laugh.

'And your hand?'

'It's really sore now the numbing injections have worn off. But Mr Ferris said any pain is good because it means the nerves are coming back.'

'You could have lost your hand . . . or the use of it.'

'No, Maman. Mr Ferris is one of the top surgeons for this sort of thing, but the district nurse will be coming every day to clean the wound and check for any signs of infection.'

'I am relieved to hear that,' Simone said. 'And now, *chérie,* I am sending you straight to bed. It is all made clean for you.'

Ronnie began to protest, but Simone held up her hand.

'You will not argue with your *maman,*' she said. 'These are my instructions from your Mr Ferris, and I will follow them.'

Ronnie slept for several hours and when she finally awoke at six o'clock she heard her mother's tread up the staircase.

'I have made you a soft-boiled egg and soldiers like I did when you were a little girl,' Simone said. 'I peeled it so I think you will manage well with one hand.'

'Thank you, Maman.' Ronnie took the tray which her mother had laid out with her best china together with a pink rose in a tiny glass vase. Feeling moved by these small touches from a mother who found it difficult sometimes to show affection to her daughters, Ronnie impulsively added, 'I know we have our arguments, Maman, but I do love you.'

A dot of colour appeared on both Simone's cheeks. She bent down and kissed Ronnie. 'I know that, *chérie*. Even though you find it difficult to show it to me.'

Ronnie burst out laughing. As usual, her mother got it completely wrong even though she'd used exactly the same words Ronnie had been thinking.

Simone shook her head as she left her youngest with her supper.

Ronnie finished her egg and carefully laid the tray aside. Keeping her hand resting on the two pillows and cushion as she'd been told to do, she lay on her back, her mind going over the horror of the explosion. Poor little Lucky hadn't been so lucky after all. Ronnie's eyes filled with tears to think she'd let Margaret down after promising to take care of the little black cat. And she'd let Sally and Jess down by leaving them to clear up the mess Hitler's terrifying rocket had caused, the only good thing being that neither of them had been hurt. They'd both promised to visit her at the first opportunity though surely she'd be back before then. But what about Michael? *That* wound in her heart was a thousand times worse than the one on her hand and no amount of numbing injections would have made the pain go away. And there was nothing she could do.

You could write to him care of the police station, her inner voice argued. *They'd pass it on to him.*

Yes, but my right hand, the one I write with, is out of order.

You could try with your other hand. Plenty of other people use their left hand.

But I'm not used to it.

That's no excuse. Try, at least.

With a sigh, Ronnie pulled the eiderdown back and went to the small table she'd set by the window. She opened the drawer and took out a pad of notepaper she'd bought at the beginning of the war. Hardly any sheets had been used, and she recalled how Raine and Suzy both used to tell her off for not being a regular letter writer. Trouble was, she hated writing letters and wasn't at all satisfied with her spelling.

Michael won't give you black marks for a letter that isn't perfect. Just write from the heart – like Dad would tell you.

She took her fountain pen in her left hand and dipped it in the ink bottle to refill it.

Dear Michael,

Her untrained left hand shook as much with the emotion of writing his name as it did in trying to form the letters. She looked at the letters she'd tried to form. The two words looked as though an infant had written them, they were so clumsy and disjointed. Her fingers felt peculiar as they held the pen at an awkward angle. Chewing her lip with concentration, and with painstaking slowness, she started the next line.

I only recieved – no, that wasn't right. It was 'i before e except after c'. She crossed out the offending word and rewrote it. 'Only received,' she said aloud as she carried on writing, *your letter of 12th February a few days ago. Somehow it had been mislaid in the motorboat. Jess found it and brought it to me. I'd just read it when the doodlebug came down. A piece of glass somehow went through my right hand. Luckily for me Sally is a nurse and made a bandage. I was in hospital nearly a week and came home this morning.*

I'm sorry I was so angry and told you I never wanted to see you again. It's not true now, and it wasn't then. And you don't need to explain anything that happened in the interview room. You were on duty and had to do your job. I realise that now. Please forgive me.

Your letter had fallen to the floor but it fell apart in the mess so I'm sending this c/o The Grand Union Canal Police. It's all I can think of. I hope you receive it. If you don't you'll never know I tried.

Her left hand ached with the strain, but there was nothing more to say.

How to end it. Nothing seemed right that she'd been taught in school. 'Yours truly', 'Yours sincerely' or just 'Yours', as Michael had written, didn't strike the right chord. When she and Lois wrote to one another they always signed 'Love' and whosever name it was.

She renewed her ink and wrote:

Love,

Ronnie

That sounded much too forward. She crossed out the comma after 'Love' and inserted 'from your friend'. There. That looked better.

At least she'd finally written it. Quickly, she scanned the badly formed letters hoping he'd be able to make sense of them. It wasn't a brilliant letter but it told him what she wanted him to know. It would have to do. And the walk tomorrow to the village post office with Rusty would do her the world of good. She glanced at her bedside clock with amazement. It had taken all her effort and three-quarters of an hour to fill one and a half sheets of notepaper.

Chapter Forty

The following morning Ronnie made up her mind to get up as soon as the district nurse had been. Maman expected her to stay in bed but she had no intention of doing any such thing. She needed some fresh air after her hospital stay and the journey yesterday on a crowded train. Besides, she had an important letter to post. She looked at her watch. Half-past eight. Goodness, she'd slept late. She could already hear Maman clattering the dishes in the kitchen. Incredible! She was obviously taking her nursing duties seriously. Ronnie couldn't help a wry smile. As far back as she could remember, Maman rarely appeared before ten most mornings, having taken ages to complete her *toilette,* as she always called it. Ronnie had to admit, she was enjoying this softer side of her mother.

The doorbell rang. Rusty pricked up his ears.

'No, it's not the postman, Rusty. He comes much earlier. It'll be the district nurse. So don't start barking at her. Not everyone loves you, even though I know that's difficult for you to imagine.'

She heard her mother go to the door. There was a murmuring of voices.

'Do come in,' Maman's voice sailed upstairs. 'Véronique was asleep when I looked in an hour ago. I was about to bring her a cup of tea.' There was a pause. 'Oh, how kind. I will not be a moment.'

I must look a sight, Ronnie thought, as she sat up, endeavouring to pull a pillow behind her back. It really was a nuisance having only one working hand. It made her feel as though she was an invalid. Well, as soon as the nurse had gone, she'd get up and have a bath. Her hair was badly in need of a wash but Maman would help her with that. The thought cheered her.

There was a light tap at the bedroom door. Rusty barked.

'Stop that, Rusty, or I'll put you out.' She looked towards the door.

'Come in,' she called.

The door opened.

'Hello, Ronnie,' Michael said casually, as though they'd seen one another yesterday instead of nearly four months ago. 'Your mother sent this up for you.' He put a cup of tea on her bedside table.

She was speechless. Unaware, she put her hand to her chest to still her beating heart. Was she dreaming?

Rusty came over, wagging his tail, to give Michael a good sniff.

'Hello, boy,' he said, bending and fondling the dog's ears. 'I think you must be Rusty. Your mistress has told me about you.'

Rusty gave another 'woof' as though to say he approved of this new friend, then looked up at Ronnie, his liquid brown eyes imploring, and barked.

'He wants his breakfast,' she said, thankful she'd finally found her tongue and it was something neutral to say. 'Go on downstairs, Rusty. Maman knows what to give you.'

As though he understood, Rusty trotted from the room.

Michael stared at her and frowned.

Ronnie's good hand flew to her face, desperate for him not to see her looking so unkempt. Her eyes were still stinging and she knew they must look like a vampire's, she hadn't brushed her hair and she hadn't cleaned her teeth. How had he found her? Why hadn't Maman brought the tea herself and warned her he was here? Oh, this was dreadful.

'Ronnie,' Michael said, gently taking her hand away, 'you don't have to cover your lovely face for me. I was looking at your eyes. I thought at first you'd been crying but it looks to me like an eye irritation.'

'It was,' she said, 'from the muck caused by the explosion. But they're not as red as they were.'

'I'm glad to hear it.' He kept hold of her hand. 'I know you've been through a terrible time and you've only just come out of hospital. I don't expect you to look like you've just stepped from the pages of *Vogue* . . . especially as you didn't know I was going to be such an early visitor.' His eyes twinkled.

'As though I ever did look like a model from *Vogue* or any other magazine,' she said with a weak smile, her mind in turmoil.

'You did at the dance.'

'Except when you saw my Wellington boots.'

'I just thought you were setting a new fashion trend.' He winked. 'Can I pull that chair up?' He gestured towards it.

She nodded. How could she begin to say what was in her heart? She'd have to take her lead from him. And he was simply being friendly, not acting at all as if he loved her. Jess was wrong. But even if he thought of her as a friend, that was something. Once her hand was healed she'd prove she could be more. Inwardly, she gave a wry smile. Go through a transformation and look glamorous? It might work for Raine or Suzy, but not for her. Try to be clever? Witty? Again, they weren't her usual attributes. She was more known for being blunt, standing up for what she believed, whatever the cost, and helping any person or animal in trouble. She didn't think any of those attributes would make a man change from friendship to love. Well, she could at least tidy herself. That would be a start.

She was conscious of her hand enclosed in his.

'Such a small hand,' he said, studying it. 'But strong.'

He leaned over and she smelt the masculine scent of him, sending an unfamiliar rush of longing through her body. He brushed a strand of hair from her face, making her forehead tingle from his touch.

'Tell me exactly what happened to your injured hand.'

She managed to pull herself together, trying to forget how near he was, as she told him, not sparing any of the gory details.

'Poor Ronnie,' he said quietly. 'But thank heavens it wasn't a direct hit on the boats. You and Jessica and the other girl—'

'Sally.'

'Yes, Sally – well, none of you would have stood a chance.'

'Lucky didn't.' A tear trickled down Ronnie's cheek. 'Jess said she was curled up on the deck. I didn't even see her when Sally took me to the ambulance, my eyes were stinging so much and I was in a daze.'

'That would be shock.'

'I suppose so. But I can't forgive myself for letting Margaret down, even though I know it wasn't my fault about the bomb. But I can't help thinking she lost her life over saving Lucky. I wish we'd never given her such a stupid name, but it seemed right at the time.'

She started to cry. Michael handed her a handkerchief.

'Try not to get upset,' he said. 'It's war. Lucky wouldn't

have felt a thing. She'd have been asleep and usually that sort of a shock just stops an animal's heart instantly.'

'How do you know that?' Ronnie couldn't keep the challenging note from her voice.

'Because I grew up with dogs and cats. I love animals. When I was a boy I read several books about how to look after them. One of them was a medical book about how harmful it was for animals to hear sudden very loud noises. It mentioned in the last war when the Germans dropped bombs that animals could have an instant fatal heart attack because their hearing is far more sensitive than ours. So that's how I know.' He smiled for the first time.

She wanted to hug him. Instead, she gave him a beaming smile.

'All right, you've convinced me you speak with the voice of authority.'

'I'm not a policeman for nothing,' he said, grinning. Then his smile faded. 'But I didn't come here to tell you about my boyhood.' He picked up her hand again and stroked it with his fingers. 'Ronnie, I wrote to you but you never wrote back. So I decided then I had to honour your last words that you never wanted to see me again.'

'Oh, but I—' Ronnie bit down hard on her lower lip to stop it trembling. She looked at him directly, momentarily forgetting her wild appearance. 'So what made you change your mind?'

'I couldn't stop thinking about you. I had to see you again. I managed to find out where *Persephone* and *Penelope* were moored but when I got there neither Jessica nor Sally had your address but they told me about the V1 exploding on the warehouses opposite – well, I could see the destruction – and that you'd been taken to hospital. I was frantic and phoned them but you'd already been sent home, and of course they wouldn't divulge where that was. But then I thought of Paul Butler – you know, the constable who first came here with Sergeant Sandford . . .' She nodded. 'He gave me your address. So here I am. And I need to know if you meant what you said about never wanting to see me again.'

Her stomach gave a somersault.

'On that table there's something for you.'

He raised his eyebrows. She nodded and he strode over and picked up the sheet of notepaper. Briefly glancing at it he came back to his chair.

'This is yesterday's date.'

'I know.' Ronnie bit her lip. 'I wrote it last night.'

She watched him as he began to read, holding her breath. Had she set the right tone? Should she have used the word 'love' at the end? He might be embarrassed by it and she couldn't bear the idea. Oh, if only she'd just said: *From your friend Ronnie*. Or nothing – just *Ronnie*. Certainly none of the 'love' stuff. Inwardly she cringed as Michael silently turned over the sheet of notepaper.

He finished reading, folded the letter carefully and tucked it in his inside pocket, then gazed at her. 'I might be repeating myself but I wanted to tell you in person, not in a letter.' He cleared his throat. 'When the inspector told us he was planning to bring Dora in for more questioning as she was still under suspicion, and he wanted her to confirm she was Will Drake's mother, and where her loyalties lay, he asked me to be there to take notes. I was happy to do it. Then he said he was bringing you in, too. I asked why as there was no chance you were involved in anything underhand. When he asked how I could be so sure, I said I knew you in a personal way. That was my big mistake. He immediately said I would be biased and he would instruct someone else to be in the interview room instead of me. I had to use all my powers of persuasion to let me be there. I knew how shocked you'd be to be called in but I thought you might be slightly more reassured when you saw me.'

'I was . . . at first. But then you gave me no sign to let me know you were on my side and I felt you had let me down, knowing we were supposed to be friends.'

'That was what was so awful. I couldn't let you know. Like I said in the letter, he was watching me like a hawk. At the first hint he would have dismissed me from the room. I had to stay at all costs.' He gazed at her. 'You'll never know how terrible I felt seeing the look on your face and having to put on such an act when all I wanted to do was to put my arms round you and tell you not to worry.'

'I thought you were worried you wouldn't be promoted if you told him you disagreed.'

'At that moment I didn't care a hoot about my career and promotional prospects. It was only you I was thinking of. Do you believe me?'

'Yes.' She looked away from the hurt in his eyes. How could she have judged him so harshly. 'I already believed you. That's why I wrote that you didn't need to explain.'

'There's something else. Something young Will Drake said when we interviewed him.'

Ronnie's stomach turned over. What now?

'He said – and these were his words – "I wanted to give Ronnie something special so I got her the camera. I love the wench but I'm not good enough for her."' Michael gave her a searching look. 'He wanted you to know that.'

Ronnie squeezed shut her eyes. Poor Will. He hadn't had much of a chance in life with a father like Leonard. Dora had tried to do her best but it wasn't enough. He needed a good father to look up to and respect. She swallowed the tears. Dear Michael. He didn't need to have told her, but he was too decent not to.

'Did you love him?' Michael studied her.

Ronnie blushed. 'I don't know. I don't think so. But it was the first time I ever felt anything about a boy. I never really bothered with them before. I was always a tomboy.' She bit her lip. 'Stupid, really, now I think about it.'

They were silent for a few moments.

'You mentioned love in your letter to *me*, Ronnie.'

Michael's sudden remark made her flinch. 'It didn't mean . . .' she stopped. Took a jagged breath. 'It was only the way I'd write to a friend.'

Oh, why did he have to bring up the exact thing she'd been unsure of?

'That's a pity. Maybe I got the wrong idea when we danced that night, but I had the distinct feeling we were much more than friends. I thought you felt the same way.'

'What about Penelope?'

'*Penelope*?' Michael jerked his head back. 'What makes you think I have any interest in *Penelope*?'

'She seems to be very interested in *you*.'

'I doubt it.' Michael's face was very near hers. 'The only person she's interested in is Penelope.'

'Oh.'

'As I was saying – I thought we were much more than friends and you felt the same way,' he repeated.

'I did,' she said in a small voice.

'I still do,' Michael said firmly. 'In fact, I'm prepared to go much further.' He put his finger under her chin and gently turned her face towards him. 'Ronnie, there's something I've been wanting to say for such a long time. Now is probably a strange time to pick when you're poorly—'

'I'm all right,' Ronnie broke in. 'I'm not ill. It's only my hand.'

'Let me finish, darling,' he said, smiling.

Darling? Her heart leapt. But then he might be the sort of person who called everyone darling – like Suzy said the actors and actresses did. But no. Michael wasn't that sort of person at all.

His face was very close now. Her lips parted a little. A thrill of anticipation fizzed through her.

The doorbell rang, echoing up the stairs, and she heard Rusty bark.

'That'll be the nurse,' Ronnie said, drawing back, disappointment flooding her body. 'I don't think she should find you in my bedroom, especially in your uniform!'

'Then I'd better go and let her in,' he grinned.

After the nurse had attended to her, Ronnie had a quick wash and cleaned her teeth. There wasn't much she could do about her hair until Maman could help her wash it. Instead, she took up her brush, and with her good hand brushed her hair vigorously to try to get rid of the last of the dust and particles from the explosion. She looked in the dressing-table mirror and was quite shocked to see the pale face that stared back at her, though her eyes had definitely improved.

At the last moment she put the tiniest dab of lipstick on, the movement clumsy as she used her left hand. She smiled and the tired girl in the mirror smiled back. Hurrying downstairs she found her mother at the kitchen sink arranging flowers in a cut-glass vase.

Simone turned. 'Your very nice young man brought me these. Aren't they pretty?' She smiled. 'He asked to take Rusty for a walk. It was his way to give us time alone.'

'He's not my young man,' Ronnie protested. She groaned inwardly. Maman was always ready to see romance in any possible situation.

'That is not what I feel 'ere.' Simone dramatically clasped her hands to her chest. 'But before we speak of him, you must have breakfast.'

'I'm not hungry,' Ronnie said.

'I have made the porridge. It only has to be heated.'

For once, her mother's porridge was perfectly edible, but Ronnie still found it hard to swallow. She was conscious Michael would be back any moment and she wanted time to warn her mother not to question him about his motives where her daughter was concerned.

As though reading her thoughts, Simone said, 'He seems a very nice young man. And a policeman, too. How did you meet him?'

'When he first came with a sergeant to inspect our boats for stolen goods,' Ronnie said. She might as well stick to the truth.

Simone's animated face fell. 'Oh, that,' she said. 'I hope they now have dropped the matter.'

'I think they have.' Ronnie childishly crossed her fingers.

'He is in his uniform, but this is a personal visit, is it not, *chérie*?'

Ronnie felt her cheeks warm. 'Yes, I suppose it is.'

'You have seen him when he is not on duty?'

'Yes. I bumped into him at a dance that Jess and I went to.'

'And did you dance with him?'

'Yes. We did a quickstep.'

'Ah, *très bien*.'

'Thanks for the porridge, Maman,' Ronnie said, putting her spoon down and hoping to change the subject.

'Michael will return soon,' Simone said. 'I let him go to

your bedroom on his own because I trust him as a member of the police force. And he is a little older than you which is good. But I must know how you feel about him and if his feelings for *you* are honourable.'

'Maman, we're in the 1940s, not the eighteenth century.'

'Maybe I am old-fashioned but I am your *maman* and I do not have Dad to ask for advice. So will you please tell me the truth, *chérie*, and I will not ask more questions.'

She had to quieten her mother once and for all. Maman would never be satisfied until she had wrung the truth from her.

'I love him, Maman,' she said.

And at that very same moment she heard the front door open and Michael's footsteps along the hall. She froze as Maman said in her clear ringing tones:

'Then if you love him as you say you do, I will be most 'appy to welcome Michael into the family.'

Michael stood at the open kitchen door, a broad grin lighting his face.

'Do you, Véronique? Do you really love me? Because I love *you* more than anything in the world.'

'You must go into the front room to talk,' Simone said, beaming triumphantly, and Ronnie couldn't help smiling. She knew it was mainly because Michael had used her full name, and even though he pronounced it with an English accent, Maman would readily forgive him.

For a heart-stopping moment Ronnie thought her mother intended to follow them, but she heard her go upstairs to carry out her *toilette*. Heaving a sigh of relief she gave Michael a half smile of apology for her mother's outburst and led the way to the front of the house. Once there she didn't know whether to stand, or pick one of the easy chairs, or make a bold move to the sofa.

But Michael answered the question on her behalf. No sooner were they inside the room, than he shut the door firmly and swept her into his arms.

'Am I hurting anything?' he said, suddenly sounding worried that he might have knocked her hand in his exuberance.

'No.'

Michael, just kiss me. Like you did before.

He took Ronnie's chin and tilted her face to his. This time his kiss was even better than before.

Chapter Forty-One

One Saturday morning, 26th August, Ronnie picked up the *Daily Telegraph*, which the paper boy had just dropped through the letterbox, and glanced at the headlines. Her heart gave a leap of joy as she read:

PARIS LIBERATED AFTER FOUR YEARS UNDER NAZIS

A small full-length photograph of Charles de Gaulle was placed by the side of the columns, which described the previous few hours. The General's expression was deadly serious as usual, but Ronnie grinned as she filled the kettle to make her mother a cup of tea. She knew Maman would hold nothing back. It was what her mother had been waiting for all these years since that fateful day in 1940 when the Germans had marched into Paris.

Once the tea was made, she popped a couple of biscuits in the saucer and tucking the newspaper under her arm she knocked softly on the bedroom door.

'*Entre, chérie.*' Simone looked up as Ronnie entered. 'You have the big smile, Véronique. Is it good news?'

'The most wonderful news.' Ronnie placed the newspaper

in her mother's hands and set the cup and saucer on her bedside table.

She watched as Maman quickly scanned the headlines and broke into a beaming smile, then kissed the photograph of de Gaulle.

'I do not approve of everything you do,' she directed her one-way conversation to the General, 'but I know how much this means to you and all French people who dream of this day.' Simone gazed at Ronnie. 'This means much to Suzanne now, you understand, *chérie.* And *naturellement,* my darling Pierre.' A shadow crossed her face, and then she brightened. 'I hope he will soon come to see us but he is still important.' She shrugged. 'The war is not over yet. But this is a very good sign, *n'est-ce pas*?'

'A very good sign,' Ronnie said, bending and giving her mother a warm kiss on her cheek.

Simone put her delicate fingers around Ronnie's face. 'A perfect heart shape,' she said. 'You could wear any hat and look pretty.'

'No chance on the canals,' Ronnie said with a chuckle, 'except a shapeless woollen one I wear day in and day out.'

Simone sighed. 'You are such a dear child, Véronique. And brave. But I hope you will not go back to those canals now your hand is nearly better. I cannot worry about all my girls in this way. It will make me ill.'

'Maman, you're so much stronger than you give yourself credit for,' Ronnie said, meaning it. 'I wanted to go back as soon as my hand felt better but it's still quite weak and you have to be really fit to pull your weight when you're working in such a small team. So I won't be going anywhere for a few more weeks.'

'That is good,' Simone said, her beautiful violet eyes looking unnaturally bright.

'What is it, Maman?'

'It means you will be here.'

'Yes, that's what I just said.'

'I mean, in time for the wedding.' Simone blushed, averting her eyes. After a moment she looked at Ronnie.

'Raine's wedding?' Ronnie stopped short when she saw her mother's raised eyebrow. 'Oh, Maman. You mean you and Pierre! So he's proposed?'

'Many times over,' Simone laughed. It was a good sound which Ronnie privately thought she and her sisters didn't hear often enough. 'But I told him not until my beloved Paris is liberated and he agreed. It is important we do not waste another moment. We can fix the proper date and inform the church.'

'Will you be able to get married in church?' Ronnie asked curiously.

'Why do you say that? I am a widow.'

'But isn't Pierre a Catholic?'

'*Non,* he is not,' Simone said firmly. '*Dieu merci.* That was the problem with my parents. Pierre is from Alsace where there are many Protestants. That is why he has blond hair. It is different in that part of France.'

'That makes life easier,' Ronnie said, 'but you need to give as much notice as possible to Raine and Suzy so they can make arrangements, as it's difficult for them to get leave with the war still on.'

For once her mother didn't reprimand her for shortening their names. Ronnie gave an inward smile. Maman had more important things now on her mind.

'That is true.' A mischievous light played across Simone's

pretty features. 'But first I must tell Pierre that this time I will accept his proposal!'

August had slipped into September and the hot weather was still holding. It was wonderful to have both her sisters at home at the same time, Ronnie thought, as she ran up the stairs, Rusty at her heels. She could hear them chatting and laughing together in their old bedroom.

'Come on, boy,' Ronnie said, barging into the room with Rusty barking with excitement.

'Can't believe you've started without me,' she said. 'I told you I only had to feed Rusty and I'd be up.'

'We haven't said anything of any importance,' Raine said, giving her a mock cuff. 'I was just asking Suzy what she was going to wear tomorrow.'

'That's exactly what I mean,' Ronnie said crossly. 'If that isn't important, I don't know what is.'

'You never used to bother about that sort of thing before,' Suzy said, pulling her blonde hair off her face and grimacing before letting it loose again. 'You always made it plain how you thought that was all girls talked about. But since you and Michael have been seeing each other it seems as though everything's changed.'

'Suzy's right,' Raine put in. 'And if you could see yourself you'd know you're as red as a beetroot.'

'Stop teasing me,' Ronnie said. 'Let me see what you've both decided.'

'I practically had to remake mine.' There was a note of pride in Suzy's voice as she went to the wardrobe and took out a lilac-coloured dress. She shook it out and held it up against herself. 'You'll never guess who it belonged to.'

'Who?'

'Jack Hawkins's girlfriend, the actress Doreen Lawrence.'

'How did you get hold of it?' Raine asked.

'She's an actress – she's lovely – they both are. They were in the play of the last ENSA troupe I was on, but Maisie, the wardrobe mistress, said the colour made Miss Lawrence feel ill and to please pass it on to Suzy Linfoot. She said it would bring out the unusual colour of my eyes – or was it the other way round?' Suzy grinned.

'It's gorgeous,' Ronnie said admiringly. She looked at her eldest sister. 'What about you, Raine?'

'I never get time to buy clothes. My boss only said at the last minute I could have the time off, so I decided it would have to be my uniform. But I'll make a concession and wear the skirt instead of the trousers . . . especially for Maman.' Raine winked.

'You always look glamorous in your ATA uniform,' Ronnie said. 'You do as well, Suzy, in your ENSA uniform.' She clicked her tongue. 'I sometimes wish I was more like you two.'

'There's no need for you to wish such a thing,' Suzy said. 'You're a true individual and we adore you as you are.'

'So you won't mind if I turn up in my shorts and a blouse then,' Ronnie said, keeping a straight face. 'Both clean and freshly ironed, of course.'

'And give Maman a heart attack on her wedding day,' Raine said, chuckling.

'I very much doubt it,' Ronnie said. 'Haven't you noticed? Maman only has eyes for Pierre when he's in the room. So just think how she'll be in church.'

'Don't you believe it,' Raine said. 'She likes us to look like well-brought-up young ladies.' She put on an exaggerated posh accent for the last few words. 'I'm not sure what she'll say about me attending her wedding in uniform.'

'She can't grumble,' Suzanne chuckled. 'Your wings make

it really special. I think she's secretly proud of all of us. But we need to sort out our baby sister.'

'Don't call me that,' Ronnie said. 'Or kiddo. Especially in front of Michael if he manages to come to the wedding.'

'Why do you say that?'

'Because he's four years older than me and I don't want to draw attention to it.'

'Just what you need to curb that impulsive nature of yours.'

'Stop it, you two, and help me with what I'm supposed to wear tomorrow. It's got to be something that goes with my shoes.'

And to her sisters' open-mouthed astonishment, Ronnie produced a pair of sparkling silver high heels.

'Gracious, Ronnie, I've never seen you in anything like those.' Raine picked one up and examined it. 'Good Lord, they're Crockett and Jones.' She looked up. 'I'm really envious. They would've cost a fortune. Where on earth did you get them?'

'It's a long story,' Ronnie said. 'They were a gift from the owner who'd only worn them once. She said she needed to let them go and I was the only person she knew who was a size four.'

'Ronnie,' Raine said, her voice coated with awe, 'these shoes are one of the most expensive makes you can buy. They're *handmade*. You simply *have* to tell us who gave them to you. All I can say is, whoever it was must be mad to give away something so special.'

'That's the very word the owner used,' Ronnie said. 'Special. Jess brought them when she came to see me a fortnight ago, saying the owner wanted me to have them as a present and to keep them for special occasions. I told her to tell the owner they'll be worn at Maman's wedding. I think she'd approve of that.'

'I shall throw you out of the room if you don't tell us who it was.' Raine gave her youngest sister her fiercest expression.

Ronnie deliberately paused. Then she grinned. 'Prepare to be astonished. It was my trainer, who I've told you all about – Deadly Dora!'

'What! I didn't think she was the sort of person who'd wear something so feminine, the way you've always described her,' Suzy said.

'People aren't always what they appear to be,' Ronnie said, then broke into a scream of laughter. 'I'm joking about *me* wearing them. They're not me. But I know someone, and they'd be right up her street.'

'Who?'

'Maman, of course. Mrs Garland invited her to the shop and let her choose one of the wedding dresses but she couldn't help with the shoes. She told Maman you couldn't buy a pair of evening shoes for love nor money, however many coupons she'd saved, so she thinks she's going to be married in an old pair of summer sandals. She doesn't know it yet but I'm giving her these for a wedding present. She and I are exactly the same size. Only bad thing is – I'll have to wear Maman's old summer sandals in return.'

6th September 1944

'Maman, I've brought your tea.'

Simone jerked up in bed.

'Oh, Véronique, put it on the table. Let me wake properly. I was dreaming.'

'A nice dream, I hope,' Ronnie said, smiling.

'I cannot remember. But there is something I *do* remember.' Simone's delicate features broke into a wide smile. 'I think today is special, *n'est-ce pas*?'

Ronnie pretended to look puzzled and shook her head. 'Sorry, Maman, I can't think of a thing. I don't know what you're talking about. It's just a plain old Wednesday.'

Her mother's smile faded as she eyed her youngest daughter.

'I think you are teasing your *maman*,' she said eventually.

''Course I am, you silly lady,' Ronnie said, grinning and giving her mother a hug and a kiss. 'Happy wedding day, Maman. I have something for you. "Something old, something new, something borrowed, something blue." You have the "borrowed" from Mrs Garland. So this is the "something old" for you to wear today. You'll have to find your own "blue".' She paused. 'Shall I leave it here?'

Her mother nodded and Ronnie put Dora's shoes, still in the same bag, on her mother's bed. Simone glanced at it but made no attempt to look inside. Ronnie smiled to herself. She knew Maman wouldn't relish wearing 'something old'. Well, she'd get quite a shock when she finally opened the bag and saw what lay inside. The shoes still looked brand new after Dora had changed into them that night in the pub and worn them for the first and only time, and that was for no more than an hour.

'Thank you, *chérie*. I will have my tea quietly and then come down to early breakfast. Today it is important that I have plenty of time to get ready. I must look a proper bride.' She gave a self-conscious laugh. 'You know this marriage is the first time for Pierre?'

'So I believe,' Ronnie said. 'Let's hope he realises what's in store for him.'

She rushed from the room before her mother could admonish her. She had a bit of titivating to do herself.

The pretty parish church in Downe was beginning to fill. Ronnie took her place by the side of Suzy, leaving a gap to her right at the aisle end of the pew. She was hoping against hope that Michael would manage to scrape in before the service began. Raine had not stopped smiling since Alec, her fiancé, had arrived in his RAF uniform, and Ronnie was proud to notice Raine's gold-embroidered wings were every bit as noticeable as Alec's. James, Suzy's sweetheart, in his naval officer's uniform, was next to join the family and Ronnie loved the way he kept hold of Suzy's hand as though he would never let it go. The two men were perfect for her sisters.

She glanced at her watch. It was just coming up to eleven o'clock. The vicar stood facing Pierre who was already in position, his back to the congregation, and without a best man. He didn't know anyone, he'd said, when the family had asked him who was doing the honours. 'I must not draw the attention to my name or marriage,' he'd told them.

On this beautiful late summer afternoon it was hard to remember the world was still at war and Pierre's situation still potentially dangerous. Ronnie noticed his jacket hung loosely but at least he'd filled out a little with a regular diet, courtesy of whoever he was working for.

How she longed to know the part he was playing in the war since he'd fled France and arrived in London with those documents, but Maman would only say he was still working for the Resistance in some kind of training capacity and she probably shouldn't have even told her daughters that much.

Whatever he was doing he was one of the Allies, and although he would never replace Dad, she and her sisters had welcomed Pierre into the family with open arms, to Maman's undisguised relief. He'd certainly brought out a softer side of their strict French mother, who was visibly more relaxed and more demonstrative to her girls as well as Pierre. Ronnie couldn't help grinning at the change.

There was some movement in the back of the church. Her heart jumped. Michael? Ronnie twisted her neck and gasped. It was Maman, on time for once, looking more beautiful than Ronnie had ever seen her. She was wearing a simple cream dress with tulip-styled sleeves that fashionably enhanced her narrow shoulders. A soft sash collar followed the deep V neckline that tied at the bust, the sash ends gently floating almost to the skirt which flared above her mother's slim ankles enclosed in Dora's silver shoes. On her dark upswept hair perched a cream hat with its own veil. She stood, hesitating, as she waited for Miss Read at the organ to start playing 'Here Comes the Bride'.

Then with the sweetest smile on her lips her mother began the short walk up the aisle on Dr Hall's arm. Pierre turned. Ronnie caught her breath. In that moment she saw in his face all the love he must have nurtured in his heart these past twenty years for their mother. She pressed Suzy's hand and her sister squeezed it in return – but not before Ronnie saw Suzy's eyes fill with tears.

This must be so strange for Suzy watching her own parents get married – strange, but wonderful.

When the service finished and it was time for Pierre to kiss the bride, Ronnie felt her own eyes well up. After everything Maman had been through, she was at last to have her chance of happiness.

When the newly-weds had signed the register, Simone, her smile radiant, took her husband's arm as they walked down the aisle to the crashing sound of Mendelssohn's 'Wedding March', which Miss Read played to full effect as her foot enthusiastically pumped the organ's pedals. As her mother glided towards the pew where Ronnie sat, she sent her daughter a mischievous wink, glanced down at her feet, then mouthed, '*Merci, chérie.*'

Ronnie leaned back in the pew, a satisfied smile plastered on her face.

Ronnie watched her two sisters talking and laughing with their respective fiancé and sweetheart in the elegant Bromley Court Hotel in Downe where Maman and Pierre's reception was being held. She glanced at her watch. It was almost noon and Michael still hadn't arrived. She knew it wasn't his fault as he hadn't been at all sure whether he could get the time off. But it would have been nice to have had him by her side. She hated playing gooseberry to Raine and Suzy, and still felt a little shy in Alec and James's company, lovely though they both were, and it was wonderful to see the two men getting along well together like old friends. And for once Maman had someone of her own. The very thought made Ronnie feel quite lonely.

And then she felt a warm furry body nuzzle her legs and heard a muted bark. Rusty. How could she possibly be lonely when she had him?

Simone and Pierre entered the room, both looking dazed with happiness. They had just begun to circulate amidst laughter and chatter when the door opened and a few of the guests turned to see who it was. Ronnie heard an audible gasp. Everyone in the room except Simone and Pierre, who were busy smiling at one another, turned to see who was causing the commotion. Then to Ronnie's amazement Suzy broke away from James and went up to the tall, elegantly dressed woman with the dark shining hair and wide smile. Curiously, Ronnie followed a little way behind and heard her sister say: 'Oh, I'm so thrilled you could come. You look sensational!'

'Thank you, darling,' the woman said. 'I thought I'd better see your mother in person as I know she didn't believe you and I were acquainted with one another. Or even that I was real.' She gave her throaty laugh and Suzy giggled.

'Come on, then, let me introduce you to her and her new husband.' She turned round and saw Ronnie. 'Oh, Fern, this is my young sister, Ronnie.'

Fern smiled and extended her gloved hand. 'Ah. I have heard about you, Véronique. You have been working on the canals, I understand. And do you enjoy it?'

Ronnie nodded, not knowing quite what to say to such a vision. 'Yes . . . a lot, but it's not so glamorous as being a famous actress,' she blurted.

'But every bit as important – probably more,' Fern said magnanimously. 'Now, come with us and find your mother.' She linked her arm through Suzy's and Ronnie's as they went in search of Simone.

'Maman, I've brought someone who would like to meet you,' Suzy said.

Simone spun round, ready to be gracious. She gave a double take. 'Fern Miller! *Ce n'est pas possible.*'

'Oh, do call me Fern,' the actress said, then added mischievously, 'Your daughter does.'

'I hope you give Miss Miller . . . Fern . . . your respect, Suzanne,' Simone said, back in Maman mood, to Ronnie's amusement.

'No, she never does,' Fern said, a delicious smile curving her lips. Suzanne laughed.

Simone took a back step, eyes wide in horror.

'Maman, Fern's teasing,' Ronnie said, laughing.

'This is an English *trait*,' Simone addressed Fern, pronouncing 'trait' in the French way. 'They like to tease. I have this always from my daughters.'

'I'd give anything for three beautiful daughters like yours,' Fern said wistfully. 'Even one would be marvellous.'

'Yes, I know I am a very lucky woman,' Simone said, as Pierre walked up to join the little group, giving Fern his charming, yet utterly sincere, smile.

Ronnie was just about to say something when a hatless figure in the doorway caught her eye.

'Excuse me,' she said to no one in particular, and rushed over. 'Michael! I thought you weren't coming.'

'I'm sorry I'm so late, darling. Something last minute at the station,' he said, giving her a swift peck on the cheek. 'But I'm here now.'

Ronnie studied him. 'There's something different about your uniform.'

He chuckled. 'Just slightly. I've been promoted.' He gave her a bow. 'Sergeant Scott at your service.'

She giggled. 'It sounds awfully grand.' She took his arm. 'Come and say hello to the happy couple. And, Michael . . .'

'Yes, Véronique. For that's who you have to be today, looking gorgeous in your pretty flowered dress.'

'I'll allow it,' she laughed. Then, honest as usual, she added, 'It's really Suzy's. She made it at the beginning of the war. She makes all her clothes.'

'You look delightful in it.' He stroked his chin. 'But I do miss the trousers and the three jumpers and the muddy wellies.'

'I must say I feel more comfortable in them,' Ronnie said, grinning.

'Whatever you wear, you are still my gorgeous Ronnie.' He took her hand and gently kissed the scar on her palm. 'That's looking much better.' He paused. 'You were also about to say something else when I called you "Véronique".'

Ronnie pretended to think what it was by frowning. 'Oh, yes. It was just that even though you're not the constable I fell in love with, I think I could rather get to like this new sergeant.'

'You're incorrigible,' he grinned, chucking her under the chin. 'Now back to the wedding. Did it go well at the church?'

'Wonderfully well,' Ronnie said. 'Maman and Pierre are the happiest couple I know.'

'No, there's another couple who are just as happy,' Michael said immediately, as he looked down at her. 'Come here. Because I don't care who knows it. Even if it *is* the famous actress Fern Miller over there.'

He swept Ronnie up in his arms.

'Maybe it will be us in that same church one of these days,' he murmured against her lips.

'That is, if you turn up,' Ronnie quipped.

'If it's *you* waiting for me, I will.' He paused and placed her a little apart, his expression serious. 'What do you say, Véronique?' He kissed her soundly.

In answer, Véronique put her hands behind his neck, drawing him towards her upturned face, and soundly kissed him back.

Chapter Forty-Two

May 1945

The war was finally coming to an end. The Russian Red Army had beaten the Western Allies last month to reach Berlin and was holding it under siege, Mussolini had been captured and shot, together with his mistress, Claretta Petacci, and two days later Hitler and his mistress, Eva Braun, had committed suicide by poisoning themselves in the Führer's bunker the day after the two of them had married. Ronnie pulled a face at the scenes her imagination produced. Good riddance to the lot of them.

She drew back the blackout curtains. It had rained non-stop this past week but today, Monday, Ronnie was thankful that for once she could see the weak rays of the sun. She opened the window and put her head out, then heard a rumble. Surely that wasn't thunder. She peered up at the sky to see a formation of aeroplanes and automatically flinched. Then she realised they were British planes. Raine had told them there would be hundreds of planes coming over to bring back the emaciated prisoners of war from captivity. Ronnie shuddered. Yet it was an uplifting sight to know that something good was finally happening to those poor souls.

She watched for a few more moments, then drew her head back in. At least it felt warmer, but the weather hardly mattered now that she and her sisters were together after so long. Raine had hardly delivered any aeroplanes in the last few weeks, so had been able to take some time off, Suzy had been home a fortnight now, and Mr Lincoln, the vet, had given Ronnie a few days' holiday.

'I reckon they'll announce it on the wireless any minute now,' Mr Lincoln had said, his face creasing into a familiar smile, 'so off you go – you need to be with your family when it happens.'

'What about you?'

'Don't worry about me – I'll be happy enough with my own company upstairs in my room with my books and my music – having a bit of time off at last with Buster and the two imps.'

Ronnie chuckled. Buster was a mature dog at eleven years old but had been given a new lease of life by the two much younger dogs Mr Lincoln had saved from being put down.

'But when it's definitely over, will you come and have supper with us?' Ronnie said.

'That's very kind of you – thank you.'

The war had taken its toll, even on those like Mr Lincoln who'd been too old to join up, Ronnie had thought, noticing his bloodshot eyes. Having to put all those healthy pets down was heart-breaking every single time, let alone not being able to save some of the very sick and badly injured animals. She was only grateful to be playing her part again, having slipped into her old job at the vet's. She'd still be doing something she loved, training hard under Mr Lincoln's watchful eye to become a qualified veterinary assistant . . . and keep an eye on Maman at the same time.

Although her hand had healed well it didn't have quite

the strength it used to, and when she'd thought about the grinding physical labour day in, day out, wielding the heavy boats and working the locks, helping to load and unload the cargo, sometimes ten or more hours a day, she'd reluctantly made her decision to leave the canals. But she'd always remember her time on the Grand Union Canal. Her first taste of freedom and responsibility. Where she'd met Michael. When she'd at last grown up.

Sally and May wrote now and again, and Jess had been to see her a couple of times. Ronnie glanced over to the wash bowl painted with roses in pride of place on her dressing table. Jess had given it to her the first time she'd visited when Ronnie had injured her hand.

'From May and Sally and me,' she'd said, laughing. 'So you don't forget us or your time on the cut. And Dora wants to be remembered to you as well.'

Dora . . . well, who could forget Dora? And her silver shoes?

Pierre had managed to come and see them, sometimes for a few days at a time, in the last year. Those visits completely transformed her mother into a more affectionate mother and loving wife until he'd have to disappear again, continuing his work with the Resistance, but now he, too, was here permanently as one of the family. Strange to think of him as her stepfather, but she couldn't think of a nicer one, and she knew Raine felt the same. You didn't even have to ask Suzy, Ronnie grinned to herself. Suzy never stopped smiling every time she looked at her father. They'd all got to know him really well and there was no doubt how happy he made Maman.

Thinking about Maman, if it hadn't been for Dr Hall rushing over as quickly as he had . . . getting her straight into hospital . . . A shiver ran the length of Ronnie's spine.

But the doctor at the hospital had said she was definitely on the mend now and tomorrow they'd all be allowed to visit her. She couldn't wait. Everything was going to be wonderful.

Later that evening Ronnie sat with her sisters in the front room, Rusty asleep at her feet. She watched as Suzanne knitted, her fingers flying over the needles. Ronnie smiled. Suzanne was always happy when she was making something. Raine was idly flicking through an aeroplane magazine, Pierre was in Dad's armchair reading a book but she noticed he hadn't turned a page in the last ten minutes. To Ronnie it felt as though the whole country was holding its breath waiting for the announcement to be made that the war in Europe was over.

'Can you switch the light on, Ronnie?' Suzanne said. 'It's getting too dark to see my stitches.'

'Oh, while you're up, Ronnie, will you put the wireless on?'

'Anything else before I crawl up to my garret after having been up since five waiting on your ladyships,' Ronnie said.

'Give me a moment and I'm sure I can think of something else,' Raine chuckled as Ronnie carried out her sisters' demands.

The programme on the wireless was a comedy Ronnie didn't much care for when suddenly there was a news flash.

'This is the Ministry of Information.'

Pierre jerked his head up and Suzanne stopped clicking her needles. Raine flung her magazine down. Ronnie held her breath.

'The three great powers will make an official announcement at 3 p.m. tomorrow, Tuesday, 8th May will be Victory in Europe day . . .'

The three sisters glanced at one another and then at Pierre who was beaming. As one they shot to their feet, hugging and kissing, shouting with joy as they danced up and down, Pierre laughing and Rusty barking his head off as he ran from one to the other for pats and hugs.

'It's not yet official,' Raine said, flopping back in her chair, 'so we shouldn't take anything for granted.' Then she grinned. 'Just kidding. Come on, let's make an early start and get the bunting up.'

Ronnie pretended to cuff her. 'Don't do that to us.'

'Couldn't help it. You should have seen yourselves.'

'I can't believe it's finally happened after all these years.'

'Whatever will Maman say?'

'Let's hope they have a wireless in the ward so we all know at the same time when we visit.'

The three sisters chattered excitedly as they roped Pierre in to help put up the bunting.

'I do wish Maman was able to watch the celebrations,' Suzanne said, as she stood on a ladder to hang one of the strings across the ceiling. Pierre stood at the other end, not needing a ladder as he reached up to fix his end. 'The village hall and the church have been making preparations non-stop lately for the street party, hoping the news might come any day.'

'I know. It's a shame,' Ronnie said. 'But when we visit Maman tomorrow we should all wear our lovely new frocks you made us, Suzy. Wouldn't she love that?'

Pierre beamed. 'She will like very much to see her beautiful daughters in their new dresses.' He tapped a drawing pin in the corner of the ceiling for the last streamer.

Raine gave Suzanne a wink. 'Did you ever think our Ronnie would be keen to wear a frock twice in one year?' She turned to Ronnie. 'It wouldn't be anything to do with the possibility of running into Sergeant Scott, would it?'

Ronnie felt her cheeks warm. 'I wish you'd stop teasing

me, Raine. He's on duty all this week. And you know jolly well I'm no longer that innocent kid since I've worked on the canals. We couldn't even think of wearing something nice when we were battling locks in the mud and snow blizzards . . . except that one time when I borrowed May's dress to go to the jazz concert and had to dance with no shoes.'

'Wasn't that where Michael saw you for the first time wearing a dress?' Suzanne said, smiling.

'That must've been the time when you realised you were a girl after all,' Raine chuckled. 'Seriously, I want to thank you, Ronnie, for keeping us all fed since I've been home. I feel a bit guilty I haven't done much, but I'll get over to the village hall early tomorrow morning and help decorate the High Street.' She smothered a yawn. 'I just didn't realise how exhausted I was.'

'We'll all help at the village hall tomorrow morning,' Suzanne said. 'Visiting time at the hospital isn't 'til the afternoon anyway.' She glanced at her older sister. 'And you needn't feel one bit guilty, Raine – not after what you've been doing all these years for the country.'

'It's just that I hate cooking,' Raine laughed a little self-consciously. 'I'm just grateful Alec has promised to take over the kitchen when we finally set up home.'

'Have you set a date for the wedding yet?' Ronnie asked.

Raine hesitated, flushing a little. 'I suppose I'll have to tell you both sooner or later.' Carefully, she stepped down from the ladder.

'Tell us what?' Ronnie demanded. 'You haven't kept something from us, have you? You know the rules—' She broke off and looked at Suzanne. 'Even though Suzy kept her secret from us.'

'Well, it's nothing quite so dramatic as our Suzy producing

her real father out of a hat,' Raine chuckled. 'That really *was* a shock.'

'So what are *you* keeping secret?' Suzanne said.

A smile crept over Raine's lips. 'Only that Alec and I are already married!'

'WHAT?' Ronnie and Suzanne chorused.

'Why didn't you tell us?'

'Does Maman know?'

'When did this happen?'

'One at a time,' Raine said. 'No, Maman doesn't know. And I can't tell her at the moment. She's got enough to worry about. But you know me – I hate a load of fuss. And Maman would have made a big thing of it – even with a war on. I couldn't bear her to take over. Alec didn't mind either way as long as I married him. We did the deed early in the New Year at the registry office, but it was on my condition we don't live together until the war ends.'

'How can you be married and pretend to be single?' Ronnie stared at Raine.

'Easy,' Raine grinned. 'You just don't broadcast it, that's all. It's far more important for us to concentrate on our jobs. Losing your concentration for a few seconds when you're flying can have devastating consequences.'

'Well, the war's ended now so you're safe,' Ronnie said.

'It's not ended in the Far East,' Raine pointed out. 'When Japan surrenders Alec and I can start looking for a flat. And then I'll have to find a new job.' She sighed. 'That's going to be the tricky part. A female pilot trying to get her commercial licence.' She shook her head. 'Almost impossible.'

'I don't know how you're going to break this news to Maman that you're married and never told her,' Suzanne said.

At that moment Pierre entered the open doorway.

'Do I understand, Lorraine, that you are already married?'

'Yes, it's true.' Raine paused. 'Do you think Maman's going to be awfully cross?'

'Cross?'

'She means angry,' Ronnie said.

'Ah. Maybe not cross but she will be *desolé*. But I will tell her it is wonderful news. And we must celebrate now in true French style with champagne.' He disappeared again and was back, carrying a tray of glasses which he set down on a side table, then went to fetch the bottle.

Expertly extracting the cork with a loud pop, but not wasting a drop, Pierre poured out the four flutes, allowing the foam to almost tip over the edge until it settled when he topped them up again. He handed one to each sister.

'To Lorraine,' he said, raising his glass. 'If you and Alec are as happy as I am with your *maman*, you will have a beautiful life together.'

'To Raine and Alec,' Ronnie and Suzanne chorused.

'And a toast to the end of the war,' Raine said. 'At long bloody last.' Her eyes flashed. 'And don't tell me off for swearing, Pierre. Put it down to being around chaps too long.'

They chatted for a few minutes and eventually Pierre said if he wasn't needed any more he was going to the dining room for a smoke and read the newspaper.

Raine waited until he left the room before she turned to Suzanne.

'You haven't told us *your* plans yet, Suzy.'

'No, I haven't.' Suzanne bit her lip. 'You're right about timing,' she said eventually.

'Hmm. Sounds like you've something serious to tell Ronnie and me as well.' Raine's smile faded as she fixed her gaze on her sister.

'ENSA has a tour lined up to go to the Far East,' Suzanne said. 'And as you say, the war's not over for our boys there. When they get to hear of all our parties and celebrations, they're going to think they've been forgotten. So if I can help some of them feel closer to home, that's what I want to do.'

There was a hush.

'Dear God, you've signed up already, haven't you?' Raine said, her brow creased with concern.

Suzanne nodded. 'Don't look like that. I'm really happy about it. Vera Lynn went out to do her bit in the Far East . . . and I want to do the same.'

Ronnie gulped. Suddenly she felt sick. It was all very well Suzanne telling them not to worry, but if anything terrible happened . . .

'I wish you weren't going,' she said. 'It's the other side of the world. You might be sent to weird places like jungles.'

'I know. But I'm really looking forward to it.'

'What does James say?' Raine asked.

'He was worried at first,' Suzanne admitted. 'But he said we all have to do what's in our hearts. He knows I'm pretty sensible.'

'I don't feel I'm doing anything half as adventurous as you two,' Ronnie said pensively.

'You're only eighteen,' Raine said. 'Look at how you stuck to the canals. It was rotten work for a girl and I know you never told us half of it. You'd still be working on the boats if that blasted doodlebug hadn't dropped. And Mr Lincoln told me only the other day when I came to see you how grateful he is that you decided to train to be a qualified vet's assistant. He needs you more than ever with most of the young people in the forces, and the animals *definitely* do. He said you were the best assistant he's ever had.' She wagged a finger at Ronnie. 'You never tell us any of all that – and by the way, he told me something else. You seem to have your own secret that Suzy and I don't know about.'

'Oh.' Suzanne's eyebrows shot up as she stared at Ronnie. 'What's that?'

'If you mean what I think you mean, I asked him not to say anything,' Ronnie said. 'I haven't even told Maman.'

'What's happened to our pact?' Suzanne said.

'Looks like we've all broken it.' Raine gave a rueful smile. 'Wait for this, Suzy. Mr Lincoln told me Ronnie gives blood regularly.'

'It's only once every three months,' Ronnie said, flushing now her secret was out. 'You're not allowed to do it any more than that, so I've only done it three times so far.'

'You've saved three people's lives in as direct a way as anyone could,' Raine said. 'If that's not doing something adventurous and rather wonderful, I don't know what is. I'd faint if I did it.'

'It's nothing really,' Ronnie said, secretly feeling pleased her sisters now knew. 'Four of us do it and we have a bit of a laugh in Dr Hall's surgery. The nurse takes it and then Dr Hall brings us a mug of tea and a tin of really good quality biscuits.' She giggled. 'That's the only reason I do it – to get the biscuits.'

The sisters chuckled.

'What made you think of it?' Raine asked.

'Michael.' Ronnie felt her cheeks flame as she said his name. 'He's given blood for five years now. He started it when he saw his first traffic accident, so I decided I'd like to do it as well.'

'You should tell Maman,' Suzanne said. 'She'd be so proud of you.'

'She'd worry.'

'Not now she has her Pierre,' Suzanne said, her voice

softening as it always did when she spoke his name. 'He's a wonderful calming influence over her.'

'He'll be away again before he's able to be with her permanently,' Raine said. 'But I'm very glad he'll be around when we all tell Maman our separate news. We need him to help soften the blows. But we'll wait until she's home.'

'And until then,' Ronnie said, jumping to her feet and going over to the window, 'I'm taking down these hateful curtains!'

'You can't!' Suzanne said, springing up. 'It's not official yet. You'll have the warden after you.'

'I don't care.' With that, Ronnie tore the blackout curtains off their rings as though she were in a tug of war. She stood back and waved through the windowpane. 'Come and do your worst, Mr Draper,' she shouted to the invisible ARP warden.

If the tremendous thunderstorm hadn't kept her awake practically all last night, then the excitement that the war was definitely going to end today would have done it, Ronnie thought with a rueful grin as she pushed up the sash early the following morning and stuck her head out. She sniffed. The storm had cleared the air. Mmm. She pulled in a deep breath. Even though it wasn't yet six o'clock there were several people scurrying below, carrying all sorts of baskets and boxes. A couple of girls, heads close together as they gossiped, their baskets piled with bunting, some of it trailing over the sides, made their way towards the High Street and village hall.

How fast things were changing. Her beloved Raine was already married, and her dearest Suzy was about to go off to the other side of the world. She wasn't happy about that with the war still raging in the Far East, but she knew nothing she or the others would say to try to dissuade her would make any difference to her sister's decision. And Maman . . . well, her mother's life had changed drastically since she and Pierre were married. Ronnie felt as though she was the only one standing in the same spot while the swirl of her family spun around her.

She shook herself. She mustn't think like this. She had her darling Michael. And today was going to be the best day ever. Victory in Europe. She pulled down the sash and at the sound Rusty leapt from his basket and licked her hand as she fastened his smart Union Jack coat that Suzy had made him. Then she threw on a dressing gown and with Rusty at her heels, barking joyfully, she ran down the stairs.

'Be good, Rusty,' Ronnie warned him as she opened the kitchen door. 'You know you're not supposed to be in here. Maman would have a fit.' She stepped in. 'Morning, Papa.' She kissed Pierre's cheek. 'That smell is making me feel hungry.'

'Good morning, *chérie*. There is some toast I have made on the stove. And some scrambled egg – with real eggs,' he added.

'Have you had yours?' Ronnie asked.

'Only coffee. I could not eat a thing.'

'It's a lot to take in,' Ronnie laughed, scooping some egg from the saucepan and placing it on a slice of toast. 'Anything exciting makes me eat double my usual.'

He gave her one of his warm smiles. 'You have a very physical job,' he said. 'You need extra nourishment.'

Ronnie grinned. 'I must say it's good to see you've put some weight on since the wedding,' she said, 'but it wouldn't have happened if Maman was in charge of the kitchen.'

'She does not like the cooking,' Pierre said. 'Lucky for her that I love it.' He looked at his watch. 'Well, I must be going. I said I will help to decorate the church.'

'Surely it's too early.'

'I will first have a walk,' he said. 'I am used to having time alone.'

Not for the first time Ronnie wondered how he'd coped in the war. But she didn't like to ask. He probably wanted to forget it.

'That sounds a good idea,' she said. 'But don't forget the bus goes at a quarter to two so we'll be at the hospital dead on half past.' She looked at him. 'I don't want to waste a minute of visiting hours.'

'Nor do I,' Pierre smiled, and it made his face light up.

Ronnie grinned back. What a handsome man he was. No wonder Maman had fallen for him the first time they met. He was different from Dad, of course, but Pierre was just as thoughtful and kind. Ronnie had to smile. Suzy was his spitting image.

'But you must be prepared when you see her,' Pierre went on. 'Your *maman* has been very weak. But now she becomes more strong each day. She will be looking forward to this afternoon with all her daughters.'

The bus to Bromley was packed with people, laughing and cheering, knowing that Mr Churchill would be making his announcement at three o'clock. Ronnie was amazed to see the villagers had already put the bunting up in the streets like a canopy, flags waving victoriously from lampposts and windows. Mothers, still in their aprons, were carrying trays of food, chattering and laughing, ready to prepare for the biggest village party they knew they were ever likely to attend, and the men, nearly all in uniform and wearing rosettes, were setting up the trestle tables. Shrieking children darted in and out, kicking balls in the empty road, and throwing their caps in the air, the older ones blowing up balloons and dangling them from trees.

'Gosh, they're even bringing out a piano!' Suzanne said, twisting her neck round as the bus began to move.

'You'll have to give them a tune when we get back,' Raine grinned.

'Bromley General Hospital,' the conductor finally called out.

Pierre alighted first and held out his hand to steady the three girls as they jumped onto the pavement. Suzanne linked her arm through his as he strode impatiently in front, Raine and Ronnie behind.

'Look at those two – they even walk the same,' Raine said, making Ronnie laugh.

As soon as they walked through the hospital door, the first thing Ronnie noticed was the bunting and balloons strung up in the foyer.

'They're really getting into the party spirit,' she said.

'Your *maman* is in Ward 8,' Pierre said. 'We go through those grand doors.'

A nurse stopped them. 'Whom have you come to visit?'

Pierre stepped forward. 'My wife, Mrs Simone Brunelle.'

It still sounded strange to Ronnie's ear that her mother was no longer a Linfoot.

'I'm afraid only two visitors are allowed at a time,' the nurse said. 'It's the rule.'

'You go with him, Suzy,' Raine said under her breath.

Suzanne frowned and shook her head.

'May I ask for an exception to the rule,' Pierre said. 'These are my daughters.' He gestured to the three sisters, and Ronnie felt a surge of warmth that he embraced all of them in his smile. 'I promise we will not stay too long.'

She pursed her lips. 'I'll have to check with Sister.'

It was the stern-faced but sympathetic Sister who walked briskly along the corridor with them. 'We've put Mrs Brunelle at the far end by the window,' she said. 'As we've stretched the rule I'm only giving you forty-five minutes.'

'Is she all right?' Ronnie asked anxiously.

'She's doing very well,' Sister said, 'but we don't want to tire her.'

'Is there a wireless in the ward?' Raine asked as Sister opened the door to Ward 8. 'I'm asking because the Prime Minister is going to make an announcement at three o'clock and we're longing to hear it.'

'We are all waiting for that news,' Sister said, taking out her watch, 'and I intend to have it broadcast over the tannoy so everyone can listen.'

Ronnie practically tiptoed past several beds, the stringent smell of disinfectant in her nostrils. She smiled at several women who glanced up from their books and magazines, no doubt waiting for their own visitors. Heart in mouth she prepared herself for her mother not looking as good, having been so dangerously ill and not allowed any visitors except Pierre. But there was Maman, propped up by two pillows, her dark hair cascading to her shoulders, and her lipstick beautifully applied.

'Oh, how delighful to see you all,' she cooed, her arms outstretched.

'Oh, Maman, you look so well,' Ronnie said, kissing her. 'And we're dying to see—'

Maman gave a theatrical gesture towards the window.

The three sisters peered over the edge of the cot at the sleeping baby.

'She's beautiful,' Suzanne said, stroking the fuzzy cheek. 'Blonde, like her papa.'

'And like you, Suzanne,' Pierre said, beaming proudly.

'But she has my eyes,' Simone said, smiling at her three daughters. 'Just like violet pansies – that is what Pierre always calls mine.' She sent Pierre a tender look and he smiled back.

'Have you named her yet?' Raine asked.

'Yes.' Simone threw them a challenging look. 'I wanted Victorine because France has victory at last, but I know you will make it short to Vicky. I will not have that. So she is to be called Denise. Your Papa has chosen it. A good French name, and impossible to shorten.'

The baby opened her eyes and stared, unfocused, at Ronnie.

'Welcome to the family, little Denny,' she said, turning to her mother with a mischievous grin.

'I think you are teasing, Véronique,' Simone said. 'And you know I do not like to be teased.'

Raine and Suzanne chuckled.

'Sorry, Maman, but you know us – we can't help it,' Ronnie said, joining in the laughter.

'I gave you all—'

'Beautiful French names that you refuse to use,' the three sisters mimicked in perfect harmony.

'Denny,' Pierre said, his brow creased in thought. 'You know, Simone, darling, I rather like it.' He sent his wife an apologetic look.

'That's who she'll be to the three of us, anyway,' Ronnie said, laughing at Maman's fierce expression. 'It'll probably even get shortened to Den!'

There was a sudden crackle from the speaker.

Denise lay like an angel in her cot, oblivious to the pent-up anticipation in the ward.

'This is London. The Prime Minister, the Right Honourable Winston Churchill.'

A few seconds pause. And then the great man spoke:

'Yesterday morning at 2.41 a.m. at General Eisenhower's Headquarters, General Jodl, the representative of the German High Command, and of Grand Admiral Doenitz, the designated head of the German State, signed the act of unconditional surrender of all German land, sea and air forces in Europe to the Allied Expeditionary Forces, and simultaneously to the Soviet High Command.'

Ronnie grabbed Suzanne's hand, squeezing it. She noticed Suzanne had her other hand gripped around Raine's arm. Pierre was sitting as close as he possibly could to his wife and Ronnie saw him quickly brush her cheek with the tips of his fingers.

Everyone in the ward was silent as the Prime Minister continued until he came to what Ronnie considered the most important bit.

'The German war is therefore at an end.'

Ronnie gasped with delight and was about to shout out when she caught Sister's eye. Sister put a warning finger to her lips and Ronnie nodded. By this time everyone in the ward was smiling but still hanging on to Mr Churchill's every word.

'We may allow ourselves a brief period of rejoicing, but let us not forget for a moment the toils and efforts that lie ahead.'

He went on to remind everyone that the war was still going on in Japan, but by now the whole ward – visitors and patients – were cheering and the local church bells pealed out for the first time in six years, the sound drifting through the open hospital windows. At the sudden strange noise Denise opened her rosebud mouth and howled. Pierre picked her up from the cot, a tender expression on his face as he gazed at his tiny flaxen-haired daughter, her mouth still open as though she wasn't quite sure whether to continue crying or not now she was safe in the arms of her papa.

'Time to go so that Mrs Brunelle can get her rest,' Sister said, coming over and firmly taking the baby from Pierre, and holding her close to her starched apron. She glanced at Denise after settling her back in her cot, then turned to Simone. 'She's timed her birth perfectly.'

'The fourth victorious sister,' Simone said with a gracious smile. 'And you, my girls, must go before *this* Sister requests you to leave, but I will ask her if Pierre may stay with me a little longer.'

'Just a little longer,' Sister repeated, smiling at the beaming parents.

'Come on,' Ronnie said, jumping up and giving their mother a kiss, with Raine and Suzanne following suit. 'The other victory sisters know when they're not wanted. Besides, they've got a street party to go to in Downe.'

Acknowledgements

Anyone who has read one or more of my previous novels will know that I do most of my writing in a cabin in the garden. But they may not know this is a mere substitute for the railway carriage I really wanted. That is, until my husband, Edward, put his foot down, warning me it would cost at least £200,000 just to crane it into the garden, not to mention the restoration it would surely need! Cheap at half the price, I told him, much to his chagrin.

But I do love my cabin. It's been my refuge when nursing a very poorly husband to grab the opportunity to sit at my desk for an hour or two and write. There I could tap out a world I was in control of, in the company of Dougie, my white rescued cat, who often curls up in my black linen Chopin bag which is supposed to hold my recycling paper.

Just before lockdown my sister, Carole, and I went to the Canal Museum near King's Cross. It's a small museum but packed with fascinating memorabilia. Best of all it contains three-quarters of a vintage narrow boat decorated with roses and castles painted by the boat people. Inside, the theme is continued in the decorated wall plates and jugs and water cans, mixed in with old framed photographs of the family. We were allowed to walk through the boat and pull down the folding bed, peer behind the pull-down table to the small larder cupboard, and admire the range which they would clean with black lead paste. Bad enough that these cramped living quarters were home to two to three boatwomen such as the trainees in my novel, but the 'real' boaters regularly had large families of six or even more kiddies (as they called them) in this tiny space. On top of that they had to carry the cargo that more often than not added to the never-ending work of keeping the boats clean. How the mothers in those days kept such spic-and-span boats, as well as their children, is beyond my imagination.

So how to do justice to all these hardworking, often very young girls and boatwomen, and the original boat people, in a subject I knew virtually nothing about? I began with the books on the reading list, but there were plenty of questions still unanswered.

A stroke of luck came from an introduction by Jo Bell, a poet who wrote the Foreword in the classic book *Narrow Boat* by L. T. C. Rolt, to a teacher and historian, James Tidy. Amazed, I learnt that he lives on a vintage narrow boat that was actually used by some of the trainee girls and women in the war! I commissioned him to read the novel and look out for any 'howlers' I may have made in my clumsy efforts to portray the workings of these boats and the details of the route the trainees took. He also answered various questions and sent me hundreds of black-and-white photographs of the girls in various stages of carrying and off-loading the cargo along the Grand Union Canal, and three more very helpful books! His input was invaluable.

As usual, I'm grateful to all those who were involved in the creation of this novel. First, as always, is Heather Holden Brown of HHB Agency. She's not only a dream agent, keeping both the editor and this author very happy, but has become a dear friend over these past years. Then there's my publishers,

Avon, an imprint of HarperCollins, who won Imprint of the Year 2020. I'm not surprised, the way the team works so brilliantly on my behalf. I'm so lucky to have my hugely talented editor, Katie Loughnane, who unerringly knows my characters (almost!) as well as I do; Sabah Khan heads PR, and consistently gets me into national newspapers and radio shows; Ellie Pilcher, Marketing Manager, works effectively in social media; and those in the graphic art department design the superb covers for my books. I thank you all.

I make up the fourth member in two outstanding writing groups. The Diamonds are: Terri Fleming, Sue Mackender and Joanne Walsh, and the Vestas are: Gail Aldwin, Suzanne Goldring and Carol McGrath. We're all published authors in different genres and are second to none at brainstorming as well as bringing our special skills to the table. We don't hold back on critiquing each other's chapters and I believe our novels are the better for it. And I haven't even mentioned the laughs . . .

I'm so fortunate to have my own critique writing partner in the form of Alison Morton, thriller novelist with the successful and long-running alternate history 'Roma Nova' series. We both love reading one another's novels in the early drafts, though the genres couldn't be more opposite. But it works like magic, as our red pens are poised to pounce on any mistakes. Just as importantly, we always feel proud of each other's successes.

Sadly, by the time I had completed the first draft of this novel my late husband, Edward Stanton, was too ill to read it. He's always been marvellous at spotting errors, particularly with anything mechanical or military, not to mention those pesky anachronisms. I hope I've managed to uphold the high standard you always set me, Edward.

Reading List

The Amateur Boatwomen by Eily Gayford
Troubled Waters by Margaret Cornish
Idle Women by Susan Woolfitt
Maidens' Trip by Emma Smith
Narrow Boat by L.T.C. Rolt
Ramlin Rose: The Boatwoman's Story by Sheila Stewart
Grand Union Canal: From Brentford to Braunston by Ian J. Wilson
Waterways Guide 1: Grand Union, Oxford & the South East (pub. HarperCollins)
The Water Gipsies by A. P. Herbert (a novel pub. by Methuen's Sixpennies in 1939)

Now you've finished Ronnie's story, why not go back to the beginning to read about her sister, Raine?

Available in paperback, ebook and audiobook now.

In the darkest days of war,
Suzanne's duty is to keep
smiling through . . .

Available in paperback, ebook and audiobook now.

Even when all seems lost at
Dr Barnardo's orphanage, there is always a
glimmer of hope to be found . . .

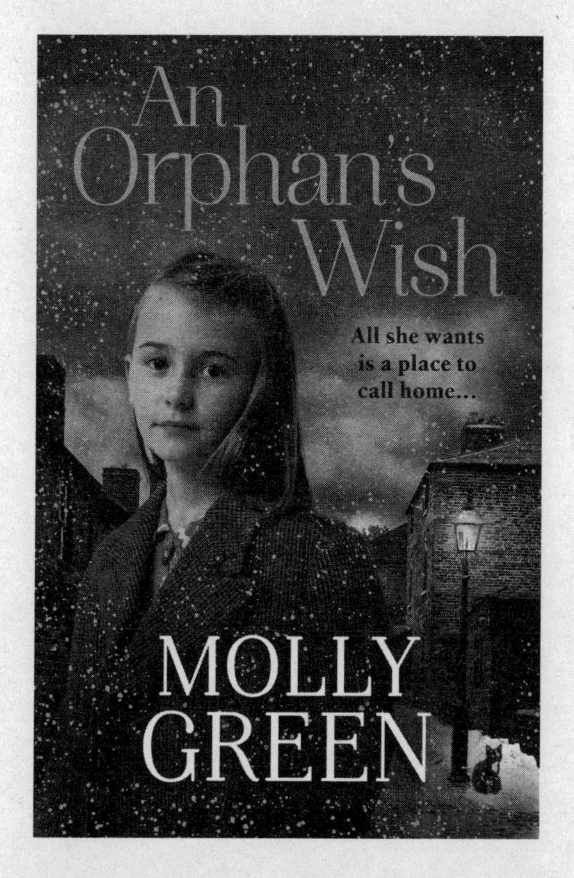

Available in paperback, ebook and audiobook now.